## About the Authors

Former PA, office manager, theme park hostess, software trainer, aerobics instructor and Wheel of Fortune contestant, **Paula Roe** is now a Borders Books best seller and one of Australia's Desire authors. She lives in Sydney, Australia and when she's not writing, Paula designs websites, judges writing contests, battles a social media addiction, watches way too much TV and reads a lot. And bakes a pretty good carrot cake, too!

*USA TODAY* bestselling author **Kat Cantrell** read her first Mills & Boon novel in third grade and has been scribbling in notebooks since she learned to spell. She's a former So You Think You Can Write winner and former RWA Golden Heart finalist. Kat, her husband and their two boys live in north Texas.

**Karen Booth** is a Midwestern girl transplanted in the South, raised on 80s music and repeated readings of *Forever* by Judy Blume. When she's not writing about dreamy fictional men and the women who test them, she's in the garden, obsessing over college basketball, or spending time with her husband, college-age kids, and bratty cat.

# A Surprise Family

# Written in the Stars

PAULA ROE

KAT CANTRELL

KAREN BOOTH

MILLS & BOON

First Published in Great Britain 2020
By Mills & Boon, an imprint of HarperCollins*Publishers*
1 London Bridge Street, London, SE1 9GF

A SURPRISE FAMILY: WRITTEN IN THE STARS


ISBN: 978-0-263-29878-9

This book is produced from independently certified FSC™ paper to ensure responsible forest management.

For more information visit: www.harpercollins.co.uk/green

Printed and bound in Spain
by CPI, Barcelona

# SUDDENLY EXPECTING

PAULA ROE

This story required an extra kick in the pants and I truly appreciate kickers Shannon Curtis and Kaz Delaney for doing that. You know how much I love you girls xx Huge cuddles to Helene Young for her wonderful cyclone information, and Gabrielle Luthy for her knowledge of all things French. And a special thanks to Kaycie from the Football Federation of Australia who went over and above to provide this soccer-challenged writer with information regarding the sport.

I also need to mention some special characters in Twitter Land who for one reason or another provided either encouragement or sweet, hilarious distraction throughout this particular story and kept this writer sane: George IV, Will Shakespeare, Prince Henry, Jack Sheppard, Philippe and Charles Brandon. Love you, guys! Lastly, to the wonderful, gorgeous people behind the epic French movie, Le Roi Danse. Because period dramas totally rock.

# One

Ten weeks ago, Katerina Jackson had spent one night in bed with her best friend. And it had been absolutely amazing.

Now, as she drove down the Captain Cook Highway, just before she got into Cairns, she was confronted with an image of the man in question, naked and smiling seductively down at her.

Kat's foot instinctively tamped on the brake, and she only just managed to avoid the car in front as it stopped at the red light. The burn on her cheeks went all the way down her body, ending in her thighs, where it pooled annoyingly in her groin. She looked up at the familiar massive billboard featuring Marco Corelli, the golden boy of France's premier *futball* league and Marseille's highest goal scorer in the club's entire history.

Well, he wasn't exactly naked. The stacked Y-fronts

left little to the imagination, though, as did his splayed hands across his low-riding waistband and the caption "Come and Feel My Skins." But it wasn't his ridged abs, popping biceps and the seductive Adonis line of muscle that disappeared into the low-riding underwear that heated her blood. It was that familiar, tempting come-here-so-I-can-have-my-way-with-you grin, the curve of his overtly lush bottom lip and the forbidden promise in those dark, sensual eyes. The way the camera had captured his hypnotic charm as he looked up from behind artfully tousled, rakish black hair, one curl lying teasingly across his forehead and cheek.

She'd had to pass that damn billboard every morning for the past ten weeks, his perfect face staring knowingly down, as if he remembered every single thing he'd done to her that night. How he'd made her sweat, how he'd made her moan. How he'd made her pant.

She snapped her gaze back to the road, glaring at the taillights as the traffic finally began to move.

"God, I am so stupid," she muttered in the air-conditioned silence. It was Marco, her best friend since high school. The arrogant former-soccer-star-turned-sports-commentator, the underwear-endorsing charmer, Mr. Flirt with a dozen different girlfriends. She was his best mate, secret keeper, sounding board, partner in crime. His plus one when he needed a date to some swish function. He was also her boss's on-again, off-again boyfriend.

She cast her mind back, sifting through her and Grace's many conversations about Marco. Yeah, they'd definitely been off for a while before that night, so there was one less moral dilemma to worry about. Which just left the main two.

Oh, she couldn't just have sex with her best friend, noooo. She had to end up pregnant, too.

*If you could see me now, Mum. All your pretty, shiny dreams of your daughter having a perfect life, a perfect career. A perfect husband surrounded by perfect, healthy children.*

The sliver of pain sliced through her, drawing blood, before she effectively sealed up the wound and pulled into Channel Five's parking lot. After flashing her ID to the guard, she parked, gathered her bag and strode into the studio. Then she tossed her bag in her office and checked her phone.

Four missed calls, one from her friend Connor, three from Marco, plus a text message. Back in town. We need to talk. Drinks on the boat? M x

She sighed then finally replied. Sorry, snowed under at work. Can't get away. Plus there's a cyclone warning, in case you haven't noticed. K x

After she sent it, she scrolled back to their texts from two months ago, a painful reminder that only rekindled her inner turmoil.

Have a good trip to France.

Hate to run and fly. We shouldn't leave last night without talking about it.

Nothing to say. Let's just blame it on booze and stupidity and forget it happened, okay?

Are you cool with that?

Totally. Erasing from my memory in three...two...one...

☺ Okaaaay. See you in a few weeks.

And that was it. Due to both their schedules, they had a mutual phone blackout during his assignments, although he always managed to send a few photos of the local scenery. But now he was back and wanted to do the usual drink-and-talk, and she had no idea what to tell him.

*You can't avoid him forever.*

"You can't avoid him forever," Connor confirmed five minutes later when she returned his call.

"What the hell, I'm gonna give it a shot."

"Don't be ridiculous. He deserves to know."

Kat slid her hip on the corner of her desk and sighed. "I can hear your disapproval all the way from Brisbane."

"Kat, I'm not disapproving. But I'm one of the few who know exactly what you've gone through these past few years. The guy deserves to know."

Trust Connor to tell it to her straight. Marco, Connor, Kat and Luke—the Awesome Foursome, they'd called themselves in high school. All so very different in personality and temperament, yet "perfectly awesome together," as Marco had put it. He'd been the cocky one, a skilled charmer, whereas his cousin Luke had had the whole bad-boy thing going on, always in trouble, always on detention. Connor was the devastatingly handsome silent-and-deep one, her unbiased sounding board who always told her the truth, uncolored by hyperbole or emotion. Sometimes it was scary how detached he could actually be, which was, ironically, what made him an exceptional businessman. He never let anyone into his private circle and she was always grateful she'd been allowed entry all those years ago.

"I...just can't tell him," she said now. "I'm already a wreck, and I can't deal with all the emotional baggage, too."

"That's unfair, sweetie. Marco would never do that to you."

She pinched the bridge of her nose and then glanced up as a runner gave her the wind-up signal, indicating she was due on set.

Kat nodded. "Look, I have to go. I'll talk to you later."

Connor sighed. "Stay safe during the storm."

"I will." She hung up, firmly pushed the conversation to one side and made her way to makeup just as her phone rang again.

It was Marco. "I do *not* want to talk to you," she muttered and slid the phone to Silent.

"Avoiding a call from the boyfriend?"

Kat slid a glance to Grace Callahan, the star of Queensland's number one breakfast chat show, *Morning Grace,* sitting in the makeup chair, getting her hair done. The woman was forty, only seven years older than Kat, but she had that polished, shiny look of someone who'd not only spent enormous amounts of time and money on her appearance, but was convinced it was the most important thing in her life. Her blond hair was curled into an artful tousle, her fake-tanned skin smooth, her body gym-honed. Yet for all her high-maintenance appearance, she had an addictive personality that attracted people by the bucket load. Which was probably why Marco kept coming back.

Kat glanced at her phone and nodded, unwilling to explain further. "No, just...a guy."

"Really?" Grace's wide eyes met hers in the mirror. "A real-life guy? Oh, my God, where's my phone? I want to take a picture of this moment."

Despite her mood, Kat smiled. "You make me sound like a nun."

"I was beginning to think you were, hon." She winced as the makeup girl pulled a lock of hair through the curler. "This is exciting—makes a change from all the Cyclone Rory news. Can I put it in the show?"

Kat snorted a laugh. "You know you can't, so stop asking. I'm not newsworthy."

"Are so." Grace waved the girl away and ripped the makeup cape from her shoulders. "You're a celebrity, and celebrities are always news."

"Please, don't remind me. I hate those people who're famous for just being famous."

"Sorry, hon, but your little scandals have fueled the gossip columns for ages. It only takes another to set it off again." She straightened her dress then walked to the door, Kat following.

Kat sighed. It was true. She was nothing particularly special: the daughter of a merchant investment banker and an events planner, a private school student. The gap year she'd spent between high school graduation and university had been twelve months of partying, but just as she was about to begin her journalism degree at Brisbane Uni, she'd been offered a job as society reporter for *The Tribune* instead. Then, she'd gone spectacularly off the rails a year later, after her mother's death.

"You never did set the record straight about everything, you know," Grace said over her shoulder as they continued down the corridor. "It'd make a fabulous feature." She swept her hands out, indicating a huge headline. "Former It Girl Katerina Jackson finally spills the dirt on her marriages, the seedy side of French football and *those* scandalous photos."

"Never going to happen, Grace."

"We could start at the beginning, make it a full show. We'd do background, talk about your childhood, your upbringing. How you beat up Marco when you were fourteen—"

"It was a shove, not a hit—"

"—and how you all ended up on detention like some modern-day *Breakfast Club* scenario—"

"I *knew* I shouldn't have told you that."

Grace laughed. "I'm not going to say anything, hon, unless you want me to. But I do find it fascinating that your closest friends are a soccer superstar, a billionaire merchant banker and the nephew of a rumored mobster. All hot alpha men. All completely different. And all newsworthy."

Marco, Connor and Luke. Her best friends since high school, since that awkwardly hilarious lunchtime detention had played out like some eighties teenage movie and they'd bonded over their hatred of school and their shared tastes in movies, music and computer games.

"What were you all there for again?" Grace casually asked as they walked to the studio.

"You know full well what."

"You'd decked Marco—"

"A *shove,* Grace. For showing off in front of his mates and getting all up in my face."

"Why? What did he say?"

"Honestly, I can't even remember." Yeah, she did —a stupid teenage comment about her lack of "womanly attributes" that, to Marco's credit, he'd apologized for later.

"Whatever. Luke had been caught defacing the toilets and… What was Connor's crime?"

"Correcting the economics teacher then threatening to bankrupt him."

"Wow, harsh."

"That was Southbank Private for you." She shrugged. "All the girls were too intimidated to talk to Luke and Connor. I wasn't. And from there we clicked. It just so happens they're guys."

"And you've never thought about…?" Grace waggled her eyebrows. *"You know."*

"What? No!"

"Not even with Marco?"

Kat threw her an exaggerated eye roll to cover up the warmth in her face. "No, Grace, I haven't," she replied as they walked onto the set. "And I have no intention of giving anyone an exclusive. I'm your research assistant now, that's it." Grace approached a raised yellow couch and coffee table surrounded by a cluster of cameras. The lights streamed down as the set director came over to go through the lineup. "The other stuff is old news. People don't want to hear about it."

"They do. But I'll just keep trying," Grace replied with a smile, taking the glass of water the runner offered.

"Of course you will." Kat accepted her usual green tea from the set assistant as Grace sat on the sofa and began to rearrange the strategically placed props on the table.

"Soooo…have you heard from Marco?" Grace asked casually.

"Not yet, no," Kat lied, fiddling with her phone. "He

was commentating the *Coupe de France,* and that was only three days ago."

"I heard he's supposed to be back today." She smoothed her dress down over her artfully crossed legs. "I'm arranging a surprise dinner for later in the week."

"Really?" Kat paused, her insides suddenly tight, and she took a sip of tea to cover up the weird feeling. "Are you two back on again, then?"

Grace laughed. "I don't think we've ever really been off. I've got plans." She took another sip of water. "Let's face it—my body clock's been ticking steadily for years. And now I have an established show and some serious credibility in this industry. It's time I started thinking about having a baby."

Kat choked, tea dribbling down her chin. She swiped at it then stared at Grace. "With *Marco?*"

"Of course with Marco!" Grace frowned slightly, eyeing the guy adjusting the lighting. "Is that a problem? I know you and he are close…"

"Oh, no. I mean, yes… I mean…" Kat took a breath, trying to steady her clenching gut. "We're close and share a lot, but we do have one rule—never butt into each other's love life."

"Really?" Grace looked intrigued. "So he's never commented on James or Ezio, not even in passing?"

"No."

"And you've never said anything to him about me?"

Kat gave her a look. "No. It's not my business. You want to have babies, it's fine with me." She gave a smile, one she'd learned to adopt out of necessity. A smile designed for intrusive cameras, when they'd been camped outside her door, trailing her on the way to work, shopping, to the gym, interrupting her family and friends and becoming so invasive she'd had to get a court order to put a stop to it.

"You sure?" Grace asked curiously as she gathered up her notes. "I always thought there was some subtle sexual tension going on with you guys, but—"

"Me and Marco? No. No way!" she denied, a little too forcefully. "I mean, he's a great-looking guy and he's my best friend, but he's…" She groped for a word. "A free spirit."

"I would've said a tart," Grace added with a smile. "And a world-class flirt. A good thing, too—he won't butt into my life and make demands on how I should be raising my child."

What could she say to that? Everything Grace said was true. Marco loved his life and lived it at breakneck speed. He had no room for a permanent partner, let alone a child.

Kat swallowed thickly, watching everyone fuss around Grace as the cameras got into position. For all her confusion, her crazy thoughts and outrageous scenarios she'd gone through these past few days, the choice was simple. He wouldn't want a baby. She most certainly didn't.

Kat adjusted her headset and sidestepped the studio camera as it wheeled toward her, watching Grace smiling into Camera One as she continued with her dialogue.

Grace could be snippy, snarky and demanding, but beneath the polished blond exterior she had a heart of gold. Kat sourced the hard-luck stories and Grace reported them, raising thousands for each charity they publicized. Grace was the public face, the ex-soapie star clawing her way back from alcohol and drugs to become the biggest-rating breakfast talk show in Queensland. Kat preferred it like that, preferred to work behind the scenes. It made a nice change, even though she still fielded a handful of interview requests every day.

No, she was content with her life. Work filled every waking moment, which meant no time for dating. Just as she'd told Connor during their regular "bon voyage, Marco" night out ten weeks ago in a Brisbane bar, she didn't do attachments or relationships anymore.

"Too much work, too difficult to navigate and way too painful when they inevitably end," she'd said, downing her drink and eyeing her friends across the table.

Marco and Luke had laughed, but Connor had had a weird look, a kind of sad-but-deadly-serious one that had annoyed her enough to order that last, fateful vodka and orange.

She swallowed an irritating lump in her throat. There was nothing wrong with her. As a teenager she'd never been obsessed with boyfriends, weddings or babies, which had set her apart from most girls in the elite Southbank Private School in Brisbane. Couple that with her preference for sport, pub bands and getting dirty over short skirts, makeup and gossip, and she'd naturally migrated toward the boys. And then there was "that incident"—as her father had called it—when she'd shoved Marco Corelli, the son of the now-notorious crime boss Gino Corelli. After the furor had died down and she'd done her counseling and detention stint, she'd realized she'd become a bit of a legend to her peers. Connor Blair, the moody silent one, had allowed her to sit with them at lunch. Luke—always so very angry—had bonded with her over obscure pub bands, and Marco… Well, he'd apologized and she'd scored a friend for life.

Complicated, complex Marco. The cocky, flirty teenager with an insane gift for soccer, who'd grown up into a gorgeous, talented, self-assured man. The guy knew her secrets, her childhood wishes, her family tragedies.

Especially her family tragedies. With her mother's death from motor neuron disease and the chances of Kat being a carrier, she'd never allowed that particular fantasy of becoming a mother take root. But now, faced with the bald-faced reality of actually being pregnant, she had absolutely no clue how to feel. After all those years of refusing the tests, of arguing with Marco that she preferred to spend her life living and not worrying, she'd actually gone and gotten tested. Now she had to wait for the results, which added extra stress to her already stressful situation.

Which was why she couldn't tell Marco. Ever.

With a sigh, she refocused on the here and now. By the time they'd finished filming the week's shows, it was eleven at night and Kat was dead on her feet. She said good-night to everyone and dragged herself to her car, fumbling with the keys as she went, her mind focused on takeout, a hot bath and double-checking her apartment for the impending storm.

Then she glanced at her car and stopped in her tracks.

Marco.

Her heart pounding, her gaze swept over him—his suit, his loosened tie, the dark hair flopping over his forehead and curling at the collar. The faint shadow of stubble dusting his firm jaw. The way he stood, all sexy and casual, hands buried in his pockets. And those wide, piercing brown eyes staring straight at her.

On another man, one with less confidence and overt sexuality, his features could almost be called pretty, if not for the overabundant aura of pure male surrounding him. His hair was a controlled crop of curls, perfectly framing those high cheekbones, lush mouth and come-to-bed eyes. And when he smiled...Lord, you could hear the knickers dropping for miles around. He reminded her of days gone by, of stocking-and-breech-clad heroes, flamboyant coats and huge romantic gestures full of wild symphonies and desperate, love-smitten poems.

And he'd been the best sex she'd had in her life.

Yes, he was adored by millions around the world. Everyone knew the story—only son of Italian immigrants, raised in Australia until a talent scout had recruited him for the French *futball* league at the tender age of sixteen. Marco, the dreamy Italian with romantic eyes and glorious touch-me hair. If that wasn't enough of an unfair advantage, he'd also acquired a hot French accent from his years living and working in Marseille and Paris. Marco, her best friend.

Her heart contracted then expanded again, and she wanted to die from the sudden ache of it all.

They'd known each other for nearly twenty years. Telling him would irrevocably change everything. Marco didn't do commitment. He loved his job, he loved women and he loved the freedom to enjoy both. And there was no way she'd lose him as her best friend after one foolish—*amazing*—night. She couldn't.

With a deep breath she continued, heading straight for her car. And the closer she got, the worse the weird feeling grew.

They'd done things—intimate things. Things she'd never imagined doing with him. They'd gotten naked, and he'd touched her and kissed her all over. Now he wanted to talk about it, and she'd rather swim with a pod of sharks than rehash her supreme stupidity that involved *that night.*

God, could it get any worse? With false bravado, she clicked off her car alarm and then crossed the last few meters to open the door.

"What are you doing here?" she asked, resisting the urge to lay a hand on her belly. Instead, she tossed her bag into the passenger seat.

"We need to talk." His unique voice—a sexy mix of French and faint Italian accents—never failed to make her shiver, but now she shoved her hair back behind her ear and steeled herself to face him. The bright security lights slashed across his face, revealing a serious expression that made her heart thump. But instead of giving in to the panic, she swallowed and crossed her arms, tilting her head.

"About?"

"We can talk on my boat."

She sighed. "Look, Marco, it's late and there's a cyclone approaching. Can't this wait another day?"

"You've been avoiding my calls, so no. And the storm's not due for hours yet."

He glanced up at the dark sky and narrowed his eyes at the barely discernible wind that had picked up.

"I'm tired."

He stared at her, irritated. "Phone calls. Avoiding."

She blinked slowly. "You're not going to give up until I agree, are you?"

*"Non."*

She sighed. "Fine. But be quick about it."

He eased off her car, moving into her personal space, and instinctively Kat took a step back, which only prompted him to frown. "You're not going to stand me up, are you?"

"No, I am not. Girl Guide's honor."

"Good." With a firm nod, he walked past her, got in his car and drove off.

She watched his taillights blink as he turned left out of the parking lot before she had time to fully comprehend what her acquiescence really meant.

*We need to talk.* Those four little words lay heavy with meaning, conjuring up a multitude of awkward scenarios from her disastrous past. Ten weeks ago, they'd not only crossed that line between friends and lovers, they'd burned it to the ground, and part of her wanted to run home and hide under the bedcovers. The other part wanted this awkward situation over and done with.

With a sigh she got in her car, fired up the engine and drove out of the car park. She couldn't run from him forever. It was time to suck it up and face whatever consequences that one night had wrought.

The marina was alive with activity, crowded with people securing their boats and belongings in preparation for the oncoming storm. Kat parked and headed down the wooden platform, eyeing the foreboding water as the dark waves lapped against the jetty. In a few hours' time, a category-four cyclone would sweep across the coast, and everyone knew all too well the devastation it would bring. The city had only just managed to recover after Cyclone Yasi had slammed into North Queensland some years before.

Marco's boat was moored at the end, a sleek, shiny thing he'd gone into great loving detail about when he'd first bought it. The only thing she remembered from that conversation was not the horsepower, the dimensions or the fuel consumption, but rather his little-kid excitement. It had made her heart flip then, as it did now when she recalled the three-year-old memories.

He stood on the deck and offered his hand as she stepped across the gangplank. Without thinking she took it.

It was weird—she'd held his hand a thousand times before, and yet right now this one simple gesture was making her jittery, as though her whole body had been put on alert and was awaiting the next eager move.

Which was stupid. Ridiculous. And highly inconvenient.

Dammit, that was what came with sleeping with your bestie. Because now she couldn't stop the memories of those same hands roaming all over her body and doing things that had gotten her all hot and panting.

As they walked aft, she managed to surreptitiously slip her hand from his, avoiding his sideways glance by determinedly staring straight ahead.

God, she hated this awkwardness. They'd gone and done the unthinkable and ruined everything, and for a second, she felt that indescribable pain slice into her heart, leaving a deep and wounding scar in its wake. Things would never be the same again. It was like one of her disastrous relationships all over again, like everything her father had blurted out that one awful time in the heat of argument.

*For God's sake, Kat, can you just for once* not *be front-page news? Stop with all the attention and drama and just be a normal person?*

The shame burned briefly as she recalled his expression, a bitter twist of anger and disappointment. Then her thoughts were interrupted by the familiar hum and throb of engines as they entered the cabin.

She stopped in her tracks. "Are you casting off?"

"*Oui.* We're going to the island."

She gaped. Annoyance quickly morphed into fury. "Are you out of your mind? No!" She strode outside but it was too late. Furious, she whirled, pinning him with dagger eyes. "I didn't agree to this! And there's a cyclone on its way, in case you haven't noticed." She threw an arm wide, indicating the dock rapidly disappearing. "The town's in lockdown. *And* my car is at the marina."

He crossed his arms and leaned back onto the rail, then absently pushed back a curl as the wind whipped his hair around his face. "First, my house on the island is designed to withstand weather extremes, cyclones included. It's probably safer than most places on the mainland. Second, I'll call someone to pick up your car. And third, the reports say the island will only catch the edge of it—the eye will hit Cairns after 3:00 a.m."

"And by that time, we won't be able to return for God knows how long. No. Go back, Marco."

"No."

She growled. "I hate it when you get pushy."

His mouth quirked briefly but he said nothing. She continued to glare, putting all her anger into it, but he merely held her gaze calmly.

"You've been avoiding my calls," he finally said.

With a frustrated growl she whirled, planting her hands wide apart on the railing. "Dammit, you can be sooooo annoying!"

"Says the woman who *still* hasn't told me she's pregnant."

A moment passed, a moment in which Kat's heart sped up, then slowed down again as she closed her eyes and dropped her gaze to the churning black water below. A moment in which those meager rehearsed words all crumbled to ashes in her mouth, and she was left with nothing but the sound of slapping water and rushing air.

"I'm going to kill Connor."

Marco raised one dark eyebrow. "Don't blame him. He thought I should know."

Finally she straightened, crossed her arms and faced him. "Turn the boat around. It's not safe to be out."

"I checked with the coast guard. We're fine for at least another hour, enough time to get to the island." He shook his head. "And we have things to discuss."

"There's nothing to discuss."

A dark scowl bloomed. "You're kidding, right? You're *pregnant,* Kat. It's not just about you. It's about me, too."

She knew that. But the bubbling frustration inside forced the words from her mouth. "My body, my decision."

He stilled, his expression a mix of shock and seriousness. "Are you saying you want an abortion?"

She blinked, shaking her head as her stomach pitched in time with the waves. "Marco, you know what I went through with my mother. She was dead within two years of diagnosis. I could be a carrier."

He dragged a hand through his hair. "So get tested. I've been telling you that for years."

"I did. Plus, I do not have one single mothering bone in my body. Babies hate me and—"

"Whoa, whoa, whoa. Back up." He frowned and held up a hand. "You actually went and got *tested?*"

"Yes. Last week."

"After all these years of 'I don't want to know' and 'I don't want that hanging over my head, directing my choices in life'? All the times we argued when I tried to convince you otherwise?"

She nodded.

She'd shocked him, if his gaping expression was any indicator. "When were you going to tell me?" he finally bit out.

"I just did!" she snapped back, inwardly wincing at his thinly concealed hurt. "And speaking of not telling, what about you and Grace?"

"What about me and Grace?"

"So there *is* a you and Grace!"

He scowled, confused. "What the hell are you talking about?"

"You and her, having a baby together?"

From the look on his face, she'd stunned him. "Since when?"

"She told me you were back together."

He sighed, hands going to his hips. "Well, it's news to me. We've been over since before the *Coup de France.*"

"How long before?"

"Way before our night together, *chérie,*" he said softly.

She swallowed, refusing to allow herself a moment of remembrance. "So, you're saying Grace is lying?"

He shrugged. "Wishful thinking?"

She snapped her mouth shut, taking a deep, steady breath before mumbling, "This is a bloody disaster."

Was it her imagination, or did she see his mouth tighten? Then he sighed and dragged a hand through his hair and the moment was gone. "Kat, I can't stop you from making the final decision about what you do. If it were me, I'd be having the baby, regardless of those test results. But it's ultimately your choice."

"Then it's a good thing you're not me," she said quietly. "You weren't there. You didn't see what the disease did to my mother, every single day, for two years. I refuse to let that happen to my child."

His soft murmur sounded more like a groan. "Kat…"

The boat went over another wave, and suddenly the day's lunch didn't seem so secure in her stomach. She swallowed thickly then took a deep breath before meeting his eyes.

"I'll be here as much as you need me to be," he said, his gaze soft. "You're my best friend, *chérie,* and that's what friends do."

*Friends.* Her insides did another crazy swoop, just before the nausea surged again. This was no confession of love, no happily-ever-after, no I-can't-live-without-you. This was Marco offering his friendship and support, just as he'd always done throughout the tragedies of her embarrassingly public private life.

She swallowed a weird swell of abject disappointment. "Marco." She shook her head. "I don't know…. I haven't made any decision. Plus…" She took a breath. "I can't—I won't—have a baby just because you want it. And once this gets out—whatever my decision—there's going to be a media frenzy. Your career is more important than front-page gossip."

"Kat—"

"You know what the headlines were like last time. Do you honestly think I'd do that to you? I… Oh, God." She clutched her stomach.

He grabbed her arm, his face creased with alarm. “What’s wrong? What—”

She turned to the railing but wasn’t quick enough. In the next second, she threw up all over the deck, right on top of Marco’s expensive Italian leather shoes.

# Two

"Guess I should've seen that coming," Marco said drily as she rushed to the railing and continued to throw up over the side.

When he placed a gentle hand on her back, she shrugged it off with a groan. "Oh, God, don't."

His gaze darted from her to briefly stare up into the dark storm clouds. It was about to rain and rain hard, and if his captain, Larry, hurried, the crew could make it safely back to the mainland before it all came down. What he needed to discuss with Kat was between them alone; he certainly didn't need anyone else encroaching on their privacy.

He returned to Kat's doubled-up figure and shifted uncomfortably on the deck. He should've thought about seasickness. She wasn't a great sailor at the best of times, and with the added pregnancy, he wasn't surprised she'd thrown up.

"Can I get you anything?" he said now, frowning as her thick breath rattled in her throat. It tore little pieces from him, listening to her force down the nausea, willing herself not to throw up. She hated being sick, and he'd held her hair back on more than one occasion, watching helplessly as she went through the motions while he'd soothingly rubbed her back and made the appropriate sympathetic noises.

She stayed like that, bent over the railing, unfazed by the wind and ocean spray on her face until they finally docked at Sunset Island's small jetty twenty minutes later. As the boat edged slowly into position, Kat pulled herself upright, swiping at her mouth and swallowing thickly with a grimace.

"Bathroom," she muttered, and he silently watched her head into the cabin.

Five minutes later, as he was going over his choices in a long lineup of conversation starters, she emerged, her face pale and grim, a swipe of lip gloss on her mouth.

When she walked out onto the deck, that weird, tumultuous, out-of-control feeling had receded, only to be replaced with trepidation. This crazy situation was totally out of his hands, and that thought freaked the hell out of him. Yet she...she looked so cool and blank as she strode toward him that he felt the sudden urge to kiss her, to dislodge that perfect composure and make her as frustrated and confused as he felt.

Stupid idea. Because Kat had made it clear she wanted to forget what they'd done all those weeks ago. And if he looked at this logically, that was the sensible thing to do. They were best friends. Throughout all their sucky personal relationships, her mother's death, his one marriage and divorce, her two, plus the crazy media attention they always seemed to attract, their friendship endured. Sure, the papers always hinted at something more, but they'd both laughed and shrugged it off a long time ago.

Yet now, as his insides pitched with uncharacteristic uncertainty, she looked almost…calm. As if she'd already made a decision and was confident in making it.

She was so damn strong. Sometimes too strong. Just one of the things that both attracted and annoyed him.

"I don't know what more we have to discuss," she said now, watching his crew prepare to dock. "This is a waste of time. Plus, with the approaching cyclone, we need to let people know where we are."

"I called the authorities before we left, plus your father, my mother and Connor," he said calmly.

"Wow. You really planned ahead for this, didn't you?"

He ignored her sarcasm. "All bases are covered. We're perfectly safe."

Her face creased with such serious doubt that he had to smother a laugh.

*Safe?* No way, not when her expression became suddenly tight and he knew exactly where her thoughts were going. If they were anything like his, it was back to That Night, replaying every intimate second over and over, despite his determination to shove it to the back of his mind. She didn't want to be stuck anywhere with him, least of all in such an intimate personal space.

Her breath snapped in, eyes darkening just before she glanced away, and his groin tightened. It was incredibly arousing, knowing she was obviously remembering their crazy-hot lovemaking. Lovemaking that had, instead of quenching the hunger, only succeeded in stoking his desire for more.

His low groan was lost in the noisy preparations for docking, yet when he gently took her arm, she shot him a dark scowl and dug her heels in.

His eyebrows ratcheted up. “You’re going to stay on the boat in protest?”

“I should.”

“Well, that’s a dumb idea. A storm’s coming, in case you hadn’t noticed.”

“You’re the one who dragged me out here.”

He sighed. “Look, *chérie,* come to the house. If you want to yell at me, at least we’ll be safe.”

She paused, seeming to go through her limited options, until her chin went up and she shot him a glare. “Fine. But as soon as the storm’s passed, you’re taking me home.”

He almost smiled. Almost. “Okay.”

She gave him a final look then swept past him, down the gangplank and onto the rickety jetty, her heels echoing dully as he commanded his crew to take the spare vessel and return to the mainland.

They took a golf buggy to the house, efficiently moving along the road that edged the west side of Sunset Island. Just like all the times before, when the place came into sight, Kat held her breath and marveled at the architecture of the magnificent six-bedroom house. It was all glass and timber walls set in a lush tropical rain forest, with natural lines, arches and a sloping roof set on sturdy stilts, perfectly sheltered among the vegetation to avoid the fiercest storms yet taking spectacular advantage of the amazing Pacific Ocean sunsets.

This was Marco's haven, a place he could relax and be himself with his friends. The guy she knew so very well. The guy who was now intimate with her body, who had made her moan and climax.

As Kat ran her eyes over the house's familiar lines and tried not to think about *that,* the buggy wound its way along the driveway, until finally they stopped at the front door and Marco got out. Again, he offered his hand and she was forced to take it, although she quickly released him as soon as she stepped out.

"We need to secure the shutters before the storm hits," he said, eyeing the sky.

Kat nodded and followed him to the long path edged with a sturdy safety railing that ran all the way around the house. As the wind slowly picked up and the trees began to sway, they both worked in silence, cranking down the storm shutters covering the multitude of windows. With the last one firmly in place, they returned to the front.

"The birds and the bats flew off a few hours ago," Marco commented, frowning into the dark sky. "They know something's wrong."

A chill ran over her skin. "The Bureau of Meteorology said the main eye is bound for Cairns."

"Yeah, they're bracing for the worst—mobile phone towers down, power outages. The ports will be closed, too. So, not the best place to be right now. Let's get inside."

"I've got nothing to wear," she said suddenly as she stepped in the door.

"You've still got some stuff from last time. And you can borrow from me if you need to."

Walking around in Marco's clothes, smelling his scent, knowing the exact same garments had been right up next to his skin? Just. No.

Kat said nothing as she walked into the familiar coolness of the slate foyer, down the hall to the back of the house, past the amazing indoor pool with wet bar to her right, the elegant water feature bubbling away to her left.

Finally she reached the heart of the house—the huge combined kitchen and entertainment area with comfy sofas, a wide-screen plasma TV, dining table to the side, curved walls with floor-to-ceiling windows and a fully equipped kitchen. She and his guests always spent their time here, eating and talking current affairs, the state of the world, his second home in Marseille and the ever-present topic, European football.

She went straight to the fridge, grabbed a ginger beer and then walked to the barricaded windows that normally displayed an uninterrupted one-eighty view of the Pacific Ocean.

During the day the simple beauty of searing blue sky stretched forever until it eventually dipped to kiss the dark ocean in the far distance. At night, the absolute blackness enveloped everything, the only respite the tiny mainland lights on the horizon. Except this time she was more than acutely aware of the brewing storm playing out behind the shutters, matching her churning thoughts as she heard Marco's firm footfalls on the polished marble behind her. The vague scent of his aftershave brought back the uncomfortable memories from that one night, ten weeks ago.

"So we should be clear of the storm here," she began, her back still to him, the cold ginger-beer bottle cradled against her warm neckline.

"Yes." He reached for the patio door handle and swung it wide, walking out onto the lit deck. "But we've still got a warning and need to take all precautions."

"Your cellar," she said as he began to collect the deck chairs.

He nodded then grinned. "And you guys teased me for converting it."

She pulled a chair inside the back door. "Well, to be fair, the worst you'd ever seen was a tropical rainstorm, not a cyclone."

"Always a first time for everything."

Those words took on a whole new meaning tonight. She watched him carry the patio chairs inside, waiting for him to break the silence as she picked at the label on her ginger-beer bottle.

He finally closed and locked the door, and after a few minutes of him shoving the chairs into a corner and saying nothing, she was about ready to break.

"Marco—"

"Kat—"

They both turned and spoke at the same time, but it was Kat who paused for him to continue. When he sighed and ran a hand through his hair, she wanted to groan out loud. She knew exactly what that hair felt like in her fingers, how soft it was, how it curled and waved with a life of its own, and how with one gentle tug at the nape she could direct his mouth to a better place on her neck....

*Oh, God, I have to stop thinking about that!*

When she glanced up, he was looking at her with

those dark eyes, assessing her every word, movement and expression until she felt vaguely underdressed. Ridiculous, because the last thing on his mind right now was getting her naked and into bed.

What a vision that conjured up. *No. No! Stop it!*

Then he abruptly turned and the moment shattered.

"You need food," he said, striding over to the kitchen and opening the fridge door. "And we need to prepare for tonight."

Her stomach took that moment to remind her of her long-gone lunch, and with a sigh she followed him over, her mind on the immediate problem of her empty belly. "What do you have?"

He waved his hand inside the fridge. "You choose. I'm going to tape up the windows."

Kat prepared bread rolls, cheese, cold meats and potato salad while Marco placed thick tape across all the windows. After they ate, they sat on the sofa and had coffee, the muted TV spurting out nonstop cyclone updates.

It was a familiar scenario—the coffee, the silent television, their seating positions: she at one corner, sprawled across two spots and hugging a pillow, he in the opposite corner with ankles and arms crossed. Yet the unspoken tension in the air was smoke-thick and just as hard to ignore.

This time it was Kat who broke the silence. "You know, Grace was arranging a surprise dinner for your return."

His eyebrow went up. "Was she?"

"Yeah."

"Right." The slight grimace in his expression spoke volumes.

"What's that look for?"

"What look?"

"Don't give me that. You know the one."

He sighed. "I don't know why she keeps bothering. We broke up months ago."

"I see," Kat said slowly, pressing her lips together. Marco would never lie to her—so *was* it all wishful thinking on Grace's part? She frowned. Yeah, Grace liked to talk up all her relationships—that TV exec three months ago, the Russian writer, the ex-soapie star.

Then Marco abruptly turned on the couch, giving her his full attention, and she forgot all about Grace's love life.

"Kat, this is me here. We talk about pretty much everything—"

"Not *everything*."

He gave her a look. "Just stop avoiding the issue and talk to me now. Let's think this baby situation over logically."

She shook her head. "Were you not listening about the tests?"

"I didn't ask that. I asked if you wanted to have this baby."

"I am *not* turning this discussion into a pro-choice debate."

He scowled. "I'm not trying to. All I'm asking is for you to consider all your options."

Her insides ached. "That's *all* I've been doing since I found out. Marco, please don't do this. I can't get attached, knowing there's a possibility it will be carrying a fatal disease. Plus, I know women are supposed to have these ticking body clocks, supposed to be filled with a great burning need to be mothers, but I am telling you, I'm not one of them."

And yet…there'd been a few moments where she'd allowed her imagination to drift, where her thoughts had been occupied by something other than work, her swish Cairns apartment and all those solitary nights stretching before her. She'd imagined an unfamiliar future consisting of a house, a garden, a husband and babies. A scary, scary thought that had her breath catching and her heart racing every time she let her mind wander there.

*No.*

She sighed. "I…I don't know what to say. I really don't."

"Well, that's a start. At least it means you're not wedded to the idea of an abortion."

"I'm not making any decision until the tests come back. I'm not going to…" She swallowed and glanced away. "Not going to get attached to the idea if they come back positive. And anyway, what on earth am I going to do with a baby? This is *me* we're talking about here."

His scowl deepened. "Don't be ridiculous. You're a great person. You're funny and gorgeous and smart, and you have people in your life who love you."

She flushed under the unexpected praise. "But a *mother?*"

"Other women begin with a whole lot less."

"But it's a full-time job. A lifelong commitment." She worried the edge of the pillow, picking at the stitching. "You can't get a do-over with these things. What if I stuff it up?"

"Nobody's perfect at parenting—just look at Connor's family. I guarantee you'd do a lot better than them."

Kat nodded. It was impossible to avoid the Blairs, especially when her father and Connor's were business partners at Jackson & Blair. Unlike her relationship with Marco's parents, she'd never warmed to Stephen Blair, a ruthlessly ambitious man with a penchant for blondes, and his wife, Corinne, a cold gym-junkie socialite with a Botox habit. Connor's childhood was a perfect study in fractured family dynamics. A therapist's dream… more so than her own.

"My dad isn't much better," she said now. "He'd rather hold a grudge about old headlines than dole out any praise."

"At least they were happy, well, until…" He trailed off diplomatically.

Until her mother's diagnosis. Kat silently filled in the sentence. They had been strict but fair, even when she'd stretched the limits with the usual teenage smoking, drinking and sneaking out to parties. Certainly not overly demonstrative in their affections. But after her mother's diagnosis, her father had turned into an angry, bitter man, always judgmental, always unhappy. And Kat could never do anything right, from her decision to drop out of Brisbane University to her crazy, wild nights on the town that were her one respite from thinking about her mother's disease.

Until one particular night when she'd stumbled home at sunrise in a highly drunken state and her father had been waiting for her, scorn pouring from every tense muscle.

*"You've had everything we could give you, and look*

*at you! Your mother is dying, so you throw in a perfectly good education to get drunk every weekend!"*

*"Maybe that's the point!"* she'd stormed back. *"It's in my head every single waking moment. I need some time to clear it out, to just forget, otherwise I'll go crazy!"*

His fists had clenched, and for one awful moment she'd wondered whether he'd give in to the temptation and actually hit her. Instead he'd cut her with words, his particular specialty.

A month later her mother had died and Kat had run away to France, where Marco was the current darling of French football. Where she'd slowly come to realize there was more to her tiny little world than short skirts, wild parties and free drinks.

Kat swallowed, pushing the memory aside. God, no wonder the press had loved to hate her. She'd been such a spoiled little rich girl.

"But you've grown since then," Marco said now. "And he's still stuck in the past, rehashing old arguments. We don't have to be our parents. Not with our child."

*Our child.* Those two words were like a blow to the chest, leaving a shallow breath rattling in her throat.

"Look, Marco, let's be honest. You've worked incredibly hard to get where you are. You've got a great career and an amazing, wonderful life. No commitment, no ties—"

"Kat…"

"No, let me finish. You can jump on a plane at a moment's notice and be on the other side of the world. You have your pick of women—and there are a *lot* of women."

"Kat—"

She ignored the warning growl in his voice and kept going. "I'm not going to force you to change, and a baby does that, in ways you can't even imagine. The media frenzy will affect both our lives and careers."

"If you choose to keep the baby, then I'll do the right thing."

She blinked. "The right thing? What, are we living in the 1950s now? You don't have to marry me because I'm pregnant."

He paused, a second too long. "Who said anything about marriage? I'm talking about being here for you. As your friend."

She frowned, the unexpected sliver of disappointment stabbing hard. Oh, so now she wasn't good enough to marry, was that it? But just as she was about to open her mouth and say exactly that, she snapped it shut. That was manipulation of the worst kind, and she refused to do it. She couldn't put Marco in that position—she wouldn't. And marriage was the last thing she wanted.

"Good thing, too. I suck at relationships," she said lightly, her hand tight on the coffee cup. "I've tried too many times, but I just don't have that particular gene. They're messy, they're painful and they always end in disaster. I don't want to ruin our friendship."

"You don't suck. You didn't force James to cheat. You didn't hand the press those photos." Marco's brows took a dive, his expression dark. "And as for Ben…"

"Please do *not* remind me." If there was a Disastrous Relationship Museum, hers would take front and center as prime exhibit number one: her first marriage to Jackson & Blair's publicity manager, Ben Freeman, when she was twenty-two. He'd turned out to be a selfish, misogynistic bastard. Her second marriage five years later, a quickie Bali wedding to Marco's teammate, annulled after just seventy-two hours when she'd caught James screwing a waitress in their bridal suite. And then her engagement to Aussie Rules' wild child Ezio Cantoni barely a year ago. *He'd* taken nude shower shots of her then "accidentally" leaked them to the tabloids.

She was done with the scrutiny, the uncertainty, the angst. It was painful and humiliating and downright tiring. For her sanity and self-respect, it was just not worth the effort. And now she was bringing a child into that?

Kat sighed, shifting on the sofa. "And honestly, Marco, how are you going to be involved? Weren't you planning to move back to France after the Football Federation of Australia's awards in three weeks?"

"That was one option."

Her brow ratcheted up. "That's not how you talked about it a few months ago."

He sighed and cast an eye to the shuttered window. "I've got a lot of things going on—the coaching clinics, the sponsorship stuff. Plus my network contract is up for renegotiation next month. I haven't decided about France yet."

She paused for long, drawn-out seconds. "Oh, no. Don't you *dare* start to rethink anything. I won't allow it."

"You won't allow it?"

"No." She ignored his irritation with a wave of her hand. "We're not married. Hell, we're not even a couple. Just…best friends who may be having a baby."

He said nothing, just looked toward the shuttered windows and then the wall clock that read quarter past one. "It sounds to be getting worse outside." He stood. "We should go downstairs."

She paused, glancing toward the windows, then nodded. "Okay."

He offered his hand and she automatically took it, the sudden urgency of the moment pushing their discussion into the background. The innocent warmth of his fingers wrapped around hers created a frustratingly intimate sensation that she was loath to give up. He took her down the hall, to a door that led to the basement and his wine cellar, which he'd modified with this kind of situation in mind.

The wine was stacked neatly to the left of the small room, and to the right sat a couch, a fixed, fully stocked bar fridge and a small generator that powered the soft lamps that were now lit in preparation.

She hesitated at the door, scanning the room as reality flooded in.

"Don't worry, *chérie,*" Marco said beside her, giving her fingers a reassuring squeeze. "We're perfectly safe."

Again, that word. The door was heavy but he closed it with ease, and when he turned to her, she swallowed the panic and offered a shaky smile.

They settled quickly in the room, Kat automatically going over to prepare coffee, Marco checking the small ventilation window high on the far wall and then the lights. After a few more minutes, they sat on the couch, Marco pulled out a pack of UNO cards and they settled in for the night.

"So how's working for Grace going? Still a pain in the butt?" Marco asked casually as he shuffled the pack.

"Oh, she's not that bad."

"Hmm." His expression was skeptical as he dealt them seven cards apiece.

She sighed. "Actually, I miss my old London job."

"What, the one you took up between Ben and James?"

"Ugh." She made a face. "My life's most significant moments reduced to a 'between exes' reference."

"Sorry." Marco's expression looked anything but. "Let me rephrase. The Oxfam job you took at the age of twenty-five when you spent a couple of years living and working in London in blissful anonymity."

She gave him a look, not entirely convinced he wasn't being sarcastic, before finally nodding. "It was only a year, but I felt better about that job than anything I've ever done. I felt like I should—" She cut herself off abruptly, her thumbnail going to her mouth, teeth worrying it.

"Like you should what?" He picked up his cards and fanned them expertly.

"Like I should do something more. Donate to charity or start up a foundation or something."

She waited for him to voice doubt, to echo her father's familiar refrain about giving up a perfectly good job for an uncertain dream when she'd casually mentioned the subject a few months ago. Instead he just looked at her and said, "You've never mentioned that before."

She shrugged and overturned the first card on the top of the deck. "I stopped thinking about it after I told my dad."

"Let me guess—he said you don't know a thing about running a charity, it's too expensive, why chuck in a perfectly stable job for a dubious flight of fancy in this economy when you'll lose interest in the first year?"

"All of the above."

He sighed and placed a yellow two on the pile. The

sudden silence sat heavy in the air now, until Marco finally spoke. "Have you done the figures? Worked out how much it would take to do something like that?"

"No."

"So work it out. Make a business plan. Talk to your old workmates. Call your accountant. Screw your father. I mean that in the nicest possible way," he added with a thin smile and placed the first card down on the table. "You're smart and clever and you have experience. You can work a crowd, raise funds and know how to handle the press. Whatever happens with those tests and the baby, you can still do this."

She stared at her hand, rearranging the cards by color as her mind worked furiously. Oh, she wanted to. In between the many fluff pieces and gossip segments *Morning Grace* aired, the human-interest stories drew her the most. The burning compulsion to do something herself, to help ease someone's burden, to bring a little joy into the lives of people who really needed it, got her every time. She always ended up donating to every cause she sourced. Every time.

"This'll be bigger than a ten-minute segment," Marco said now. "You'll be able to give things more media coverage, follow it through, devote more time. Really make a difference."

She put a Draw Two on the pile and murmured something noncommittal, signaling the end of the discussion.

Marco said no more and for the next half hour they played cards and pretended everything was fine, even though the faint sounds of the creaking house and the wind as it picked up forced their attention from the game a dozen times. Finally Marco turned on the small radio and the room was filled with a steady stream of weather updates.

When the lights suddenly went out, Kat jumped. Yet when the generator kicked in seconds later and the lights clicked back on, it did nothing to assuage her growing panic.

"What are we even doing here?" she muttered, flicking her thumb along the edge of her cards, eyeing the lights, then the generator. "We went out in a cyclone warning, for God's sake! This is stupid, not to mention dangerous."

"We're not in its direct path. Would I honestly do something to put us in danger? Trust me. We're safe."

When she shivered, he handed her the blanket from the couch, draping it around her shoulders, tucking it close. She half expected a tender forehead kiss to finish. Damn, she was actually wishing for it. He'd kissed her before, an I-love-you-you're-my-best-friend kiss on the cheek or the forehead. And they'd hugged more frequently than she could count. But tellingly, he'd never kissed her on the lips. Until That Night.

For the next twenty minutes they kept playing cards as the rain and howling wind picked up, the updates morphing into location reports and interviews of people in organized shelters and those who chose to stay in their homes and see the storm through.

Half an hour later, it hit.

Card game now forgotten, they sat in tense silence, hip to knee on the couch, glued to the radio. The wind screamed past the house, ripping through the trees and banging the shutters in their frames. From inside their refuge, they could hear the rush of air, the snap and crack of trees bending and breaking under the raw elements, debris being thrown around. The house remained firm but the wind and slashing rain was a constant, picking up in waves then petering out until the minutes stretched like hours.

The radio spat out crucial information as the cyclone careened across the coast, and as time crawled into an hour, then two, and the cyclone finally passed through Cairns and headed south before dying down a few miles out to sea, details began to trickle in. Details of devastating damage, heart-wrenchingly revealed via the mainland survivors.

*"We're gonna have to start over. We've lost everything."*

*"We have family, friends, community. We'll survive this."*

*"I don't know whether we can rebuild. We weren't insured."*

*"Well, you just pick up and move on, don't you? You just get it done."*

*"Please, help us. Our house...everything. It's gone. We need help."*

Kat's breath caught, the sob forming low in her throat as she listened to that last one, a woman and her family who'd been right in the storm's path. It ripped at her like claws, and she unashamedly let silent tears well as the extent of the damage was slowly and thoroughly detailed over the course of an hour.

When Marco's hand went to her knee, patting reassuringly, she jumped, eyes flying to his.

The look on his face undid her, a mix of sorrow and understanding that reflected everything she'd tried to keep inside. She watched him swallow, her gaze following his thumb as he leaned in to gently wipe away her tears.

"Don't cry," he said softly, knuckles and thumb resting firmly on her cheekbone. "It's okay."

Her breath jagged. "But all those people..."

"They'll rebuild. You know that. No fatalities have been reported, so that's one good thing. It'll be okay. We're safe."

She sniffed, unable to look away from his concerned gaze. "I was scared."

"I know." He cupped her face and leaned in, placing his warm mouth first on one cheek, then the other. Years ago, the familiar French-style greeting had amused her. But now, with his lips so very close to hers, and then as she watched him slowly pull back with a soft smile creasing those dreamy eyes, her heart leaped.

*Keep calm, Kat. If you stop acting normal around him, he'll know something is wrong.* But could she honestly do all those little things, the smiling, the hugs, the casual touching, and not be affected by what they'd done?

Her gaze darted to that mouth, that lovely, lush mouth that seemed like an evil conspiracy on a man already so beautiful.

Yes, *beautiful* was the only word to describe Marco Corelli. Outwardly he appeared cocky and confident, working the crowd, the camera, the press with smooth ease that trod a fine line between charming and practiced. He always got what he wanted, be it an interview, a prime restaurant table or a woman. But she also knew him better than anyone else and knew that public persona was only a small part of what made him tick. He was generous. Fiercely loyal. Fiery and passionate about the things and people he loved.

She could feel his eyes on her, taking in her expression, every single movement, and it was then that she realized she'd been staring at his mouth and daydreaming like some mooning soccer groupie.

With a suddenly dry throat, she darted her gaze to his.

And her breath stuttered all over again.

# Three

Kat didn't know what happened because it was instantaneous, although in reality it probably took a little longer than that. All she knew was one second she was sitting there, heart pounding, his hand still cupping her face, the imprint of his warm mouth on her skin. Then his gaze slipped to her lips, she parted them, he made some choked sound and suddenly he swooped down and they were kissing.

Her arms went around his neck as if they belonged there. She groaned, opened up for him and was gone.

He dragged her to his chest, cradling her, almost as if inviting her to sink into him. So she did.

During the long, hot, unbelievable kiss, she felt his hands everywhere, tugging her clothing, sweeping over her skin, caressing and touching until she was all heated up and her heart throbbed hard against her ribs. Then he pushed her back, bunching her skirt around her waist, and she was grabbing his shirt, yanking it from his pants and fumbling with the waistband.

"Let me." He pushed her hands aside, quickly dragging down his pants, his urgency fueling her arousal as her mouth locked on his. Her blood raced as he jammed a knee between her legs, pushing them roughly apart then settling his hips against her before suddenly and swiftly entering her.

A harsh breath hissed from her lips, matching his as she stared into those dark eyes that bled black with passion, and she nearly lost it then and there. Then he uttered a low growl, hitched her leg around his waist, pinned her hands above her head and started to move.

She couldn't think, couldn't breathe, from the raw, animal sensation of being filled, fully and completely. He wasn't tender or slow. He didn't offer romantic words of love. He simply took, and when she got over the shock of the moment, she took, too, welcoming him, grinding her hips hard into his, her breath rushing out in a harsh groan, her teeth nipping the sensitive spot where his neck met shoulder. He cursed softly when she did that, upping the pace so she slammed into the sofa, the cushions grazing her skin. She gasped but kept moving, knowing full well she'd have wool burns come morning but totally beyond caring. Instead the moment took her, wiped away any reality until it was just them, their harsh breath coupling in the eerie silence and the air full of the familiar scent of sex and need.

Breathless and throbbing, she impatiently rocked her hips against his, eager for the final release. And when her climax came, it rushed in with little warning, and she was left floundering as the waves crashed, leaving her shaking and panting. Dimly she was aware that Marco still had her hands pinned, his deep murmur of release against her lips as he followed her, his body jerking into hers. She shook, his satisfaction heightening hers, and she tightened her leg around his waist, cradling his body, taking all of him with a groan that ripped from deep inside.

It was…he was… She groaned again and closed her eyes, willing reality to stay away for just a moment more so she could just enjoy this, them, here and now.

But of course, it wasn't possible. Reality always intruded.

The air cooled her naked flesh. His breath on her neck slowed. The shudders racking her body subsided. And soon, the angry wind against the house broke into their private moment. When he gently released her hands, blood rushed into her fingers once more. And slowly, so very slowly, she felt him slip from her body and then stand.

They'd done it again. After everything she'd told herself, every warning she'd mentally listed.

She opened her mouth to say something, closed it and then opened it again before giving up. Instead she sat up, yanked her skirt down and began to button up in the embarrassing silence, pointedly ignoring Marco as he did the same.

But when they were done and literally had nothing else to distract them, Kat sighed and finally looked up.

Marco had moved to the far end of the couch and was packing up their card game.

"Marco…" she began, her throat dry.

"Hmm?"

"I... We..." She paused, hands going to her lap as he continued to tidy. "Can you stop that and look at me?"

When he paused and finally met her gaze, she had to bite back a soft groan. He looked so serious, the raw curves of his face drawn into such a solemn expression that she was sorely tempted to trace her finger down his cheek to coax a smile from his full lips.

Lovely lips that she'd had the thorough pleasure of just moments before.

"What on earth are we doing?" she said now, acutely aware of the warm flush heating her skin. "How did we get to this?"

With a sigh, he flopped into the chair and crossed an ankle over one knee. "Well, the first time, alcohol was involved."

"And this time there's..." She waved a hand, indicating the storm outside that had eased into a dull rumble. "But that's not what I meant. I've never...thought of you in *that* way before."

"I see."

She couldn't meet his eyes without getting embarrassed, and that realization just flustered her further. Truth was, she'd thought about it more than once but every time refused to indulge for more than a few moments. Giving the fantasy more than that would've been weird, not to mention futile. He'd never seen her as more than a best friend, so what was the point? She'd been content with the tag for all those years.

Until now, apparently.

Dammit. She felt her entire body warm under his scrutiny, until the desperate need to move overwhelmed her. So she rose, went to the small bar fridge and fished out a bottle of water. With her back to him, she rolled the bottle over her neck then down, welcoming the icy shock on her hot skin.

She was exhausted, so tired of thinking. She had no idea where she stood. Her head was a mess, and she couldn't even blame this lapse on alcohol as she had last time.

The heat of the moment? Yeah, nah. She could have stopped if she'd really wanted to. She just didn't want to. She *wanted* to taste his mouth, have his body slide over hers. Wanted to feel his hot breath on her skin and have him fill her in the most primitive way possible.

He made her forget things, just for a while.

She twisted off the bottle cap and took a slow swig, her thoughts churning. She shouldn't be distracted, not now. She had other things to consider, important, life-changing events.

Swallowing the water, she stared at the small ventilation window that would herald a new morning, full of light and promise. A brand-new morning revealing the wild chaos of a passing cyclone. As the radio had revealed these past few hours, so many people had lost everything, and not only their homes. Personal effects, memories, things that meant so much to them, had been swept away by Mother Nature in the space of a few hours. It really was a miracle no one had died.

Relief surged, shaking her for one second before she swiftly got a handle on it. She was alive. So was Marco. They'd eventually return to the mainland, check over any damage to their homes, and she'd get the results of her test then make an informed decision based on those results.

Belatedly, she realized Grace would want her on the cyclone coverage, would need her expert digging to find that unique special-interest story that would spearhead the show's donation line. They'd done it for the Queensland floods, for the bushfires, even New Zealand's recent earthquake. Yet as she stood there with the cyclone's aftereffects thinning outside, punctuated by the constant radio chatter, all she could think about was…

Her test results.

Marco. A baby.

Their *baby.*

And her thoughts scrambled once more, rendering speech useless.

Marco kept his gaze firmly on her as she pointedly ignored his scrutiny. Her warm brown hair was sexily tousled, her neck flushed with faint stubble burn and the buttons on her shirt were crooked where she'd hastily tried to gather her composure.

"I guess," he finally said in answer to her previous question, "that we're giving in to some latent sexual tension, which is only heightened by the storm outside."

Startled, she flicked him a glance as she took another drink. "Sure."

He waited for more but she remained silent, all her attention firmly on her water bottle.

So of course, his eyes wandered, lingering on those long legs, the dip of her waist. The almost nonexistent curve of her stomach.

And suddenly an overwhelming bolt of emotion shot through him, a mixture of desire and fierce protection for both her and that unbelievable spark of life growing in her belly. No one except a handful of people knew the real Kat—the loving, fun woman who'd do anything for a friend, who'd wrestled with her parents' overprotective influence her entire life. Who'd been dragged through her own personal hell thanks to her mother's illness, front-page headlines and a bunch of loser men who frankly didn't deserve her.

She was intelligent, passionate…and stubborn. Way too stubborn. Once she made her mind up about something, there was no way she'd change it back.

Like that damn stupid decision not to get tested. It twisted like a splinter in his gut every time he allowed himself to think about it, every time he tried to convince her to just go and find out. And now she'd finally done it.

Even though she was avoiding his eyes, he knew she knew he was staring. The tension in her shoulders, the way her mouth tightened, all gave her away. And stubbornly he kept on staring.

After half a minute's standoff, he gave up and turned up the radio. Eventually she came over and sat in the chair opposite and they listened in silence, the weather updates and on-location reporters slowly charging the air with a sense of growing concern.

Finally she said, "Is it…? Do you…feel weird?"

He glanced up, but her eyes remained firmly on the radio. "What? The cyclone?"

"No, us."

He felt many things, but weird wasn't one of them. "No, actually. You?"

"Yes. No." Her gaze darted to a spot past his shoulder before returning to the radio. "I…don't know."

"Okay."

She sighed, her elbows on the table, her thumbnail going automatically to her mouth before she stopped halfway and dropped her hand. “This is…” She finally shook her head. “It’s… We shouldn’t have done this.”

“A bit late now, *chérie.*” He swallowed the small blow she dealt with no outward sign. “Although I totally expected that response.”

Her eyes snapped to his. “Did you?”

“Mmm. You have a tendency to run when things get too…intimate.”

“I do not!”

He lifted one eyebrow at her outrage. “You do.”

Her eyes narrowed as she leaned back in the chair and slowly crossed her arms. “Ben was a selfish bastard who dumped me when he realized I was serious about not wanting kids.”

“I wasn’t talking about *him.*” His hands involuntarily clenched at the memory. “And I still think you should’ve let me deck him.”

“And have you charged with assault? No way.”

He shook his head. “Anyway, I’m talking metaphorically as well as physically.”

“James was screwing a woman in our hotel room. Ezio took naked photos of me and sold them to a gossip mag.” She shoved a stray strand of hair back off her shoulder. “These are all deal breakers for me.”

“And what about us, Kat? Is best-friend sex one of your deal breakers?”

“Sex *always* ruins things.”

He frowned at her too-quick answer. Again, she was dancing around the question. But when she glanced away, hiding her expression from view in an uncharacteristically shy move, man, the sudden desire to kiss her pulled low and tight in his gut. Instead he swallowed the urge and remained where he was.

"So what are we going to do now?" he asked, deliberately casual.

She shrugged. "The media—"

"Screw the media," he growled, putting both palms flat on the table. "What do *you* want to do?"

"Marco…" His name came out as a groan, her fingers going to her temple, where she rubbed firmly. "I'm tired. I know it's your thing to talk things over ad nauseum, but can we just not right now? Please?"

He took in how she was reclining in the chair, her half-lidded eyes, the creases bracketing her mouth, and a sliver of guilt shot through his gut. "You should really get some sleep."

For once, she didn't argue. "So should you."

He shrugged. "I'm still on European time. Not that tired. Here." He stood and rearranged the pillows. "Sleep."

After a second's hesitation, she went to the couch and sat, then stretched out. He quickly dragged the blanket up over her.

"Thanks," she muttered, her eyes heavy as he covered her feet.

He moved to the single armchair and had just settled into it as her eyes closed. Moments later, her breath slowed and she was asleep.

With a small smile he got comfy, crossed his arms and ankles and let his mind drift.

He swept his gaze over her, from the dark lashes resting on the soft curve of her cheek and the soft hair streaming down her neck, to her long, lean body, which took up the entire couch. They'd been friends forever, ever since that embarrassing moment in Year Nine had changed everything. Fourteen was such a cocky, self-indulgent age, and he'd been the worst, so full of attitude and mouth. He'd made a stupid comment, showing off to his friends, and Kat had surprisingly struck back, shoving him so hard he'd fallen on his ass. He'd jokingly admitted that had been the start of his adoration, and their combined detention plus her innocent smile, offbeat humor and fierce loyalty had only cemented their relationship.

From then on they'd been a tight quartet—him, Luke, Connor and Kat—until he'd been offered the unbelievable opportunity to play European football and left Australia for France when he was sixteen. Then their individual lives had taken over—him with his soccer career, her with her mother's illness and her various tabloid exploits. He'd been shocked to see her three years later, barely a month after her mother's death, but he'd never questioned it, instead taking up right where they'd left their friendship. They'd traveled, she'd crashed at his house in Marseille for a few months and from there she'd bounced between Europe and Sydney for close to six years. It was like she'd been trying to find her place in the world, and until her stint in London, he wasn't sure she'd find it. But then, three years ago, she'd landed the *Morning Grace* job, and since then, she'd actually been happy. Sure, they'd both had relationship woes and she'd been his shoulder through the excruciating years his father had been dragged through the press, then an inquiry, before finally being cleared of money-laundering charges last year. She'd been his go-to girl when he'd been in between girlfriends and needed a date for some function or event. She was his wingman. His best friend. And now his lover.

She was having a baby. His baby. Theirs.

He swallowed thickly, a dozen emotions churning as he imagined her—his Kat—growing big with their child. Glowing, smiling. Happy.

*But she isn't, is she?*

His brows took a dive. *Don't think about that.*

For once, she wasn't talking. Odd, because they'd never had any problems talking about any topic, from exes to family to everything in between.

Well, almost everything. The ban on relationship talk was still in force, even though he'd wanted to overstep that boundary dozens of times. But for her, he'd bitten his lip and stayed frustratingly silent.

His speculative gaze ran over her sleeping form again. She might project a haughty, almost cool confidence to the world now, but to her closest friends she was just Kat Jackson, filled with doubt, frustration and a dozen dreams she worried she'd miss out on. She had a wicked sense of humor. She read literary fiction as well as popular crime novels. She was a *Star Wars* fanatic but adored the *Star Trek* reboots, had an insane collection of anime art and eighties retro music. She hated pickles on her burger, loved penguins and handbags, was funny, gorgeous, impatient, argumentative and incredibly intelligent.

And yet the press had first tagged her as ditzy and shallow, a party girl of the craziest kind with a penchant for bad boys. It didn't help that she'd gone overboard when she'd turned seventeen, bouncing from one publicity event to the next, dressed in designer heels and revealing clothing, getting snapped drunk by every single reporter eager to plaster Keith Jackson's spoiled baby girl all over the gossip pages. Not surprising that she'd taken up a position as society reporter, a job that had lasted until her mother's death.

He'd been living in France, where he'd quickly become Marseille's *Ligue 1* star forward on a million-dollar contract, treated like a rock star wherever he went. Ridiculous really, for a kid barely out of his teens to be suddenly thrust into celebrity life, rubbing shoulders with the rich and famous, dating supermodels and actresses, all while his best friend had been wrestling with life-changing events.

A low growl forced itself through clenched teeth before he bit it back. She'd turned up on his doorstep a week after Marseille had won the *Coupe de France* and broken down in his arms. Then they'd spent three months during his off-season backpacking through Europe, clearing their heads and getting their friendship back on track.

Those months had been a wake-up call for him, too. He'd stopped drinking, started making responsible choices, investing his money instead of blowing it all on thousand-dollar bottles of champagne, designer jewelry he'd never wear and vintage cars he'd never drive. And it had also been a turning point in their friendship. Now they were both thirty-three and had never gone longer than two days without a call or a text, except when he was traveling on business. And they told each other everything, no matter how private or painful. Well, except for that no-go relationship zone.

He still couldn't believe she'd actually gone and gotten tested. God, he still remembered that huge argument, a week after her mother's death, when they'd nearly ruined their friendship for good.

*"How can you not want to know?"* he'd demanded.

*"Because I don't! I don't want a death sentence affecting how I live my life!"*

She wasn't alone in thinking that, either. He'd done the research. He knew more people chose to remain in the dark about being a fatal-disease carrier. Yet it still didn't stop his heart from contracting every time he thought of her, his Kat, suffering the same fate as her mother. Dead within two years of diagnosis.

Marco released a long, slow breath, his eyes darting to the ventilation window at the far end of the cellar. The wind had downgraded to a strong breeze, the low hum of radio chatter white noise against it all. He grabbed a bottle of water and unscrewed the top, downing the contents in a few swallows, and then shoved a hand into his hair, dragging slow fingers through it.

This "let's not talk about it" attitude wasn't Kat. She always told him the truth, no matter how painful, and he did the same for her. And the only thing that had changed was the sex. Which meant it was already messing things up. She was awkward and self-conscious, holding things back, keeping her thoughts to herself. He didn't like this new Kat, not one bit.

With a scowl he shifted in the chair and tried to get comfy. Pretty soon, the wind outside lulled him and he managed to fall asleep.

# Four

Marco was the first to wake. After glancing at the still-sleeping Kat, he quickly checked his phone—no signal—placed it back on the table and then cast an eye at the softly glowing lights, before to Kat, now yawning on the couch. She was rubbing her cheek where the cushion had imprinted, looking so adorably sleepy that for one crazy second, impossible thoughts of permanently waking up next to her rushed through his brain and his breath caught.

"What time is it?" she asked, voice hoarse with sleep.

"Seven a.m.," he replied, glancing away. Desperate for something to do, he grabbed his phone again, determined not to focus on the way her long legs swung from the couch to the floor, her normally straight hair all mussed up and her half-lidded eyes still languorous. And of course, his mind latched on to the one thing he'd been trying to avoid. *That* moment. That hot, amazing moment on the couch when she'd crumbled beneath him.

"Phones are still out," he said, then turned the radio up.

Pretty soon they were up-to-date with the full aftermath of Cyclone Rory.

"The ports are closed, then," Kat concluded, combing her fingers through her hair.

"And there's no planes going in or out, apart from emergency ones." Marco rose, stretched and cracked his back, working his knee firmly back and forth.

"You okay?"

"Mmm."

She studied him for a moment. "Does it still ache?"

"Only when I sit for too long."

"Must be weird having pins in your knee."

He smiled thinly. "You get used to it. Could have been worse."

She nodded, knowing exactly what he meant. The on-field injury had ended one stellar career but he was lucky—it could've left him unable to walk. The bitterness still burned sometimes but it was something he refused to dwell on, not when all the other amazing opportunities had opened up for him a few months later.

"There'll be debris in the water, so they'll have to clear that up first," he continued.

"So we're stuck here until further notice."

"Until they give water traffic the all clear in a few days." At her unexpected smile, he tilted his head. "What?"

"I could name at least a dozen women who'd give their left leg to be holed up on a private island with you."

He sighed. "Why do you do that, Kat?"

"Do what?" She looked confused.

"Always bring up the women."

"I..."

She looked so genuinely flustered that his irritation quickly dissolved, leaving only an odd frustration. He sighed. "Look, forget it. We should go and see if there's any damage to the boat."

"I was only teasing."

"I know." When he held out his hand, her brief hesitation before she firmly grasped it and stood was telling.

It only increased that vague sense of wrongness.

He walked down the hall, a half-formed scowl on his face until he swung open the front door and their attention was immediately commanded by the outside world.

The warm air was rife with the smell of rain and dirt. The blue sky was cloudless, the sun already streaming through the trees to heat everything up. The palm trees still stood, but many were leafless; downed branches and debris were strewn over every inch of wet ground. As they stood there, taking in the damage, the familiar screech of rainbow lorikeets as they returned to their nests echoed.

Marco waited until they were in the buggy, making their way carefully down to the dock, before he said softly, "You know it'll be different with your own child, right?"

Her gaze snapped to him but he kept his focus ahead, avoiding the fallen branches and clumped mountains of dirt the rain had swept across the road.

"Will it?"

"Sure it will. *Je vous le—*"

"So help me, Marco, if you say that stupid catch-phrase I will seriously do you damage."

He snapped his mouth shut but couldn't completely keep the amusement from his voice. "Still don't like it, huh?"

"*Je vous le garantis.* I can guarantee it? It's lame. No one can guarantee something."

"The press seems to think so. Everyone awaits my game predictions with bated breath."

"Full of yourself much?" She snorted. "And you *have* called it wrong before."

"Only you would remember that. Three times in two years," he reminded her, grinning as he saw her mouth quirk. "Uh—I saw that smile."

"Was not a smile."

"Sure it was." He glanced at her. "I hate seeing you so serious and angry, *chérie*."

She crossed her arms and stared right ahead, her mouth twitching. "Keep your eye on the road. There's debris all over the place."

They finally reached the windswept dock, the trees familiarly bare, the water full of flotsam. But thankfully, his boat was still moored securely, bobbing in the water, jammed up against the jetty.

He cast an eye over the lines from bow to stern, then made his way on board to inspect further. Ten minutes later, satisfied there was no damage, they returned to the house.

It was only after they returned to the house, opened all the shutters and then went back outside to inspect the filthy pool that Kat's stomach began to rumble so violently the ache made her wince.

"I need food," she said as they walked in the patio door.

"Sure." Marco moved to the kitchen. "What do you feel like?"

"I can do it."

He huffed a sigh. "Seriously? What, you've had lessons since I was last home?"

"Don't be facetious," she sniffed.

"You haven't. Which means *I'll* cook. You—" he glanced over toward the bench "—do your usual and make the coffee."

"Fine." She opened the cupboard and grabbed the gourmet coffee beans, then the grinder. It felt so surreal, going through the motions of this familiar task when all around them everything had lost grip on reality. A cyclone had raged over the coast, devastating lives. A once-strong friendship had cracked from one impulsive night. And a baby would change their lives forever.

*Stop.* She stared at the grinder as it tossed the beans. She couldn't make that decision yet, not when the test results were still to come.

With that tiny mantra echoing in her head, they made breakfast then ate at the table, watching the TV reports outlining the damage, filling them in on every single detail, flashing up familiar scenes of devastation, until Kat's head buzzed with overload. She glanced at Marco and then away, focusing on her plate until the silence began to cloy and she was desperate to break it.

When it got unbearable, she finally said, "So, I hear you're up for a Hall of Fame award at the FFA dinner next month."

He nodded. "Yep."

"You taking anyone?" she asked casually.

When his gaze met hers, she winced. That totally

sounded as if she was fishing, when it was definitely not the case.

"You, if you want."

"Sure." Her response was automatic. The Football Federation of Australia's annual awards dinner, a three-course dinner in a five-star Sydney hotel, was always a good night. Ironically, in a nation where sport ruled supreme, soccer barely rated a mention on the national networks, and that included the biggest soccer awards event of the year. Which suited her low-key life down to the ground.

June. Three weeks away. *Three weeks plus ten weeks means...* She scowled. *No. Don't think about that.* "So you're staying in Australia until then?"

He nodded. "I have the coaching clinics to set up, plus a new shoot for Skins. And a guest appearance on *The Big Game* when the new season starts in October."

She smiled. "Still in demand. I knew that knee injury wouldn't slow you down."

His mouth curved. "Always right, aren't you?"

"Always."

As they finished their food, Kat asked, "So what else is news?" Marco took such a long time to answer that she glanced up from her empty plate with a frown.

"Ruby's on the cover of next month's *Playboy,*" he finally said.

Oh. She waited for him to share, and eventually, with a clatter of fork on plate and a deep sigh, he did. "She's my ex-wife. I shouldn't care what she does."

Kat nodded. "True."

"We've been apart for four years, divorced for two."

"Yes."

He sighed, linking his fingers together on the table.

"Call me old-fashioned, but I draw the line at having my ex-wife's hoo-ha on display for every guy who's got ten bucks to spare. Those things are private."

She looked him straight in the eye. "I agree."

He picked up the fork and continued to toy with the remains of his food in silence for a few more moments. "She didn't even ask me. I don't care about the whole media thing. I just would've liked to be forewarned."

She nodded again, knowing that the situation cut deeper than he let on. It wasn't about the damage to his reputation, although the media attention had already started to swell following the sneak peek of Ruby's cover two days ago. It was more personal than that. It went to the core of who Marco was—a deeply honorable man who respected women, who valued manners and was known in the French *futball* league as a true gentleman, despite his multitude of girlfriends and on-field arrogance.

"You know, we should get married."

She stilled, the fork halfway to her mouth. "I'm sorry. Did you just say…we should get *married?*"

He nodded, his expression deadly serious as he leaned in. "Totally."

She gaped for one second. "Why?"

He stared at her, as if waiting for her to say something more. But when she just continued to gape at him in shocked silence, he shrugged and said, "Why not?"

*Because you should be madly in love with me when you propose.* Kat swallowed the words as her brow dipped. "Because we don't have to?"

"So you're *not* worried about your pregnancy hitting the papers?" He tipped his head.

"Of course I am. I'm worried about everything hitting the papers. But I can't live my life in a bubble because of it." She eyed him. "Anyway, what does that have to do with marriage?"

"Because we can lessen the damage. If we—"

She held up a hand. "I'm sorry, what?"

He sighed. "Look, just hear me out. For over twenty years you've not shown one symptom, so let's assume the results are negative until otherwise proven, okay? Like it or not, marriage is still a respectable option. You'll be pregnant with my child. Once the cyclone news dies down, the press will be on the lookout for the next big story, and they're going to love this. The attention they give it will be off the charts. They'll hound you, your family, and when they find out I'm the father, they'll come after me." He held up a hand, cutting her off. "The papers are going to rehash every romantic involvement, including our marriages and divorces. And you can bet they'll find a way to bring my father into it. Someone at my network is going to listen to all that crap, and there'll probably be repercussions because I do have a code-of-conduct clause in my contract. Grace will probably demand an exclusive. The attention will drag on and on. Even better, they'll bring the romantic 'holed up during a cyclone' angle into it."

"Marco—"

"Now think about the alternative. We get married in a private ceremony then put out a press statement. The deed is done. Everything's announced how we want it, when we want it. The media have their story for a week, two, max. We'd have to tell Grace, of course, but there'll be no backlash for me at the network, no comparisons to the past. And everyone returns to their normal lives."

She stared at him for a moment and then slowly placed her fork on the plate. “It’s not that simple.”

“Well, obviously not.” He followed with a frown. “It won’t stop the attention, but it will lessen the time we’ll spend on the front page. Then they’ll go back to real news.”

She shook her head slowly. “You would seriously marry me?”

He shrugged. “Why not?”

She said nothing, just stared at him for the longest time. She’d be Marco’s wife. Mrs. Corelli. For one second her heart swooped, an alarming response that sent her into a panic before she swallowed and it all crashed back down to reality. He wanted to marry her, but for all the wrong reasons. Duty. Respectability. To avoid publicity. Not because of love.

*Wait, what?*

This was Marco here. He didn’t think of her in that way. Oh, she knew he loved her, but he wasn’t *in* love with her, which was a huge difference.

Anyway, she didn’t want him in love with her. Not at all.

“You know it makes sense,” he said, chewing on the last piece of toast.

There were those annoying words again. *Sensible. Smart. Logical.* Everything she’d wished for after Ezio’s betrayal. Everything Marco was offering.

She drew in a slow breath. “I don’t want to get married.”

“What, ever again?” His brow went up. “Or just to me?”

“I’ve done it twice already.”

"I know, *chérie.* I was there to pick up the pieces, remember?"

Her heart squeezed. Yeah, he was. He was always there. Through the divorces, the horrific tabloid attention. Through the aftermath of her mother's illness. He was her rock, more dependable than any of her girlfriends or family. He'd dropped everything to listen to her rant, then cry, then get solidly drunk and make a complete fool of herself at some swanky French nightclub. Then he'd dragged her backpacking around Europe in blissful anonymity.

And now he was offering again, stepping up and taking on the responsibility for their one lapse in judgment.

"I can't marry you, Marco," she said now. "That would be selfish."

"Why? I suggested it. And it's not as if we have anyone else lined up."

"Oh, that makes me feel so special."

He laughed, much to her chagrin. "You are. You're my closest friend."

"What about Grace?"

He sighed. "What about her? We're over, I told you. It's all in her head."

She crossed her arms and leaned back in the chair, trying to get a grip on her jumbled thoughts. "Marco, this isn't the solution. I don't want to force you into something you'll come to resent. No, let me finish," she added when he opened his mouth. "You love your freedom. You love being able to pick up and go away on assignment. I totally get that. But I need someone constant, to really *be here.* Fly-by parenting doesn't work. I know that firsthand. A child can't just be an appointment in your schedule, someone you see whenever you have a spare few weeks."

He stared at her for the longest time, until he ran a hand through his hair in frustration, his eyes narrowing. "That's ridiculous."

"Which part?"

"Oh, just about all of it." He braced his hands wide apart on the table and pinned her with his dark gaze. "Don't tell me what I feel, Kat. Sure, I love my job, but it's just a job."

"Are you kidding me? Soccer is your life. It's a part of who you are. You would die if you couldn't do it."

"You say that like I'd be giving it up. Which I'm not."

She sighed. "And we're back to where we started. Being Marco Corelli takes you all over the world. You'll be away from your child for months on end." *Away from me.* She prudently swallowed those words.

"So what's stopping you from coming with me?"

She blinked. "I have a job, in case you've forgotten." Boy, he just didn't let up, did he? Her head whirled with all the scenarios, emotions running riot until she had to take a mental step back. It was all just speculation, pipe dreams. She couldn't make a decision based on that, not when she might not even have a future.

The black moment engulfed her, stealing her breath so suddenly she shoved to her feet.

It was too, too much.

"I can't think. I need some air." Without waiting for his response, she turned and walked down the hall to her room.

Thoughts still churning, she pulled open a drawer and rummaged through the clothes she'd left from her last visit. She took a denim skirt and white linen shirt from the chest of drawers, slathered on sunscreen and then swiftly changed. When she emerged fifteen minutes later, Marco was nowhere to be seen.

After digging out sunglasses from her handbag and picking up yesterday's newspaper, she stalked over to the patio doors and slid them open, thankful Marco was not around.

That was good, wasn't it? It meant a respite from the questions she had no answers to. A break from thinking for once. And a reprieve from those annoying emotional responses that kept hijacking her thoughts whenever he smiled, shoved back his hair or touched her…or…

Simply breathed, it seemed.

With a deep sigh, she stepped outside. The tiles that ringed the eternity lap pool warmed her feet and the morning air teased over her bare arms, making her hairs stand on end.

Blinding sun speared across the deep blue ocean, the sky unmarred by clouds. She shoved on her sunglasses and assessed the now-familiar storm debris scattered over the deck and tiles, the leaves and filth floating in the pool, and then padded over to the small storage room, removed a broom and pool skimmer and set to work.

It was good to have something to do, and she set to her cleaning task with singular concentration. The sun shone brightly down, making her sweat through her shirt as she first swept the deck and surrounding tiles, then took up the skimmer and went to the pool. By the end of the repetitive skim-and-tip, her shoulders pleasantly ached and her brow was damp. Finally, she walked over to a lounge chair and settled back with the paper.

Five minutes, that was all it took, and her mind

began to drift back to what she'd effectively avoided the past hour.

With a sigh she closed the newspaper, folded it and stuck it under her leg.

"Test results aside, do you want a baby?" she asked herself aloud now, as if by voicing the question, she was giving it the proper gravitas.

"I don't know. Maybe." Pause. "Kat," she added, her voice dipping lower as if she was conducting a self-interview, "are you thinking about what others think again, and not what *you* think?"

Yeah, she was. Her father would be livid when he found out she was pregnant. The press would have a field day with this seemingly unsurprising return to form. Grace would… Well, she wasn't exactly sure what her boss would do.

On the flip side, Connor and Luke would offer support and be happy if she was, and honestly, their opinion meant more to her than all the others put together.

"Just forget about the test results for a second and think. Would having a child make you happy?"

With a sigh she recalled that odd thought from a few weeks back, the one where she'd allowed her mind free rein and had imagined a home and husband and a family.

*Oh, Lord.* Her breath hitched as her chest tightened, sending her emotions haywire. Maybe it was the aftermath from the storm. Maybe it was because she'd suppressed so many urges for so long. Or maybe it was because deep down inside, she didn't want to be that woman whom everyone pitied, who projected a fierce "I don't care" attitude, but inside died every time someone made a joke about her staunch opposition to having kids.

She'd thrown herself into researching motor neuron when her mother was first diagnosed with the debilitating disease that attacked the muscles but left the mind clear. The statistics, the chances of survival, the death rate… It broke her heart piece by tiny piece with every detail she'd uncovered. So after a few weeks of agony, she'd bundled up the research papers, untagged all the bookmarks and cleared her computer history, then solemnly made the choice not to get tested.

She'd come to terms with that decision, even made her peace with it. Outwardly, she'd projected that capable-career-woman persona, had brushed off any discussions about family and babies. Of course, her mother's illness wasn't a huge secret, but she'd refused to let that be a reason for people's pity. To the outside world, she'd made a conscious decision to remain childless. If everyone wanted to pour scorn on her because of that, that was their choice. Her skin was tough—she could handle it.

*But now...*

A baby. A family.

"Emotional stuff is scary," she said to herself now and then paused.

She sat back on the lounge, blinking out over the ocean view. There. She'd said it. It was *scary.* Opening herself up meant she'd be vulnerable. She'd done it so many times with relationships, and it was getting harder and harder to get over it when they inevitably ended. Most often badly, too.

She'd opened up once before, when she'd revealed to Ben why she didn't want kids, and he'd asked her for a divorce via text the next day.

*Hang on. This is Marco we're talking about.* Marco would never hurt her. He got her as no other guy did. He understood her offbeat pop-culture references, and he sang along to the music she played in her car. He let her choose the movie more often than not, and he discussed, argued and laughed with her.

He was her perfect partner.

She sat up abruptly, alarm tightening her muscles. No. Definitely not. She would *not* go there, not with him. He was her friend, not a future ex. She was supposed to be thinking about this baby, not romanticizing a one-way attraction.

"Right," she huffed, shoving her hair off her sweaty neck. "The baby. Think about the baby."

She paused. Okay, since when had she started thinking about it as an actual baby?

With a soft groan she tipped her head back. "You're going to keep it, then?"

She let that question hang in the midmorning air, the wind picking up around her, rustling the trees. The parrots squawked, the only sound punctuating the silence, and she placed a hand over her stomach and closed her eyes, cautiously giving her imagination free rein.

A baby. A miniature of her and Marco—a gorgeous child with wild curls, a beautiful mouth and high cheekbones. Marco's dreamy brown eyes…or maybe hers—sharp blue to contrast with masses of black hair. A fierce, adventurous child with charm and attitude. A combination of both, but also entirely unique, not a black-and-white copy but one that had been enhanced with color and shape and form.

She felt the catch in her throat and was helpless to stop it, until it came out as a gasping sob.

She wanted this baby. She *actually* wanted it.

Wow.

After all those years of not caring, not wanting. She wanted. It was like an epiphany, a shiny new revelation that actually made perfect sense the more she thought about it.

Marco was right: things would be different with her child. Yes, the prospect of becoming a mother was scary, different and way out of her comfort zone.

She'd never allowed herself the luxury of thinking about a family. She was Katerina Jackson. She'd handled paparazzi, the crème de la crème of society, weird celebrities and total-jerk boyfriends. She'd come through two divorces a stronger person. She was fortunate enough to have money, friends and support. And when the blood tests from the geneticist came back negative, the only obstacle remaining would be gone.

"A mother," she said softly, skimming a hand over her still-flat belly. "Me. That's…incredible."

She had to tell Marco.

# Five

Kat swiveled her feet to the tiles and stood, then padded across the courtyard and back into the house.

"Marco?"

Loud in the silence, her voice echoed off the walls. She tilted her head and paused, her brow furrowing in concentration as she listened.

Was that…music? Violin, to be exact.

Her frown deepened. Marco liked a collection of hard rock, Europop and Top 40, but he'd never professed a great love of classical. She slowly followed the thread down the corridor to the closed doors that led to the indoor pool and paused, her hand resting lightly on the sliding door's handle.

He was obviously in a private moment. The verticals were drawn, door closed, music cranked up.

And yet this had to be done.

Before she could talk herself out of it, she clicked the handle and walked in.

Just like all the times before, this room stole her breath away. The low whitewashed arches, the concrete floor with Grecian tiles leading to a kidney-shaped heated pool, the fully stocked wet bar in the middle. And to the right, an intimate entertaining alcove that always made her think dirty thoughts.

Dirty thoughts that suddenly morphed into reality when she spotted Marco lying shirtless, listening to music.

*Oh, God.* She sucked in a silent breath, frozen in her tracks. He was facing her, his eyes shut tight, expression creased in concentrated passion and his hand moving through the air as he focused on the piece—a beautiful, haunting piece that made her heart swell and thump, a soft groan sticking in her throat as it echoed off the walls.

She ran her gaze hungrily over his figure, from those jet-black curls, noble nose and defined jaw, to shoulders of corded muscle, broad chest, ridged abdomen and lean waist. By the time she'd reached his firm thighs, encased in pants, she'd become more than a little hot. Who would've guessed that watching him as he listened to the music—his expression moving in rhythm, his hand conducting as the notes went through the dips and troughs—would be so arousing?

But damn, it was. It was as if her insides had suddenly been set on slow burn, and coupled with the hot music as an erotic sound track, everything began to slowly melt, making her steadily damp the longer she stood there and stared.

And stare she did. It was as though the music possessed him, commanded him. Touched him. And she couldn't look away from his expression as it moved and morphed, his hand swaying in time.

She'd never been turned on so much in her life.

Then the song abruptly finished, his eyes springing open on the very last note, and she was caught standing there gawping like some weird, obsessive stalker.

He noticed her almost immediately, so she couldn't even preserve their dignity by retreating. His dark eyes fixed on her, his expression blank as he stared for long moments, a light sheen of sweat glistening under the soft overhead lights. Slowly, he wiped his brow, shoving his hair off his forehead, and Kat's mouth went dry.

Marco was her best friend. He infuriated her. He made her laugh, made her yell. He was her rock, her shoulder to cry on. And she was his plus one whenever he needed her, his sometimes clothing consultant, drinking buddy, confidante. Of course she loved him, just as she loved Connor and Luke.

But now, as he sat there and stared right back at her, residual emotion slowly bleeding from his expression, all she could think about was how much she wanted him.

He was glorious. A perfect example of passion and beauty, all wrapped up in dark Botticelli curls and a classic European profile that had women swooning even before he opened his mouth and that dreamy French accent came out.

She twisted her fingers in the ties of her shirt and said faintly, "Since when have you been interested in classical music?"

He slowly stood. "Since last year."

"And you didn't tell me?"

He shrugged.

*Odd.* "What was that piece called?" She forged on with a small frown.

"*Idylle sur la Paix* by Jean-Baptiste Lully." He absently plucked at the hem of his trouser leg.

"Never heard of him."

"Seventeenth-century French dancer and musician. He invented baroque music."

"Oh." She smiled. "No one important, then."

His mouth quirked. "He was King Louis XIV's court composer—a musical genius who also knew how to get what he wanted. Best friends with playwright Molière. A fascinating character, but unfortunately there's not a lot about him, unlike Mozart or Beethoven."

"That's a shame."

"I've got a couple of books and a French movie, but not much else." He slowly reached for the stereo remote and clicked it off. "You should see the movie—you'd like it." He smiled. "Especially the costumes. Historically inaccurate but still flamboyant."

"You'd have to translate for me."

"I could do that." He dragged a hand across his chin then put both hands on his hips, and Kat couldn't help but linger on all that casually exposed skin—the taut shoulders, the defined ridges of his abdomen, that tempting Adonis belt disappearing beneath his waistband.

Her heart began to canter and her mouth was dry when she finally met his gaze. His expression was unreadable, but his eyes darkened in an oh-so-familiar way as he leisurely took in her warm face and neck, then farther down to her torso partially exposed by her shirt. He finally finished his perusal at her legs before returning to her face, and her fingers involuntarily clenched hard into fists.

"Kat..."

Her name tripped so deliciously off his tongue in that beautiful accent, and she was gone. He must have realized it, too, because all he had to do was hold out a hand and crook his finger in a "come here" gesture and she leaped to do his bidding.

She walked, slowly and purposefully, around the edge of the pool, her bare feet on the cool tiles a welcome relief compared with the warmth curling in her belly.

When she finally stood before him, her lungs emptied on a shaky breath. *Lush:* that was the perfect word to describe Marco Corelli. Lush and romantic, especially with those dark curls and perfect lips.

He'd be a hit, of that she was sure.

She held her breath as he slowly reached out and curled a lock of her hair around his finger, tugging gently on it for a moment before pushing it behind her ear.

Then he leaned in, inch by agonizing inch, until his mouth was a whisper away from hers and she could feel his warm breath feather across her skin.

"Kat," he murmured, his dark hooded eyes dropping to her mouth, then back up to her eyes.

She swayed, every single cell in her body tingling from anticipation, breath rattling low in her throat. "Yes?"

"Kiss me."

With a soft groan she jerked forward, demolishing the divide between them and bringing her lips to his.

His mouth was warm and tasted faintly of peppermint. As she pressed her lips urgently against his, she heard a moan low in his throat a second before his hands were on her shoulders, dragging her to his chest.

*Yes.* She felt the excited flush sweep her from head to toe and, with another groan, put her arms around his neck and deepened the kiss.

Breath mingling. Hearts racing. Skin heating. It all happened in an instant, as if her body had been waiting for this exact moment to spark to life. When his tongue expertly parted her mouth, diving inside to tangle with hers, she gasped, legs wobbling, and immediately his arms tightened, taking all of her weight as her insides melted. They stood like that for ages, tasting each other, the room echoing with soft moans and heavy breathing. And finally, after she'd been thoroughly and skillfully aroused just short of the point of frustration, he began backing her up to the daybed.

She went willingly, clinging to him while his mouth continued to make her breathless. He took her bottom lip between his and gently sucked, his hands sliding down her lower back to firmly cup her bottom then press her urgently into him.

She gasped, feeling the hardness of his arousal against her clothes. The sudden urgent desire to be naked, to have him cover her, have him inside her, flamed.

"Marco," she groaned as her legs hit the edge of the bed.

"Hmm?" His lips were trailing over her jaw, then down her neck, and when they hit her most sensitive spot where her neck met her shoulder, she sucked in a gasp.

"Take your pants off."

She felt his mouth curve on her neck just before his hands went to his waistband, quickly unsnapping his pants and dragging them down, and she barely had time for the reality to sink in—*Marco is getting naked!*—before he went for her clothes.

Soon she was shirtless, and he was pressed up against her, his mouth returning to hers for a deep, breathless kiss before he slowly made his way down her neck.

She swallowed thickly, the heat from his lips trailing small shudders across her skin. Dimly she was aware of her bra being removed, and then he was pushing her gently down onto the bed, his hand cupping one breast. Her back curved, arching into his touch, and with a soft murmur he obliged, his thumb sweeping over one peaking nipple before he took it in his mouth and sucked.

She shuddered, which was unbelievable considering the amount of control she normally had over every single waking moment of the day. But with Marco it was different. He had suddenly become chaos in her ordered world, and she was experiencing all sorts of things for the first time. As his mouth and tongue worked magic on her skin, coaxing her nipple into an achingly hard peak, she shoved any doubts she had into the back of her mind and just let the moment take her.

Her hands went to his boxers, hooking her thumbs in the waistband then slowly taking them off. And when she reached for him, his soft exclamation in her ear only fueled her desire.

Then he leaned back and her eyes flew open to stare into his dark depths.

"Kat…" he groaned, expression twisting. "Do you want to…? Should I…?"

Her breath came out slowly, heavily, as she cupped

his face with one hand, emotion and desire and need roiling in her stomach in one heated mass.

"Yes." She placed a soft kiss on his mouth. "I need you." Her teeth gently captured his bottom lip. "Deep." She sucked on his lip, her breath ragged, matching his. "Slow." Darting her tongue out, she licked the curve of his mouth. "Please."

His eyes closed on a thick gasp, and she watched his throat work, swallowing slowly. Then his knee was nudging her thighs apart. When his hand went between her legs, her body jerked.

His long, skillful fingers teased and tempted, his thumb coaxing the swelling nub of her arousal over and over as she trembled with every stroke, rocking her hips into his hand, grinding firmly as she whimpered beneath his mouth. With a low chuckle he continued, sliding first one finger inside, then another, working her with a steady, sensual glide that swiftly reduced her to a quivering mass of need.

"Marco!" She was beyond caring how desperate she sounded, how much she needed him, how damp he made her. Because right now, all that existed was his mouth, his hand…and suddenly, his throbbing manhood as he swiftly positioned himself and pushed inside with one hard thrust.

*Oh...!* Everything shorted out, until all that was left was thick heat and a hard pounding heartbeat echoing inside every single nerve. And when he slowly shifted his hips and inched deeper, she gasped, eyes flying open to meet his.

His face, that beautiful face, was so close to hers she could smell the arousal rolling off him. Her entire body pulsed from it, hot and breathless. How could she withstand these sensations, this glorious heat, the tightness, the pure friction of taking him deep inside her? Then he moved again and she knew she'd do more than withstand it. She'd revel in it, enjoy the pure moment of claiming him in the most primitive way possible.

She groaned, rocking back to meet his thrusts, the friction of him steadily flaming her arousal. Her thickened heartbeat throbbed wildly in her head, and she pushed back into him, hard, squeezing her eyes shut, groaning. "Marco…"

"Hmm?"

Instead of answering, she grabbed his hand, sliding it to where they were intimately joined. "There. Touch me there."

He did as she asked, moving his fingers over the hot, sensitive nub of her arousal. "Oh, yes…" She bit down on her lip, her hand still on his, losing herself in the sensation of his fingers, his mouth on her nipple and him hard inside her as he slowly and firmly moved.

They remained that way for excruciating minutes, rocking together, his finger flicking her intimately over and over, until she was sure she'd explode from it all. And then he surprised her by suddenly flipping her onto her stomach, looping a hand under her hips and pulling her up onto all fours. Before her brain could register the interruption, his hand swept over her butt. He nudged her legs apart and entered her from behind.

Her breath came out in a harsh gasp, and she had to brace her hands wide on the mattress to accommodate all of him. He paused, a palm gently sweeping over the curve of one butt cheek.

"Kat? Are you okay?"

Was she okay? Hell, no. She was about to die from

every single piece of her exploding in joy. Instead, she managed to get out, "Yes…yes."

"You sure?" His hand stroked her back, her hip, before slowly easing around her waist to cup one breast.

"I won't be if you don't keep going."

His chuckle—partly amused, partly dirty—nearly did her in. Instead she pushed back into him and felt no small satisfaction in hearing his harsh intake before he gripped her hips and began to rock.

She gasped as sensation took over; she felt his mouth as he leaned over and bit gently on her shoulder, his hands firmly cupping her breasts, and the hot, sweet sensation of him deep inside, filling her completely, creating such an arousing, intimate friction that a whimper welled deep in her throat.

Then it hit and she went down to her elbows, unable to hold back as the shuddering release swept her entire body, and she heaved in great gulping breaths, welcoming his weight as everything pulsed in pleasure.

"Marco…" For the third time, his name ripped from her mouth, like a mantra, and she felt the stinging sensation of his teeth grazing her neck, then her name echoed and the room filled with their harsh cries of release.

Dimly, she was aware that she'd collapsed on the bed, and Marco's body was flush on hers, damp and heavy in the aftermath of passion.

"That was… You are…" She groaned into the mattress, chest heaving.

His hand went to her face, gently turning her to him, his mouth seeking hers. "Kiss me."

She did, sweetly and softly, and a groan escaped his lips when he finally broke away, lifting his body off hers. "Sorry. I'm way too heavy to be lying on you, especially when..."

He petered off, letting her fill in the blank, which she did way too quickly.

It was a definite mood killer.

She sighed, watching him move around the shadowed room, picking up his boxers and pulling them on. With a flush she glanced away from his perfect form—long, corded thighs; strong, muscular back; and perfectly shaped behind.

"Marco, we need to talk."

He finally turned to her, hands on hips, and she couldn't help steal a brief glance at his chest before quickly forcing her gaze to his eyes.

She didn't know what she expected—amusement over her perusal, a sarcastic eye roll over the clichéd relationship line they both hated. Even residual lust wouldn't have been unusual. But there was none of that, only a carefully blank countenance that accompanied the vague sense of anticipation in the air.

"I think we should."

*Right. So far, so good.* She gathered the sheet around her, covering her breasts, before continuing. "Okay, so I don't want to make any major decisions without the test results, but I do know one thing. If the tests turn out to be negative, I want to keep the baby."

The silence fell like a blanket, and yet he still said nothing, just waited for her to elaborate. The simple fact that he knew there *was* more was as unnerving as it was disturbing.

"And here's the thing, Marco," she continued. "I don't want this child to have a part-time parent. You're either totally in this or not at all."

He frowned. "What makes you think I'm not in this?"

She sighed. "I don't want you making major decisions based on what *I* want. You want to go back to France, you go."

The frustrated growl was low in his throat. "You can't throw out something like that and then tell me *not* to think about what you want. That's not the way I operate."

"I know. But you have to. I'm giving you permission to walk away from all the craziness now."

"You're not making any kind of sense." He raked her with such a look that she felt her cheeks flush. "First you say I should be in this totally or not at all. Then you say I should do what I like." His hands went to his hips, his expression darkening. "Let me ask you this—knowing me so well, do you actually think I'd walk away?"

"That's not what I'm saying."

"Oh, that's exactly what you're saying." His expression remained tight, almost too tight. "That's pretty low, Kat. Thanks. Thanks a lot."

She blinked. Had she hurt him? His face said no, yet the brief flash in his eyes said the opposite. "I just…" She swallowed when she saw his scowling countenance. "I don't want you to feel trapped."

"How long have we known each other?"

She paused, calculated. "Nineteen years."

"Right. And in all that time, have you known me to do something I didn't want to do?"

She hesitated. "No."

"There you go." He yanked on his pants, slid up the zipper.

"But—"

"Dear Lord, Kat, can you stop? Just…stop." He finished dressing, then gave her a frustrated look. "If all you're going to do is lump me in with past boyfriends, then I'm going for a shower."

She opened her mouth for a second and then closed it. "Great. Fine. Go."

He narrowed his eyes. "So we're done here? You've said everything you need to?"

"Looks like it." She scooted to the edge of the bed with as much dignity as possible, anger welling up inside. But when he stalked out in long, ground-eating strides, she collapsed back on the mattress. Could it be more uncomfortable? From best friends to arguing lovers in the space of a day.

Must be some kind of record for her.

This wasn't what she wanted. Not at all. But how in the hell could she fix it?

Good Lord, Kat was so stubborn.

Marco was in the kitchen, gathering up food and utensils for lunch with more noise than necessary, his thoughts dark, before moving onto the patio, to the huge four-burner barbecue.

She was so determined to make her own decisions, to not even consider a different opinion unless she'd thought of it first.

Sure, his long absences from home were sometimes inconvenient, and there were times when he felt he was playing catch-up with people's lives. But after his knee injury had forced him into early retirement and the network had offered him this prime job, he'd jumped at the opportunity. And from that choice, a whole new bunch of opportunities had opened up—his Skins contract, the football clinics. He couldn't afford to regret any of it, not when things were as pretty close to perfect as he could get.

But right now, at this moment? A flame of frustration had flickered to life, refusing to be quenched.

Damn, he missed everyone, missed being able to drop everything and catch up with a meal and a beer. But with Luke and Connor in Brisbane and he and Kat up here in Cairns, plus their work commitments, it was a logistical nightmare trying to sync their schedules.

With an irritated flick he threw the steaks onto the hot plate, his bad mood momentarily rewarded by the satisfying hiss.

For example, if they were all together right now, they'd have this issue picked apart and solved within an hour. Instead of what had really happened—his making a lame marriage proposal, her getting all offended for some reason and now this weird standoff.

After a few minutes of grilling the hell out of the steaks, a movement through the glass caught his eye. He turned to see Kat standing in the middle of the living room, her attention commanded by the TV.

The sight hit him low and hard. She was barefoot and wide-eyed, looking sexily rumpled in nothing but short-shorts and an old gray T-shirt that skimmed her thighs. Magnificent thighs.

His head flashed back to what they'd done in the pool room. Then, further, to the larger issues they were both determined to avoid until hard evidence left them no choice.

He scowled. He'd never craved—yet dreaded—the outcome of a test so much in his life. The knowledge would change their lives forever, for the better or the absolute worst, and it wasn't until this moment that he understood why Kat had deliberately chosen the path of not knowing. It took a strong person to fight, but it also took someone equally strong to choose the other path, to live their lives with impunity when somewhere, in the back of their minds, they would always be wondering, thinking, considering.

Kat was way stronger than he even thought possible.

Humbled and angry, he turned his attention back to the grill and waited for her to approach him.

He hadn't long to wait—a few minutes was all it took.

"Can I do anything?" she asked, standing in the open door.

He glanced up briefly then back to the grill. "We need drinks."

"Sure."

He watched her pad to the kitchen, his eyes skimming over her long legs. He took in the way her back remained firm and straight, and he swallowed the lump in his throat.

Quickly he served up the steaks then went inside.

When she took the plate he offered, a whiff of scent hit him, tightening his gut. "What are you wearing?"

She glanced down and plucked at the T-shirt. "This? It's a sleeping shirt."

"No. Your perfume."

"Oh." She looked disconcerted for a second then said faintly, "Lemongrass and cloves. I keep it in my underwear…drawer…"

Her words trailed off at the exact same moment he grinned. He could practically read her thoughts—*Great,*

*Kat, just talk about your knickers, why don't you?*—and his mouth curved wider.

"Is that enough?" Marco said.

"Hmm?"

He nodded at her steak. "Do you have enough?"

She swallowed. "Yes, thanks."

He watched her take a seat at the table, her gaze darting up to his before she steadfastly focused on the food, and the brief moment of amusement was gone.

What the hell was wrong with…?

*Riiiiight.* He sat in his chair, his eyes going anywhere but to her. She was nervous. But why? He'd teased her a hundred times before, and about things a lot more personal.

Yeah, but that was Marco-the-best-friend, not Marco-the-lover. Like it or not, things had changed. It was almost as if…she was uncomfortable now.

He swallowed a curse. What the hell was he supposed to do with that?

"Kat," he said in a low voice.

"Hmm?" Her attention remained firmly on her plate.

"This is weird for me, too."

Her eyes darted to his. "What, specifically?"

"You and me."

She blinked. "Is—?" He watched her swallow. "There isn't a you and me."

*Isn't there?* The unspoken question just hung in the air, the seconds gathering, until he realized he was frowning, and she'd darted her gaze back to her plate.

"So we're just occasional bed partners, then."

The sarcasm was lost on her. "I don't think that's a good idea."

He stared at the top of her head in silence, and finally, reluctantly, she brought her eyes up to his and he stifled a groan. Soft skin. The indent of her waist, the curve of her butt cheek. Her damp body shaking as he took her, desire raging hard and fast. And her moans of pleasure as they both reached their climax.

His thoughts raced, nostrils flaring with remembrance, but he let the silence drag, until her eyes widened and she swept her gaze back to her plate. "You're my best friend, Marco. I don't want to ruin our friendship."

"It's not ruined. Just…" He searched for a word and finally settled on "Different."

"Different," she repeated with a small scowl.

He nodded. "Of course. We've slept together. We're having a baby. How can those things not make it different?"

"I don't *want* it different."

"You've made that perfectly clear," he snapped back and then took a breath. "But denial is stupid."

Her head jerked up. "Are you calling me stupid?"

"No! Jeez, Kat…!" His breath was sharp on the intake as he tried for calm. "I'm not calling you stupid," he said deliberately, rising from the table with his plate. "But wishing the past was different is a waste of time. You know that."

When she said nothing, just slid her gaze away and refused to meet his eyes, he swallowed a groan. It was her infuriating you're-right-but-I'm-not-going-to-admit-it look. God, that annoyed the hell out of him!

"It was fine the way it was," she said now, her gaze now on her plate.

The blow hit him like a stray free shot. She didn't want him.

No, that wasn't right—she didn't want *anyone.* She'd made that clear. He shouldn't take it personally. Yet how could he not, when they'd been together three times now and every time she'd indicated she'd rather be friends?

He knew exactly what she was doing. Things were getting emotional and she was pushing him away. She'd done it with everyone when her mother had started getting sick, and she was doing it now. Only this time, she had to deal with not only pregnancy hormones but the mental effort of waiting for those damn test results.

If this was what she really wanted, he'd let her have it…for now. He'd keep his thoughts and hands to himself, support her and stand by her as a best friend, and only that. But eventually, after they got off this island and went back to their reality, things would change. They had to. Because they'd stepped over that line and he was damned if he'd remain on the sidelines, where she was so determined to push him.

# Six

The next morning Kat lay in her bed, staring at the ceiling as the sun slowly crept through the blinds.

They'd spent the evening in uncomfortable silence. Even the constant TV chatter did nothing to ease the awkwardness. She'd finally excused herself and went to bed, then lay for ages staring at the window and listening to the sounds of the night creatures rustling around outside.

Marco as her lover? Ridiculous.

Yet every time she'd lost her head, forgot who he was and just let the moment take her. It was crazy. Exciting.

Dammit, she couldn't stop those hot memories from filling her thoughts at the most inopportune moments. The way he kissed her, as if he couldn't get enough. The way he touched her, his fingers making her shiver in anticipation. And the way he took her, hard and possessive.

*Yeah, and you've given him the "just friends" talk. Which he accepted without argument.* She'd told him he was the father of her child, nothing more.

The question was, did she want him as more? Did she want to start something that could end in disaster? Or worse, drag him into an emotional mess when she had no clue what those damn tests would reveal?

*You can't.*

With a hitched breath, she rolled over in bed and hugged her pillow. This was Marco Corelli, a guy she knew better than anyone. Yet in this one thing, she had absolutely no clue.

And then there was the matter of Grace.

She groaned and gave the pillow a vicious thump. Everything was such a mess, and on top of that, she had to figure out something to tell Grace. Oh, she'd contemplated not saying a thing, but experience had taught her it was better to be honest. And anyway, she liked and respected her boss. She deserved to know.

*Sorry, Grace. The guy you wanted a baby with? He's having it with me.*

She winced.

*Grace, I know you had plans for Marco—*

Urgh. Terrible.

*Grace. I need to tell you about something that happened....*

She rolled her eyes. It sounded so much better in her head. Come to think of it, lots of things sounded better in her head. Truthfully, she had no idea why she was practicing—she worked much better off-the-cuff. And it was something she should really think about *after* the test results came through.

"I can't wait to get off this bloody island," she muttered.

When she walked into the living room half an hour later, the breakfast things were already laid out on the table. Marco was dressed in a white shirt and jeans and was flicking through the TV channels.

"What's the situation with the cyclone?" she asked as she sat and reached for the cereal.

"They're saying the phone towers may be up and running in a few hours," he said as he moved into the kitchen and pushed down the toaster.

"Good."

"Eager to escape, *chérie?*"

His smile lacked warmth, which only made her feel bad. "I'm eager to know the results of my tests," she said slowly as she poured the milk then grabbed her spoon.

He nodded, his attention riveted to the toaster.

"Marco…"

"Hmm?" He remained focused on his task and she bit her lip, her gaze sweeping over him before darting away.

"Nothing," she mumbled and shoved a spoonful of cereal in. "We should watch that DVD you were telling me about. After breakfast, maybe."

He glanced over at her, his expression unreadable, and then back to the toaster as it pinged. "Sure."

Just as they did yesterday, they ate in silence, their attention focused on the TV. *It's still happening,* she realized, her eyes determinedly fixed on the news updates. She hated this awkwardness, as if they were waiting for the other to address the elephant in the room.

It was excruciating.

When he got up with his plate, she couldn't help but lift her gaze to follow. He had a way of walking, a kind of fluid motion that had earned him many women admirers when he'd played for Marseille.

Actually, he still had a few.

She sighed and rose. Three times now they'd ended up in bed, and every time it still amazed her. But to voice her need, her wish to have him as a friend *and* a lover…that was too damn scary. She'd be a fool to start something, only to have it implode if the test results came back positive. Because then she'd have to deal with that on top of everything else, and she was damn sure she didn't want to put Marco through even a millionth of what she'd suffered, watching someone she loved slowly wither away.

She walked over to the sink to rinse her bowl and unthinkingly settled her soft fingers on the warm flesh of his waist to nudge him out of her way.

He jumped like a scalded cat, which in turn made her jump.

"Sorry," she said when he shot her a look. Her face was a hairbreadth away from his shoulder—within kissing distance, she realized dazedly. Yet his small shiver had her frowning as he slowly moved to her right.

"Your hair," he murmured, removing his plate from the sink. "Tickles."

"Sorry," she said again unconvincingly, leaning down to open the dishwasher. Her breath caught when her arm skimmed his chest; she knew she'd gotten to him when she heard the snag in his throat.

The heady feeling of power winded her. "You should put a jumper on."

"Huh?"

She nodded at his bare arms, now littered with goose bumps. "If you're cold you should put a jumper on."

He sent her a closed, indecipherable look that confused as much as aroused. How on earth had she been able to look at that face, into those dark eyes, without feeling her pulse spike before? But she had. She'd hugged, laughed and touched with impunity, secure in their platonic-friend zone. But now…now all she wanted to do was touch him. Kiss him.

Get him into bed again.

With a thick swallow, she called on her thinly shredded control and turned away.

"Let's watch that movie."

From the very first minute, the very first strike of classical music booming through the speakers, she was hooked.

Of course, it was all in French and Marco had to translate. Her breath caught every time he leaned in, his deep voice soft over the lilting on-screen French. The music was rich and powerful, the costumes beautifully flamboyant, and she could feel her senses spike in response. And of course, there was Marco sitting close, his body heat and faint cologne a frustrating accompaniment to the period drama. She had to stop herself from squirming after one intimate scene, to firmly focus on the screen and not turn and kiss him as he bent in to translate a particularly hot piece of dialogue.

She swallowed, suppressed a shudder and made a move to rise. "I need a drink. Do you want a drink?"

She squeaked when his arm went around her, pulling her back down. "No. Wait until after this scene. It's awesome."

"Just let it play. I won't be a second."

He groaned and clicked Pause. "You always do that. I hate it!"

"It's only a few seconds," she said, grabbing his fingers and pulling. "Let me go."

"No. Louis is about to confront his mother. You'll miss something important."

She worked at his fingers but he held her fast, and she couldn't help but stifle a giggle. A giggle that rushed out in a gasp as he yanked and she ended up sprawled in his lap. "The drink can wait."

"But—"

"Quiet, woman. I'm trying to watch the movie and you're ruining the mood."

With an exaggerated sigh she settled her head on his thigh and watched the scene.

When Marco casually draped his arm over her waist, an involuntary shiver coursed down her back. She was suddenly very much aware that his hand was curled at her hip, his hard thigh beneath her cheek and the back of her head in his lap.

*Oh, dear.*

She tried to focus on the movie, but it was no good. Amid the powerful scene, full of heightened tension, coupled with Marco's soft translation, she could feel her body heat up.

Her breath hitched. She couldn't take her eyes off the screen, and she couldn't switch off her senses because Marco was everywhere—his hand resting lightly on her hip. His scent, all male and clean. And that voice, so achingly intimate that her insides just seemed to shudder every time he opened his mouth.

When she stirred, she felt his thigh beneath her cheek shift and tighten, and she had to clench her fists to stop herself from involuntarily stroking that hard muscle.

She closed her eyes, swallowing thickly as his hand suddenly left her hip to gently toy with her hair.

*So soft.* Marco heard her faint sigh, barely discernible against the rich baroque sound track. Yet his senses went on high alert at the sudden tension riding her back as he continued to stroke her hair, the silky chocolate strands twining around his fingers. The sudden urge to bury his face in that hair, breathe deep and never come up for air winded him.

"Marco?"

His name, warm and whispery on her lips, sent a bolt of heat to his groin.

"Yes?"

"You should stop."

He didn't pretend to fake ignorance. "I don't think I can."

She turned her head in his lap and he groaned under his breath. Her wide blue eyes stared up at him, and he couldn't help himself. He needed to kiss her. Now.

So he did.

She had ample time to protest or move away, but she did neither, just watched him get closer and closer until his lips gently brushed over hers, tentative at first, then with more urgency.

Her sigh ended on a groan and told him everything he needed to know.

They spent long moments that way, just exploring

each other's mouths with lips, tongue and breath until Marco finally pulled back with a soft curse.

"What the hell is this, Kat?"

She stared up at him, eyes wide. "I have no clue. But…can we just…not talk about it?"

"Kat—"

"Please, Marco. With everything else going on, let's just not…not analyze this."

His hand skimmed over her jaw then down her neck to finally rest across her collarbone, a frankly possessive gesture that she ignored. "We're going to have to at some point."

She sighed. "I know. Just not now, okay?"

When she tentatively leaned up, lips seeking his, he pulled back, and for one brief second he saw her tense, as if preparing herself for rejection, and it just about killed him then and there. With a groan, he cupped her head and captured her lips in a deep kiss.

They kissed for ages, the rich music and French dialogue a sensual background that only flamed his need, urging him to do more, to touch, to possess.

He abruptly pulled back. "We should…"

She swallowed. "Stop?"

"Are you asking me or telling me?"

He heard her breath rattle as he studied her, taking in the curve of her lips, the mix of emotion in her darkened eyes. Did she…? Would he…?

Impossible.

Or was it?

"You're right."

He gently eased off the couch and moved away to the kitchen, leaving her in silence. She'd surely stop him, say something, if she thought any different, right?

But as he went through the motions of getting a drink, the silence was loud and obvious.

He hadn't mistaken that look—a mix of want and trepidation. He'd seen it so often in other women.

But this was Kat. His Kat.

No, not his.

Annoyed, he lingered in the kitchen as she sat on the couch, until the unmistakable ping of his phone broke the silence.

He paused. "Did you hear that?"

"What?"

"My phone pinged."

"That means the towers are working," she said.

He frowned and then quickly strode over to his phone, flicking it on. She picked up hers and did the same, hurriedly scanning through the messages.

Disappointment curled in his belly as he read. Ridiculous. They couldn't stay here forever. They needed to get back to their lives, to reality. Which meant work, test results. Press coverage.

He groaned softly, dragging a hand over his face. God, they'd have a field day with this trapped-alone-in-a-cyclone scenario. And Grace, she'd definitely want in on that story. Then there were Kat's test results that frankly scared the crap out of him.

He glanced over and saw her staring intently at her phone and frowning. They'd all want a piece of her. She could skillfully avoid the press, but Grace… Yeah, Kat's boss was demanding and challenging. It took a special person to work for her, and he knew she bugged Kat for an exclusive at least once a week. So far she'd held out, but after the past few days he wasn't entirely sure Grace would keep taking no for an answer.

The sudden urge to escape, to take Kat somewhere where they could relax in blissful anonymity and just ignore the realities of the outside world, swept over him, and his grip tightened on the phone. Japan, maybe? The Himalayas? Alaska. Alaska was nice….

Or they could just stay here.

Her soft exclamation broke through his thoughts and he quickly busied himself with the cups.

"The geneticist called. They have my results."

He spun around, but she'd already pulled open the patio doors and stepped outside. The soft click of the door was as final as any slam.

She'd shut him out.

Damn. He busied himself with coffee, refusing to look further into it. As always, she'd tell him in her own time, and as always, he'd be there for her, whatever the result.

He paused, and damn, the panic he thought he'd managed to ignore these past few days just swept right back in, leaving him floundering in a pool of helplessness.

He couldn't lose her. Not his Kat. Not the woman he'd just realized he was totally and completely in love with.

Wait, what?

Before he had a chance to let that realization take bloom, she'd reopened the door and was standing, pale and still, in the middle of the room.

"Kat?"

"I know they're not supposed to tell you over the phone," she said slowly. "But Dr. Hardy and my mother go back a long way, and I wasn't sure when we'd return to the mainland and—" She stopped, took a deep breath and looked him in the eye. "Sorry, I'm rambling.

I just…" She dragged a hand through her hair with a sigh as he just stood there, his heart lumping in his throat, blood pounding way too loud.

"Kat, you're killing me here," he said softly. "What did he say?"

"They're doing another test, to double-check the results," she began. "But…"

"Yes?"

"Preliminary tests were…" Her eyes rounded, disbelieving. "Positive." She swallowed, her voice cracking. "They were positive."

Oh, dear God.

For one second the world stopped spinning. He realized he'd gotten out a thick "What?" but the shock quickly drowned everything else out. She was… She had…

No. Just no.

*NO.*

He realized he was staring, silent and disbelieving, until he saw her tears spilling, slowly coursing down her cheeks, and his heart just shattered into a million tiny pieces.

Nononononono—

He surged forward just as she let out a gut-wrenching sob. In a few strides he'd crossed the room, and then he was crushing her against his chest.

She collapsed into him, and when he felt her begin to shake, he just held on tighter.

Impotent fury surged because he couldn't help her, couldn't stop her tears, couldn't do a damn thing but hold her, muttering totally useless sentiments while she cried and cried and broke his heart over and over.

He swallowed thick gulps of air, tightening his embrace as she trembled in his arms. She was so damn strong all the time, and it killed him to see her so broken now. After her mother's death, she'd never allowed herself to think about this possibility. She'd been determined to live her life without a death sentence tainting every moment. But now…now…

He held on tight, feeling her body shake, her tears dampening his shoulder, and he swallowed again and again, sucked it all up and bit back all his pain even as he felt his own tears spill on his cheeks. She needed him to be the strong one here. He'd be useless to her any other way.

Yet how could he when everything inside him throbbed with pain and fury and the injustice of it all?

That anger took flame, growing with each second, until thankfully he managed to force back the tears. "We'll get another test," he muttered against her hair. "And then another. They could've made a mistake—it happens all the time."

She muttered something unintelligible, and when she finally lifted her face to his, her expression so broken and torn, he couldn't help himself.

He leaned down and kissed her, hard.

She kissed him back just as fiercely, her small whimper warm in his mouth, her cheeks wet against his. When he angled her head and thrust his tongue between her lips, she groaned, welcoming him, her hands fisting in his shirt to pull him closer.

His brain shorted out as lust instantly exploded. He grabbed her arms and kept kissing her, her gasps of pleasure feathering over his lips, her hands grappling with his shirt, yanking it from his pants.

And then she was backing him up, and suddenly they

were sprawled on the couch with her on top, mouths still locked.

He couldn't think, couldn't speak. The emotion of the moment had completely hijacked any thought of common sense. With frantic hands they worked his pants open then off, then attacked her shirt, ripping it with their urgency. This was lust at its highest, the kind of clothes-ripping, skin-biting rush that left no room for soft words of love. It was just about the physical coming together of two people in desperate emotional need to connect, to prove they were still alive and were far from done yet.

He yanked up her skirt then dragged down her knickers, briefly reveling in her soft skin, in the warm, throbbing life of her, before she was bracing her hands on each side of his head. With mouths still locked in a desperate kiss, he grasped her hips, shifting her slightly, before plunging her straight down onto his aching manhood.

Her gasp rent the air and he groaned against her hot mouth, feeling the hard pulse of his arousal buried deep inside her. For a dozen breathtaking moments they remained still, intimately joined but unmoving as their eyes locked and they shared one breath.

It was…she was…incredible. Amazing.

With shaky hands, he swept his thumbs over her cheeks, sweeping away the last of her tears, before placing a slow, agonizing kiss first over one eyelid then the other.

"Kat…"

Her expression crumbled. "Please, Marco. Don't talk." Then she swooped down for a kiss, silencing him, and began to slowly, sensuously rock.

Instinctively he gripped her hips, taking charge of the rhythm, commanding her body. His heart pounded thickly, blood racing. He may have heard her whimper; he wasn't sure because his heart was beating so damn fast it felt as if the whole room echoed with it. And past that, there was the faint, sensuous sound of flesh on flesh coupled with their heavy breathing.

She rolled into him, biting her lip. "Marco…"

"Yeah?" His gaze met hers, and the raw need etched on her face blew him away.

"Touch me…"

He did as she asked, and her eyes closed in pleasure, her hands covering his as he skimmed over the velvet flesh of her stomach, her waist, then up over her ribs to finally cup her breasts. His thumbs teased her already sensitive nipples and she hissed, grinding harder into him.

She leaned down and he took her mouth in breathless kisses over and over, until he was about to explode, until the friction and heat where their bodies joined escalated to the point where they were both on the brink.

He felt her tighten around him and he groaned, gripping her hips and thrusting hard, until she panted against his mouth, her eyes squeezed shut. Then, with a soft cry and a ragged breath, he felt her go over the edge.

He shuddered, a deep, satisfied groan wrenching from his lips as he followed her. She collapsed on his chest as he murmured her name, his breath against her cheek, arms tight, holding her close. He felt her response against his neck, her body damp and shaking as she wrapped her arms around him, legs tightening with a sigh. "Don't move. Stay right here."

"I'm not going anywhere, *chérie*." His fingers went

into her hair, stroking her nape as the tight throb in his body began to slowly ease.

He blinked.

He loved her.

Just when the hell had that happened? And how? He searched his memory, going over each moment with determined concentration. Had it happened since that night ten weeks ago? Or sooner?

A frown furrowed his brow. It really didn't matter when, just that it *was.* He loved her as a best friend, as a lover. As a smart, amazing, funny, gorgeous and incredibly vulnerable woman. He loved that fourteen-year-old girl with the perfect hair and bright blue eyes, who'd stood up to his teasing. He loved that vulnerable, crazy nineteen-year-old, the one who'd needed him so desperately, the one who'd leaned on his shoulder, who'd needed *him* in her moment of grief. The woman who'd made mistakes in love and life and still continued to get back up, to forge her way and give the finger to all her critics.

The woman who had just received the worst possible news you could ever get.

No. He couldn't stop reality from intruding, but damn, he gave it his best shot. He knew the moment she felt it, too; her breath shook just a little on the intake and her arms tightened around him.

"No, don't," he said softly.

Too late.

She slowly slid off him in silence. As she fiddled with her underwear and pulled her skirt down, he took the moment to quickly adjust his pants. When he swung his feet to the floor, his breath snagged at her expression. How much effort was she exerting now, just to remain so calm, so in control? She was trying to hold it all together so he wouldn't see her at her absolute worst.

When she turned her back to him to do up her buttons, the curse he swallowed hurt like jagged glass. *Don't you dare lose it. Not when she's managing to keep it all together.*

"We should find out when we can go back to the mainland," he said softly, her back still to him. He had a few seconds to admire the smooth skin of her thighs, the gentle curve of her hip, the strong shoulders as she squared them and finally turned to face him, pushing back that mane of hair.

"Yes. I'll need to make some more calls, too."

"Kat." He leaned forward, looped an arm around her waist and pulled her to him. Surprisingly she offered no protest, just went into his arms silently. He held her, without passion and without subterfuge, just two friends sharing an embrace.

Finally he said, "Let's not jump to any conclusions here. They want to retest you. We should wait until that happens before we start making decisions."

He felt her nod against his chest, knew without confirmation that she was already thinking, planning. Making decisions. Her brain never stopped working, and now, of all days, she needed to make logical, sensible choices.

With a sigh she finally pulled away from him, and reluctantly he let her go. She went over to the table and grabbed her phone. "I have to make a few calls."

# Seven

After Marco confirmed that the port at Cairns would reopen in a few hours, Kat used all her negotiation skills—and a few pleas—to wrangle an appointment with the geneticist for the very next day. Then they made a number of calls to let people know they were alive and well.

From what they gathered, Cairns was a disaster area. Parts of the city still had no water and electricity, and phone coverage was spotty. With the tropical climate, it was crucial those services be up and running again as soon as possible. It would be an arduous task, one that required a coordinated effort of all rescue services, plus private contractors. At least when the ports were clear and operating, supplies could be shipped in, and the massive cleanup could begin.

Armed with that information, they set about doing

physical tasks around the house—ripping the tape off the windows they hadn't already gotten to, and clearing more of the debris that would probably take a few weeks to get into some semblance of order, because all services would give priority to the mainland.

It was good to keep busy, to just focus on the pure physicality of lifting, clearing, moving. She'd assumed there'd be no time to think about tests, babies, Grace or the situation with Marco, but as they worked and sweat quickly soaked Kat's shirt, she found her mind was not so easily swayed.

*You can't have this baby.* She couldn't. It was the exact reason she'd vowed not to have kids. Her heart squeezed painfully and she scowled, putting more force than necessary into her raking task.

What her mother had gone through, what *she'd* gone through, watching her slowly wither and die from that death sentence… It was a pain so unfathomable that she'd willingly shift a mountain to prevent it from happening. It was one thing to cope with having the disease, to know exactly what she'd be facing every single day for the rest of her short life. But to willingly bring a child into that equation? No. Never.

Her eyes flicked briefly to Marco, then away. Yes, the pain of termination would cut deep, but it was preferable to a lifetime of anguish, of knowing she could have prevented it but selfishly did nothing. She would not put a child nor Marco through that.

*Ah. No. Don't think about it.* But she couldn't help it—her thoughts were already there, crowding her head with every single possible scenario until it was the only thing she could think about.

She gritted her teeth, wielding the rake with such

force that she heard the handle creak. *Damn. Something else. Think of...the cyclone. Work. Yes, work.* Grace would want her on top of this, sourcing stories, digging up information. She'd be so busy she wouldn't have a second to scratch herself, let alone think about…*that.*

She winced. And so it would begin again—Grace would choose the stories worthy of their effort and attention, the appropriate donation lines would be set up and a dozen other untold issues would remain just a couple of sentences in her notes.

The futility frustrated her.

And so she spent the next half hour focused on cleaning up, and eventually, with her arm and thigh muscles aching from the effort, they managed to clear a good part of the mess surrounding the house.

Finally Marco straightened, grabbed a bottle of water from beneath the tree and took a swig, then picked up his phone. "We should finish up."

Kat paused, scratching at a thin bead of sweat running down her neck as he handed her another bottle. "Okay."

"We'll probably make the mainland by three."

She nodded, one hand on her hip as she took a long swallow.

When he fell silent, she could feel his eyes on her. "Kat…"

Her gaze snapped to his as she finished the water, and the look in his eyes had her insides crumbling all over again. "Marco," she breathed. "Don't."

"But I have to say—"

"No," she said, a little too forcefully. "Don't say a thing. We did that already and look where that's gotten us. I don't want to say anything more until I have those follow-up tests in my hands. Until I know for sure." She studied him for a moment, taking in the tightness bracketing his mouth, his slightly clenched fist. "Promise me. No talk until we know."

As the seconds stretched, she held her breath, willing him with her mind. She'd coped with her mother's illness by not discussing, by not talking. She couldn't recall having one single deep and meaningful conversation with her father about what was going on, how she was coping, what he was feeling. He wasn't a talker at the best of times, but in this his lips had been perfectly sealed. Not talking was the only way she knew—that and partying until the nights had all just become one big, glitzy blur.

If Marco made her discuss just one more thing about this mind-boggling situation, she was sure she'd dissolve into a bawling mess on the floor.

"Fine."

Her breath whooshed out, relief flooding in. "Thank you. Now—" she attempted a smile but it fell way flat "—I don't know about you but I definitely need a shower before we head back to civilization."

How she managed to keep everything together for the entire day, Marco would never know. It was a testament to her inner strength, to her willpower, that she went through the motions of the boat trip strong and silently, pale-faced but determinedly swallowing her nausea.

And slowly, as the mainland came closer and closer, their attention was commanded by the shocking result of Cyclone Rory against the mainland of Cairns.

The radio reports had done nothing to prepare them for the devastation. It looked as if someone had stomped through in giant boots and created total havoc. A dozen private boats were all bunched up and shoved against the harbor wall like toys. The majestic palm trees were flattened, some crushing houses, some merely uprooted. Debris, sand, trees, glass, broken buildings and belongings… Everything had been displaced and reorganized into odd clusters, like the small speedboat half-buried in a luxury beach house. The kid's bike hanging from a lone palm tree. A cracked plasma TV lying in the middle of a now-sand-covered Esplanade pool. There were ripped roofs and scattered belongings and broken dreams left bare and torn.

Everywhere they looked, the cyclone had transformed the coastline into something neither of them recognized. In solemn silence they managed to dock, even though flotsam still floated in the water, then picked their way across the amazing wreck that was The Esplanade, to the next street, where Marco had arranged for a car to pick them up.

The drive north through town was made in similar silence as they were guided through the traffic snarl and stared out at the damage, trying to wrap their heads around the utter devastation the storm had wrought.

Physical devastation to accompany the emotional.

Marco swallowed, his gaze going briefly to Kat in the passenger seat, then back to the litter-strewn road, his eyes firmly on the police and rescue workers directing traffic and controlling the dozen news cars competing with business owners and volunteers eager to start the cleanup.

No, he had to stop those thoughts right now. They didn't know. Not until—as she said—she had the hard evidence in her hand. Then they would deal with whatever needed to be dealt with. So he bundled all those horrible thoughts, the possible future scenarios, and locked them up tight.

Her ringing phone provided some respite. After a brief conversation that mostly involved her listening to the caller, she hung up and said, "Grace needs me." He simply nodded.

"I'll drop you off."

When they pulled up outside the studio, Kat swung from the car and then glanced back.

"Thanks. I'll let you know how I go."

"You sure you don't want me there?" he asked for the third time, studying her face carefully as she leaned in.

She nodded. "Grace confided in me. I should be the one to tell her. And the sooner she knows the better." Her ironic smile was brief. "Preempt that press statement I just know she's been working on."

He snorted but said nothing more, so she gave him a smile, said "Thanks" again and left.

But as she strode into the studio, her mind was still on the island, far from the Grace situation. It was as if the time they'd spent there had been their own personal bubble. Now it was back to reality.

She sighed as she dug out her ID and then swept into the building. Time to focus on what she needed to tell Grace.

"Just say whatever comes into your head" had been Marco's advice on the boat. And he was right. Some of her best stuff for *The Tribune* had been spontaneous and off-the-cuff. Too much rehearsing had felt overedited and scripted. This was one time where she didn't want things to sound forced.

With a pounding heart, she clipped down the corridor straight to her office, grabbing a runner on the way to determine Grace's whereabouts. She eventually ended up at the canteen, pausing in the doorway to scan the room, her eyes eventually landing on the TV star at a corner table with their executive producer.

Right. This was it. She took a deep breath and strode over, a smile on her face.

Grace spotted her a few feet away, and a second later she gasped and shot to her feet, commanding everyone's attention.

"Kat! Oh, my God, it's great to see you! How've you been?"

She was quickly enveloped in a warm Estee Lauder–scented hug, and then firmly cheek kissed. "You were so vague on the phone—you were with Marco on the island, right? Did the cyclone hit there or pass by? Was there much damage? Did you take photos? Sit and tell me everything!"

Acutely aware of the sudden attention, Kat went through the motions of nodding and smiling, accepting hugs and arm pats then thanking everyone for their good wishes until her face started to ache from the smiling. Finally, when the minor fuss had settled and everyone moved back to their tables, she leaned in to Grace. "I need to talk to you. Privately."

Grace's unlined brow went up. "Sure. Let's go into my office."

It took a few minutes to get out of the canteen and then down the corridor. But finally they were in Grace's vibrant yellow-and-blue office, the air smelling faintly of Estee Lauder's Beautiful, her signature scent.

"So, what's up, Kat?" Grace smiled curiously, closing the door behind her. "Did you want to run a new story idea past me?"

"No." Kat eased onto the edge of the sofa, her insides churning. "It's about Marco."

"Oh?"

"Yes." Boy, this was awkward, way more awkward than she'd thought. It was because it was Grace, someone she cared about. Someone who'd be hurt, no matter how skillful or pretty or unscripted her words were. It was personal this time, and she hated every single minute of it.

Still, she had to put on her big-girl knickers and get it done. So she took a breath and plunged right in.

"Grace. Marco and me…me and him… Well, we're kind of…" Kind of what? *Together? Bed partners? Having a baby?* "Involved," she finished lamely.

*Oh, way to go. Put those media skills to great use there.*

Silence reigned, somehow made thicker by the soft fragrance permeating the air, as the expression on Grace's perfectly made-up face went through the emotions in a matter of seconds—amused surprise, confusion, disbelief—until she settled on a dark frown. "I'm sorry…what?"

"Marco and I are…involved."

Grace slowly crossed her arms. "Yes, you said that. But what does that actually mean? You guys are always involved in one way or another."

"We slept together."

Grace's eyes rounded. "What? When?"

Kat swallowed, her gaze firm. "Ten weeks ago, just before he left for France." *And these past few days...* Although she didn't need to spell that out, because judging from the look on Grace's face, she'd already assumed that.

Grace's slow blink and sudden laden silence said everything and yet nothing at all. So instead of elaborating, instead of trying to justify an action that had obviously cut deep, Kat waited.

Grace slowly sat down behind her desk then leaned back on the plush office chair, her face carefully blank. "I see. A little farewell private party, was it?"

"Grace..." Kat's chest tightened. God, this was hard! "You two weren't together at the time—"

"Oh, thanks for checking on that." The brief grimace slashing Grace's features twisted a little knife in Kat's belly. "It makes me feel so much better."

"I meant, I didn't plan on—"

Grace held up a hand. "Stop. I really don't need to know the details." She paused, raking her gaze over Kat until the burn of humiliation and betrayal had formed a small pool of sweat at the base of her spine.

"You knew when I mentioned wanting a baby," Grace finally said.

Kat nodded.

"And you said nothing."

Kat nodded again. "And I'm really sorry about that. I didn't know what to say. At that point, the thing with me and Marco was just a...a...one-time thing. We'd both decided to just ignore it and move on. But now, after these last few days, we've talked and it's all become a bit more...um...complicated."

"How?"

Kat flushed. "Just...complicated."

Grace's eyes narrowed. "You're not pregnant, are you?"

The shock of having it put right out there made Kat gasp, and she had to scramble for a breath. "Wh—what?"

"Are you pregnant?" Grace repeated, her expression tight.

Because it was Grace, a person she admired and respected, a person she'd come to trust with parts of her personal life, Kat hesitated over her automatic denial. But it was the small hesitation that gave it away, gave Grace clear and direct confirmation. And when the older woman's face creased into a small smile, Kat's conflict grew a thousandfold.

*Please don't ask. I can barely wrap my head around it all myself...and the test results just totally screw everything up.*

Kat bit her lip and slid her gaze away. "No comment."

Silence descended for a few moments, silence in which Kat firmly swallowed every emotion she'd been battling the past day. Damn, she couldn't lose it again. She *wouldn't* lose it again. She'd had her moment of weakness with Marco, had let the overwhelming feelings command her, make her vulnerable. She couldn't do it every single time someone mentioned it. Otherwise she'd just be a blubbering wreck on the floor.

Grace finally sighed and said, "I can't deny I'm hurt, Kat."

She grimaced. "I know. And I am really, really sorry about that. But it wasn't planned. If there's anything I can do to make it right for you..."

"An interview."

Kat blinked, her brow furrowed. "What?"

"You can give me that interview we were talking

about." Grace stood swiftly, hands wide on her desk, a gleam in her eye.

*Oh, wow. That was a bit...* Kat's head spun a little. "That's…uh. No."

"You're still saying no?" Grace lifted her brow. "After what you've just told me? Knowing nothing in this business is kept a secret for long?" At Kat's look of alarm, she waved a hand in the air. "Oh, honey, you should know by now it won't be me leaking details to the press. But once others get involved, it's inevitable."

Kat remained silent as Grace gave her a long look, then fished out a makeup bag from her desk and went through the motions of reapplying lipstick. It was true. A secret was kept only by one person, and over the next few days more and more people would be involved, like it or not.

"The offer is still there," Grace finally said, unplugging her phone and scrolling through her messages. "We'd do it your way, with your final approval. And you know I don't often say that."

Kat paused, trying to get everything straight in her head. "So you're okay with the Marco thing?"

"No." Grace smiled thinly.

She swallowed. "Grace…is this going to be awkward between us?"

"Most likely." The older woman eyed her, her expression still tight. "You denied it too much, you know. I always knew you had a thing—one that predates my claim—so I shouldn't be that surprised."

Kat swallowed her guilt, glancing away. "That's not what—"

"Oh, please." Grace rolled her eyes theatrically as she

walked to the door and pulled it open. "Give me some credit here. You and Marco have *always* been a thing."

Kat followed her out the door then down the corridor in silence, until Grace finally turned and eyed her. "So when are you going public?"

"*If,* Grace," Kat said. "If we go public."

Grace threw her a knowing look over her shoulder. "Oh, it's a 'when,' hon. Trust me."

Kat frowned. "That's not something we've thought about."

"Really?" Grace kept walking. "Well, you'd better start. Gossip has a way of getting out, you know."

Kat stared at her back. Was that a threat? That definitely sounded like one. And to be honest, she couldn't deny Grace her bitterness. If she could make this right with her, she'd gladly do it.

Even giving her an exclusive?

Ugh. That thought lay heavy in her gut for the rest of the afternoon, until she finally made her way home, barely made it through a shower and finally collapsed into a blissful sleep coma on her bed.

# Eight

The next day Marco and Kat sat in Dr. Hardy's waiting room, nervously waiting for her name to be called. Most structures in North Cairns had survived cyclone damage and it was still a surreal sight to see: half the town had been flattened while the other half stood tall and proud as if everything was normal.

Instead of offering empty it'll-be-okays and you'll-be-all-rights, he remained silent, loosely holding her hand, occasionally brushing her knuckles with his thumb as the minutes ticked by.

One minute.

Five.

Ten.

He glanced at the clock then scanned the pristine waiting room for the umpteenth time. Life still went on, despite the destruction outside. People still needed results, still needed diagnosing, needed to know what was wrong and how to fix it. Only a few people waited with them—a young couple, an elderly man, a woman with two small children—and briefly he wondered what each of their stories was, how they'd come to be here, right now. How they would cope with bad news, what they had vowed to change if the prognosis was good.

He watched the young mother settle her toddler with a book, and he smiled at her as their eyes met over the child's head.

That could be Kat in a few years' time.

Or not.

"Thank you for coming with me," she said now with a small smile.

"I wouldn't be anywhere else, *chérie.*" He squeezed her hand, careful to keep his worry firmly under wraps as he met her gaze. She needed him to be strong, whatever the result. He was there as her best friend, not the man who loved her so much he'd willingly sell his soul to trade places if he could.

Her finger softly traced his frown lines with a half smile. "Don't," she said softly.

He captured her hand, kissed it gently before his gaze slid away. "Sorry."

"Please, Marco. I really couldn't cope if you fell apart on me now."

He nodded, breath catching for a moment before he slowly huffed it out.

*You need to tell her.*

He grimaced, his gaze firmly on the floor. *No.* She had told him quite firmly they were friends. Nothing more. He had no doubt if he did tell her, that it would be the end of their friendship. And fighting about that now, proving to her that they should be together when she had so much more on her mind, would take everything he had. Waiting was not something he did well, but he wanted her in his life. He'd damn well have to wait for now, regardless of how it frustrated him.

Just not for long.

The door suddenly opened and all eyes went to Dr. Hardy as he walked purposefully over to them with a pleasant smile.

His heart thudded, hard.

"Good afternoon, Kat. Thanks for coming in." He said it softly, but still the people closest to them heard. A gentle murmur of recognition rippled, followed by all eyes swiveling to her as she stood with a flush. To her credit she ignored it all, just tightened her hand in Marco's and followed the doctor down the hall.

"Have you seen the town?" Dr. Hardy began as they settled in his office, his elderly face creased into concerned lines.

"Yes. It's unbelievable."

"Not quite as bad as Yasi but pretty grim."

She nodded, her expression neutral. Yeah, she was impatient, though. Marco could tell by the small muscles bracketing her mouth, the slight dip of her eyebrows.

"So," Marco said. "The tests. You ran them again?"

"We did." Dr. Hardy coughed then slowly removed his glasses, tossing them on the file.

"And?"

He spent interminable seconds shuffling through the file, then finally pulled out a piece of paper and read, pausing way too long.

Kat leaned in with a frown. "What?"

Dr. Hardy flushed. "First, I want to offer you my heartfelt sympathies for what you've been going through. We do have strict protocols, and regretfully I broke from that because of the history I had with your mother." He coughed. "But right now I can confirm that..." He stared at the paper before returning to her. "There was a mix-up at the lab. Some samples were mislabeled. And as a result, you have tested negative for motor neuron disease."

It was like taking a football to the chest, meted out by the world's best striker. Marco's gasp mingled with Kat's softer, higher one. Her hand went still in his as she froze, eyes wide. Her voice, when it came, wavered as if she'd just raced up a flight of stairs. "I'm sorry...what?"

"Your blood-test results have tested negative for motor neuron disease. You are clear and healthy, and—"

Marco's pounding heart drowned out the rest. She was healthy. The tests were clear.

The relief was unlike anything he'd ever known in his life. Nothing compared—not national selection, not the not-guilty verdict from his father's trial. Not even the positive results after his knee surgery telling him that yes, he would be able to walk. This...oh, this...

Joy, pure unadulterated joy choked his breath, and he felt the crazy laugh well inside, just before he choked it down.

*She's going to have a child. Our child.*

His expletive came out like a shot, and then he was turning to her and dragging her into a hug that was way too tight, way too emotional, but damn, she was clear, and the joy that swelled was too hard to contain.

She was going to live to see their child grow up. Take its first steps. Go to school, go on dates, get married.

Damn, she was going to *live.*

Eventually he pulled back enough to cup her teary face, knowing his smile stretched from ear to ear, because hers matched it.

"Clear," she whispered, her joyful expression a watery mess.

"Clear," he repeated, then slowly added, "We're going to have a baby."

Her eyes widened for a second, and then a small nod followed. "Oh, we so are."

Kat swallowed. She had tested negative. She was having a baby.

She couldn't even begin to quantify these two life-changing statements. She'd done enough survivor stories to know the emotion involved in processing this kind of information. The mix of elation and sheer panic running through her mind right now was...overwhelming. Overpowering. It choked her breath, snagged a laugh in her throat, forced tears to her eyes.

She stared at Marco as he brushed her damp cheeks with a shaky hand. How many times had she nodded sympathetically when all those survivors had tried to verbalize their feelings, tried to compose their thoughts into some semblance of control yet let everyone know of the emotion behind it? But she didn't know, not really.

Until now.

The adrenaline rush was amazing. She wanted to cry and laugh and dance and take on the world. She wanted to do reckless things just for the hell of it. She wanted to fulfill all those silly, crazy dreams she and Marco had laughingly thought up in ninth grade, trying to outdo each other on the ridiculous scale. Bungee jumping off the Eiffel Tower. Hiring Disneyland for the day. Biking down Everest. Flying a fighter jet.

She wanted to *live*.

After all these years of steadfastly refusing to get tested, pushing the worry and doubt to the back of her mind, then those agonizing hours of unbelievable anguish, she had finally been cut a break.

Everything seemed surreal, as if she was walking through a dream where nothing and no one could touch her. And couple that with Marco's gentle kiss, his obvious joy at her results, and there was no better moment than this, right here.

It was… Well, she couldn't even find the words to describe it. *Amazing* and *unbelievable* were way too tame for such a life-changing occasion.

She wasn't sick.

Dr. Hardy's discreet cough, when it came, had them both turning in surprise. He sat in the same position, leaning forward on the desk, arms bent, his expression professional.

"Thanks, Doctor," Kat got out, the smile stretching her face until it ached. "That's the best news I could've had."

"You're welcome." He leaned back in his chair, a hand brushing over his sparse gray hair. "There is, however, one more issue."

"Yes?"

He cleared his throat and focused his gaze on her. "Your mother's blood group is O, correct?"

She nodded. "Yes, it was in the hospital documents."

"And you are AB."

"Yes."

"Well, here's our problem."

She shook her head. "Sorry, I'm not getting it."

"Kat, normally I'd recommend further blood tests, make the standard speech about getting more results, seeing your doctor, etc., etc. But I knew your mother for a long time and I owe you this." He sighed. "I'm saying an O parent cannot have an AB child."

She blinked then shook her head with a snort. "Well, obviously there's been a mistake. We need to test it again."

He fixed her with a look, part sympathy, part concern. "I'm sorry. It's been done three times already. There's no mistake."

*What?*

Kat stilled, her thoughts all crammed in tight as she tried to decipher what this meant.

Okay, so her mother was O. She was AB. And O and AB couldn't be related. Which meant…

Her hand suddenly tightened in Marco's. "Hang on, you're saying it's impossible for my mother to be my *mother?*"

Dr. Hardy nodded.

"No," she croaked, and then more firmly said, "No, the tests are wrong. Just…just…" she stammered, her head whirling. "Just like with my first results! An accident. Human error."

"No, it's quite correct. We were very careful this time around. Everything was done properly." He paused, taking in her pale face and thinning mouth. "Kat, look, I can put you in touch with someone who—"

She stood so quickly, the blood rushed to her head. "I can't…I can't…" She didn't finish that sentence, just strode over to the door and stalked out.

Impossible. Ridiculous. It had to be a mistake.

She made it out the waiting room, then down the corridor, oblivious to Marco calling her. The elevators gave her pause, and she viciously punched an elevator button as her mind tried to make sense of these past few days, put them in neat little boxes and bring her some order and peace.

She couldn't. She was as far from peace as she could possibly be right now. She'd had a life-threatening disease for a day and everything involved in that—the feelings, the worry, the entire universe of emotion that came with the ordeal—had drained her. Yes, she'd managed to wrap her head around it, even though part of her deep down had refused to accept it. And now here she was, her greatest wish come true. She was disease-free....

But she had no clue who she was.

Who was her real mother? Was her father even her father? Did she have brothers, sisters out there somewhere? Where was she born? Did she look like anyone in her family?

Had someone given her up and then turned around and walked away without another thought? Was she stolen? Or had her parents loved her and been involved in some horrible accident?

A sob caught in her throat and she lifted a shaky hand to her mouth, determinedly glaring at the elevator doors as she felt the tears form.

It was as if someone had just suddenly erased her entire past, every single moment and memory effectively wiped and replaced with...what?

A million questions.

She sensed rather than saw Marco standing beside her, a silent presence that did little to calm her chaotic insides.

Was her real name Katerina, or was that another lie? Did her father know? Did *anyone* know?

Just who the *hell* was she?

She choked back a sob just when the elevator doors swung open, and she silently entered, hand still on her mouth as if to hold in all those raw, spilling emotions.

Marco pressed the basement-floor button and finally broke the silence. "What are you going to do?"

Her eyes remained firmly on the doors as she desperately tried to gain control, swallowing thickly and blinking over and over. She would not break down here, not now.

Later, yes. Not here.

"I'm going to see my dad."

A pause. "Flights will be limited until the airport's given the all clear."

"I know. I'll take the next available to Brisbane."

"I'll come with you."

Desperate for something else to focus on, she pulled out her phone and tapped on the travel app. "You don't have to do that."

"I want to."

"Can you take time off work?"

"I'll make time," he said firmly. "This is important."

She chanced a glance at his determined expression and then quickly looked away. *Of course you want him there.*

Just as during every other emotional time in her life, his presence would give her the necessary strength to get through this. He was her first and last choice.

"Okay. I'll let you know." The elevator opened and she walked out the foyer, then through the automatic doors. "Can you drop me off home?"

"Sure."

They walked across the car park to the vehicle in silence, and when she finally slid onto the soft leather seat with a groan, she closed her eyes. She was physically and emotionally drained. Thank God Marco said nothing, just drove in silence.

They finally reached her apartment block, and still not a word had been said.

What could she possibly say? She'd been through the emotional wringer and her brain was desperate to focus on something else. Yet when she crawled out of the car and glanced back at him, the small frown furrowing his brow and the look on his face crumbled her composure. "Kat, are you okay?"

She gave him a shaky smile. "No, actually. But I will be."

"Do you want me to come up?"

She pulled back, shaking her head. "No. No, thanks. I just need some time alone. Time to sort some things out."

"Okay." His blatant skepticism almost had her smiling. Almost.

"I'll call you." With that she turned and walked off, her disappointment echoing with every click of her heels on concrete.

What was she expecting? She'd said no, and he'd taken her at her word. End of discussion.

Except her reality had been ripped from her in the space of one afternoon, and she had no idea what to think or feel anymore. So instead of focusing on the whole messed-up bag of her parentage—the sensible thing when she had no clear answers—she latched on to the other issue she'd been avoiding.

Her and Marco.

Marco's reality was being absent six months out of the year. And the truth was, she didn't want him 30, 50, even 80 percent of his time. She needed his 100 percent commitment. But she also knew she couldn't ask that of him.

She unlocked the door to her third-floor apartment and went in, tossing her bag onto the kitchen counter and yanking open the fridge.

Honestly, it'd be easier for both of them if she raised this child by herself.

She could do that. She'd take time off work, hire a nanny. Women did it all the time, and she was in the fortunate position of having a healthy bank account to ease the burden.

And yet…

Hadn't she always resented her parents' piecemeal approach to parenting? Oh, her mother had been there when she could, but she'd been so involved in her work as an exclusive events planner she'd missed the bulk of Kat's high school activities. And her father… Well, she had as much chance of flying the starship *Enterprise* as she had of seeing him there for her. It would've been a shock to actually have her father attend something.

Their long and pointed absences had hurt the most, the overwhelming feeling that they'd just simply lost interest, gotten bored or had something more important to focus on shaping her insecurity all the way through high school. The familiar thread of instability still made her gut tighten even now.

Except she wasn't her mother's daughter, was she? Maybe they hadn't been totally committed because the blood bond that tied normal families together wasn't there. Maybe she was a disappointment, someone they'd not come to expect much of. And when her mother had become sick—

A sudden sickening realization swept over her, and she grabbed the bench for support.

If Nina wasn't her biological mother, and they'd known all along…

Then they'd know she wasn't a carrier or infected.

They had *known.* And not told her. For nearly fourteen years, her father had had so many opportunities to reveal this information, to put her mind at rest. But he hadn't. He'd let her go on believing every single day that her body was a ticking time bomb and that she could fall sick at any time.

The cry that erupted from her throat was almost primeval. She actually felt physically sick.

How on earth could the secret of her birth be more important than her physical and mental health?

Her hand shook as she poured a glass of juice and then quickly placed the carton on the bench. Her head hurt just trying to sort through everything. She could either make herself crazy going around in circles about it, or she could do something. Except until she saw her father, there was nothing *to* do.

Wrong. She could start to preempt the damage.

She grabbed her phone from the bench and scrolled through the contacts, finally calling a Brisbane number she'd never thought she'd need again—the publicist who'd skillfully navigated her around her last disastrous divorce, then those awful photos.

"Emma?" she said when the woman picked up. "It's Kat Jackson. I need to hire you."

# Nine

Three days later, after Kat had begged off early on Friday afternoon, she and Marco managed to get a flight into Brisbane, and Kat arranged to meet her father at work during his lunch hour. Not that he actually took one, she thought, as they both rode the elevator up to the executive offices of Jackson & Blair International Investments. She'd grown up on the stories of how her father and Stephen Blair had overcome the odds of humble family beginnings to develop their business. How they'd used their trademark determination and ruthlessness to throw every penny and waking moment into what was now one of Australia's top-ten investment companies.

And with such a sacrifice came a price. She barely remembered her father during her childhood. Instead he stood out by his lengthy absences—the times her mother had brought her to the offices for their "quality time," the weekends vying for his attention when he'd been on the phone, in his office or hunched over some important papers. In that, she and Connor had bonded, recognizing similar upbringings but rarely needing words to confirm it.

If Keith Jackson had intimidated her growing up, Stephen Blair had done so tenfold. Even now, passing by his office on their way to her father's, catching a bare glimpse of his towering, expensively suited presence in heavy discussion with similarly suited men, was enough to set her nerves on edge. He was a man who silently judged, for whom perfection meant everything, and nothing was good enough unless it was his way.

What a nightmare for Connor to have a father like that.

Five minutes later, Kat left Marco in the waiting room and strode into her father's office, a mix of anger, intimidation and frustration congealing in her belly.

*Calm. Stay calm.* She had the truth on her side, and she had the courage to confront him because what he did was wrong.

"Katerina," Keith Jackson said with a thin smile as she walked into his office then closed the door behind her. "I'm surprised the network let you go amidst all the cyclone coverage."

"It's only one afternoon." Not to Grace it wasn't, and she had the feeling her boss would be calling in the favor fairly soon.

"So, what's so urgent you had to fly down to Brisbane to talk to me?"

She took a seat opposite him, saying nothing. On

the two-hour flight south, she'd rehearsed this over and over, until her head spun and she'd exhausted herself.

It simply wasn't possible for her father *not* to know. Which meant beyond a shadow of a doubt that he also knew the chances of her having her mother's disease were low to none.

He could have told her anytime. They both could have told her. Instead they'd said absolutely nothing, letting her go through the pain, the anguish, then the ultimate decision to not get tested. Anger had surged every time she thought about that, so she'd vowed to not think about it until she had confirmation. Then she could silently go to pieces.

"I need to ask you something and I need you to tell me the truth, okay?"

His eyebrows went up, mouth in an impatient "okay" expression, as if she'd just told him she was buying a new handbag or going to the Gold Coast for the weekend.

"Dad," she said without preamble, her gaze direct. "Am I adopted?"

His expression froze, a perfect display of shock and confusion all rolled into one. She waited calmly as he leaned back in his chair with a dark frown, his face faintly flushed.

"What kind of question is that?" he said tightly.

"A perfectly legitimate one, considering it's impossible for Mum's blood type, O, to produce a child of my AB type."

His long pause was telling. "And why on earth are you getting blood tests? I thought you didn't want to know."

"I'm pregnant, Dad." Wow, that came out way smoother

than she'd practiced. It felt liberating, actually. "And I wanted to know if I had the disease. I don't, by the way. But then, you probably already knew that, considering Mum isn't really my mother."

She'd never seen him so still. Wow, she'd actually robbed him of speech—an ironic first. Swallowing the hysterical little laugh, she just slowly folded her arms and stared at him. And yet, he said nothing.

Great. It was up to her, then.

"Did you have an affair? Did the woman leave you with the baby?"

"No!" He flushed again, this time deeper. "That's ridiculous."

"So I'm adopted."

His nod, when it came, was frustratingly short.

She clamped down hard on her anger, but it still ended up bubbling over. "Oh, my God, Dad! I've had that disease hanging over my head for *years,* sitting there in the back of my mind, a death sentence." She sprung to her feet, fury flushing her face hot. "How the *hell* can you justify not telling me? Why on earth would you let me go through all those years of worry, of thinking…of thinking…" She couldn't stand there and finish the sentence, not with her father's face twisted into such uncharacteristic lines of pain that it hurt her heart just to look at him.

It was like the night of her mother's death, the only time she'd ever seen him weak and vulnerable, a man without power, without control. Just a man.

It had scared the hell out of her. Just as it did now.

She slowly sat, hands gripped on the armrests. "So why adopt? And why keep it a secret?" Her gaze softened. "Dad, if Mum couldn't have kids, it's nothing to be ashamed of. Why didn't you just tell me?"

He sighed, leaning back in his chair. "Because we made a promise."

"To whom?"

When he shook his head, her irritation spiked again. "Dad, tell me!"

He scowled. "Why bring this up now, Kat? Don't you have other things to worry about—like how the press is going to react to you being pregnant?"

She blinked and bit back a curse. *That* was what he was worried about? "I'm handling that."

His expression was borderline skeptical. "Right."

Dark, hot anger surged, making her skin tingle with the power of it, but her voice was calm, unwavering. "We're talking about my blood tests, Dad."

Oh, she desperately wanted to spill the entire story of the past few days, throw the false positive in his face and reveal her anguish, anger and every other single emotion that had accompanied it. She even choked on a sob as the words caught in her throat, but at the very last minute she clenched her fists and bit her tongue.

He lapsed into silence again, and she just stared at him. She knew her face reflected all the thoughts and emotions bubbling to the surface, every single one of them. When he broke eye contact first, she took just a little joy in that.

"Your mother wanted to tell you, you know," he said, carefully moving his coffee cup from the corner of the desk to the middle. "Many times."

"Why didn't she?"

He sighed. "The timing was never quite right. Because she knew you'd start asking questions, and she couldn't answer any of them." He slid her a glance. "That was why we never pushed you to get tested. The likelihood of you being positive was practically nonexistent."

She swallowed, dragged in a shaky breath as the past few days crashed over her. *You're negative. The test was negative, remember?* "Who are my birth parents?"

He paused a moment. "I can't tell you. I gave my word."

"Who on earth would make you promise something like that? Who would hold either so much power or so much loyalty...that...that..." She petered out, her mind clicking through the possibilities until she finally latched on to something crazy, something so far-fetched that she realized it fit perfectly.

No. It couldn't be *him*.

And yet...

*It so totally could.*

But that would mean...

Her back straightened in the chair. "It's Stephen Blair, isn't it?"

"No," he snapped quickly, the tight lines bracketing his mouth deepening.

It was so quick she barely had time to register it—the tiny twitch of a muscle near his eye, the clench of his hand. The almost imperceptible thinning of his lips. All signs of guilt.

"It so is." She stood, head spinning. "And I'm going to ask him."

"You will not!"

Her father's harsh command stopped her midturn. Slowly she turned back to face him, and his expression—

a mix of fury, tension and…yes, fear—was enough to temper her anger.

"Tell me, Dad," she said softly. "Please."

He paused, pursing his lips. She could practically see his brain working through the different outcomes of telling versus silence.

Thankfully, he made his decision quickly. "You can't say anything. Not even to Connor."

She blinked, gripping the chair back for support as the implication suddenly sank in. *Oh, God. Connor was…*

Connor was her *brother.* This was…

She couldn't even wrap her head around this. Connor. Her brother. Stephen. Her father. So…

"Who's my mother?"

He sighed then nodded to the chair. "Sit."

Marco sat in the waiting room, flicking through his phone and resisting the urge to get up and pace. For the fifth time he glanced up at the receptionist, and just as she had those five times before, she quickly dropped her gaze and hurriedly pretended to be doing something else.

Finally he strode over to the huge twentieth-floor window, to the panoramic view of Brisbane spread before him.

He sighed. When Kat was growing up, Keith Jackson had been the quintessential workaholic, but where he was gruff, terse and had little time for people other than his social circle, Kat's mother, Nina, had been his polar opposite. Whenever Kat talked about her mother, her face lit up, her eyes alight with love, even though she hadn't been a perfect parent herself. Marco had lost count of how many times he'd watched Kat swallow disappointment over her mother's prior commitments and broken promises. Yet all of that had become unimportant in the wake of her illness. And boy, he clearly remembered the time Kat had turned up on his doorstep in France, barely a few weeks after her mother had died. It was as if something essential had been stolen, something he wasn't sure she'd get back. But slowly, over time, she'd found her way back to who she was—his Kat. Changed, with added maturity, yes. But still Kat, deep down.

"I'm sorry, but aren't you Marco Corelli?"

His thoughts scattered, and as he glanced up at the receptionist, he quickly put on an automatic polite smile. "I am."

Her grin widened. "I knew it! My little brother plays local league and watches the European games religiously on cable. He's so excited for the World Cup selection next year, I can't tell you." She laughed. "He'll be so jealous I got to meet you."

Marco couldn't help but return her smile. "Thanks. We're all pretty excited about the selection, too."

"So will you be calling the match again? Our whole neighborhood stops to watch, you know," she added, rising from her seat, clutching pen and paper.

"That's the plan." When he held out his hand, she shook it in silent awe, and for the next few minutes, he answered her breathless questions, signed an autograph and smiled for a photo.

"Congratulations on the FFA award, by the way," she said, finally returning to her seat as the phone began to ring. "My cousins in Sydney will be stalking the red carpet on the night." She paused and picked up the handset with a smirk. "I'll have to text them that photo and make them jealous. Good morning, Jackson & Blair. How may I help you?"

"Marco?"

His soft laugh abruptly cut off and he whirled at the sound of Kat's voice, her pale face choking off the last of his amusement. He said nothing, just pushed the doors open for her, sent the receptionist a smile and a wave and followed Kat to the elevators.

"Well?" he asked as they rode down to the ground floor. "What did he say?"

She opened her mouth once, then closed it, then just stared at him, a dumbfounded expression on her face.

He gently took her shoulders. "Kat?"

"I am…" She shook her head, as if she couldn't believe it. "My father is…"

"Yes?"

She dragged in a harsh breath. "My birth father is Stephen Blair. Connor is my half brother."

His soft expletive bounced off the walls, but she barely winced, just turned back to the elevator doors, staring as the descending floor numbers lit up.

"Apparently Stephen had an affair with his housekeeper's daughter and I was the result." Her mouth thinned. "This was after my mum discovered she had motor neuron and decided not to have kids."

"And where's the housekeeper now?"

"They paid her off and she moved back to New Zealand. She died a few years ago."

He scowled.

"So they adopted you? Why keep it a secret? And how?"

"They went to the States for a year to hide the fact

my mother couldn't get pregnant." She sighed. "Stephen begged my father not to say anything—gave him the whole 'my wife will divorce me, my life will be ruined, the company will suffer' spiel. Dad agreed."

"And your dad just told you this voluntarily."

"Well, not at first." Her mouth thinned.

He paused, digesting that information.

"So are you going to tell Connor?"

The doors slid open and they walked through the elegant marble and crystal ground floor. "If you were him, would you want to know?"

He nodded. "Yes, I would. What about Stephen? Are you going to tell him you know?"

She remained silent as they pushed through the turnstile doors out onto George Street.

"I don't know." Her expression tightened. "I think it's a fair bet to say he won't care."

"Yeah." He glanced around then leaned in. "Whatever you decide, if you tell Connor—things always have a way of getting out." At her look, he added, "I'm not saying any of us would deliberately say anything. But the more people who know, the higher the chances."

She nodded then cast a casual glance up then down the busy Brisbane street, scanning the people going about their day. He noticed one or two do a double take as they passed, and he knew it was Kat they recognized and not him. The pull of her celebrity still amazed him, even after nearly a year of absence from the headlines.

Except that would soon end, and in spectacular fashion. His network had already fielded a handful of calls about his whereabouts during the cyclone, and he knew Kat had hired a publicist to issue a statement. Plus there was that thing with Grace, who was still on her case about an exclusive. After she announced her pregnancy, the press would start to piece things together, and then the nightmare would really start.

He suppressed a groan, remembering what it had been like the last time for her. All that stress, all that anxiety. Outwardly she'd handled it with aplomb, but he knew firsthand how much damage it had caused on the inside to her confidence, her self-esteem.

Not good for the baby.

They walked into the parking station, paid for the ticket and then made their way to his car, both wrapped up in their own thoughts until he glanced at his watch. Three hours before their flight.

With a frown he turned to face her, leaning against the door.

"Kat."

"Marco," she said in the same serious tone. God, he'd missed her humor. These past few days had drained him to the point that he wondered if things would ever get back to normal again.

He just wanted to see her smile again. Was that too much to ask?

"You don't have to do this, you know. You could just issue a statement then move into my place for a few weeks, until it blows over."

She stared at him for a moment and then slowly shook her head. "I have a job, Marco."

"One that Grace is making very difficult, so you said."

"She's angry. I understand that."

He let out a breath. "So if you're not going to take my suggestion or give Grace her exclusive, then tell me again why getting married would be a bad thing?"

Her expression twisted, telling him it was precisely the wrong thing to say. “Marco, please…”

He sighed. “Look, I’m trying to wrap my head around this and work out the best way to deal with everything.”

“And you think I’m not?” She scowled. “My head is a mess. My life is…crazy. And my past, everything I just assumed was real? Gone. All thirty-three years of it.” She slashed her eyes away from him, her frustration palpable. “Asking me to marry you is—”

An audible gasp interrupted her, and they both whirled to find two girls, shopping bags forgotten at their feet, busily clicking away with their cell phones.

One of them jiggled on the spot, a wide grin on her face. “Ohmygod, are you guys getting *married?* That is so awesome!”

*Click, click, click.*

Marco flushed, his hand instinctively going up to shield his face as he glanced to Kat, but she’d already moved and was yanking open the car door. She scrambled inside a moment later, and after he quickly joined her, he fired up the engine and they pulled out of the car park.

Her soft curse in the still air said it all, as did her glare in the rearview mirror. “That was—”

“Probably nothing,” he said, taking the next turn to get them onto the highway. “A couple of fans.”

“A couple of fans with cell phones and social media at their disposal,” she muttered, glaring out the window, her face tight with emotion. Just as during the times before, he knew exactly what she was thinking.

*Here we go again.*

The phone calls, the questions, the borderline stalking. Her family getting hassled. Photographers camped on her doorstep, at work, at the gym. TV and radio dissecting and analyzing their every move, offering expert damage control.

And there wasn't a damn thing he could do about it.

"Kat..." he said now, but she quickly held up a hand and made a call.

"The press statement will be out today, for whatever good that'll do me," she said when she hung up.

"Maybe it's not that bad."

She gave him an "Oh, really?" look. "Trust me, something will show up."

He couldn't argue with that.

They drove another twenty minutes in silence, until they finally pulled into the airport parking station and Marco turned to her.

"I have to be in Darwin tomorrow," he said.

She glanced from the window to meet his eyes. "Oh?"

He nodded. "One of the remote coaching clinics I set up. We're doing a grand opening with the mayor."

"When are you back?"

"In a few days. I fly in Monday."

She nodded. "Okay."

"Listen, Kat, I don't want to leave you in the middle of this, but I also have a thing in Melbourne, then Sydney. I won't be back until the day before the FFA awards."

She shrugged. "It's okay."

"No, it's not." Her cavalier attitude irritated him—as if she expected his absence.

"I have an appointment for an ultrasound next week," she added.

*Damn.* He scowled. "Why didn't you tell me?"

"I'm telling you now."

He frowned. "I could've rescheduled."

She gave him a look. "Not when you're booked months in advance. And anyway, it's only an ultrasound."

He dragged a hand through his hair. "I'm not abandoning you, Kat."

"I know. But until I make a public announcement, I think we should keep you out of it, don't you?"

He gritted his teeth and grabbed the handle, swinging the door wide. "No, I bloody well don't. Honestly, this is getting ridiculous. There comes a time when you just have to say, 'What the hell,' ignore what everyone says about you and live your life."

He got out of the car, slammed the door and, with long-legged strides, headed into the airport terminal, Kat following. And thanks to that little encounter earlier, he spent the whole time surreptitiously glancing around at the crowd, wondering if someone somewhere was taking photos, eavesdropping on their conversation. It was bloody unnerving.

Finally they made it through departures, past the check-in counter and into Qantas's private VIP lounge, which consisted of a bar, dining area, plush lounges and a communications center. They settled in and ordered drinks and food, but otherwise the silence stretched out between them. Marco checked his phone. Kat opened her iPad for her mail. Still not a word.

Was this how a friendship ended? he thought as he stared at his phone screen. Not with a spectacular all-out screaming match, but in a forced silence so uncomfortable she couldn't even bring herself to look at him.

It wasn't an argument. They didn't hate each other. He just… She just…

She didn't want to marry him. And he wanted her to.

He scowled at his phone. They had nineteen years between them, and he was damned if he'd let her push him out of her life. Once they dealt with this current situation, they'd have a serious talk about everything—including marriage.

It must've been some kind of record. Barely a day later, their "marriage proposal" hit social media, then the national papers, spreading out what could have just been a one-off article into a planned series on celebrity weddings and divorces, which were advertised with annoying regularity on TV. Marco and Kat were, of course, given plenty of airtime through the media, and, with the tabloid press, including the TV networks, setting up camp at her home, she'd had to hire a driver to take her to and from work.

Some photos still managed to leak out—one of her getting out of the car at the station. One when she'd not quite closed her curtains all the way. And some old cringe-worthy celebrity shots of her in full party mode.

That last one had been published two days ago, and she hadn't heard from Marco since. A dozen times she'd picked up the phone, ready to call, but stopped herself every time. It was something they needed to talk about face-to-face, not get into over the phone.

Of course, Grace had been mega-pissed about the attention, and the pressure at work had been high, compounding her stress about her family issues. After each day of her Job from Hell, she'd come home and collapsed on the sofa, finally allowing herself to think about the whole adoption thing, not to mention where to start finding out if her biological mother had had family, which in turn would be *her* family.

How did you tell someone you were his sister? Granted, it was Connor, one of her closest friends, but still. She wanted to do it right.

Armed with a laptop and a bowl of cereal, she crawled into bed and started on some research. Thanks to a bunch of online forums and chat rooms, she'd gathered heaps of information, read about people in similar situations and how they'd gone about connecting with their biological family.

That evening, after she'd bookmarked the last site and closed down the laptop for the night, her mind swung back to the physical part of her reality. In less than seven months, she'd be having a baby. The appointment she'd scheduled for next week loomed on the horizon, and suddenly her body went prickly with nervous tension.

She curled up in the bed, gently sweeping a hand over her belly. An official appointment. In writing. Out there.

It was really happening.

And Marco would be away for it.

She squeezed her eyes shut, refusing to let the guilt get to her. There was nothing she could do, right? He couldn't reschedule everything for her. It was as she'd said—just an ultrasound. There'd be plenty more opportunities for him to be involved.

Except she'd told him she didn't want him to be.

Did she even know what she wanted anymore?

Unable to answer that question, Kat buried herself in her work the next day, in the frantic energy of detailing Cyclone Rory's tragic path and sourcing stories that were all too depressingly bountiful now. Yet during their regular staff meeting when they argued the merits of each story and rearranged and reworked them for maximum viewer impact, she couldn't help but refocus on Marco's suggestion to follow her own dream.

A charity. A foundation where she would be in control, raise money and see each case through to completion from beginning to end.

So she began drafting a list, slowly filling in more details until she had two pages of handwritten notes. That night, during her usual hour on the treadmill, she reorganized it all in her head, until she finally had a semblance of a game plan. And the more she thought about it, the more excited she became. She'd even reached for her phone, eager to discuss it with Marco, but ended up balking at the last minute.

He was obviously busy, which was why he hadn't called.

She pressed the end button on the treadmill and grabbed her bottle, downing half the water as she cooled down. As amazing as it had been, the stupid sex thing had ruined it. She was thinking like a woman in a relationship, not as a best friend. Best friends didn't care who called whom first—they just *called*. They didn't stress about how many days, hours, minutes had passed since they'd spoken. And they certainly didn't let the other person get away with such a lengthy silence.

Just as she finally stepped off the treadmill and picked up her phone, it rang.

It was Connor. "Hey, stranger," she answered, way too cheerfully, as she grabbed her towel and walked into the kitchen.

"What are you doing tomorrow?" he asked.

"Saturday?" She jammed her phone under her chin then flicked on the hot water jug. "Oh, the usual. Watching TV. Eating by myself. Hiding from the hundreds of paparazzi camped on my doorstep."

"Where's Marco?"

"Swanning around in Darwin, I believe."

There was a pause as he picked up on her tone. "Did you guys have a fight?"

Kat sighed. "No, we are having…a difference of opinion."

"Anything to do with this engagement thing the press is going crazy with?"

She walked slowly back to her lounge room, clicked on the TV and muted the sound. "Partly. I just…" She sighed. "It's complicated. The baby. This press thing. Work. And I feel guilty that his appearances have been overshadowed by the media craving a sound bite. Did you know someone actually asked him about us during a ribbon cutting yesterday?"

"The press is full of idiots. Which is why I'm coming to see you."

She perched on the edge of her lounge. "If that were the real reason, you'd have come to see me way earlier than this."

His chuckle brightened her mood. "We'll lounge around and ignore the press together, eat pizza and watch *The X-Files.*"

She couldn't help but smile. "Sounds divine."

"Or, you know, we could just go to Marco's island. Plenty of privacy there."

"God, don't you start. Next they'll be hooking you and me up instead of Marco."

He laughed again. "I dunno—I do like the sound of 'Kitco.' Much better than 'Markat.'"

"Shut up." When he laughed, she reluctantly joined him. "You're an idiot, Connor."

"Shh, don't tell anyone. You'll ruin my reputation."

She was still grinning when she hung up. Yes, her emotions were all over the place, and she had too many questions to ask and no idea how to approach Stephen… if she even wanted to. Frankly, the man scared the hell out of her and always had. But the one thing she had no issue with was accepting Connor as her brother. She loved him like a brother. More, actually, because she'd had years to appreciate him as a friend without any pressure or family obligation. As she walked down the corridor to the bathroom, she had to admit that she was looking forward to telling him. She had no idea how he'd react, but hopefully he'd feel the same way.

The next night, barely thirty minutes after she made it through her door with a relieved sigh, her intercom beeped.

"Chez Jackson?"

"I heard someone's having a pizza party."

She grinned at Connor's commanding voice. "Yep. With beer and juggling monkeys."

"I'm so there."

She buzzed him up and then unlocked the door. He stepped through the door five minutes later with an overnight bag, a steaming-hot Crust pizza and a huge grin.

"You are my savior." She hugged him then took the pizza and stepped back to allow him entry. He strode in with his usual lanky gait, his broad frame filling her space.

He dumped his bag near the couch. "Midnight must be a bit late for the paparazzi. I didn't see anyone about."

She shoved the pizza on the coffee table. "Oh, they're there—you just can't see them. Like cockroaches."

His laughter followed her as she went into the kitchen to get drinks and plates. When she emerged, he was scowling at his phone.

"What's up?" she asked.

"Everyone's got marriage on the brain." Connor slowly placed his phone on the table and sprawled on her couch. "My mother's been bugging me about it. Apparently a successful thirty-three-year-old guy needs a wife to appear more stable to our conservative European investors."

Kat patted his hand sympathetically. "Well, between Marco and me, I can honestly say it's not what it's cracked up to be."

Connor snorted. "Yeah. Two apiece, right?"

"I'm two. Marco is one and a half."

Connor centered a coaster on the table and placed his beer bottle on it. "So is there any truth to the rumors?"

"Which ones?" She flopped down on the single-couch chair.

"The marriage ones. Because everyone's waiting for the real press statement, you know, not the lame 'no comment' one."

"I know." She fixed him with a look. "Yes," she said at length.

"Yes, what? Marco actually asked you to marry him?"

"A few times, yes."

His breath came out in a whoosh. "Wow. And?"

Kat shook her head. "He only offered to avoid the nightmare PR—which is ironic, considering we're in the middle of it anyway. I haven't even announced I'm pregnant yet, so imagine what that'll do," she said as she flipped open the pizza lid and inhaled deeply. "Anyway, enough about that. I've got something more important to talk to you about. I need to—"

"Hang on, reverse." He leaned in. "More important than you being happy?"

"What?"

He sighed. "Can you not see it?"

"See what?"

He thumped a palm on the table. "You and Marco. You're perfect for each other."

Kat felt the tingle of embarrassment all the way down her spine, her eyes quickly darting away. "It's not like that, Connor. He's my—"

"Best friend, yeah, yeah, I know." Connor rolled his eyes. "You've both been preaching that old chestnut for so long, I'm ready to strangle someone. Why don't you guys just admit you love each other and put yourselves out of your misery?"

"I do love him, Connor. I love you, too."

He grinned. "Ditto, sweetheart. But you're not *in love* with me."

She frowned, the denial on her tongue, but instead she just pressed her lips together. "Look, forget that for a moment. I need to talk to you about something." She leaned in, hands tucked between her knees. "You know how I went for that blood test last month?"

Connor paused, midchew. "Yeah?" At her look he slowly placed the pizza on the plate, wiped his hands on a napkin and gave her his full attention. "Ah, Kat, don't tell me they got it wrong again…."

"No, nothing like that," she said quickly. "Okay, so the reason why my test was clear was…because… well…" It was still unbelievable, no matter how many times she tried to process it. Saying it aloud only made it more real. "Keith and Nina aren't my biological parents."

A deathly silence permeated her apartment.

Connor's brow dipped. "What?"

"I had a blood test. Nina and Keith are not my biological parents," she repeated patiently.

Connor's jaw dropped, eyes rounding. "No way."

Kat nodded. "It's true. My blood type and Mum's aren't compatible. Then we flew down to see my dad and he confirmed it."

"We? Marco went with you?"

She nodded. "And there's more."

He huffed out a breath. "Jeez, what?"

Kat smiled. "Connor…" She held his gaze unwaveringly. "My father is Stephen Blair."

Everything was still for a few seconds, maybe more, until Connor's loud bark of laughter split the air like a shot and she jumped. Frowning, she watched in silence as he sat there, chuckling and shaking his head. What did that mean? Was he…upset? Happy? Freaked out?

"Are you okay?" she finally said after a few moments.

He shot to his feet. "No, actually. Give me a moment."

She watched him pace, with one hand running through his hair, the other on his hip. It was worrying, not knowing if he'd taken the news as a good thing or not.

Finally, after a few interminable minutes, he turned to her. "You know, I just knew it was something like this. I *knew* it."

"What?"

He paused, taking in her expression, and shook his head. "About ten years ago, I caught the tail end of an argument. Couldn't hear much but I did eventually work out Mum and Dad were talking about a child. Oh, I didn't realize at the time that it was you," he hastened to add. "I never would've worked that one out."

She blinked. "What did they say?"

"Well, Mum was pretty pissed off—that was clear. Dad didn't want to talk about it, as usual. Then after, Mum ended up with a new Prada handbag and a necklace from Paspaley, and everything just seemed like normal."

Kat sat back in her chair, processing that information. "You didn't say anything about it to us."

Connor gave her a look. "I don't tell you guys everything."

True. Connor was extremely private when it came to his family—it had taken years for him to share even the most basic of details. It was only because they'd witnessed his parents' arguments firsthand that they knew about them at all. It was a deep source of embarrassment for him.

"Mum's always going on about Dad's affairs. You know that," he said now, picking absently at the label on his beer bottle.

Kat nodded, her expression solemn.

"So I overheard a bit more than usual. Apparently my mother still hasn't forgiven him for being in bed with another woman the day I was born."

Kat's mouth thinned. Connor projected such a hard and capable facade that people refused to believe there was a heart of gold under that swish Armani suit and classically handsome face. She knew that mask was to protect him from feeling too deeply, but she'd known him long enough to realize that he sometimes felt more than any of them put together.

"My sister, huh?" he said now, taking another swig of beer with a smile. "How do you feel about that?"

She was his sister. She had a *brother.* With everything else going on in her life, she'd pushed the impact of that detail to the back of her mind, but now, faced with a grinning Connor and the familiar way his eyes creased, the easily recognizable sweep of his nose, it was unmistakable.

She felt her mouth stretch into an answering grin. "Do we need to hug to mark this momentous occasion?"

"Hell, yeah." When he opened his arms, she got up, moved toward him and was enveloped in his embrace. The relief, the utter joy she felt at this moment, when it had just been bad news after bad news, was like a weight off her shoulders. She leaned into the hug, into his solid, hard warmth, and felt the tears well up. She couldn't believe how happy this actually made her.

Damn pregnancy hormones.

"Are you going to tell your dad that you know?" she asked, muffled against his shoulder.

He pulled back with a grimace. "I have no idea. After all these years of keeping the secret, do you think he'd want us to know? Plus, it could create a backlash with yours."

She nodded. "And it doesn't really change anything, him knowing, does it? I mean, I'm not going to demand in on the will or anything."

Connor laughed. "But it would be fun to call him Grandad in seven months' time." He glanced pointedly at her belly.

"You're terrible."

He laughed again, and again she felt the burden of the past few weeks shift.

Finally, something was going right. If only she could fix things with Marco.

Her expression must've given something away, because Connor's brow suddenly creased.

"Problem?"

"Oh, besides the gossip, pregnancy hormones and the fact Marco won't speak to me?"

"Well, you're not exactly speaking to *him,* are you?"

She opened her mouth to deny it but wisely closed it instead. "Plus his network contract's up for negotiation, so naturally they're speculating on that, too."

"They won't drop him. He's too much of a draw." Connor leaned back, cradling his beer with a small smile.

"What's that look for?"

"It's awesome you two are finally a couple. I always knew there was something, despite your denials."

"Connor, we're not. We're not speaking."

"Only because he's not here. Wait until you guys see each other again…next week, right?"

"Yes. At the awards thing."

"There you go. You'll be in Sydney, in a hotel. A

perfect opportunity to talk alone." When Kat remained silent, he impatiently tapped a finger against his bottle. "Listen. Is moping around with a head full of what-ifs better? No. Just say you love him, then kiss and make up."

"But I don't—"

"Sure you do."

"No..." *Yeah. You do.*

It was like a revelation. As if something fundamental had changed deep inside her. The false positive, the adoption, the baby had all added bit by bit to this moment, forcing her to see what was truly important in her life. To reassess again, to work out what was of true value to her.

The answer was so blindingly simple she gasped from the impact.

Marco. He was the one.

She sighed. "I told him we're just friends a few times, Connor," she said softly, voicing the doubt that had plagued her the past few days. "Surely there comes a time when he actually takes me at my word."

"You're talking about Marco here," Connor said. "And anyway, you're his best friend and you're having a baby together. He can't cut you out of his life permanently."

Kat nodded, saying nothing. Three times she'd pushed him back into the friends zone, and three times he'd not put up a fight.

Surely that said something?

She sighed, leaning back into the sofa. Either way, she'd have her answer next week.

She took a shaky breath. This was scary, so much scarier than anything she'd ever done in her life. Because in laying everything out there, there was a real possibility of rejection.

He could reject her. Say he just wanted to remain friends. And the question was, would she be satisfied with that?

# Ten

The next five days were a crazy, breathless mess of activity. Kat was flat out at work, working on the Cyclone Rory stories, the follow-ups, the charity lines, but the overwhelming media attention on her personal life had started to impact on her work, with some sponsors severing their partnership at the last minute, leaving her frustrated and angry. Outwardly, Grace didn't seem overly concerned, but Kat knew she was furious. Couple that with their already cool tension, and work was not a pleasant place to be.

Marco had managed to call her once, the day of her ultrasound, but other than that, their texts had been short and sweet. And it broke Kat's heart, knowing their friendship was showing those irreversible cracks.

Finally something had to give. So the day before she

was due to fly to Sydney, she walked into Grace's office and firmly closed the door.

"I'll do it."

"Do what?" Grace asked, glancing up from stirring her morning coffee.

"The interview. An exclusive." She quickly put up a hand as Grace started to speak. "But everything—and I mean *everything*—has to go past me first."

Grace blinked slowly, then her face broke out into a huge grin as she shot to her feet. "Kat, this is brilliant! Wonderful! Oooooh..." She rounded the desk and embraced her in a cloud of perfume. "This has made my week...my month—hell, possibly my entire year!" Kat slowly pulled away, smiling thinly as her boss perched on the corner of her desk, beaming. "Can I ask you why now?"

Kat shrugged. "Timing. It's the right time."

Grace paused, watching her closely. "Really."

"Yep. Time to set the record straight once and for all. About everything." She met her boss's gaze unwaveringly, and in that small pause, an understanding passed between them, one that needed no words. This was Grace's moment and Kat was giving it to her. They both knew there'd never be another opportunity, just as they both knew things had fundamentally changed between them these past few weeks.

She knew it and Grace knew it.

"When?" Grace finally asked.

"Next week. After Sydney."

After another moment's pause, her boss nodded. "I'll set it up and let you know."

"Okay. And can you wait until after the awards before you start publicizing? The night should be about the players, not me," she added with a thin smile.

To her surprise, Grace nodded. "Sure."

"Thanks." Kat moved toward the door, unprepared for the wave of sadness that engulfed her. They both knew it wasn't just an interview date they were setting: it was Kat's quitting date, too.

Even knowing she was moving on to something bigger and better, something that really made her heart sing, didn't make leaving hurt any less. Despite the stress, the imperfections and the recent personal issues, this job had come at a perfect time, when she'd needed it the most. She'd always be grateful for that.

"Grace," she said now. "I want to thank you for—"

"No." The older woman shook her head, smiling softly as she reached for her ringing phone. "I thank *you.* It's been a pleasure working with you, Katerina Jackson."

Their gazes held for a moment, then Grace answered her call and it was Kat's cue to leave.

Kat flew into Sydney on Saturday and spent all day getting massaged, primped and fussed over, satisfied she'd gained at least some control over the spiraling situation. Meanwhile, Marco spent hours under harsh studio lights dressed in nothing but his underwear, fulfilling his Skins contract, so the first time they actually saw each other was half an hour before the limo picked them up for the FFA awards ceremony.

When she heard the knock at her hotel door, she nervously smoothed down her pale blue satin dress and pushed her hair behind her ears. All the half sentences she'd barely had time to practice crumbled on her tongue when she opened the door and saw him standing there, looking incredible and perfect in a designer suit and tie, his hair casually tousled and a familiar this'll-be-fun smile on his generous mouth.

His eyes swept over her thoroughly, taking in every last detail from her tight elaborate updo, to the dangling earrings and the strappy floor-length ice-blue ball gown with a respectable amount of ever-growing cleavage on show.

Then he held out his arm, said softly, "You look beautiful," and her heart just melted.

Twenty minutes later, stepping out of the limo onto the red carpet together, Kat took a moment to note the familiar players currently in European competition, now all returned for this special night that honored Australian-born sportsmen and women. As usual a smattering of die-hard and local fans stood behind the roped barriers, taking photos, and she felt her mouth curve, her expression calm.

She was ready to face the crowd.

She spent minutes gaining more confidence, her tension relaxing as she mingled with people she knew, chatting casually to old acquaintances.

This was going to be a good night, she thought as they made their way slowly down the carpet. No intrusive press, no focus on her. Just dinner and the awards. Yet as she turned, midsmile, and saw a familiar figure stride across the carpet, she faltered.

James Carter. James Bloody Carter.

Marco's former Marseille teammate, the Irish-born center who'd charmed her for over a year then convinced her to get married in a quickie Bali wedding. Then had promptly shagged some woman in their bridal suite seventy-two hours later.

It was too much to expect that he'd gotten fat and ugly in the years since she'd last seen him. If anything he was more handsome, more toned. Broader in the shoulders, leaner at the waist. His flashy suit set off a healthy physique so discreetly that to the untrained eye it might have seemed effortless. Kat knew better.

"What?" Marco was squeezing her arm, and she glanced up to see the concern in his face.

"James is here."

His mouth twisted briefly. "Really?"

She frowned, ignoring the fact they were on a red carpet with cameras within recording distance. "Wasn't he supposed to be in Italy or something?"

"Yeah." He took a step forward and they kept on walking. "Look, he's just a presenter. He'll be onstage most of the time, not at our table. He won't come over, and if he does, just say nothing."

"Easy for you to say. He's not the one who cheated on you."

Marco sighed. "Just…be cool, okay?"

She snorted. "I am *always* cool."

"Uh-huh."

He squeezed her hand, she grinned at him, and suddenly it was just as it was before, where they'd been so familiar, so close. So comfortable.

Damn, she missed that. It'd been three weeks since she'd seen him, and boy, she hadn't realized how much she'd missed him until he'd turned up at her door dressed in a formal suit and one of his expensive silk ties. And when he'd smiled…it had taken a massive effort not to tackle him then and there.

Now, with the heat rising in her belly, she glanced around at the smattering of people who'd stopped to rubberneck, the long red carpet that led into the plush foyer and the familiar faces of Sydney's football community. With a deep breath, she put on a smile and firmly shoved everything else from her mind. This was Marco's night, and she should just enjoy it. There was time enough for stress and worry later.

The ballroom easily seated two hundred and was elegantly decorated, with tiny blue downlights in the ceiling casting a cool glow over the round banquet tables. The tables themselves featured art deco–style centerpieces. People hovered around the bar, and a slide show above the stage was playing highlights of the past season backed by a classic-rock sound track.

Surprisingly, despite the presence of cameras and James, Kat was less tense than she thought she'd be. For one, the evening was about the awards and the players, not her. There were no intrusive questions or random photos or the usual stares-and-whispers from complete strangers. Sure, there were cameras, but she could smile nicely and handle a few shots. And as long as James kept his distance like he'd been doing for the past hour, she'd make it through the night unscathed.

She smoothed her gown down, thankful for the flowing empire style that hid her growing belly, only just managing to stop herself before placing a telling hand on the thirteen-week-old bump as she walked over to the bar. Even though this was a private function and she was fairly relaxed, everyone was still equipped with a camera and a Twitter account.

After she reached the bar and ordered drinks, she casually scanned the room, a small smile on her lips. A smile that immediately fell when she felt a guy standing way too close behind her. She frowned, preparing to say something, but when she glanced back, all the words just stuck in her throat.

"Hi there, Kitty."

James Carter was standing there, all casual as you please, hands in his pockets, face creased into a charming grin. After darting her gaze around to see who was watching—and seeing the coast was clear—she sent him a withering look.

"What do you want?"

James's smile was perfect—too perfect. "What—no hello? No 'how've you been these last few years?'" His faint Irish accent oozed over her like thick molasses, bringing with it a wealth of conflicting memories.

"I have nothing to say to you, James," she snapped.

His mouth quirked. "Is that any way to greet a long-lost—"

"A long-lost what? A friend?" She snorted. "Let's call it like it is. You're my cheating ex—a drinking and gambling ex with a serious money-management problem."

"Kitty, darlin'..." His expression was pained. "Don't be like that. I didn't come over here to rehash old wounds."

"Don't call me that." She frowned. "So why? You want to give people *more* to talk about?"

"No." He drew a slow hand over his eyes. "But you're kind of a one-woman pap magnet—the magazines and papers are all over you. I flew in for the awards and—"

"I'm not interested in your life," Kat interrupted, turning back to the bar.

As she waited for her order, she could feel his scrutiny. *Dammit, don't take the bait. Just ignore him, and then go back to Marco. Ignore it, ignore it. Ignore—*

With a sigh, she turned to him. "Fine. What do you want, James?"

"Forgiveness."

Kat blinked. "Sorry. Fresh out of that."

James took a step closer, and instinctively she stepped back against the bar. He winced. "Believe me, Ki-Kat. I'm truly sorry."

"Are you."

"Yes."

Kat flushed. "Well, 'sorry' doesn't cut it."

"What do you want me to say?"

"Nothing. Absolutely nothing." She nodded to the barman and then took the drinks.

"You know, after the divorce I spent a year working my way down to rock bottom," he began stiffly, following her as she made her way across the room. "I got into a car accident, spent forever in rehab. I'm a completely different person now."

She stopped. "I know. I read all about it." Briefly she recalled the headlines, the shock then relief she'd felt at reading about his struggles. "But I don't see what this has to do with me."

"I told you. I want to make amends."

"Fine. You've apologized. Now I'm going."

"Wait." His hand shot out, grabbing her elbow, and she stilled, staring at him.

Slowly he withdrew then self-consciously looked around at the clusters of noisy people milling about the room.

"You can't expect absolution just because you ask for it. This is so typical of you, James." She scowled.

"So selfish. I was your trophy girlfriend and then you cheated on me. There's no forgiving that."

"I know." His expression dropped, and for a second he looked genuinely contrite. "I can't excuse my past behavior."

"No, you can't."

She moved off, hoping he'd get the hint, but still he followed, until she got to her table and she finally put the drinks down.

James's mouth thinned in frustration. "You never let me explain. I wanted to talk on our honeymoon, but you stormed off. And anyway, you weren't such a saint yourself."

"What?"

"Yeah. You had this chip on your shoulder the size of Alaska. You carried around your toughness as if it were some goddamn bravery badge, instead of the defense it really was. And I always had to compete with Marco. The perfect, do-no-wrong, everybody-loves-me Marco Corelli."

"He is my *best friend!*"

"Really. Can you swear, right here and right now, that you never thought of him as more?"

"Of course not!" But she'd hesitated a second too long, and the look on James's face said it all.

"Did you sleep with him?"

She sucked in a sharp breath, gaze darting to the people around them. "Oh, my God, James, I am so not doing this with you. This is ridiculous!"

He glared at her, his handsome face twisted into angry lines, until he finally let out a breath, hand going to the back of his neck. "Look," he muttered, his gaze firmly on the floor. "I didn't come here to argue. I just wanted to—"

"You okay, Kat?"

Kat whirled, the words dying on her lips as her eyes collided with the steel of Marco's at the same time his arm looped loosely around her waist.

She was so stunned by the suddenly intimate gesture that she totally forgot to step away, to create a more platonic space between them. And Marco… Well, it was as if someone had cast a spell and turned him to stone, he was so still. Yet beneath that stillness, that cold expression, Kat could sense his body coiled as if he was ready to spring into action any second.

Dangerous.

"James," Marco finally said, his voice low and painfully polite.

James looked startled but swiftly recovered, holding out his hand. "Hi, Marco."

Marco slowly and pointedly looked at it and remained where he was. "Congratulations on your award. Player of the Year is quite an achievement."

James shot Kat a look of part frustration, part wariness. "Thank you."

She had to hand it to him—her ex was smooth. From the top of his expensively shaggy haircut to the soles of his shiny black dress shoes, the man had all the right props. He was someone who used charm and looks to get what he wanted.

When he flashed a perfect let's-all-be-friends-now smile, she couldn't suppress one of her own. *Oh, you're good, aren't you? So smooth. And Marco can see right through that.*

"So, Kat," James was saying, "we need to talk some more. I'm in room fourteen-oh-five."

"She won't be coming," Marco cut in smoothly before she could reply.

She gave him an irritated look then turned to James. "We've got nothing to discuss, James. End of story."

James scowled, his eyes going from Marco back to her. "Whatever you might think, Kat, I'd like to smooth out our differences. Start a clean slate."

A pause. Then, "Do you have a hearing problem?" Marco asked coolly.

"Butt out, Marco," James snapped. "This is between me and my wife."

"Ex-wife. She's my fiancée now. Oh, please, be my guest," he murmured as the other man clenched his fists.

"Fiancée? So you guys *are* getting married?" James's eyes widened, his gaze darting from Marco to her. "Huh. Guess that confirms things, then." As Marco bristled, he pulled himself up to his full six foot five and glared back.

*Oh, for heaven's sake.* It was like watching two dogs snarl and growl over a bone.

"No, we're not." She couldn't believe Marco had said the *F* word.

With a snort she moved out of Marco's embrace. "Okay, you need to leave now, James."

James sighed. "Look—" he stuck his hands on his hips "—I didn't want to do this here, but you leave me no choice. I've been asked to write my biography, a kind of inspirational, overcoming-the-odds thing. And I can't do it without mentioning you."

She sucked in a breath. "No."

James eyed Marco then came back to her. "Like it

or not, Kat, you were a part of my life. I'd like your approval on the chapter, but I can still publish it without your consent."

"James…" She took a deep breath, waiting for her brain to catch up. She could sue him, but that would take money and time, plus attract more attention to the book than it was worth. Or…

"If I don't like what I read, can I change it?"

"It depends what it is. But sure." He nodded. "I'm open to amendments."

That didn't mean a thing, but it was all he was offering. With a short nod, she said, "Fine. Email me the chapter when you have it."

James nodded and his mouth tweaked, a hint of what she used to think was the most devastating smile in the French soccer league.

She watched him leave in silence, her mind still halfway in the past. But at the last minute, as he was walking by the video tripod that had been filming the night, he abruptly turned.

"Congratulations on getting engaged," he called loudly, causing a few conversations to halt. "I knew that press release was a smoke screen—very clever. I hope you'll be happy. For what it's worth, I could totally see it coming."

A dozen people in earshot quickly turned to first James, then to Marco and Kat, and all of a sudden a chorus of cheery woo-hoos erupted.

*No. Oh, no.*

Kat's stomach bottomed out yet she refused to let it show. She simply shook her head at the closest group of well-wishers. "We're not… No, we haven't…"

Too late. The damage was done.

Embarrassment leached into a low, slow burn, one

that tightened her back, then her neck. She gritted her teeth, smilingly denied everything and stalked through the crowd, straight for the doors leading outside.

A handful of curses ran through her mind as she went. Damn James. Grace's exclusive was supposed to set everything straight, but now he'd gone and ruined it. Which meant they'd have to bring the interview forward.

Just as she dug out her phone and was about to reach the balcony doors, Marco grabbed her arm. "Kat. Stop."

"Marco…" She was barely holding it together, and his concern only tipped the scales.

She turned slowly to him with a dark frown. "Your fiancée?"

Marco shrugged, eyeing the people passing them by and giving them a casual nod. "I thought he needed a little encouragement to leave."

"With a lie?"

Marco studied her for a heartbeat. Then he said, "What upsets you more—the unwanted attention or me staking a claim?"

"You've no right to claim anything."

"Not even when you're having our baby?" he murmured.

Kat put a hand to the wall for support. Now that she was alone with Marco, she could no longer hold the memories at bay. They all came rushing back, making her skin heat and her head spin with remembrance. His lips and what they'd done to her. His warm breath, teasing her skin. And his wonderful hands, hands he now shoved aggressively in his pants pockets.

"Do you have any idea what this is going to do?" she said tightly. "How people are going to—"

"Going to what? Gossip?" A hand dived into his hair. "Christ, Kat, I'm really sick of hearing about it. I'm trying to help but you keep saying no. Stop complaining when you know you could fix it with one simple yes."

"Marco, this, on top of everything else…I just can't deal—"

"I know that." He leaned in, his face tight with anger. "I'm only guessing how things are for you because you haven't called, haven't wanted to discuss anything. It's like trying to get information from a goalpost."

She blinked, frowning. "Marco, I…"

"Look, this isn't the right place to talk," he said, curling his fingers around her wrist. "Let's go."

The automatic refusal was there, but she quickly swallowed it, giving him a brief nod. And when he turned and began to lead her firmly through the crowd, her breath quickened in anticipation.

This was it. They'd finally put it all out there. It would either be the end of their relationship or the beginning of one.

God, she was praying for the latter. Because the former would be like cutting a vital piece of her heart out.

There was no way she could do that. Ever.

# Eleven

They stood in the middle of her hotel room barely ten minutes later, and as Kat watched him work his tie loose and slowly peel it off, everything just flew out of her mind.

It was incredible how her heart reacted to his presence. Her body just went all tingly, her blood heating as her eyes hungrily took in his broad frame, his strong cheekbones, his hair.

Everything.

When his gaze met hers, his expression was deadly serious. Not good.

He gestured. “You first.”

She swallowed thickly. Could she honestly lay everything out in the open, finally? How on earth was she supposed to do that? Her nerves shook at the very thought.

And yet what was her alternative? Live with this painful ache, always wondering if things would have worked if she'd just had more courage to voice her feelings?

She barely had time to sort through her thoughts before he was right there, next to her, his expression unreadable.

She shoved her clutch onto the table and then threaded her fingers together, trepidation suddenly engulfing her. And all of a sudden she was left just staring at him, the words stuck in her throat. And that made her incredibly, annoyingly nervous.

"I'm waiting."

"I'm thinking."

"Okay." He crossed his arms and studied her, which made it that much worse.

"Stop looking at me!"

His eyes suddenly creased. "Sorry. Where would you like me to look?"

"Just… I don't know. Anywhere. The view." She waved to the window displaying a magnificent night panorama of Sydney Harbour. "You're making me nervous."

"That is not my intent, *chérie*."

She sighed. "I know. Look, there are a lot of things I have to get through and I wanted to tell you face-to-face, so you might want to take a seat, okay?"

"Is it the baby? Is everything all right?"

"Yes, it's fine. Everything is fine there." She took a deep breath, one that shook on the exhalation. "I was just reading about your contract negotiations."

He shrugged. "You know how the press likes to beat things up."

"So you're not going to move back to France, then?"

"It's one of many options on the table right now," he said cautiously.

"Right."

She let the silence fall, chewing on the inside of her lip as she tried to gather the right words.

He crossed his arms with a frown. "Kat, this isn't you, always second-guessing your words. Just come out and say it."

He was right. She'd handled more than her fair share of difficult situations. She could do this now. However she'd planned to do this, whatever preparations she'd made, this was it. She had to tell him.

And yet…her determination just seemed to crumble, making everything ache from the gaping hole it left. She may want to, so very badly. But it wouldn't be right. Or fair. Not when she was desperately in love with him but he just saw her as his best friend and marriage as a way to handle her PR nightmare.

She didn't want to marry him when he wasn't in love with her. That wasn't selfish, right? It was noble. It was good. It meant she cared for him way too much to see him unhappy.

Even if it killed her inside.

God, she was killing him! Marco's control had gone from torn to shredded in the space of a few moments as he sat there, waiting for her to say something, until he'd finally had enough.

"Kat." When he got abruptly to his feet, her surprised gaze followed him, and for another few seconds he chewed over the words, discarding a dozen imperfect ones, until he finally came up with everything he needed to say. "I love you."

She stilled, eyes wide, expression frozen for one horrible second. Then she shot out a soft breath and her small smile ripped at his heart. "I love you, too."

"No," he repeated, dragging in a breath. *Suck it up and just finish it already.* "No, I really love you."

"And I—"

"Kat, you are not getting it." He shook his head, heart thudding. "I am *in love* with you. I want to marry you, but not because of some press stunt, or out of any moral obligation. I want to marry you because I am desperately and hopelessly in love with you. I want to be with you, but only if you want that, too."

*Shock* didn't begin to describe the look on her face. She just stood there, silent and gaping, and for one horrible moment every terrible rejection he'd ever faced came bubbling up to the surface.

Her soft groan, the twisted expression, cut him swift and deep, but he could do nothing but stand there, waiting with his heart laid bare, waiting for her to let him down gently.

"I…" She floundered, frowning, then took a ragged breath.

"Kat…" he said, hating the way his voice came out all husky. "Say something. Anything."

Her eyes closed briefly, then opened again, and in that gaze he saw the truth. "These last few months—hell, these last few weeks—have been crazy for me. A baby, a pregnancy, this whole adoption thing. My head's been in ten different places, and I'm sick of it. Nothing is perfect, Marco, and I've just realized it doesn't have to be."

He remained silent, giving her nothing until she finished saying what she needed to say. He didn't have long to wait.

"It's taken all of this to make me see what is truly important," she said slowly, as if it was a revelation to herself, too. And when she reached out and took his hand, he offered no resistance, just let her link her fingers through his, the intimate glide of skin on skin sending his heart racing.

"And that's you. I don't want to spend the rest of my life wishing I'd had enough courage to tell you how I really feel, and I don't want to spend another day without being with you, talking with you. Loving you. If that means I only get you six months of every year, then, by God, I want those six months to count."

He closed his eyes as if her words had somehow cut, and Kat held her breath, waiting, waiting as the seconds ticked over.

*"Dieu."*

When he finally opened his eyes, the expression there had her going weak at the knees.

And suddenly, he was dragging her in for a kiss, a deep, hungry kiss full of emotion and feeling and heat. She squeaked in surprise then opened up for him, her arms going around his neck.

"Kat," he finally murmured against her mouth, hands slowly stroking her hair. "God, do you know how much I missed you these last few weeks?" Then he groaned, capturing her mouth for another kiss, and she was sure she was going to die from the joy of it all.

When he finally broke away, the look on his face was unmistakable. *"Je t'adore, chérie."* He cupped her cheek in his hand, placing his mouth softly on the corner of hers. "I've loved you for such a long time, but you've been so damn stubborn and I—" His breath caught in a growl and he kissed her again, a little more desperate, a little more hungry.

She whimpered against his mouth, her body pressed hard against his, every single inch of her skin tingling with awareness.

He loved her. How was that even possible? After everything she'd been through, how on earth had she managed to score this amazing, wonderful guy—her best friend—as her lover, as well?

"Come here."

She led him into her bedroom then closed the door, her entire body beating out a loud pulse as her blood rushed to every corner. With a trembling hand she shoved her fingers under his shirt and swept the outline of his ribs. After she lifted his shirt, she followed with her lips, kissing softly.

She took a deep breath, trying to calm her nerves, but it only succeeded in filling her lungs with his unique scent. "You smell amazing."

His chuckle did crazy things to her gut. "Thanks. You don't smell so bad yourself."

She grinned against his skin, her lips grazing across his hip, her hand curling around the other. "Is that a murmur of appreciation I hear?"

"Yeah." His guttural response made her flush and smile. "Kat…"

"Yes?"

"Stop talking."

When she began to mouth her way slowly across to his navel, he groaned and relaxed back on the couch, her kisses flaming a path while she stroked his hip and he muttered in Italian. He had the most perfect voice. Perfect hands. Perfect everything.

"You're perfect," she muttered against his skin.

"No..." he ground out.

"Yes," she countered. "And this part, right here—" her hand skimmed over the defined muscular V-line flanking his hips, the Adonis belt "—is such a temptation."

"Yeah?" His breath came out in a rush as she continued to stroke.

"Yes. Just above your waistband. Drives me crazy every time."

"How crazy?"

"Like this." Quickly she unsnapped his jeans and placed her mouth on the spot, softly trailing her lips over the muscle, before heading back to the center, tracing the thin line of hair downward.

His sharp breath as she finally eased his jeans down fueled her already stoked fire. He raised his hips a little to help, and when she'd tossed his pants aside, she couldn't help but swallow thickly at the sight of him lying there.

Wanting *her.*

"Kat..." It was only one word, yet the raw vulnerability behind it made her heart contract.

She slid her hands up along his corded thighs, gripping his hips, and then took him in her mouth with firm command. When his hips bucked, she placed a steady hand on his stomach.

"Shh." She continued to pleasure him, reveling in the heady power and the wonderful hard-velvet feeling of having him in her mouth.

And when she felt his body finally tense, she stopped.

His gasp and obscene curse echoed loudly. "Kat? What the hell?"

She slid up, her naked body gliding against him, and she stopped to nibble on his bottom lip briefly before straddling him.

"Impatient," she muttered against his mouth.

"Tease."

"No way." Eyes locked on his, she positioned her hips then swiftly eased down on him with a sharp breath.

They moved together in perfect time, two people in love, experiencing joy in each other, reveling in the pure physical moment. And when everything just became too much, her emotions so overwhelming she couldn't take any more, her release crashed in a wave of pure ecstasy, leaving her trembling and spent. With a soft groan, Marco followed her, his arms wrapped tight, holding her in place as their damp bodies slid together as one.

The minutes ticked by, the thick air punctuated by their ragged breathing. Kat lay there, soaking up his heat, a thousand words on the tip of her tongue but reluctant to say a thing because she didn't want to shatter this most perfect moment.

But finally, as their bodies cooled and their heartbeats returned to normal, Marco glanced over at the clock on the bedside table and said, "Maybe we should be getting back to the ceremony…"

Kat followed his gaze. "I guess."

He chuckled. "So enthusiastic."

"Well, given the choice, I know where I'd rather be."

"I know how you feel."

They remained perfectly still, as the moment stretched.

"Marco…" Kat finally said. "I'm quitting my job."

A pause. "Really?"

She nodded, glancing up at him. "I'm going to start up a charity. Not sure what, yet. I'll think about it while I'm busy with being pregnant." She smiled faintly.

When his hand slid to her stomach, palm moving possessively over the gentle swell, her breath caught. Then he smiled and leaned down to kiss her, and everything just choked her up all over again.

"I don't want you to overdo things," he murmured softly against her mouth.

"I can hire people. Delegate."

He spent a few moments lazily kissing her. "So you really want to do it?"

"Do you think I *can* do it?"

"*Chérie,* you can do anything you want."

She basked in the warmth of his smile, until seconds passed and realization began to seep in.

"Sooooo..." she said softly. "About that marriage thing—"

"Yes?"

"Is the offer still on the table?"

He blinked. "No."

"What?" She frowned.

He cupped her face, brought her to his mouth in a gentle kiss. "It's not a business offer. I am asking you to be my wife. To be with me for the rest of our lives. To have my children, to make me happy and to let me make you happy. It's a marriage proposal made with love."

*Oh.* Breathless, all she could do was stare at him, at the tender look in his dark eyes, at the curve of his mouth. And she fell in love with him all over again.

That was...absolutely perfect. More than perfect.

It was Marco.

She felt the tears well a second before he reached

out and caught one on the tip of his finger, his smile gently warming her.

"Tears, *chérie?*"

She sucked in a breath. "It's the hormones."

"Sure. Not tears of happiness?"

She sniffed, blinking furiously. "Maybe." At his look, she laughed, a weird watery sound. "Probably."

"I know." His kiss was tender, soft and everything she could have wanted to mark this moment. "So," he breathed against her lips, "will you marry me?"

"Of course I will," she replied without hesitation. "You're my best friend. My Marco. I love you."

"And I love you. My Kat."

* * * * *

# THE PREGNANCY PROJECT

KAT CANTRELL

# One

In one of life's great ironies, Dr. Dante Gates, PhD, had a chemistry problem he couldn't solve.

Not one single data point from his doctoral thesis had provided clues to this puzzle. Nothing he'd researched in the name of his hit TV show, *The Science of Seduction,* had revealed even a hint of an answer. Even the work he'd done on proving the effectiveness of quantum chemical models for protein analysis—which had nearly landed him a Nobel Prize—hadn't helped. And Dante was beyond frustrated by the lack of progress in unraveling this chemistry problem named Dr. Harper Livingston.

Dante and Harper had been friends for a decade. She was the standard by which he judged all other women. Which meant Dante spent a lot of energy being irritated that he could never find a woman as beautiful or as smart as Harper. She did it for him, in all the right ways.

Or *wrong* ways, more like. Because they were *friends.*

His relationship with Harper was the one constant in his life, the only thing he could count on. They had a sacred bond he valued, one he refused to disrupt.

Dante had pretty much convinced himself the only reason he had such a thing for Harper lay solely in her unavailability. Surely if they tried taking their relationship to the next level, it would be a dismal failure. Once he had a taste of that forbidden fruit, Harper would instantly lose her attractiveness. He'd never think of her *that way* again.

The problem was that once he'd started imagining just how delicious that fruit would be, he couldn't stop.

This morning, Harper had called to say she was at the Dallas airport, about to get on a plane and would be at his doorstep in two hours. She hadn't come to visit him in Los Angeles in the three years since he'd moved here. Something big was up. Seemed like the opportune time to solve his chemistry problem, one way or the other.

LAX was one screaming baby short of hell. Like always. Only Harper could drag him to the airport when he had no plans to fly. Dante checked his Breva watch, which featured an anemometer that he'd geeked out over even though he didn't sail. Harper's plane had landed ten minutes ago but no passengers had disembarked yet.

Finally, a stream of people carrying backpacks, pillows and water bottles burst through the gate. Dante leaned against the nearest post, arms crossed, to wait for the woman he'd come to collect.

Harper wasn't hard to spot. Her flame-red hair stood out from the crowd, and she carried herself differently from everyone else, barreling ahead with no fear. In Harper's world, hesitation was for losers. It was his favorite of her qualities.

She caught sight of him and instantly lit up with a

whole-face smile that whacked him in the gut with unexpected heat. Before he could process that, she dropped her bags and flung herself into his arms. Automatically, he balanced his weight to take on hers, snuggling her deep in his embrace, because holy God she felt good.

"Hey," he murmured into her hair, breathing it in.

Harper's perfume wound through his senses, infusing his blood with her essence. Which was not how perfume worked. At best, the scent should remind him of food and thus something his body needed to survive. It was supposed to smell nice, not make him want to kiss her until she couldn't breathe.

He ignored the heat. It wasn't easy, but he did have a lot of practice.

Harper—mercifully—pulled back enough that Dante didn't have to worry about her noticing the inappropriate stuff going on down below.

"What are you doing here?" she exclaimed as she drank him in with her bright gaze. "No one has picked me up at the gate since 9/11. I forgot how nice it is. How did you get past security without a plane ticket?"

He chuckled. "Simple. I bought one. Surprise."

Dante traveled so often for his job as a TV show host that he could always change the ticket later when he planned to actually use it. Or if not, so what? Harper was worth blowing a few hundred bucks over.

She socked him on the arm. "You didn't have to do that. But I love that you did. I thought you were filming today. I was totally expecting to take a cab."

And if she'd been anyone else, he'd have sent a car. Shrugging, he picked up her carry-on bag and shouldered it. "We finished early and now I'm off for two weeks, which I plan to spend with you. Perfect timing for an impromptu visit."

Perfect timing to figure out how to kill his attraction to her. Surely it would only take a kiss. One simple kiss, it would be weird and he'd be done. Back to being friends.

"Your girlfriend won't expect to spend time with you? The supermodel. What's her name?" Harper snapped her fingers a couple of times as if to jog her memory.

"Selena," he supplied. "Actually, we're not really an item anymore."

He'd lost interest in Selena as soon as he'd started seeing her, what, like six months ago? But it was good for his career to be photographed with her, and the sex wasn't terrible, so he'd held on much longer than he should have. She was a sweet girl in a long line of sweet girls who developed instant Vacant Eye when Dante dared throw X-ray crystallography or self-synthesizing materials into conversation. Harper was the only woman he'd ever been able to talk to about anything and everything.

"That's too bad. I'm sorry. But I'm sure it's for the best since there's no way she was good enough for you." Harper grinned. "Oh, I forgot to tell you. Cass is pregnant."

"That's fantastic," he said and meant it. Babies were great. For other people.

Harper and Cass had been friends a long time, since college, when they'd devised a plan to open a company together, along with two other friends, Alex and Trinity. Fyra Cosmetics had thus been born and Harper had made a place for herself as the chief science officer. He was so proud of what she'd accomplished since getting her doctorate in analytical chemistry. Dante had known all four ladies for a decade, but as he had the most in common with Harper he'd naturally become closest to the redhead.

"Gage is making a big deal out of it." Harper sighed dramatically and rolled her eyes. "As husbands go, he's perfect for Cass. But I would shoot him if he treated me the way he does her. 'You're working too much,' he says. 'Let me take care of you.' And my favorite, 'You might be craving potato chips, but you need to crave vegetables.' Men. Like they know anything about pregnancy."

Dante couldn't imagine a woman as fierce as Cass letting Gage railroad her. "His heart is in the right place. How is Alex doing, speaking of pregnancy?"

"Much better now that she's further into her second trimester. No more morning sickness."

He hadn't realized so much of what was happening with Harper's friends revolved around babies. The whole subject made him vaguely uncomfortable, no doubt because of his own history. Sure, people started out wanting kids, but no one could know that they'd still want one next year, or the year after that. After being shuttled from home to home as a foster kid, Dante knew that fickleness firsthand.

Dante guided Harper toward baggage claim. She laced her fingers with his and held his hand as they walked, chatting about her friends and business partners.

It was companionable. Or at least that was probably how *she* viewed it.

Dante had a burning awareness of her that was only heightened by the glow radiating from Harper's face. That glow was new. Where had that come from? He adjusted his trademark horn-rimmed glasses with his other hand, but the corona didn't fade. Why the hell was she so much more beautiful today, of all days?

He might have to get to that kiss sooner rather than later, or this whole trip would slide into disaster.

"Did you have a good flight?" he asked.

Harper pushed her soft, red curls behind her shoulders and nodded. "Not bad. But the vending machine by my gate at DFW didn't have any Reese's Peanut Butter Cups and that's the only thing I want. I'm starving."

"Come on." He pulled her into a newsstand shop and scouted until he found the candy in question, picked up the entire box from the shelf and handed it to the clerk along with his American Express.

"Dante!" Harper laughed. "I just wanted one, not twenty. You'll have me looking like a blimp if you keep that up."

The cashier did a double take as she zeroed in on Dante's face, then she glanced at the credit card, her eyes rounding. "Dr. Gates! I'm a huge fan of your show. Please, can I get a picture with you?"

She held out her phone, because of course the answer was yes. Fans were part of the gig, and as the producers of *The Science of Seduction* funneled millions of dollars into Dante's bank account to host it, he couldn't really complain. But secretly, he hated nearly everything about the show.

Money was nice, he could not deny it, but he missed *real* science. The kind that made a difference in the way people understood the known universe. Helping a guy hook up didn't amount to a whole lot in the grand scheme of things, no matter how good Dante was at his job. Science had long been his refuge when the rest of the world didn't care, yet he'd abandoned his roots for sensationalism.

He let the cashier fawn over him as much as she wanted because fans had made him a celebrity, and he did not take that for granted. Harper watched with no small amount of amusement.

Finally, he extracted himself from the cashier and the newsstand, handing Harper the bag of candy. "Sorry about that. Comes with the territory."

With a snort, Harper grinned. "Are you kidding? That was awesome. I rarely get a chance to see you being Dr. Sexy. Due compensation for losing your attention."

He matched her grin. "I have to live up to my tag line."

*Dr. Dante Gates Brings Sexy To Science.* That line had graced magazine covers, promo for his show, you name it. Never in a million years would Dante have assumed that agreeing to host a show about how to use science to attract a lover would mean he'd become the poster boy. Of course, he *had* positioned himself as an expert in the subject. He should have realized women would come out of the woodwork to beg him to test his theories on them.

The attention flattered him. At first. He was only human. The field research alone made the women worth his time, and he'd long ago acknowledged that being abandoned by his birth mom to foster care had created a craving for acceptance and connection. It wasn't a crime. The real travesty was that not one of the truly inventive and quite beautiful women had eclipsed his attraction to Harper.

Because she was the only one he couldn't have. Probably.

Harper rolled her eyes as they arrived at the baggage claim area for her flight. "You don't need to appear shirtless in a dish soap commercial to be sexy, silly. Your brain is the most attractive thing about you."

Something about her smile caught him sideways and he nearly did a double take. He'd let her reference to Dr.

Sexy roll off because...well, that was part of his TV persona. But now this. Was she *flirting* with him?

Interesting. Had these nuances been there before and had he missed them in his struggle to keep his thoughts about Harper in the friend zone?

After all, she'd just admitted she found him attractive, which he liked far more than he should. What if she'd been shooting him subtle signals this whole time, hoping he'd make a move? She probably thought he was blind. This impromptu trip to LA might have been solely designed to correct his vision.

With that in mind, he guided her to a secluded spot in the very back of baggage claim, between two dark, locked offices. The milling people around them were focused on the stationary carousel, which meant he had Harper all to himself for a few minutes. At least until luggage started arriving.

"Hey, in case you've forgotten, scientists are not known for their six-packs," he murmured and leaned in, eliminating the space between them. "I worked hard to put on muscle after spending so many years hunched over pages of equations. If someone wants to pay me to take my shirt off, I'm not going to say no."

All this talk of shedding clothes had set off serious sparks. Did she feel them, too?

She blinked as she looked up at him, her smile slipping a touch. Her tongue darted out to drag across her lips and he followed it pointedly with his gaze, then shifted back to her eyes. The heat in her cheeks mirrored the flare in his gut as he let the moment drag out.

Would wonders never cease? She *was* feeling it.

Maybe she'd clued in that he was a hot property. Not that he'd let any of his press go to his head. But come on. Women flocked to him. Empirical evidence suggested there was something about his spiky brown hair, horn-rimmed glasses and fit body that they liked.

It was way past time to get his inconvenient attraction to Harper worked out. If he'd read her wrong, they'd laugh about it and go on. He'd prove there was nothing here other than a healthy appreciation for a great woman. The electricity in the atmosphere and the heightened sense of anticipation was nothing more than the product of his imagination.

Without taking his gaze from hers, he reached out and traced the line of her jaw. Not as a friend. Not companionably. But with intent.

"What are you doing?" she asked as a line appeared between her brows. "This isn't… I mean—we're not…"

"Haven't you ever been curious?" he interjected smoothly. "About what it would be like between us?"

"Be like? What *what* would be like?" Her eyes widened as his meaning must have registered.

There was still time to backpedal if taking things up a notch ended up being the worst idea ever conceived, but that window of opportunity rapidly shrank the longer they stood here in this blanket of awareness.

"I've thought about it. A lot," he continued, since she hadn't pulled away and hadn't fled in horror. "No time like the present to find out."

Before logic could kick in and remind him of all the reasons this could go south, he sank his hands into Harper's soft red curls, spread his fingers across the back of her head and tipped it up. Slowly—because he wanted to give his body plenty of time to soak in the lesson to be learned here—he lowered his lips to Harper's and claimed them in a sweet kiss.

Which instantly caught fire. Heat erupted where

they'd joined, sensitizing him, claiming him. Harper flowed through him, waking up his blood.

And that's when he realized his mistake—one kiss and all he'd proven was that he was *not* done. Not even close.

*Dante was kissing her.*

Shock opened Harper's mouth without her permission and he took it as an invitation, swirling his tongue forward to find hers and *oh, my God.*

The sensations overwhelmed her and all she could do was cling to his shoulders. She'd meant to push him away. She didn't do this, not with Dante, not with any man. And then she wasn't pushing him away because *wow.*

The chemical reactions firing off inside her body were fascinating, amazing. Unprecedented. She wanted more. That was the most shocking thing of all because normally she avoided this sort of contact.

Her lips tingled as he reshaped them. Little pulls in her abdomen increased the urgency and she leaned into him, her hands drifting from his shoulders to his back. Hard. Strong. He felt good under her palms and she dipped lower, eliciting a groan from deep in his chest. It vibrated her own, teasing her breasts, and that's when she realized their torsos were touching.

That sculpted chest was pressed up against hers. Dante was kissing her and she was kissing him. *In the airport.* Oh, God. This was all wrong. What was she doing?

She sprang back, wrenching away, and he followed for a half second until he realized she'd stopped. Hugging the wall behind her and legs shaking, she stared at the man who had been her best friend for a decade. "I'm sorry."

His big brown eyes watched her from behind his horn-rimmed glasses, which sat slightly askew. Her fingers flexed to fix them automatically, as she'd done a hundred times. But she didn't.

"For what? I'm the one who kissed you."

*Yes, he had.* For God's sake, why?

Some better questions were why she'd kissed him back. Why it hadn't felt weird. Why her body felt like it had been twisted in a knot and dipped in a volcano. Why of all men, Dante had jump-started her sex drive.

The problem was, Harper knew exactly why. How was she supposed to explain that she'd completely overreacted due to an influx of hormones that her body didn't know what to do with? That she'd hopped on a plane to share the most exciting news of her life with her friend?

Somehow, she hadn't envisioned blurting out *I'm pregnant* in response to being kissed by the man she'd come to for support.

"I'm the one who didn't stop you," she said instead.

"No. You didn't."

When he didn't ask how come she hadn't, the swirl of uncertainty under her skin pulled the response from her throat anyway. "I was…curious. But please, don't take that the wrong way."

He already had, she could tell. Dante wasn't inexperienced, not like she was, and he'd noted how much she'd liked kissing him. It was a surprise to her, too—she hadn't been kissed in years and even then, it had been a horrible experience, never to be repeated.

This kiss…it had been the stuff of teenage dreams and an R-rated movie all rolled up in one. Because Dr. Harper Livingston's body reacted to conception by suddenly craving the touch of a man. Apparently. What was she supposed to do with that—ask him to kiss her again?

"How could I possibly take that the wrong way?" he asked.

She was botching this and if she didn't fix it, she'd lose everything important to her. "It can't happen again. Dante, I need you. As a friend. Please don't change anything."

God, this was all backward. The results of the four positive pregnancy tests she'd taken that morning weren't the only reason she'd hopped on a plane to LA. Her career had imploded over Fyra's decision to develop a product that required FDA approval, and she really wished she'd known that snafu was coming *before* she'd visited a fertility clinic.

On the brink of both professional and personal disaster, she'd run to the one person who had always been there for her, who was one-hundred percent on her side… only to smack headlong into something she had no context for.

A foreign expression popped onto his face. "Harper. I wanted to kiss you. Surely you realize there's something new happening between us—"

"No!" Her lungs hitched and somehow, a lone tear squeezed out before she could catch it. "Nothing new. I need everything to be exactly the same as it's been. You're so important to me. As a *friend*."

Friends had each other's backs. Friends were there through thick and thin and she needed the promise of knowing she had that in him. That he'd be the way she'd thought of him every day for the last ten years. Until this one. She'd responded so readily to his experimental kiss that he'd gotten the wrong message.

His eyes narrowed behind his glasses. She knew that look. He was about to argue with her and she could not do this right now.

With a strained smile, she touched his arm, like she'd done for years and years, before thinking better of it. "Let's just forget about it for now. Would you mind getting my bags?"

Ever the gentleman despite the tense circumstances, Dante firmed his mouth and did as she asked, then ushered her into a sleek, red Ferrari. The silence laced with weirdness settled heavily in the car, nearly choking her, as they hurtled down the freeway toward his home in the Hollywood Hills. She scarcely enjoyed the unfolding LA scenery, but what could she say to get everything back to where it was supposed to be?

Dante rolled the Ferrari to a stop at a gated drive, then pointed a clicker at the black wrought-iron gate. It opened, allowing him to drive onto his lush, expansive property, where he parked on the circular drive in front of the sprawling Spanish villa. All without uttering a word.

Which lasted only until they cleared the doorstep. He dropped her bags on the Mexican tile under their feet in the spacious foyer and faced her, brows lowered. "We've been friends a long time. Why would that change just because we're exploring what else might work between us?"

"Because I don't want to do anything more," she burst out. "All of this scares me."

How could she get through the problems at Fyra, pregnancy, birth—good grief, the next eighteen years with a kid—if she didn't have the friendship that had carried her through the last ten years?

"Come here."

Before she could blink, he whirled her into a deep hug, the kind she'd welcomed so many times in the past, but it was different now as his strong body aligned with hers.

*So* different. The tease of his torso against hers set off tingles in places that shouldn't be *tingling* over Dante. She tore away, devastated that she couldn't stay in the circle of his embrace, devastated that things had already changed without her consent.

Hurt sprang into his big brown eyes but he banked it and crossed his arms. "So now I can't hug you?"

"Sure you can, if you drop twenty pounds of muscle," she shot back before realizing how that sounded. Quickly, she amended, "I want things like they were before you turned into Dr. Sexy."

And that wasn't much better as explanations went. He'd been Dr. Sexy for a long time—what she really meant was before she'd become aware of it. But he had her all flustered.

A brief smile lifted his lips. "I thought you liked that side of me."

She did. That was the problem.

Dante was one of the few friends she had left who was still the same as he'd always been—she'd *thought*. She didn't make friends easily. Cass and Alex, two of the three women she'd built Fyra Cosmetics with, had moved on to new phases in their lives, marrying great men and starting families. Which was amazing, and she didn't begrudge them their happiness. But Harper felt… left behind.

Which was why she'd decided to have a baby of her own. But minus the husband, who would expect things of Harper she couldn't fathom giving. Intimacy. Control. A promise of everlasting romantic love that no one could guarantee because it was nothing more than a series of confusing chemical signals in the brain.

Men complicated everything.

"How many friends do I have, Dante? Should be easy for you to count them. No advanced degree required to get to four." She ticked them off on her fingers. "Cass. Alex. Trinity. You. Now imagine that two of those friends have recently gotten married and started families. Everything's changing around me and I can't stop it. I need you to stay the same."

Because she was the one who had already changed things, the one who had gone off and gotten pregnant, and by default, Dante had to be the constant in this equation.

Understanding dawned in his eyes. "You're scared of things changing."

"I'm pretty sure that's what I just said."

Instead of backing off, he leaned in and captured her arms, holding her in place. "You did. I'm just catching up. So it's not that you mind the idea of me kissing you. You're just scared of losing our relationship. But I don't want to lose it, either."

Those melty chocolate eyes speared hers, and all at once, she didn't like the way he was looking at her, as if she held the secrets to his universe. Except he'd always looked at her like that and she'd explained it away as affection between friends. But now that he'd veered completely off the friendship track, it made her uncomfortably aware that he'd just had his mouth on her in a very non-friendly way.

"You're practicing selective hearing." She shook her head and tried to back up a step so she could breathe. And pick up her luggage, so she could...do something with it. "I do mind the idea of kissing. And everything that goes along with it. Or comes after it."

"Everything?" he murmured and somehow she was still in his arms. "You mean sex?"

Heat leaped into his expression and that was so much worse than the melty eyes because her body flared to life at the promise of feeling the way it had when he'd kissed her. *More. Now.*

"Yes." She squeezed her eyes shut, groaning. "I mean, *no.* No sex. Geez, what is this conversation we're having? I came here to visit my *friend.* How did we start talking about sex?"

"You brought it up," he reminded her needlessly. "I was just trying to clarify."

"Sex is not a part of this conversation."

"What if I want it to be?" he countered softly and his fingers slid up her arms to grasp her shoulders. "Your hearing is bordering on selective too if you can so easily ignore what I've been trying to tell you."

Caught, she stared at him, taking in his familiar horn-rimmed glasses and spiky hair, desperate to get back to a place where she could be secure in her relationship with him. "What are you trying to tell me?"

"Our friendship is the most important thing in my life. That's why I'm trying to save it. I can't unkiss you. There's something here that isn't going away until we explore it. Harper…" He drew out her name reverently and the sound sang through her suddenly taut body. "Kiss me again. Think of it as an experiment. Let's see how far this thing goes, so we can deal with it, once and for all."

Her eyelids slammed shut because *holy mother of God.* "That's a hell of gauntlet to throw down."

"Tell me no and I'll step away."

"No." Instantly, his hands moved from her arms and his heat vanished. She opened her eyes to see him standing a few feet away, his expression hooded and implacable.

"Can I at least know what your major objections are? In case there's something—"

"I'm pregnant, Dante." She didn't know whether to laugh or cry. "And that's only the first in a long line of objections."

# Two

All of the blood in Dante's brain drained out. "You're… what?" he whispered.

"Pregnant," she repeated and the word still sounded like *pregnant*.

"With a baby?"

"Science has not yet successfully crossed human DNA with any other species, so yeah," she confirmed darkly. "I didn't want to tell you this way but you gave me no choice."

Blindly, he stuck out a hand and sought the nearest hard surface to sink onto. Happened to be an end table in the adjacent living area but so what? His knees wouldn't have held up much longer.

"I don't understand how this happened. Are you seeing someone?"

There was no way. Not as eagerly as she'd responded to his touch. Not as close as he'd have sworn they were. She'd have said something about a man in her life.

Wouldn't she? He thought back to the last time she'd mentioned a guy—all the way back in college.

She shook her head. "No. Artificial insemination."

"Why in the world would you do something like that?" He bit off the syllables, not bothering to temper the harshness.

Babies needed a family. A father. She'd deliberately set herself up to be a single parent. It was inexcusable.

Her face froze as she took in his expression. "I wasn't interested in sharing parenting duties with anyone long-term. So a donor who was willing to sign away his rights seemed ideal."

This got better and better. Or worse and worse, more likely. He laughed without humor. "Most people have a life partner they decide to have kids with. Because they're in love and want to raise a family together. Did that ever enter your thought process?"

"Not once." She tossed her red hair. "A romantic relationship would only complicate everything."

"A baby needs a male influence," he insisted. "That's not an opinion. Study after study shows—"

"I know that, Dante!" Hands on her hips, she towered over him as he perched on the end table. "Why do you think I said I needed you, you big moron? That's why I'm here. I want *you* to be the male influence. Dummy me, I thought our friendship was strong enough to add a baby and then you had to go and kiss me."

Dumbfounded, he blinked. "Did you think to ask me about this before you got pregnant?"

Because he would have talked her out of it if she had. This was the most ridiculous idea she'd ever heard.

"It's my life and my body," she announced as guilt flashed through her expression.

She must have guessed he might react like this, because she knew his history, knew how he felt about kids. And had done it anyway. "You know anonymous donors don't always tell the truth about their medical history on those questionnaires. There's no telling what kind of genetic mess you've created in there."

He jerked his head toward her abdomen. She had a baby in her womb and it was suddenly a sacred place, not available for desecrating with the kind of activities he'd had in mind mere minutes ago.

He'd actually been strategizing on how to get her back into his arms so they could finish that kiss. How else would he exorcise his attraction to her? What small taste of her he'd been granted had thus far only whetted his appetite for the main course. Hers, too, obviously, despite her denial.

Dante was an expert after all. She wanted him as much as the reverse was true.

But she was already shaking her head. "That's why the donor wasn't anonymous. I did a lot of research into this before I made my decision and I carefully selected my baby's father. Dr. Cardoza is the perfect—"

"Dr. Cardoza? Dr. Tomas Cardoza is your baby's father?" Red stained Dante's vision, his hands curling and uncurling as he fought to keep from unleashing his frustration on the drywall.

"He's a renowned chemist," she explained as if he might be confused about Cardoza's contribution to the planet.

"I know," Dante somehow got out through clenched teeth. "If you recall, he's the reason I didn't win the Nobel."

Harper's eyes widened. "Well, yeah. But that was ages ago. Surely you're over that, especially given that you've moved into another field."

He couldn't help it. The laugh bubbled out and he pinched off his glasses to wipe his eyes. Of all the people she could have fathered a baby with, she'd picked Cardoza, the sorriest excuse for a human being that ever walked the earth, and that included Dante's parents, whoever they were.

No. He wasn't *over it*. Cardoza was the reason Dante had been forced into TV. If Cardoza hadn't cheated on his methodology, he'd never have won the Nobel and Dante would have at least had a fair shot. After Cardoza had won, all the interest in Dante's research had dried up, leaving him lab-less, fundless and desperate for someone to give him a new opportunity.

*The Science of Seduction* had been born.

Of course, it had been lucrative beyond his wildest fantasies. But a nine-figure bank account didn't make up for having his long-held scientific goals stolen out from under him.

"Just out of curiosity," he said once he thought he could talk without betraying the wash of emotion beating at his breastbone. "How did you manage to pick Cardoza?"

*Of all freaking people.*

"Oh. I ran into Tomas at a convention recently. The thing I told you about in St. Louis? He was presenting a paper and I loved his conclusions. When I saw him later in the hotel lobby, I introduced myself and we got to talking."

"Got chummy, did you?" Dante practically sneered. *Tomas*. Like they were all friends here.

"Sure, he's a brilliant man. Great cheekbones. His genetics were the main reason I became interested in him."

Something black bloomed in Dante's chest. "He hit on you."

"What? No. Well, okay, yeah, I guess if you count the fact that he asked if I'd consider getting pregnant the old-fashioned way 'hitting on me.'" she accompanied her words with air quotes, oblivious to the way Dante's stomach had lost its lining. "Then I guess he did."

Dante massaged the ice pick that had formed between his eyes. "Please, for the love of God, tell me you said no."

She scowled. "Of course I said no. I have no interest in that kind of relationship with any man."

Relief flooded his chest so fast, he almost saw stars. The thought of Cardoza putting his filthy paws on Harper—he swallowed the bile. Thankfully, she'd handed the horrible man his hat.

With anyone else, this would be the point when he'd ask if she meant that she preferred women. But he'd felt her reaction when he'd held her in his arms.

She was straight, 100 percent. "No interest in any man except me, you mean."

"Uh, no. Not with you, either," she corrected. "Haven't you been listening?"

Oh, he'd heard every word, much to his chagrin. "You're interested, Harper. You're so interested you can't stand it."

The way she'd curled into him when he'd kissed her, the thrill of her eagerly offered tongue against his—he'd be reliving that in need-soaked dreams tonight. She was interested. And not happy about it, clearly, as her reaction to the kiss had prompted this little game of true confessions.

*Pregnant.* As mood killers went, that one took the cake.

"I don't know when you developed that industrial-sized ego," she said primly. "But it can go anytime."

"Please." He snorted. "Lie to yourself, but you can't lie to me. Not when my mouth was on yours. I could feel your interest clear to my bones."

Not ego talking. Okay, maybe a little, because it did warm him up plenty, even now, to recall how fervently she'd responded. She'd thrown herself into the kiss, no holds barred, like she did everything, practically climbing into his pants while he kissed her, and he'd have let her.

The attraction between them was mutual. Whether she liked it or not.

A blush worked its way across her cheeks. "That's just hormones."

That got a chuckle out of him. "Yeah. That is generally the way it works, or have you forgotten everything you learned in college?"

To his surprise, she sank onto the couch and buried her head in her hands. Her shoulders started shaking and that's when his bad mood vanished in favor of the mood he should have had all along—concern for the woman he cared about.

He wedged in next to her on the couch and gathered her into his arms, holding her without a word because what would he say? He'd already ruined her big announcement, one she'd only made under duress because he'd been pushing her past her comfort zone.

In another shocker, she relaxed into his embrace and it almost felt like normal. Sure, the smell of her hair crossed his eyes like it always did, but he'd been ignoring the physical pull of Harper for a long time. He could buck up for his friend, who'd spelled out her need for him in no uncertain terms.

"I'm sorry," he murmured into her hair and she nodded. "I just don't understand. Why a baby? And via artificial insemination to boot?"

"I told you," she mumbled against his shirt. "Romance is not my thing. It's all a bunch of chemical reactions that people mistake as an emotion greeting card companies tell you is love. Then those reactions stop and what are you left with? My way is so much easier."

The arguments against all the mistakes in her theory bubbled to the surface and he almost started firing back facts from the hours and hours of research he'd done into the chemistry between people, but he cut it off at the last second. She didn't need his opinion, professional or personal. Not right this moment. Not when she'd already made the decision.

"Congrats, regardless." He bit back the rest of that, too. Foster care had colored his view of people who had children and the various ways they ended up making the kid's life hell. Until he could be objective about Harper's baby, he'd shut up. "For the record, those chemical reactions come with a hell of a kick."

"I wouldn't know," she said, her voice so muffled he almost didn't hear her.

All at once, the subtext whacked him over the head and he realized she wasn't talking solely about love. "You're still a virgin?"

Pieces of this puzzle started falling into place at a rapid clip. She'd confessed as much one night back in college, but he'd assumed that somewhere along the way she'd—but then, she'd probably have told him if she had. Idiot.

She froze. "I've been busy getting a doctorate and then building Fyra's product line from the ground up. Who had time?"

His head fell back against the couch and he stared at

the ceiling. Some doctor of seduction he was. He'd totally missed the most important aspect of the dynamic at work here.

Harper was scared of what he'd made her feel. He'd tied up a normally fearless woman in knots because she'd never been properly introduced to the pleasures between a man and a woman. That was a travesty of the highest order.

And a blessing. His resolve solidified. Dante had been gifted an amazing opportunity to be her first. Then he'd finally have one up on Cardoza, that was for sure, and he wasn't going to apologize for being smug over it. He and Harper could burn off their attraction, get back to being friends, and go on. Win-win in his book.

"It doesn't change anything," she said defensively. "I'm still pregnant and I still need your support, regardless of your opinions about my choice of donor or methods of impregnation. I can't do this alone. Can I count on you to be my *friend*? To be there for me?"

The realities of the situation crashed down on him. His best friend was pregnant with the offspring of his most hated rival and all he could think about was claiming Harper in some kind of testosterone-filled territory grab.

She knew him well enough to hone in on his biggest conflicts, but naming it and claiming it didn't change his views on babies. If he said he supported her, he had to do it. Keeping his word meant something to him. This friendship meant something to him. He had to put his money where his mouth was.

"Of course you can count on me."

And she could. But he wasn't going to back away from the attraction between them. Instead of scaring him off, she'd inexplicably created a challenge he couldn't ignore.

He wanted her. Perhaps even more now than he had before, thanks to her confessions.

New plan. Nothing but a full-bore seduction would do, and he had an undeniable urge to put every ounce of his energy into verifying the strategies he promoted on his TV show actually worked. Even on a woman who'd never had a lover before. Even on a friend. A *pregnant* friend. Was he an expert or not?

Dante had the next two weeks to find out.

Dante's sprawling home in the Hollywood Hills had enormous charm and Harper loved it. A housekeeper showed her to the guest suite, pointing out the kitchen, the dining room, the back terrace with the multilevel swimming pool on the way.

*Wow.* Harper craned her neck as the housekeeper breezed past the triple set of French doors overlooking the pool. Cerulean water rippled in the sunlight, and beyond the bougainvillea and palmetto palms camouflaging the wrought-iron fence around Dante's property, Los Angeles unfurled at the base of the hills, urban and busy, but stunning despite the layer of smog.

Dr. Gates had done very well for himself.

Heavy exposed beams stained the color of triple-strength espresso held up the high ceiling in the breezeway to the back of the house. The housekeeper opened one of the doors and stepped back. Harper blinked at the lavish sitting area off to one side, complete with a flat-screen TV. A large mission-style bed had been placed opposite the sitting area. What a beautiful room.

"The bathroom is through those doors," the housekeeper pointed with a polite smile. "You need anything, you let me know. I'm Mrs. Ortiz, and my daughter, Ana Sophia, cooks for Mr. Dante. No request too small or too big. We live in the old coach house near the gate, and Juan, my husband, keeps the grounds."

"Oh, okay." Dante had servants. More than one. Had any of them overheard the conversation in the foyer earlier? Harper shut her eyes for a beat. Too late now. Would have been nice for Dante to warn her that they weren't necessarily alone as she went around blabbing about personal stuff.

But then, he'd apparently decided to make blindsiding her a habit. She didn't especially care for it.

"Thanks, Mrs. Ortiz," Harper said as graciously as she could. It wasn't this nice lady's fault her boss had gone slightly off the deep end.

The housekeeper nodded and closed the door behind her as she left. Harper spent a few minutes unpacking but it didn't take nearly long enough to settle her trembling insides.

After that fiasco of a kiss had forced her to drop the pregnancy bomb, Dante had melted away, presumably to give her time to settle in, but probably more to give them both breathing room. Or was she the only who'd needed it?

Before she'd gotten on a plane to LA, her relationship with Dante had made sense. Her feelings for him were uncomplicated, easy and eternal, unlike what would inevitably happen in a romantic relationship. That was why she'd never entertained the slightest notion of having one with any man, let alone one she liked as much as Dante. Friendship had so much to recommend itself.

Until Dante had flipped everything upside down by kissing her.

What could she do to get back to the place where she had her friend by her side, holding her hand through this new adventure?

Because she needed him. Badly.

Pregnancy was freaking her out.

She was scared she'd made the wrong decision. Scared that she'd picked the wrong time, given that her career might be in the toilet. Scared that she'd failed to cross some *T* when dealing with the legal aspects of using a donor. She'd never second-guessed a decision like this and the only thing she wanted to do was crawl under a blanket, let Dante stroke her hair and tell her everything was going to be okay.

That was all wrong. She'd wanted pregnancy to be a happy experience. One that would create a new bond with Alex and Cass, who were also new mothers or soon-to-be, and strengthen the bond she had with Dante because of course he would be her baby's favorite...uncle-like person.

She hoped.

The look on his face when she'd said, *I'm pregnant...* she never wanted to see that again. But the shock coloring his expression replayed in her mind on an endless loop. Apparently she'd miscalculated how he'd feel about it, but she couldn't figure out if he was upset because she hadn't consulted him or because he still had residual bitterness over losing the Nobel Prize. Or both.

There was every possibility that despite claiming he'd be there for her, Dante might change his mind. He might end up not wanting anything to do with her baby. That would be devastating.

Angst was killing her. What had happened to her usual logic and reason? *Poof.* Add a baby and suddenly she was a mess.

She changed out of her plane suit and slipped on an unstructured sundress with spaghetti straps that she'd bought in anticipation of an expanding waistline. Wishful thinking, since she hadn't confirmed her pregnancy until this morning.

None of this heated introspection would resolve the open issue—how to get back to normal. Harper worked best with absolutes and only Dante could give her those.

*Get the data, formulate the problem and then solve it.*

Her relationship with Dante was going to be the same today as it was yesterday, or she'd die trying to keep it that way. She refused to let either the baby or the kiss put a wedge between them, not when so many other things were out of her control. The FDA rejection being exhibit A.

Determined, she wandered through the open floor plan toward the kitchen in hopes of finding Dante and a cup of hot tea, and not necessarily in that order.

"Called it in one," she murmured as she caught sight of his dark head bent over something.

She walked in and skirted the island. Dante glanced up.

His gaze softened behind his lenses, instantly turning his gorgeous eyes the color of melted chocolate. If he looked at other women like that, it was no wonder they were tripping over themselves to get to him.

Which was a totally uncomfortable thought, all at once. *Did* he look at other women like that, with that same blend of concern and affection? And why would she care? She didn't. Dante was her friend and he could look at a woman any way he chose.

Except her. Definitely he could not look at her like that.

"I was just about to make a pot of tea," he said as if nothing had changed.

Nothing *had* changed, she reminded herself sternly. He'd kissed her in some sort of misguided notion that there was something between them. She'd disabused him of that notion, and it was over. "That would be great."

She cleared the squawk from her throat and wished the tension could be so easily dispelled.

Tea was one of their shared passions, one she cherished. When Dante came to Dallas, he always picked up a fresh bag of Gyokuro Imperial Green Tea—her favorite—from the Teavana shop at DFW airport and they drank it on the patio of her condo, which overlooked Victory Park. She loved their ritual more for the conversation and easiness than the tea, though it only took the barest whiff of the scent to make her mouth water.

He handed her a press pot and nodded to the loose-leaf tea in a container printed with Chinese symbols, which sat on the counter near his elbow. "I'll boil the water if you scoop the tea."

The familiar rhythm soothed her, and she moved around both the kitchen and the man with more ease than she would have expected. Maybe the weirdness was all on her. If she acted like everything was cool, it would be.

Tea made, they took their mugs onto the lanai that overlooked the lush pool and outdoor kitchen. Dante settled onto a cozy love seat and patted the next cushion, which she gratefully sank onto.

"Your house is beautiful," she commented. "Why did it take me so long to visit?"

"A fair question." He nodded once. "And the answer is?"

"Busy." Her gaze drifted back to the landscape as she searched for the truth. "Fyra's been a mess lately and Cass and Alex have had personal things going on. Leaves me and Trinity to hold the seams together."

Regardless, Dante had always made time to come visit her. She'd written it off as a function of his insane travel schedule; of course it was easier for him to pop into Dallas. It was one of the major US airport hubs.

In that moment, with every nook and cranny of their relationship under a microscope, it felt…wrong. Unbalanced.

“Why did you come this time?” he asked quietly, and it was the opening she’d been looking for.

“I took my first pregnancy test this morning,” she admitted and forced herself to go on, no matter how uncomfortable the subject. Because regardless of what he’d said earlier, it still felt like an elephant in the room that they had to work through. “And then I took the next three.”

Surprisingly, he flashed a smile. “Because four gives you better odds of getting an accurate result.”

“You know me so well,” she joked automatically, but when his jaw tightened, she wished she hadn’t said it.

“I’m hoping to learn more,” he returned cryptically. “How did it feel? When you saw that it was positive?”

So many things had flooded her chest in that instant. How did she catalogue them for someone else—and a man at that? “The clearest sense of awe. Glee. Accomplishment.”

She’d picked the right donor, clearly, since the procedure had worked the first time. Of course she had. She’d done extensive research into genetics, legalities, odds—and Dr. Tomas Cardoza had been the obvious choice. Tomas had two doctorates, impressive Spanish ancestry and dark skin that would hopefully guarantee her child wouldn’t have to slather on as much sunscreen as its Irish mother. He’d agreed to be her donor, including signing away any paternal rights, and that was that.

Somehow, she didn’t think Dante would appreciate those details.

“I hate this.” She set her mug down and swiveled to

face him, one leg bent underneath her. "I feel like I'm walking on eggshells, like I have to watch what I say or it'll start another fight."

He cocked his head. "*Another* fight? We're not fighting. Are we?"

"Well…yeah. Earlier. When I told you I was pregnant. That was a fight." Wasn't it? He'd been so angry and disappointed in her.

"It was a conversation," he corrected and set his own mug down in favor of taking her hand, holding it tight as he caught her gaze. "About something going on in your life. I didn't handle it well. You surprised me, that's all. But I care about you and want to know everything. It's not okay that you think you have to hold one single thing back."

Warmth spread across her palm, feathering outward. She stared at Dante and all at once, he morphed back into the man she'd loved for ten years. And then the warmth climbed into her chest as he smiled at her. It was so normal—and such a relief—she nearly wept.

Except she was changing things. That was really her biggest fear, that she'd irrevocably damaged their relationship by getting pregnant. She and Dante told each other chemistry jokes and talked about quantum mechanics, not diapers and breastfeeding.

She centered herself with a string of biofeedback techniques. Everything was going to be okay.

"Then I want to start over. Dante, I'm pregnant."

His eyebrows shot up in mock surprise, bless him. "That's fantastic news. Congratulations. I can't wait to meet the little version of you swimming around in there."

And that, against all odds, made the whole thing *real*.

She had a life growing in her womb. A baby. One that would be hers and hers alone, who would be a brilliant addition to the world of science from an early age. She would raise him or her with all the best educational opportunities and be this baby's everything, since she'd be a single parent.

That was when the panic started.

It was a baby. A helpless tiny thing who couldn't communicate its needs. She'd have to figure it out. By herself. The flutter behind her breastbone grew nearly audible. And then she realized that was the sound of her heightened pulse thundering in her ears.

*Breathe. And again.* She'd wanted it this way. Love between mother and child was absolute. Preordained. There was no potential for error, like there was when romance entered the picture, confusing everything with signals her brain couldn't interpret. Thus, this baby would fill a need in her life that no man could ever hope to. She'd never be lonely again, yearning for something she couldn't quite put a name to.

Plus, it would solidify her place among her business partners who valued the institution of motherhood. Or at least Alex and Cass did. Trinity had and always would march to the beat of her own drum, but regardless, she and Harper had long agreed about the value of a permanent man in their lives—zero.

Except this one. She squeezed Dante's hand and swallowed. "I'm scared."

"What? Why?" Clearly puzzled, he tucked a lock of hair behind her ear and smoothed it back, exactly as she'd envisioned he would when she admitted her fears. "You're the most capable woman I've ever met. You've got this, hands down."

"There's some...other stuff going on. Fyra is in trouble."

"What's going on?" he asked softly. "Whatever it is, we'll deal with it."

The thick bands around her chest loosened. She'd come to LA precisely because Dante was the one person in her life she could turn to. If she could just talk about it, maybe a plan would come to her, some way to haul herself out of the professional hole she'd fallen into. Then the pregnancy decision wouldn't seem so…ill-timed.

"Something happened with Fyra's FDA approval for Formula-47," she blurted out. A sudden burning behind her eyes mortified her. She never cried. Was this how it was going to be then? Emotions out the wazoo around the clock?

"What? Tell me," he demanded instantly.

Formula-47 had been her first baby, conceived and crafted in her lab with one sole purpose—to heal scars and wrinkles better than plastic surgery because it used revolutionary nanotechnology that she'd developed. It was brilliant. And it might never see the light of day.

*No.* She would fix it.

She took a deep breath. "Phillip—Senator Edgewood—you know how I told you he was helping us grease the FDA wheels in Washington?"

"Sure, because you're releasing your first product that requires FDA approval. I remember."

"The committee suspended the request."

It was nearly the worst moment of her life to hear those words come out of Phillip's mouth. The process should have been easy. Submit an application for approval for Formula-47, which she'd poured two years of her life into perfecting, give the committee a tour of the lab, explain her formulary methodology, send samples and research. Done. Approval to sell the formula as a product would be in the bag.

Nothing had gone according to plan.

"What?" Dante's expression mirrored the righteous

indignation of his tone. “Why would they suspend the request?”

“They had questions about my samples. And my lab.”

The expletive Dante muttered made her smile.

“Your methods are beyond reproach,” he groused. “How dare they question anything about your lab.”

She couldn’t help but revel in his unconditional support, which was precisely what she’d come for. None of her partners really understood what the allegations had meant to her professionally. Personally.

Dante got it. Understood instantly why the whole thing felt like someone had driven a railroad spike through her gut.

“There’s more. I think the questions cropped up because someone deliberately sabotaged the samples.” Even uttering that heinous suspicion aloud nearly caused her stomach to revolt.

Because that was the bottom line. She had a traitor in her lab. *Her lab.* Her sanctuary.

Until she got that sorted out, she was afraid she’d never fully embrace or enjoy the next nine months.

# Three

Dante smoothed Harper's hair back again because she was still trembling and that needed to stop. She didn't have to know that her hair felt like satin under his fingertips and thus the soothing motion benefited them both.

"Sabotage," he repeated and scowled. "That's not cool. Who do you think it is?"

"I don't know."

She shook her head against his palm and he feathered a thumb across her temple, which shouldn't feel so intimate, not in the midst of her crisis. But he couldn't help the fact that step one in his seduction plan included getting Harper relaxed with him again.

She was upset. She needed him. Which naturally led to him comforting her and *voila*. Here they were, holding hands on a small love seat. His fingers toyed with her hair. They were a couple of millimeters shy of an embrace. One small sway forward and he'd have easy access to her lush mouth.

But he didn't move. Not yet. Step one wasn't complete. He couldn't execute step two until he got her good and over her freak-out from the first time he'd kissed her. His mistake had been assuming one kiss was all it would take, and then they'd go back to normal, with his attraction to Harper easily handled and resolved.

Episode twenty-six of his show had been dedicated to that exact phenomenon. The mind played tricks on you sometimes, leading you to believe you had chemistry with a person, when in fact, the moment you locked lips, it became apparent there was nothing there. That's why he'd thought it was best to get that part established immediately, especially since he'd been seventy-five percent sure the attraction between them only existed because of another very well-documented phenomenon—the allure of look-but-you-can't-touch.

Hadn't worked anything close to how he'd hypothesized.

And the whole game had changed with the addition of Cardoza, Harper's pregnancy and her virgin state. A mere kiss wasn't going to cut it. He wanted it all. And had no issue whatsoever with working for it.

They could go back to being just friends later. After he'd introduced her to the pleasures to be had when a man took his time with a proper seduction. After they'd burned out this spark. After he'd had the opportunity to revel in the fact that he might not have bested Cardoza at winning the Nobel, but he'd sure as hell beaten him in all the ways that counted.

"This FDA mess sucks," he said simply. "What can I do?"

"You're already doing it."

She sighed with a little smile, oblivious to the way her chest rose and fell under her dress. She'd changed into a flirty number that dipped between her breasts, cradling them provocatively. It wasn't even all that low-cut, but it didn't matter. On her, it was sexy.

Off her, it would be epic.

"How about if I do something that actually solves the problem?" he growled because he couldn't keep the awareness from his voice. "I'll come with you back to Dallas and we'll tackle this together."

It was perfect. So much so that he couldn't quite believe this opportunity had fallen into his lap. He'd have every excuse to spend night and day by her side, just the two of them in a place that turned them both on—a chemistry lab—and then he'd swoop in at the eleventh hour to solve all her problems. He'd be the hero, short only of the white horse as he rode to her rescue.

Harper was both a virgin and a scientist. He couldn't use run-of-the-mill strategies to get her into his bed and have any hope of success. As seduction plans went, this one was killer.

Harper's eyes widened. "I can't ask you to do that."

"You didn't. I volunteered. I have two weeks off from filming and nothing planned. Do you have the option to give the FDA new samples?"

Nodding, she bit her lip, her sharp mind clearly working through the idea. "But it's a lot of work and my job, not yours. I have to fix this."

She wasn't connecting the dots fast enough. The idea of getting his hands on a real test tube made him nearly giddy. When was the last time he'd gotten dirty with the periodic table? Ages.

Harper and chemistry at the same time? He could not think of anything he'd enjoy more unless it involved her spread naked on the lab worktable, beakers shoved aside and forgotten, as he pleasured her with his mouth until she screamed his name.

Okay, that image had to go or he'd blow this carefully planned seduction.

"You're pregnant, scared and said you needed my support," he pointed out. "What better way can I support you than this? Let me help you create the new samples. I want to. It'll be fun, not work."

In response, she closed the gap between them, throwing herself deep into his arms in enthusiastic agreement.

His body reacted instantly, hardening in places she would surely notice in about two seconds since she'd nearly climbed into his lap. An erection the size of Minneapolis was impossible to hide.

"I thought I wasn't allowed to hug you anymore," he muttered darkly.

She stiffened and pulled back. *Idiot.* That's what he got for opening his big mouth, but holy God, what was he supposed to do when she was clinging to him like Saran Wrap and smelled like something he wanted to take a bite out of?

"Sorry, I got carried away in my gratitude."

Cursing inwardly, he willed back the rush of heat and grimaced. With any luck, it might look like a smile if she squinted. "I like hugging you. I was just—"

*Enormously turned on. Gauging whether I could actually feel your nipples through your dress. Thinking about how seriously hot that kiss was.*

He should quit while he was behind. Step one in his seduction plan did not include alienating Harper, confusing her or making a move too soon. She needed time and space to acclimate to him again or step two would die a nasty death.

Seduction was a science, not an art. There was no room for missteps.

Dante cleared his throat. "I'll call my assistant in the morning to book me on your return flight. No arguments. We're in this together."

Her tremulous smile went a long way toward smoothing over his blunder.

"Thanks. You have no idea what this means to me. I finally feel like I'm back on track."

That made one of them. But the genuine relief radiating from her expression warmed him. Not as well as her body had mere moments ago. But nicely enough. Because he did care about her and wanted to help. It was just a really awesome coincidence that the problems in her lab so neatly coincided with his agenda.

"I'm excited." She clapped like a five-year-old presented with a birthday cake. "We haven't spent two whole weeks together in…forever."

"Not since college." And even then, they hadn't been under the same roof. Living in the same dorm, sure. But the dynamic had been completely different back then. He'd attended college on an academic scholarship and every grade counted. The hours he'd spent with Harper had most often happened at the library or in the computer lab. Studying.

"Ooooh, we'll get to relive our glory days. It'll be just like it was back then."

"You mean when we had to exist on ramen noodles and four hours of sleep a night?" He grinned, only half kidding. "Speak for yourself, but I much prefer being able to afford a steak anytime I want it."

And this time around, he had a much better idea how to get this woman into his bed. He'd had his share of girlfriends in college, mostly due to simple things he'd never have dreamed would be such chick magnets: manners, an old-fashioned insistence that a man should pay for dinner and zero interest in sports.

Harper had always eluded him, though he'd felt a buzz the very first time he'd laid eyes on her.

"I *loved* college. Remember the spring break when neither of us could go home because we'd grossly underestimated the reaction of that substrate to the graphene?" She touched his arm enthusiastically, lost in her story. "We had to do the whole experiment over again and the project was due in like a week and a half. I was so panicked but you were Mr. Calm."

"I remember," he murmured, but not the same way she did, obviously.

Dante hadn't gone home for spring break ever. Or Christmas, summer break, random weekends. Because his foster home hadn't been a *home*, it had merely been where the people who'd agreed to raise him lived, and when he walked out the door at eighteen, he'd never returned. He'd loved college, too, but only because it gave him somewhere to go, somewhere to succeed. A place to belong.

A friend in Harper Livingston.

"Those were the days. We didn't have much, but we had each other." She smiled fondly, and his own return smile bloomed automatically.

Harper had been the first person in his life to really care about him, what he thought, whether he was eating well. He'd conveniently forgotten all of that in the heat of the moment, focusing so hard on how to get to the next step with her that he'd lost sight of why Harper had stayed so firmly in the friend zone all these years.

He needed her, too, as the one stable relationship he'd ever had. The only person who had ever demonstrated what it meant to value one another. It was the closest thing to love he'd ever felt.

Was he confusing that with attraction?

Guilt and agitation squeezed his chest and he didn't like it. There was a reason they called him Dr. Sexy instead of Dr. Emotional Expert. Physical chemistry he understood, very well. The psychology of the unquantifiable feelings between people, not so much.

If he succeeded with seducing Harper and got her naked and breathless, would that screw up their bond?

No, surely not. They were both adults and neither of them had much use for the emotional part. It was one of the many reasons they were still friends after all these years. They had a lot in common. The squiggle in his chest was nothing more than a reminder that he had a stake in ensuring nothing ever affected their friendship, even sex. Especially not sex. He'd keep one hand on the ripcord and shut down his seduction campaign if even a hint of a complication reared its ugly head.

Harper slid a cool hand up his arm to squeeze his shoulder, leaning in to kiss his cheek. Somehow, he managed to mask the sound of his lungs strangling over a breath as he fought to keep from turning his head to capture her lips with his.

"I'm so glad I jumped on a plane," she said brightly, thankfully clueless to the mayhem happening on his side of the wicker love seat.

He should be thrilled. Clearly, she was back to being relaxed around him. Step one could be labeled a rousing victory, *rousing* being the operative word. Unfortunately, step two promised to be more of the same since the goal would be to make her aware of the spark between them. So she could act on it when *she* was ready.

"Let me take you to dinner," he returned hoarsely.

He had to get some traction on step two before he lost the lone speck of sanity he had left.

Harper spent an inordinate amount of time dressing for dinner, taking a hot shower to wash the airport from her skin, then using the enormous three-way mirror to carefully apply a spate of cosmetics that she'd personally had a hand in developing. A swipe of Prague Sunset lipstick finished off the look.

The results sang, if she did say so herself.

She stepped into a dress the shade of cotton candy, which should have competed with her hair, but didn't because Harper had a near-savant ability to mix color. It was what made her exceptional at her job.

She had a healthy appreciation for how chemistry improved a woman's natural assets. She'd built a career on it. Only to see the culmination of her dreams screech to a halt due to tainted lab samples. And for the first time in a month, she finally felt hopeful about the future of Fyra. Dante was going to help her fix the problems and the FDA would approve the new samples. Simple.

That more than anything had dissolved the weird tension between her and Dante. He'd brightened at the thought of helping her and honestly, it sounded like fun to her, too.

Her stomach rumbled. She hadn't eaten lunch and after the…fiasco at baggage claim, the Reese's Peanut Butter Cups had lost their appeal. Dinner sounded like exactly what the doctor ordered.

She went in search of Dante through the labyrinth of halls in his enormous home, wandering toward the sound of running water. Being unfamiliar with Dante's house, she didn't realize it emanated from his shower until she was already in the doorway of his bedroom.

She raised a hand to knock just as he strode from the adjoining bathroom, bare chested, towel draped over his lower half. The terry cloth had settled low on his lean hips, almost to the point of indecency. But the uncovered part was enough to set off all sorts of bells and whistles in her head.

And other places.

A brilliant green dragon tattoo spread over his left shoulder, spiraling down around his upper bicep, accentuating sinewy muscles that she'd never seen before, but had certainly felt. His torso had turned sleek and brown, as if he'd spent time in the sun, and crisp hair lay against his chest in a trail leading to the stuff underneath the towel.

Her mouth went dry and her legs locked. Her brain might have melted, too. Or she wouldn't have stood there staring as he caught sight of her and grinned, totally unaffected by his state of undress.

"Hey," he said and casually pushed his glasses higher on his nose, as if she'd seen him wearing nothing but a towel a dozen or more times.

Because she had, especially in college when they'd lived in the same dorm with a communal bathroom. But that was before he'd filled out so much. Before he'd decorated his skin with something as…*sexy* as a tattoo. Before she'd deliberately introduced a plethora of hormones to her body that obviously rendered her stupid and prone to being affected by the sight of Dante's bare chest.

*Before* he'd kissed her and she'd felt all those muscles pressed up against her.

A blush prickled her cheeks and she spun, turning her back to the half-naked man that she couldn't reconcile with the one she'd known for years and years. Things were supposed to be back to normal. The *same.* What had happened to her sweet, slightly banal feelings toward her friend?

God, she'd always thought of Dante as sexy in a sort of detached way because of course he was good-looking. *Sexy.* It was just a word, but all at once, the root of the meaning became painfully clear because there was nothing *detached* about what was happening to her body.

"Harper. Are you okay?"

His voice washed across her skin as he called out from behind her. He'd said her name before. Lots of times. Using that same voice he'd always had. And yet it was not the same *at all.*

It was deeper, with more color. Was he also remembering that kiss that should be forgotten but clearly couldn't be removed from her memory? Was *he* thinking about how it would feel to try that kiss again while he wore nothing but a towel?

Oh, God. He was wearing nothing but a towel. Awareness raised goose bumps on her bare arms and sent a sharp pull through her abdomen. What the hell?

She'd hunted him down. Served her right for coming upon him in his bedroom going about his business. Naked.

"What's the matter?" He'd come up behind her and settled one hand on her shoulder.

She nearly yelped as his palm burned her skin. Why had she picked a strapless dress?

If she stepped away, wiggled out from under his touch, did anything other than stand there, she'd tip him off that she was midfantasy about turning around so she could get evidence about whether the second kiss would feel like the first.

Because protesting about wanting things between them to stay the same wasn't necessarily the same as protesting the kiss itself. Though she might have presented it that way. It was entirely too...*wrong* to be thinking about kissing him.

Didn't make the image fade.

"Nothing. I just...um, didn't know you were, ah..." *Naked. In your bedroom. Tattooed.* "Sorry. Your door was open and—"

Her throat seized. What was wrong with her? This was *Dante*. They'd gotten back to normal. No more crazy talk about "something between them," which she planned to deny had a grain of truth.

*Hormones, hormones, hormones.* She was stronger than her body's chemicals.

"Yeah. If I had anything to hide, I would have closed the door." He sounded amused. At her. Because she was being silly by refusing to look at him, like that would change the hyperawareness of his state, so of course he'd gotten a good laugh out of it.

"You should. Close the door," she amended lamely. "Now that you look like that."

"Like what?"

Oh, God. Somehow she was supposed to explain that he'd gotten her all flustered and confused, and then come right out and admit that he'd elicited a physical reaction from her? She barely understood it herself. There was no way she could explain it to him, not even with a dictionary and a copy of *Human Sexual Response* with notes in the margin written by Masters and Johnson themselves.

"Like *that*."

Twirling her fingers in the air didn't knock loose any good phrases from her brain to describe the sight of a man any other woman would have called hot, gorgeous or delicious. But not her. Because it was Dante. They were buds, intellectual equals, platonic. She shouldn't think of him as someone to be ogled. *Shouldn't.* But that didn't make it stop. He was a finely built man aesthetically speaking, and no one could possibly argue with that.

Could he tell? She shut her eyes as her mortification grew. Did he at this very moment realize that she'd developed an awareness of how sexy he was? This could *not* be happening.

"You, um…have a tattoo now," she explained.

*Yes.* Stick with the facts. Do not mention the riot of hormones that had exploded all over their friendship. *How* would she brazen this out with someone who knew her so well he could practically read her mind?

"I got it a few months ago. I generally try to keep it covered because it's mostly for me, not public consumption. Do you hate it?" His voice rumbled in her ear as he stuck his arm out, presumably so she could review it again before answering. "They edited it out of the dish soap commercial because they said it was too fierce for their target demographic."

She eyed the dragon from her peripheral vision. Wrong. The tattoo added to his appeal, but she'd take that notion to the grave, especially since any further discussion of that subject would mean she'd have to come clean about how she'd never watched his shirtless commercial. It seemed silly to objectify a man to sell dish soap, but now that she'd gotten an eyeful of the goods, it was a wonder the company hadn't developed an instant shortage of the product.

"I don't hate it," she mumbled.

"Then what's up?"

She needed space. Air. Distance. Before she uttered another word, she had to get back on an even keel or she'd ruin everything by admitting he might have a point about dealing with this…whatever it was between them that had cropped up out of nowhere.

She didn't want to deal with it. She wanted it to go away so she could work with him in her lab and not be constantly reminded of how his mouth felt on hers.

And that was only in the next two weeks. What about all the weeks after that, when she panicked about the baby, or being a mother, or some other unknown? Dante was her center, her constant, and there was nothing about this situation that felt the slightest bit *centered*.

"Nothing," she squawked. "Jet lag maybe. I probably need to go to bed. By *myself.* I mean, not that you were thinking I meant with you—"

Oh, God. *Shut up.*

"Dinner," she corrected hastily. "I need dinner. Let me know when you're not naked."

She fled. Pregnancy had completely and thoroughly scrambled her genius-IQ brain.

# Four

The first thing Harper did when she got back to work on Monday was call an emergency meeting with Fyra's C-suite. And then she spent twenty minutes in the bathroom of the company she'd helped build from scratch puking her guts out.

Seemed as if her body had finally figured out she was pregnant. Better it happen here than at Dante's den of temptation. Of course the flight back to Dallas hadn't been much of a reprieve, either. The wide first-class seat should have been comfortable enough for her to relax, allowing her to catch up on some much-needed sleep, but the stewardess had recognized Dante zero-point-four seconds after takeoff.

Honestly, Harper had been shocked the woman's shameless giggle hadn't jump-started a precursor to the yak-fest currently going on. Dante had been just as shameless, flirting outrageously and calling her Candy like they were…intimate.

To be fair, the stewardess's name tag had prominently displayed her name. But Dante didn't have to say it with that hint of wicked in his voice, like he wanted to lick her in order to find out if she tasted as sweet as her name.

It didn't matter. Or rather it *shouldn't* matter. The fact that it bothered her—then and now—was yet another problem Harper did not want to deal with.

Finally, she got her faculties somewhat stable and freshened her makeup while sucking on a peppermint that succeeded in settling her stomach quite well. No mystery. It was a time-honored remedy for pregnant women. Harper had done extensive research on all the stages of pregnancy so she would have a handle on what to expect.

Unlike the suspension of Fyra's FDA approval for Formula-47. That was not something she could quantify or gather enough data to explain. Her business partners needed to know that Harper had it under control. That she had a plan and had brought in expert reinforcements to help.

She left Dante in her office with a terse, "Be right back," and pretended like it was easy to keep her mind off the image of what he looked like naked.

She ducked out of her office before he could comment, and hightailed it through the beautifully appointed halls of Fyra. Purple, the company's signature color, graced nearly every surface and matched their packaging perfectly. Fyra, the Swedish word for four, had been a dream for so long…and someone wanted to undermine all their hard work. That wasn't going to happen.

When Harper arrived in the conference room, Cass Branson, the chic-as-hell CEO of Fyra, already had a virtual meeting session up and running on the large flat-screen TV. The face of Fyra's CFO, Alex Edgewood—beautiful even in a T-shirt and wearing no makeup—filled the screen and she smiled as Harper came in view of the webcam. Alex lived in Washington, DC, with her husband, a US senator, and only came into the office a few days a month.

A second later, Fyra's chief marketing officer, Trinity Forrester, rushed into the room, a volcano in Versace who couldn't spell the word tranquil with a dictionary.

"Am I late?" she asked breathlessly, though it was clear they hadn't started yet. "I was on a call with our Facebook rep, hashing out some ad placement."

"No problem." Since she'd called everyone here and the next steps in the FDA approval process belonged to her, Harper should be the one to lead the meeting.

Except all at once, as Harper glanced around the table at her three friends, her throat closed and right on schedule, her eyes turned into faucets.

"What's wrong?" Cass rounded the table instead of taking a seat at the head like she always did.

"Sorry," Harper gasped and fumbled for a tissue from the box in the center of the table. "I don't know what's wrong with me."

"You're stressed about the FDA fiasco?" Trinity suggested mildly. "You're working too many hours a week in compensation? Jet lag? Take your pick."

Harper pressed the tissue to her eyes, thankful at least that the smudge-proof mascara she'd developed as part of Fyra's premiere product line allowed her to cry without fear of looking like a raccoon. Small victories.

"I don't think so." Alex, sharp and analytical even from over a thousand miles away, zeroed in on Harper's face. "Do you have something you'd like to tell us?"

Oh, God. Really? Was the fact that Dante had kissed her bleeding out of her pores or something? Could everyone tell that she had a near-constant hyperawareness of the man who had been her friend for a decade? Her brain was officially fried.

Mortified, Harper sank down in her swivel chair a quarter of an inch and blurted out the first distraction she could think of. "I'm pregnant."

"I knew it!" Alex exclaimed over the sounds of Cass and Trinity absorbing that news with their own comments. "I couldn't figure out why you'd suddenly developed an interest in taking me to the doctor, asking all those questions about what it felt like to be pregnant. Congratulations."

Cass hugged Harper and then pulled back to peer into her eyes, warmth in her gaze. "How far along are you? If you need a rec for an obstetrician, mine is wonderful. I'm seeing Alex's doctor, Dr. Dean. I'll text you her number."

"Not far enough along to have a doctor picked out," Harper returned, absurdly grateful no one had jumped on the third-degree bandwagon, like Dante had. She had a list of doctors a mile long, of course, but why spend a few hours sorting through all that data when she could trust Cass's recommendation?

Trinity raised a brow. "Is no one else's jaw on the floor besides mine? Come on, ladies. This is huge news. Who did you finally do the deed with, honey? Because if you say anyone other than Dante, I'm going to be really disappointed."

Harper blinked. It sounded an awful lot like Trinity had expected Harper to confess not only that she'd lost her virginity, but that Dante had fathered her baby.

"What are you babbling about? Dante and I are *friends*," Harper stressed vehemently. "I got a sperm donor."

Trinity shot back a mock gag that set her dark angular bob in motion. "Are you kidding me? The only fun part about getting pregnant is sex and you denied yourself that? You're certifiable. Especially when you've got a man who looks like Dr. Gates at your disposal."

"Thanks for the support." Harper scowled. Dante was not at her disposal. "Some of us don't think of sex as a recreational sport, and I would never compromise my friendship with Dante to that degree."

That was a mantra she should stick to. If she repeated it a thousand more times, maybe her stupid hormones would finally get the message that Dante was off-limits.

How dare he put her in this position with that stupid kiss. This was all his fault.

"Too bad." Trinity waggled her brows. "I bet Dr. Sexy has some smooth moves. If I had to pick someone to be my first all over again, that man would be at the top of the list."

"Can we stop talking about my sex life?" Or lack thereof, which her friends well knew was by design. Harper appealed to Cass with a pointed plea. "We have much more important things to discuss."

"Like why Dr. Gates is hanging out in your office, maybe?" Cass suggested brightly. "I wasn't expecting you to bring him home with you when you announced last week that you were taking a personal day to fly to LA."

"Yes, exactly." Relieved to be back on track, Harper cleared her throat. "When I told him I suspected sabotage, he volunteered to help me create new samples. Really, it's a great plan. We don't know how the original samples were tainted, but odds are good our culprit is in the lab."

It still baffled her. The lab was sacred, the place where

the magic happened. Who hated her enough to desecrate the samples designed to take Fyra to the next level?

"So Dr. Gates will act as an expert consultant," Alex supplied and Harper nodded gratefully. "I'm in favor of having an independent third party involved. I'll run it by Phillip, but I think the FDA committee will view it as a good step toward resolving the issues with our lab."

*Issues with our lab.* The very concept threatened to bring on another round of toilet-hugging. But in reality, harsh or not, the FDA committee didn't care if the original samples weren't the ones Harper had intended to submit, that someone had switched them, or tampered with them. All they knew was that Fyra had presented the samples as products of Harper's lab and they were not acceptable. So there must be a problem with Harper. As she held the title of chief science officer, they were right.

Everyone looked at Cass. The four women shared equal stake in Fyra, but as the CEO, Cass had the final say. She nodded. "Let us know if Phillip has a problem with Dr. Gates's credentials."

"What?" Harper nearly came out of her seat. "What's wrong with Dante's credentials? He's a respected scientist with a doctorate from the same university I went to. Plus, he's not Dr. Gates," she mimicked in a sing-song voice. "Like he's some random guy with letters after his name. You've all known him for years and years."

"He's certainly qualified but he does bring a level of… celebrity that may dampen the enthusiasm of the FDA committee." Cass smiled to soften the message. "And of course this is not a reflection of our personal feelings toward Dante. I'm glad he's here for you."

Harper huffed out an uncomplimentary grumble but having seen firsthand how women fawned over Dr. Sexy, she really couldn't argue. "Fine. But since he's already here, I'm going to show him around the lab and get him acclimated. I have to produce new samples, regardless."

Trinity leaned forward, a crafty glint in her eye. "I think you guys are being too by the book. The only question here is whether we advertise the fact that Harper outsourced creation of the samples to a TV show host." She shrugged. "Who cares how they were produced? Let Harper and Dante play around in the lab. Who has to know?"

"I would know," Cass countered. "We still haven't caught the person who leaked the existence of Formula-47 to the industry."

As reminders went, it was a harsh one, especially since the leak had happened several months ago, starting a cascade of problems that had ended with the tainted samples. Harper had a fairly decent hunch that responsibility for both lay with the same culprit.

And it was someone under her own nose.

"That's why Dante is so critical," Harper threw in. "Because I can't let anyone else get their hands on these samples. He stays, no matter what."

She needed him for moral support, regardless. Her other friends had their own lives—hence the reason she'd decided to have a baby in the first place. Once Cass turned off the television, Alex's image would fade and she'd be inaccessible to Harper. Oh, yeah, they could text and call. Email. But it wasn't the same.

Gage lived in Austin, which meant Cass spent all of her extra time traveling back and forth from Dallas to spend time with her husband and their son from Gage's previous relationship. Trinity—well, she and Harper had never liked the same things, and now that Harper was pregnant, she didn't expect their friendship to get tighter.

Dante was her constant, and she couldn't begin to say how much it meant to her that he'd volunteered for this project. Her righteous indignation over his audacity in kissing her faded. A little. And then a little more. He'd only been trying an experiment. She was the one who'd blown it out of proportion.

As long as she could keep her mind off that kiss, and on the job at hand, everything would be great.

"That's a fair point." Cass stood, effectively ending the meeting because she probably had a million other things on her agenda. "Just keep in mind that the leak could just as likely spill the beans about Dante's presence here. We need to be aboveboard. In everything. Especially now. But I don't have a problem with giving him special temporary clearance to the lab. Ask Melinda to get him a guest badge."

Harper nodded and beelined it to the receptionist's desk before anyone got started on that third degree. The last thing she wanted to discuss was her pregnancy, or rather the reasons she'd elected to have one.

But as she rounded the door of her office, newly minted badge in hand, Dante glanced up from his laptop, his eyes turning that melty chocolate that threatened to liquefy her panties right off her body. What was *wrong* with her?

Correction. The last thing she wanted to discuss was why Trinity had zeroed in on Dante as the man most likely to pop Harper's cherry. Because she feared she'd done a terrible job of hiding the fact that her body had other ideas about what was appropriate behavior between friends.

And if she couldn't hide it from Trinity, she sure as hell wouldn't be able to hide it from Dante. Especially not in the confines of one very small chemistry lab. Well, she'd have to figure it out. They had work to do.

Harper's lab reflected the organized, thorough style Dante had always associated with the woman. Clean white counters, modern cabinetry and cutting-edge equipment invited him to dive in.

Science—real science—went on here and his heart should be leaping for joy over that alone.

Too bad he could scarcely keep his attention on the tour Harper was dragging him through. Who cared where she kept the disposable pipettes when step two had gone well enough that all he could think about was how quickly they could get to step three in his seduction campaign?

The only experiment he could fathom conducting right now involved his mouth, Harper's body and a hypothesis that she would taste better than the ripe peach she smelled like. Only a round of rigorous testing could prove that theory and he was fully prepared to go the distance. In the name of science, of course.

"Dante?" Harper paused in her recitation of the raw materials available in that particular cabinet, one eyebrow arched. "Am I going too fast? You seem a little distracted."

"It's the thrill of being in the lab again," he improvised smoothly. It would not do to get ahead of himself.

The problem was that step three involved a very intricate series of rational arguments designed to lead Harper to the conclusion that she wanted to take things to the next level.

But he didn't want to talk. He wanted action. Progress—and Harper wanted to show him where Fyra stored talc and deionized water. *Distracted* might be an understatement.

Harper smiled. "I'm glad you're thrilled. I wasn't sure if you'd volunteered for this solely to help me, or because you had a burning desire to do some rudimentary chemistry again."

"Both." He grinned back and wondered if it would be out of line to admit he was an enormous fan of Harper in white. Her long coat hid all her curves, but it made him yearn to strip her out of it. "Spending time with you in a lab is my idea of nirvana."

"I'm not kidding about the rudimentary part." She wrinkled her nose. "I'm almost embarrassed at how simplistic some of the formulas are. Someone with your advanced abilities will most likely find all of this...boring."

That hit him right where it counted. When was the last time someone thought of him as a serious scientist—and an advanced one at that? A big wave of Harper spread through his chest, warming him with equal parts affection and something the opposite of friendly.

Given the fact that every nerve in his body was poised to execute his slightest command—as long as the action involved yanking Harper into his arms—boring was not the description he'd have chosen. "It's been a while since I've picked up a test tube. Entry-level chemistry is right up my alley."

And hers. The parallel didn't escape him. Harper still had a ways to go before she'd be comfortable with a man's hands on her skin. Entry-level chemistry all the way around.

He wanted her to enjoy the experience, to have fun. To be unafraid to do anything she so desired. Losing her virginity was a big thing and he loved the thought of being the one to make it great for her.

A few staff members buzzed their IDs and entered the lab, chatting. All three women skidded to a halt when they caught sight of Harper and her guest.

"Good morning, Dr. Livingston," they recited, all three pairs of eyes on him, not the lady in question, likely calculating whether they could fawn over a celebrity in front of their boss.

She waved them over with the tiniest eye roll. "Dr. Gates loves selfies, so don't be shy."

Of course this would be the one time she'd cater to his ridiculous craving for acceptance. Any other day, he'd welcome a vigorous chat with fans. But not when he had an incredibly long and difficult step three to wade through. And a semi hard-on. Long lab coats that hid a man's boner, for the win.

The three lab techs took their sweet time gushing about how much they loved *The Science of Seduction*, throwing out twenty-dollar words to make sure Dante understood they liked it from an intellectual level as well as a practical level. While he appreciated that fans gleaned great tips from his show, he still didn't quite get what about *him* they found so compelling.

Or maybe he was still stuck on why everyone else in the world couldn't get enough of Dante when the woman at his side held him at arm's length, despite knowing very well that she'd been as affected by that almost-naked scene outside his bedroom door as he had. He'd half thought they might skate right through step two and pick up step three right there in the hallway. But she'd taken off instead of responding to the spark.

*Patience is a virtue*, he reminded himself.

By the time the lab techs had posted pictures of themselves and Dante on their social media accounts and drifted off, his patience had largely unraveled. Virtues were overrated.

The redhead lounging against one of her pristine white counters shot him an amused smile. "Sure you wanna dip your toe back into the lab? Looks like psychology is your field after all."

He scowled, and not just because Harper had pointed out his issue with his new job—it was *psychology*, not hard science. And pop psychology at that. "The show is not my field. It's entertainment. Any idiot with half a brain could figure out how to read a woman's subtle cues without my help if he really wanted to."

Crossing her arms, she cocked her head. "Really? What am I thinking right now?"

Oh, thank God. A perfect segue. And he intended to take full advantage of it.

"That's not a fair experiment," he countered smoothly and swept her with a once-over that held the slightest tinge of heat. "I'm not an idiot and I've known you a long time. I have a lot of practice paying attention to you."

Curiosity filtered through her expression, cascading all the way down to her mouth, which tipped up at the corners. "Yet you're still standing there not mixing samples."

Yeah, yeah. They were here to fix her sample problem. He got it. And they would. Later. His hands already knew the shape of a beaker and how to hold it. He wanted to educate himself on the feel of this woman, what would make her gasp. Laugh. Sigh. Moan. He wanted it all. Samples could wait one more day, at which point he might actually have a shot at concentrating.

That was the goal here, after all. Kill the lightning-hot buzz between them and move on. Been there, done that. Back to being friends and scientists, where they talked for hours about nothing and everything, laughing over shared jokes, being each other's sounding boards.

"Samples, Harper? Is that really what you were thinking about?" Casually, he leaned on the counter, decreasing the distance between them without making it obvious that he'd boxed her in. "Because that's not what your subtle cues are saying."

She glanced at his hand, which happened to be about four centimeters from where her hip rested against the counter.

"My subtle cues might be saying *feed me*," she said with a half laugh that didn't fool either of them. "It is close to lunchtime."

"It's ten thirty." He caught her gaze. "What's really going on is you're thinking about that kiss. You can't forget how it felt. Or all that heat burning up the atmosphere when you were checking out my tattoo. You're thinking you're a little freaked about it."

Guilt flashed through her gaze. Holy hell. He'd only said that to steer the conversation away from samples and toward his ultimate goal. He had not expected to get an immediate reaction.

Intrigued, he did a quick assessment. How freaked out *was* she? Was she freaked because she wanted him to do it again and didn't know how to ask? Or freaked because she was still in the friend zone with no exit ramp in sight?

"I'm not, either." She tossed her hair behind her shoulder. "We talked about it and things aren't weird anymore. What is there to be freaked out about?"

Door number one then, he decided with no small amount of glee. If she wasn't thinking about doing it again, she'd have trotted out her *we're friends and nothing but* excuse.

"Well, that's a very good question." One he definitely planned to get answers to. "I'll answer that with a question of my own. Why didn't you take Cardoza up on his invitation to do the baby making the old-fashioned way?"

"What?" She crossed her arms and used the action as a poor cover for moving her hip an inch further down the counter. Away from his hand. "How did we circle back to that subject?"

"Easy. You want to know why you'd be freaked over me kissing you. I'll tell you. It's the same reason you shot down Cardoza when the poor man obviously has the hots for you."

Imagining the disappointment on the jerkwad's face made a nice addition to the Kick-Cardoza's-Ass box in his head.

"Yes, well, that's too bad for him," she shot back. "I didn't take Tomas up on his invitation because he's not the man I want to lose my virginity with."

Oh, really? Her bold statement ratcheted up the heat a notch as a zing of energy accompanied the sentiment. Obviously she had a name in her head and it wasn't Dr. Cheater.

"Who is?"

Harper flinched, color flooding her cheeks. "No one! That came out wrong. What I meant was, I don't have any interest in sex. I mean, like none. Zero. Nada. It's just a series of chemical reactions that people would pay a lot less credence to if they really understood the way it works."

What was the *Hamlet* quote? The lady protested way too much. Or something like that.

"Pretend I'm someone who doesn't understand how it works," Dante murmured, clenching his hand into a tight fist so he didn't actually reach out to feather a thumb across that pink staining her delicate features. "Explain it to me."

"Don't be ridiculous. We're in a cosmetics lab." Her tone dropped to such a low register it only made sense to lean in. So he could hear her. "Where I work."

What the hell was she wearing that smelled like peaches? It was mind-boggling. Did she actually think she could lace her skin with a scent like that and he wouldn't notice? That he wouldn't want to sink his nose right into the juncture of her neck and shoulder?

Focus, he reminded himself, and soon he'd have all the peach-scented Harper he could take.

Glancing around, he jerked his head toward the open space behind him. The lab techs had gone into another room, leaving them blessedly alone. "Which is empty. What better place to discuss chemistry than a lab?"

"But we're not discussing chemistry," she ground out. "You're just fishing for intel about Tomas. Out of, I don't know, jealousy or something."

This time, her casual use of first names didn't burn a hole through his gut, which allowed room for a genuine chuckle. "What do I have to be jealous of Cardoza for? You didn't kiss him."

"I shouldn't have kissed you, either," she muttered darkly.

"I beg to differ. How else are you going to find out how wrong you are about your conclusions if you don't kiss me?" He gave her a minute and then leaned on that button again. Hard. "That's why you're still thinking about it. That's why you're freaked out. Because you're curious and you can't stop yourself from wondering. What's all the fuss about?"

Her crossed arms said she wasn't backing down. "I know what the fuss is about. People confuse synapses firing with something mythical and otherworldly, which, in turn, colors the experience. Sexual response is no different than hunger pains."

Oh, what an apt comparison. It was time to help Harper find out exactly how ravenous she was.

# Five

"Good for you for not denying your curiosity. So, let's talk about that, shall we?" Dante suggested smoothly and Harper did not like the look in his eye.

Thus far today, she'd inadvertently blurted out the pregnancy news to her friends, fallen into Trinity's cross-hairs regarding the suddenly hot topic of her virginity and then stumbled into a discussion about sex with the one man she did not want to talk about sex with.

Could the universe just give her a break, for crying out loud? The nightmare of the FDA issues would have been enough to deal with, thanks. And the way Dante kept twisting her words depending how he wanted to play it—all of it was wearing on her.

"I'd rather not talk at all. Samples," she reminded him, and was sure he didn't miss the touch of desperation behind her words. "They are not going to make themselves."

"Hmm," he fairly purred and her spine tingled as he leaned in a little closer, his gaze wandering down her body with a spark of…something she didn't have any clue what to do with. "I'll make you a deal. Give me ten minutes to make my case. Then we'll get started on your samples and I'll shut up. Scout's honor."

She eyed him as he held up two fingers. "I think that's the 'live long and prosper' sign, not the Scout sign. Clock's ticking."

*Bad idea.* The worst in the history of bad ideas. But Dante was nothing if not tenacious. She'd give him his ten and cut him off cold. They had work to do.

He eyed her right back. "You know I'm going to win. If proving a theory was a competitive sport, I'd get a gold every time. You must want those samples pretty bad."

Ha. He was obviously forgetting that time in grad school when they'd chosen opposing techniques to catalyze the photo-splitting of water. Photoelectrochemical—also known as Harper's idea—had been the clear frontrunner.

"I don't even think *you* know what case you're trying to make. Therefore, it was a calculated risk, weighted heavily in my favor," she countered primly, only to strangle over her statement as the space between them vanished.

Mute, she stared at him, drowning in his big brown eyes. His glasses showcased the riot of colors that created that yummy chocolate hue she'd seen in her dreams last night.

What were they talking about?

"My hypothesis," he began, and his voice dropped, likely in deference to their public proximity, but that didn't make it any less…affecting. "Is that you *used* to believe sex was just a series of chemicals and that you weren't interested. But that's recently changed.

And you're curious about how. Why. You're a scientist, Harper, and this lack of understanding is killing you. Of course you want more data. I'm offering you a chance to get it. It's an experiment."

"Wait a minute. We're still talking about kissing. Only. Right?"

The sizzling once-over Dante slid down her length answered that question, even as he shook his head. "You know that's not what I'm proposing."

Oh, God. She barely wanted to be talking about kissing. When had sex entered the equation? Harper's body woke up instantly, and her blood heated so fast, she saw stars. *Yes. That's exactly what you want*, her newly aroused lady parts insisted.

*No*. She scowled. That was the hormones talking and when had they gotten so bossy? "That's a hell of an experiment. What if your hypothesis is wrong?"

His smile did all sorts of interesting things in her lower regions and dang it, her brain was off and running. Because yeah, she was curious.

Why now? Why Dante? What *was* all the fuss about? Trinity's comment about denying herself the fun part of getting pregnant couldn't be pushed out of Harper's mind. It looped through her brain on a continual repeat, like an earworm that wouldn't stop bleating, no matter what other songs she sang.

What if she was the one missing something?

"I'm not wrong, Harper." He drew out the syllables, his eyes on her mouth the entire time, and her lips tingled as if he'd actually touched them, but he hadn't, and *oh, God*. She wanted him to.

Insanity.

"There are all sorts of ways what you're proposing can go south," she murmured, and was that her voice?

It had gone all *sotto voce,* too, and the sound of it put a fascinating glint in his eyes. "We have a friendship that I can't lose. What if I hate it? What if *you* hate it?"

Yes. That was the issue here. Kissing was one thing—a huge thing, which, by the way, had already changed their relationship against her will—but sex? That was an unknown that had *giant risk* painted all over it. Too much of one.

By way of answer, he reached out and she nearly jumped out of her skin, but he just took her hand, smoothing his thumb over it like he'd done a million times. Except she had a full-body awareness of it that flowed through her with an amazing, thick flood. Hormones, she reminded herself.

Oh, who the hell cared? It felt good. She liked it. That was his whole point.

Her knees weakened as she watched him watch her and she had a feeling he'd clued in to her minor capitulation. That was an error she could not repeat, not if she hoped to keep him focused on the roadblocks firmly in the way of his insane plan.

"You're right," he said. "We can't lose our friendship. That's why this is so important. If we both hate it, that's perfect. We laugh, chalk it up to Dr. Gates's faulty logic and go on."

"What if only one of us hates it?"

*Shut up.* This was not the conversation they should be having and she definitely shouldn't be letting on that his careful argument was swaying her. Because it *wasn't.*

"It doesn't work like that," he said.

Really? Dang it, now he'd thoroughly intrigued her. "Why not?"

"Well, that's the best question of all," he acknowledged and his thumb found a particularly sensitive spot on her hand that she'd have sworn he'd touched before, like a quadrillion times. But it had never rocketed through her with something akin to a lightning bolt.

She scarcely held back the gasp.

"Tell me," she choked out instead and his smile made it clear he knew exactly what he was doing to her.

"It's more of a show kind of thing."

Well, that felt strangely inevitable.

His gaze burned through her, which was completely ridiculous. He wasn't a superhero with laser vision. A man looking at her shouldn't cause a physical reaction. Of course, if she planned to hold that line, neither should thinking about him, hearing his voice, stewing about his audacity to speak to another woman or God forbid, remembering his bare torso with the line of crisp hair that disappeared into a loosely tied towel.

Yet *all* of them induced a physical reaction. What would it feel like to introduce corporal stimuli to the mix, but this time, with permission to experiment?

Weary of fighting herself, she shut her eyes and waited for the brush of his lips against hers. Her body bowed up, poised to feel all those luscious muscles rubbing her breasts again, primed for the rush of those chemicals she'd deny to her grave she craved.

Because yeah. Dante wasn't wrong about his hypothesis, not that she'd admit that to him. Her curiosity would be her undoing, apparently.

She waited.

*Nothing.* No lips. No rush. No Dante.

She cracked one eye open. He hadn't moved from his spot against the counter, and embarrassment replaced some of the desire she'd been reveling in.

"Um, when does the showing start?" she squeaked,

and geez, had he really maneuvered her to the point where she was begging for it?

Nonchalantly, he shrugged. "I don't know."

Disappointment crushed the air from her lungs and she yanked her hand free of his so she could wrap her arms around her stomach. It didn't hold back the tide of confusion. "So you're not going to kiss me?"

For the love of God. After all that? Really?

"Oh, make no mistake," he countered, and a slow, wicked smile spread across his face. "There's going to be kissing, among other things. But you're the one who's going to be doing it. This is your experiment, not mine. Tell me what you want me to do, Harper. Your wish is my command."

A hodgepodge of X-rated scenarios leaped into her mind, like a dozen browser windows had opened all at once and every one featured something not safe for work. She shut it down. Somehow. There was no way she could initiate anything of the kind. She could barely imagine admitting she'd pictured lurid details involving Dante.

And no way in hell would he ever find a way to convince her to kiss *him*. This was his deal, not hers. She was—almost, sort of, maybe—along for the ride.

"That doesn't make any sense. You kissed me first. You're the one who introduced all of this to our relationship." She glared at him and he didn't even have the grace to look chagrined. "I'm making a huge concession here that you might have a point about there being something between us that we need to deal with and you're forcing *me* to be the lead on this experiment?"

His other hand slid across her jaw, tipping her face up and all at once, she couldn't breathe as time stopped, suspending in a hazy glow. Everything in her peripheral vision faded and the fine details of Dante's face imprinted themselves on her soul. The smattering of freckles across his nose. The little nick on his jaw where he'd cut himself shaving at fifteen and it hadn't ever healed. The indentation high on his cheekbone that was almost a dimple but wasn't until he smiled. Details she'd noted a dozen times a day or more, but never as a whole, and they all belonged to the man she'd have sworn she knew inside and out.

But didn't. There were a thousand nuances of his face that she'd never explored. What would the almost-dimple feel like under her lips, for example?

"No one is forcing you to do anything." His gaze speared through her, sending shafts of heat clear to her toes. "I want you to be fully aware of what we're doing, what's going to happen to you. The choices you're making. The boundaries you've set and the lines you won't cross. If you're in control, nothing happens unless you say. That's how you make sure the other person doesn't hate it."

God, that was so up her alley. Of course it was. Because he knew her, knew that would be exactly the right button to push. But then that begged the obvious question. "How do I know I'm not forcing you then?"

That got a gorgeous smile out of him, and she could not tear her eyes away from that ridiculous dimple that she'd never had trouble ignoring before. How dare he come into her lab and flash that thing around, enticing her into fantasies about it?

"I'm good. I know what I'm getting myself into."

"I hate being at the intellectual disadvantage," she groused.

Something else she hated? His insistence that she make the first move. What was that, but some macho ploy designed to feed his ego? Like she couldn't resist him or something. All the other women in the world flocked to his side, but Harper didn't, so this was all a way to get her to cater to his need for attention.

Plus…she had no idea what she was doing. For someone used to being proficient 24/7, that was a hard pill to swallow.

"But that's easy to resolve. Jump in," he advised with raised brows. "You only gain experience from here and who better to experiment with than someone you trust implicitly? I would never hurt you and you already know I care about you. If I'm right, intimacy just makes our already great relationship better."

The reminder poked at her self-righteous stance. Of course she trusted him. He wasn't some random guy looking for a hookup and trying to talk her into doing something she didn't want to do. That was the whole point. He wanted her to make the decision and he wasn't going to force the issue.

"If nothing else," he continued, "resolve your curiosity now. With me. Once the baby is born, you'll be a busy single mom. Moms don't get unique windows of opportunity like the one I'm offering you."

"So I'm just supposed to kiss you? Right now?"

"When you're ready." His thumb stroked over her cheek again and his hand dropped away. "Time's up."

"Hmm. What?" She blinked as the phrase registered.

*Give me ten minutes.*

He'd made his case and now he was done. Instantly, the raw, achy places inside got rawer and achier as his heat faded from her skin. As her body started to cool, her temper flared. Oh, so that was how he wanted to play it. Lay out the premise that she could experiment to her heart's desire, set boundaries, be in control. How *dare* he appeal to her sense of logic and reason? That was dirty, through and through.

"That wasn't ten minutes," she informed him with a toss of her hair.

His brow lifted. "It wasn't?"

"Not even close." There was no clock in this part of the lab and both their phones were deep in their coat pockets. It could totally have been seven or eight minutes. How would he know? "I'm not done here."

Dante leaned back against the counter, arms crossed. "I've got nowhere else to be."

There was too much Irish in her blood to put up with all his feigned nonchalance. He'd started this and he was going to finish it. "In case you've forgotten, I have no idea how to kiss a man. I've never done it before. Seems like I should find someone to practice with. Maybe Tomas is free."

Instantly, Dante stiffened and something wholly feral streaked across his expression. "Maybe you can forget that idea."

*Not so calm, cool and collected now, are ya, Dr. Gates?*

And was it terrible that she liked provoking him? It was only fair. He'd been doing that to her since she got off the plane in LA. "Seems like you threw out some ground rules that sounded an awful lot like I was supposed to be doing all the kissing. You were just going to stand there and look pretty."

He processed that with a gaping fishmouth that warmed her competitive soul. If she did nothing else today, she'd prove that he was wrong. That she wasn't curious, that she wasn't freaked out, that she had no desire to experiment on him or anyone.

"I explained my reasons for allowing you make the first move," he ground out. "For your own peace of mind. What do you want from me?"

"I want you to kiss me," she fairly shouted.

"Yeah?" A wicked smile flashed across his face as he jerked his head. "Come and get it. I dare you to."

Red stained her vision. He didn't think she could do it. What a...*man*. Who was wrong. Of course, that was redundant.

That smile decorating his smug face needed to go. Harper grabbed his lapels and yanked.

His mouth landed on hers with enough force to drive her backward against the counter and his hands took possession of her hair. Moaning, she fell into the kiss with every ounce of pent-up frustration and longing and hormonal imbalance rioting through her body.

God, it was glorious. His mouth. *His hands.* The heat and pressure built until she thought she'd explode.

Something snapped inside and *poof.* No more thinking. This was supposed to prove something but her brain had melted and all she could do was cling to Dante's shoulders, marveling at how solid they were under her fingers.

Tilting her head, he drank from her, his mouth a conduit that pulled all of her strength from her body, weakening her knees. She nearly collapsed into a little puddle of nothing but nerve endings.

But he caught her in his strong arms, holding her tight against his torso. All the delicious hard planes of his body aligned with hers, and *oh, my.* The sensations flooded her. *More, more, more.* And he gave it to her, heightening the dizzy spiral inside until she feared she'd incinerate in his arms.

His heat inflamed her skin, sensitizing it, and she needed...something at her core.

Hips tilting of their own accord, she sought it blindly, until she accidentally hit the steel length of what had to be Dante's erection. Mortified, she froze, but his hand snaked down her back, leaving a trail of fire as it went, until he cupped her bottom, fingers nipping in.

He shoved her mound hard against him, circling until he groaned, and the raw, sensitive place at her core lit up. It was too much. *He* was too much.

Harper tore out of his arms, leaving most of her composure on the floor near his feet.

Torso heaving, she shut her eyes against the wholly affecting sight of Dante's kiss-stained mouth. Her body had other ideas about the distance, swaying toward him in hopes of getting all that lovely sensation back.

"I'm sorry," she whispered. "I can't do this."

That had been a complete and total mistake, because now she couldn't pretend she had no interest in kissing him.

Except she hadn't known he was going to make her feel like *that*. Or touch her in places that had never been touched.

Embarrassment filtered through her, coalescing in all the places Dante had filled her moments before. And now everything was weird again. Had she actually believed that they'd laugh about this and go on?

"Hey." Suddenly, Dante was there, his warm hand on her shoulder, familiar and comforting. "I'm at fault here. I goaded you into it before you were ready. I'm the one who's sorry."

"I made the choice. Like you asked me to." He'd played her exactly right. Ridiculously well, actually, and she was not happy about it, especially since she couldn't even blame him. "You were just indulging me in my experimentation."

"God, Harper, seriously? Did you not feel what you do to me?" He huffed out a frustrated breath, cursed and pinched off his glasses to rub at his eyes. "I goaded you into it because you make me crazy and I wanted you in my arms. And I'm not going to stop wanting more."

*Sex.* He meant sex. That was the "more."

Her heart froze, refusing to beat and she struggled to drag air into her lungs. If this was the aftermath of a simple kiss, what would it be like if they'd done…other things? Touched each other? Put their mouths against bare skin? Her stupid hormones had pushed her out of her comfort zone, pushed her into a place she did not want to go. Her pulse jump-started again, stumbling over itself in a race to catch up.

Shaking her head, she did some backing up herself. "No. That's not what I want. I…hated it. I was trying to figure out how to tell you."

He put his glasses back in place and cocked a brow at her, clearly unconvinced. "Don't do that. If you're scared, it's okay."

"It's *not* okay."

*And I'm not scared.*

But she couldn't keep lying to him in that moment any more than she could fly. She was terrified that if they did go down that path, their friendship would disintegrate in a vast sea of weirdness, that she'd do more shameless things in the heat of passion, that she'd be unable to look at Dante without thinking of his hands on her. Without imagining all the wicked things she'd done or would do or wanted to do.

Most of all, she was scared of how easily he could make her stop thinking. That was the real danger, because then what would happen? She'd always relied on her brain to guide her. The body's baser needs were not a reliable source of direction.

Dante cupped her jaw with both hands, forcing her

to look at him. "Harper, I understand that this is strange and you're nervous. No more pushing, no deals. I swear to you I will let you go at your own pace. If you want to kiss me, do it. If you want to strip off all my clothes, have a ball. If you don't, then don't. But don't deny what's happening between us because that *will* hurt our friendship."

With that warning ringing in her ears, Dante glanced around the lab. "Where do I start?"

The chemistry required to make cosmetics was relatively simplistic in the grand scheme of things, but Dante could hardly see through the haze of sexual chemistry painting his vision. Good thing Harper wasn't asking him to do something really difficult, like walk and chew gum at the same time. He'd be screwed, and not in a good way.

Who was he kidding? He'd been screwed since the second the words *I want you to kiss me* left Harper's mouth. That sweet phrase had wound through his blood and gotten him so hot and bothered that he'd thoroughly ruined all the progress he'd made thus far.

If Harper hadn't been freaked enough before to run scared, she certainly was now. It bothered him. A lot. He hated being responsible for upsetting her, because he did care about her—more than anyone else on the planet.

The problem was that he wasn't doing a great job of helping her see how things could only get better between them.

Dante held the test tube in his shaking fingers and willed Harper not to turn around. She'd taken a spot at the lab table near the window, while he'd chosen the furthest seat away from her. The last thing he could afford to do was let on how difficult it had been to let her stop that kiss. How he was still caught in the throes of it, his mouth watering to get her into his arms again.

But he couldn't push her—he'd made a promise. And he should definitely be shot because all he could think about was breaking it. She was his friend and that was not how you treated one.

"Got that reaction under control?" Harper called over her shoulder.

Not even a little.

Bobbling the test tube, Dante firmed his suddenly slick fingers. Practicing her mind reading, was she? Or was the fact that no blood had returned to his brain more obvious than he'd hoped? "I'm good."

"Great." Harper faced forward again, concentrating on her own task. "Those nanoparticles have a tendency to be volatile. We don't want any accidents."

He nearly groaned. Truer words had never been spoken, but he'd bet every last million in his bank account that the double entendre was completely lost on her.

What was the matter with him? This was a God-honest lab, with exciting technology at his very fingertips. He had free rein over every last piece of lab equipment and a well-funded corporation backing it. If he said he needed a different electron microscope, Harper's lab manager would procure it within twenty-four hours, as Harper had generously explained.

Hard science, exactly as the doctor ordered. What was he doing with this golden opportunity? Watching Fyra's chief science officer as she bent over a scale, measuring...something.

Her backside had been firm and sweet under his palms, and he'd ached to sink into her. She'd been hot and ready. And then he'd obviously made a serious blunder by taking things to the next natural level.

Okay, he hadn't been thinking with his brain when he'd ground against her, but who could blame a guy for losing his marbles when a hot redhead tilted her hips against his blazing erection? And then she had the audacity to lie to his face about hating the kiss, when she'd been a hair's breadth away from a fully-clothed orgasm. Which he would have gladly given her if she hadn't stopped.

But she had. He'd respect her boundaries no matter how certain he was that death might be preferable to being forced to shut it down like that again. Not only that, he'd had to soothe her through the remnants of her freak-out. Watching the genuine fear skitter through her expression had cut like he'd swallowed broken glass.

Not to mention the fact that he needed her calm so they could actually get some work done.

Or rather so she could. His attention was fully engaged in hashing out step four: get Harper used to his hands on her. Without breaking his promise.

She needed a little more encouragement, a little more space and a lot more reminders of how off the freaking charts their chemistry was. At great personal expense, as his aching groin liked to remind him.

All at once, he didn't feel like so much of an expert. Apparently seduction was much easier when the female in question started out interested in sex.

Harper pulled away from her scale and set aside the vials she'd been working with in favor of peering over Dante's shoulder. Her breasts brushed his back and he nearly dropped the test tube as all the air in the lab vanished. Good thing. If he breathed in right now, it would smell like peaches and he didn't think he could take that at this moment.

Of course she thought nothing of getting close to him

like this. Because he'd done everything in his power to set things back to rights between them after that fiasco of an experiment.

"I thought you said you had the reaction under control," she tsked. "Those particles have almost completely absorbed the dye. You were supposed to keep them separate."

"Oh, yeah," he said hoarsely. "I was curious if it would change the consistency of the lotion."

She frowned. "I worked on this formula for two years. It's sound."

Crap, he hadn't meant to insult her. Maybe fate had steered him away from hard science for a reason—he'd lost his edge. Or Harper was slowly draining him of every ounce of his intelligence. "Of course it is. This was more for my own curiosity."

The word pinged around inside him, reminding him of the last time he'd said it…when he'd been pushing Harper to absolve hers. In his arms.

All at once, he realized why his seduction skills weren't working like he'd expected them to. He was going about this all wrong.

Harper was a scientist, sure. But she was also a woman. And he'd done absolutely nothing to romance her. Episode twelve of his show had featured that exact subject and at the time, he'd covered a lot of ground regarding the things normal women liked: flowers, moonlight, fine wine.

The woman he wanted would never be impressed by stuff like that. If he hoped to have Dr. Livingston draped naked across his bed any time before the next century rolled around, he needed to get off his ass and figure out how to woo her properly.

# Six

By dawn the morning after The Lab Kiss, Harper had slept maybe two hours total.

When she'd invited Dante to stay in her guest bedroom—because hotels were for strangers, not best friends—she hadn't realized she'd develop a sixth sense that allowed her to hear him breathing through the walls.

Nor would she have guessed his presence would induce an achy restlessness she could not shake no matter how many times she recited the periodic table. The problem was that she couldn't forget Dante's parting shot…that to deny the spark between them would affect their friendship.

She got the point. The moment they started lying to each other was the moment they had no trust between them. That scared her more than anything. It had never occurred to her that *she'd* be the one to mess up what they had.

So she'd given herself permission to try out the idea

that she was attracted to Dante. That it was okay to think of him as sexy in every sense of the word. That her base reaction to him had nothing to do with her brain and everything to do with the way his mouth set her core on fire.

Hence the achy restlessness with no relief in sight.

Oh, she had a pretty good handle on how the logistics of that relief might come about. It wasn't like she'd been absent the day they taught human sexuality. Hell, she'd sat through more than one R-rated movie with Dante filching her popcorn as they watched the on-screen couple get it on.

What she did not have a handle on was her own reactions. Because sex was all she could think about. What it would feel like. What Dante might look like under the towel. She had a great imagination or she'd never have come up with something as revolutionary as Formula-47...but the odds of her mind conjuring anything close to the real deal when it came to specifics of sex? Not a chance.

Of course, the second she decided to get a glimpse of the doctor's naked body, she had explicit permission to start unzipping his pants whenever. That was also something she could not envision.

Which put her firmly at square one. Dante had sworn to keep his hands off her from now on. All the balls were in her court and he'd demanded only one thing of her—be truthful about her feelings, no matter what they were.

She'd rather jump off a bridge.

The clock blinked 6:30 a.m. Groaning, she rolled out of bed and trudged across the hardwood floor to the cavernous, lushly appointed bathroom that had been one of the main reasons she'd bought this condo in Victory Park. She showered the grit from her eyes well enough to see, but lacked the proper skill set to also eliminate the grit from her brain.

Why did everything have to be so hard?

When she got out of the shower, she stood naked in front of the floor-to-ceiling mirror in her hundred-square-foot closet, objectively cataloging her body. Soon, her belly would expand, rounding with the child she'd longed for. She'd hoped some of the changes might have started already but everything appeared to be exactly the same as last month and the month before.

The mess with Fyra and the FDA had robbed her of the chance to have a girls' night in with her other pregnant friends so they could compare notes, talk about delivery methods, eat a gallon of ice cream because they were all going to be fat anyway—or already were in Alex's case. She was carrying twins and had ballooned a few weeks ago.

Of course, Harper had only seen that secondhand on a Skype screen because Phillip didn't want Alex to travel unless it was absolutely necessary. And nothing fell in the category of "necessary" where her husband was concerned.

Girls' night in had become a pipe dream. Harper couldn't relax with her friends anyway, not until she'd fixed the problem that she'd caused for her business partners by failing to detect the switched samples.

Yesterday, she'd gotten zero traction. Today had to be better.

Dante stood in her kitchen holding a press pot full of Gyokuro Imperial Green Tea. He smiled when she walked in as if everything between them was A-OK, except his eyes were glowy with something new, or maybe she'd just never paid attention to how beautiful he was. All at once, her heart fell out of cadence.

Great. Now she'd developed an arrhythmia in addition to an awareness of Dante.

"Good morning," he said cheerfully.

Of course he was cheerful. He'd probably slept all night, content in the knowledge that he'd had Harper's number the whole time. Her mood soured.

"It will be a great morning if I can get some workable samples done today," she snapped and immediately regretted her cruddy attitude when he nodded as he poured a cup of tea, hustling her to the table in the small breakfast nook adjacent to the kitchen to sit her down with the mug.

"Then consider it done," he said and shot her another smile that shouldn't have made her as suspicious as it did.

"What, like you're going to put your nose to the grindstone instead of coming up with new and inventive ways to distract me?"

She flinched at her tone. He was being super nice to her, even after she'd barked at him. What was her problem?

"Yes." He settled into the opposite chair with his own mug of tea. "I told you. Next move is yours. In the meantime, you asked for workable samples by the end of the day. I'm going to give you that or bleed while trying."

Her brows arched involuntarily. "You can't bleed in my lab. That's a health code violation."

His dark, rich chuckle spread through her like honey, dang it, and her greedy, hormonal, Dante-starved body soaked it up, begging her to find 187 other ways to get him to laugh like that again.

It was just a laugh. He'd laughed at her jokes in the past. Nothing to see here, she advised her lady parts and scowled at Dante.

Who promptly held up his hands. "No bleeding. Yes,

ma'am. I was merely demonstrating my commitment to the project using figurative language. I note the boss is not a fan. We will stick to literal language the rest of the day, then."

She rolled her eyes. "I'm not the boss of you."

Something sizzled through his expression that heated her already jazzed body. "Oh, but you are. I'm ready, willing and able to be commanded at a moment's notice."

And yeah, she still had enough working brain cells to be quite aware they were no longer talking about samples. She cleared her throat. "I'll keep that in mind."

Which, she had a feeling, had been precisely his intention. And of course, her creative brain had no trouble following that lead. She'd have to watch it or her highly independent mouth might accidentally spill one of those fantasies and he'd take it completely the wrong way.

Dante drove Harper's Mercedes to Fyra because, as he insisted, she should take advantage of having a slave around and relax. Who could relax with all the shimmery electricity arcing between his fingers on the gearshift and her bare knee, mere inches away?

"Let me take you shopping on Saturday," he commented out of the blue.

"For what?"

He shrugged. "Baby stuff. A new car. Groceries. Whatever you need or want. I'm here to help."

"What's wrong with my car?" She'd just bought the cute two-door Mercedes less than six months ago and she loved it. It was sporty and…oh. No backseat. She hadn't gotten that far in her pregnancy planning because she had plenty of time. But she wouldn't have Dante around at her beck and call for more than a couple of weeks.

In a few months, she'd be doing all that baby stuff solo. In a new, more mature car.

That blackened her mood further. Not that she wouldn't give up her cute car for something more sedan-like—she'd gone into the idea of being a mom with a totally open mind—she just didn't like that Dante had been the one to think of it. And make her tea, like he was her personal lackey, ready, willing and able to be told what to do, no matter what her suddenly X-rated mind came up with.

Sinking down in the seat, she crossed her arms and glared out the window because it wasn't Dante's fault her pregnancy hormones had turned her into a lunatic. Instead of craving meat or orange juice, like normal women, she craved Dante. It was totally not fair.

The lab, typically her refuge, reminded her of the kiss from yesterday and reminded her that anytime she wished for a repeat, the man at her side would be totally on board.

But then she'd have to admit that she wanted him. Because in the crazy, mixed-up world she lived in now, their friendship depended on her being honest about that.

Somehow, she focused long enough to get into a rhythm. At first, she'd been leery of letting her guard down long enough to get comfortable with Dante, but soon they were side by side, knee-deep in ingredients, equipment and sheer bliss.

"Did you check on the sodium caseinate?" she muttered to him at one point. "It's about time for it to come out of the homogenization process."

"I did just a minute ago," he confirmed. "It's done."

That was the beauty of working with him. His analytical process mirrored hers and they rarely had to talk through a concept. Things were easy between them, like they had been in college, and when Dante glanced at his watch and noted with surprise that it was lunchtime, the real surprise was that she had indeed relaxed.

And she and Dante had made huge strides toward her goal of working samples. They'd gotten far more accomplished than she could have done on her own. "This has been very productive. I'm a little in awe."

Dante elbowed her good-naturedly. "You say that like you're shocked. I had a chemistry set when I was ten, I'll have you know. This makeup stuff is easy."

She laughed and it felt good, especially in light of her crappy mood from earlier. Dante stood, held out his hand to help her off her stool, and announced that he was taking her to lunch.

Gratefully, she nodded and clasped his hand without fear. She didn't let go, and wonder of wonders, he didn't comment. He just held her hand companionably as they strolled through the building. Like it always had been between them. And she nearly wept at how much she'd needed that in the midst of everything going on in her life.

"Thank you," she choked out around the lump in her throat as they settled into her car. "For being here."

Instead of starting the car and driving, like she'd expected, he turned to meet her gaze, his hand settling into place against her jaw. "I will always be here. We both need that constant."

Something passed between them as she absorbed his touch into her skin. Not heat, not the precursor to a kiss. Something else that was warm and safe and tender, and she reveled in it.

His hand fell away before she was ready and he chatted as he drove. The sound of his voice washed over her, soothing her, and she stopped listening halfway through his conversation. Her head drifted back against the seat. A long sleepless night crashed into her and that was all she wrote.

The car lurched, startling her awake.

Blinking, she oriented herself. “Did I fall asleep?”

Dante ruffled her hair. “Yeah. In the middle of my scintillating conversation, no less. If I didn’t know that pregnant women needed more sleep than normal, I’d be offended.”

“How do you know that?”

He shrugged. “I did a lot of reading about it. Can’t be too prepared when your best friend is pregnant and you’ve never so much as held a baby. I also know that you’re not supposed to eat sushi, certain kinds of fish and we’re going to avoid things that are high in sugar because it’s far easier to develop glucose intolerance when you’re pregnant.”

Oh, no. There went her heart arrhythmia again. Speechless, she processed his casually thrown-out admission that he’d researched her condition. Surreptitiously, she rubbed her heart to get it to start beating normally again. Except she was worried she might need defibrillators because when he came around to her side of the car to open her door and help her from the low-slung seat, she glimpsed the sign near the parking lot he’d pulled into.

“You brought me to the Perot Museum for lunch?”

“Is that okay?” He apparently took her earlier hand-holding concession as gospel because he didn’t release hers as he guided her toward the crosswalk. “The café is run by Wolfgang Puck and the menu sounded pretty good when I looked it up earlier. They give away a free dinosaur mask with the purchase of a kid’s meal. I’ll let you have mine. You know, since you’re masking for two.”

As black-mood lifters went, dinosaur masks might be her new number one favorite. Especially when Dante put one on and then stuck his glasses back on his face over the top of it. Harper couldn't hold back the giggles and before long, he had one tied around her stomach, too. Out came his phone so he could take pictures and she couldn't help but feel a little smug that her selfie with Dr. Sexy included evidence that he'd well and truly accepted her pregnancy with good humor. And that they hadn't lost the ability to have fun together.

The picture was precious. In more ways than one.

After lunch, Dante pulled her toward the mezzanine where they sold tickets to the museum itself. "Take thirty minutes and walk through the exhibits with me. I haven't been here yet and you know science museums are my crack."

That made her grin. She liked that he could be silly with her, no holds barred. And she liked the museum, too.

Since they'd made so much progress on the samples—and she genuinely didn't want the great mood he'd teased out of her to vanish—she nodded. "But I'm paying. You sprang for lunch."

He waved it off. "I picked this date. You pick the next one and I will generously allow you to pay."

She blinked at his back as he handed his black credit card to the clerk behind the counter. This was a date? Like a really real, God-honest date and somehow she'd missed the memo?

Surely he hadn't meant it that way. It was just a word, one they'd both used before to describe an activity, like *I've got tickets to the new Star Wars movie. Wanna be my date?*

But that had been before he'd kissed her. Before she'd

kissed him. *Way* before she'd allowed her attraction for him to come out to play…

Maybe she could just roll with it and stop being so neurotic.

"Ready?" Dante put his hand at the small of her back as he guided her to the escalator, then kept it there as they maneuvered through the crowd.

It should have been weird, given all the other stuff swirling between them. They were physically connected and she was aware of it, but instead of convincing herself it was friendly, or worrying that it sent the wrong message, she eased into it.

Dante didn't seem to notice that she'd basically adhered to his side. They talked about the dinosaur skeletons, pointed out their favorite birds in the bird hall and stood in line for the earthquake simulator, cracking jokes and laughing.

After Dante made a big deal over ensuring that it was okay for a pregnant woman to ride the earthquake simulator, they wedged onto the platform near the railing. Twenty or so other people crowded around them, forcing them face to face. Or rather, her face to his shoulder, which she didn't mind, even when Dante wrapped his arms around her.

Especially then.

"Just in case," he murmured in her ear and his lips nuzzled her in a way that seemed totally casual and highly suggestive simultaneously.

"In case of what?" she muttered back. Spontaneous combustion? Because that seemed likely the longer she stood in his embrace with heated flares jumping through her abdomen unchecked.

But then the simulator started up, jolting the platform. She nearly lost her balance but Dante's arms tightened as he shifted to take her weight. Somehow, her thigh ended up between his in an intimate press that rubbed her in all the right ways.

God, that felt good.

"In case of *that*." His voice rumbled in her ear over the virtual earthquake sounds. "I live in LA. Earthquakes are a thing. Suspected you might not be ready for what was coming."

Understatement of the year.

"Yeah, didn't see that coming," she agreed readily and imagined what it might feel like if she rubbed against his leg a little harder. Or better yet, if she admitted she liked it and asked him to touch her there.

Lust jackknifed through her so fast and so hot that her vision hazed.

"It's okay. I've got you," he said.

Yes, he did. And when she glanced up into his eyes, the answering heat reflected there nearly undid the fragile seams holding her together.

But he didn't close that tiny gap between them. Didn't ease his lips onto hers for a slow, wicked kiss that would be oh, so amazing given the fact that the earth was already shaking beneath their feet.

He didn't because he'd promised her he wouldn't.

And she had ample evidence digging into her stomach that he was as turned on as she was. The iron will he'd been exerting thus far deserved a medal.

Or maybe they both deserved something. But she needed a little bit of help to get there. Otherwise, the sheer terror coursing through her veins would win. Again.

When they got back to Fyra, she gave Dante a few pointed instructions about some tasks he could perform without her oversight and ducked out mumbling about a meeting. Which wasn't exactly a fib. Then she tracked down Trinity in her office, which was a little like bearding a lion crossed with Lady Gaga in its den.

But there was no one else Harper could turn to in her hour of need than a woman who regularly got top marks for her sex-capades.

"Ms. Forrester, are you in?" Harper called and rapped on the open door, which was kind of a joke between them. Trinity hated being called Ms. Forrester because it made her feel old, so of course Harper teased her about it.

Trinity's dark hair swung back from her left cheek as she glanced up. The right side of her hair had been sheared close to her scalp in an angular cut that fit the woman to a T. Last week, she'd colored it all purple but had quickly grown tired of it. That was one thing Harper admired about Trinity—she never let the grass grow under her feet.

And the woman was fearless with a capital *F*.

"S'up, girlfriend," Trinity said with a grin. "Do I sound like a part of the millennial intelligentsia who can sell cosmetics to teenagers?"

"More like a desperate marketing executive staring down the barrel of thirty and none too happy about it."

With a scowl, Trinity stuck out a wrist to show off the new butterfly tattoo she'd gotten a couple of weeks ago. "I'll have you know this thing marks me as super cool when I go to career day at Hockaday."

"Hockaday is a private girl's' school that costs more than my doctorate did," Harper countered and plopped into Trinity's visitor chair. "I'm not sure that demographic is going to give you the most balanced viewpoint into what's hot among seventeen-year-olds."

Out came Trinity's pierced tongue in defiance. "Did

you want something? Something other than to watch my self-esteem slide onto the carpet like yesterday's trash?"

Harper rolled her eyes. "As if that would ever happen. Which is kind of why I'm here."

And now that she was, she couldn't figure out how to actually bring up what she wanted to talk about. They'd been friends a long time, but they had so little in common. Mostly Harper looked to Trinity for fashion advice, especially as it came to what was hot, trendy or was already passé. Together, they'd come up with some of Fyra's most well-received product lines.

It was a little more difficult to lay out a personal problem. Especially one that Trinity would no doubt laugh at.

Trinity laced her fingers together and planted her elbows on her desk, then rested her chin on the ledge she'd created. "You're here because you need dating advice."

Blinking, Harper sank down an inch or two in the chair but only succeeded in wrinkling her pantsuit as opposed to disappearing. "Am I that transparent?"

"Sweetie, I'm not blind. I see what's going on between you and your hot lab partner. The real question is, do *you*?"

Oh, yeah, Harper saw it all right. In living color. In her dreams. When she caught sight of Dante from the corner of her eye and couldn't help but watch him as he measured acrylate into a beaker.

"Maybe," she muttered. Did everyone know that Dante had kissed her and vice versa? Was she walking around with a big neon sign on her back that said *pregnant lady with hormonal imbalance finally discovers her libido*? "It's...confusing."

And private. Embarrassing. Ridiculous. No one else had trouble coming right out and telling a man they wanted something from him. But what if she let her hormones rule and it turned into a disaster? She couldn't deal with that.

"Lay it on me. Wait!" Trinity jumped up and closed her office door, an act of mercy that Harper dearly appreciated, then she sank into the other visitor's chair, rubbing Harper's arm sympathetically. "Clearly we're going to skip the birth control lecture. So what do you need to know?"

Her friend's wry tone actually made Harper smile. Which meant she'd come to the right place for help. "So that's part of the problem. I guess my body reacts to conception a little differently than Alex's or Cass's."

"You've got an influx of hormones, do you?" Trinity chortled. "That's classic. I believe that's known as irony."

"Yeah, hilarious. Dante isn't helping."

"That's a flat-out lie." Disdain made her friend's carefully plucked and penciled eyebrows shoot up. "He is nothing but interested in helping. I can read males from three hundred yards and that man is into you. Always has been. Which is a crying shame, because I'd have tapped him years ago otherwise."

An image of Trinity and Dante together settled into Harper's stomach with a sour lurch. Except he'd slept with lots of women and likely would in the future. Which was none of her business. "I don't own him."

"Please." Trinity snorted. "That doesn't matter. He wouldn't look twice at me, not when his googly eyes are so firmly fixed on you. Do I need to kick him in his very fine backside? How is he not helping?"

By breathing, eating and sleeping in close proximity to Harper. Being sexy and understanding and logical and fun. That was the opposite of helping because it made her yearn for things she'd never realized she could yearn for. Things she didn't know how to ask for. "He's insisting that I make the first move."

"That rat bastard. How dare he?"

"This is not funny," Harper spat back as the reality of the situation overwhelmed her. "I have no idea what I'm doing, and everything is so confusing. How can I make a rational choice when my hormonal state is so unreliable?"

"Honey, if you think rationality is the goal here, you're doing it wrong." Crossing her arms, Trinity leaned back and put Harper under the microscope of her arresting blue eyes. "How does he make you feel?"

"Like I licked Satan himself," she said without hesitation. "Hot, sinful and wicked."

A purely blissful smile lifted Trinity's lips. "Aww, yeah. That's when it's the best. So make the first move. What's stopping you?"

"I just don't want to mess up our friendship."

That was the bottom line. Once that line had been crossed, they could never go back.

Trinity shrugged. "Then don't mess it up. You know what messes up relationships? Emotions. Letting your heart engage is a sure ticket to misery. Emotions aren't a part of sex. Ever. Take all that noise out of the equation and let that man make you feel good. It's a woman's right to have as many orgasms as humanly possible before death."

*Emotions*. Harper processed that. It made a certain sort of sense. She'd been scared of losing their friendship because…she didn't know why. But it seemed like people who had romantic relationships ended up crying in the break room when they ended. And they always ended.

How had she never seen that the key here was to separate the body from the heart and mind? This was no love affair with the potential to go wrong, leaving broken hearts scattered in its wake. She and Dante weren't romantically involved and never would be.

She could love Dante as a friend but sleep with him as a woman—and be as shameless at that as she wanted to because they'd leave their hearts at the door.

It was sheer brilliance. And humbling. Some scientist she was. Dr. Livingston sure hadn't analyzed that one correctly. At all.

But her friend wasn't done with all the startling disclosures.

"I'll tell you a secret that Cass and Alex told me," Trinity leaned in like someone might overhear, even though the office was empty save the two of them. "When you're pregnant, there's a lot of extra blood flow to your lady parts. Sex is apparently out of this world."

Not that Harper would have any basis for comparison. But that made sense, too. She'd often wondered if something was wrong with her because she'd never been tempted to "see what all the fuss was about," as Dante so succinctly put it—until she got pregnant.

It was almost a relief to hear that pregnancy might be affecting her body in a completely normal way. That made it acceptable to indulge herself, didn't it? Not just acceptable. Practically required. "You don't say."

Trinity nodded. "I have it on good authority. It's kind of a shame I'll never get to experience that."

"Not jumping on the pregnancy bandwagon?" Harper didn't blame Trinity. Every woman had to make her own choices.

The look on the other woman's face could have scalded milk. "Are you out of your mind? Could you imagine *me* as a mother? Besides, I dare any man's swimmers to get past three kinds of birth control. So, are we good here? I answered all your questions?"

"Oh, no." Harper shook her head, renewed in her determination. "I'm just getting started. Tell me how I get Dante into bed."

Something wholly wicked stole through Trinity's expression. "I thought you'd never ask."

# Seven

When Harper had finally returned to the lab after a two-hour meeting, she'd wasted no time in announcing to Dante, "I have an idea. For our next date. You, me and dinner. At my place."

And his concentration for the day left the building.

Dinnertime took approximately four hundred years to roll around, but once the antique clock on Harper's wall chimed seven, Dante had the strangest lack of appetite. For food.

Apparently Harper had liked the idea of dating. Better than he would have ever guessed, especially since he hadn't meant it like *that*. The science museum had been a spur-of-the-moment thing designed to get him the hell out of the lab before he busted something.

"Are you sure I can't do anything?" he called to Harper in the kitchen.

She'd unceremoniously ordered him out of the way because, as she put it, this date was her pick. And she owed him for the science museum. Not that he'd felt any particular need to be repaid when he'd been lucky enough to get her into his arms during the monumental shift in their relationship that had somehow happened in the middle of an earthquake simulator. She'd not only welcomed his touch, but melted into his arms. He couldn't have conceived a more perfect way to put a cap on step four than that.

He'd call that serendipity but he'd worked too hard for what he hoped would be the culmination of the evening to chalk it up to fate.

This was his woman to lose. And he didn't intend to.

"I've got it." Harper breezed through the entryway between the kitchen and the dining room, plates extended in both hands, then placed them on the table. "See? All done."

"Yeah, I see." But his eyes were on her.

How could food capture his attention more thoroughly than Harper, when she'd changed out of her snappy work pantsuit and donned a flowing ankle-length dress the color of sunset? She'd left her hair unbound and brushed it out somehow so it waved down her back instead of springing up in curls.

His body stirred to life in apparent appreciation, and the date—particularly the torture part—was officially underway.

Before she could sit down, he leaped up to pull her chair back because an erection was not an excuse to forget his manners. He got her all arranged and pushed her chair up to the table without touching her, though he had little hope he'd have that strength again. She smelled divine, like peaches with a hint of something sharp, like alcohol. Which reminded him of how much he enjoyed the lab and did not help matters down below.

"I'm sorry I didn't have time to cook," she apologized unnecessarily. "We left Fyra too late."

She worried her bottom lip with her teeth, oblivious to the enormous sexiness of the sight. Or maybe she knew exactly what she was doing to him; after all, she'd announced plans for a second date mere hours after they'd finished the first. During that amazing earthquake simulation—which, by the way, felt almost nothing like the real thing—his erection had been happily squished up against her soft stomach and there was no way she'd missed it. And her response? Dinner.

He considered that a huge step forward.

"I don't expect you to cook for me," he told her as he picked up his fork. "We were doing something much more important in the lab. By the way, if I haven't already told you enough times today, Formula-47 is brilliant. I'm not just saying that to get into your pad thai."

They'd stopped at one of the Thai restaurants near American Airlines Center and brought the takeout home. The extent of dinner prep had included heating up the food and plating it, but Dante did not take a hot meal for granted, even after three years of being able to order everything off the menu at the priciest five-star restaurant in LA.

Harper laughed as she dug into her own food. "Thanks. That means a lot coming from you."

"Yeah, because Dr. Sexy's scientific opinion is sought after worldwide." Wow. He hadn't meant for that to come out with such bitterness. But facts were facts. He had changed fields, thanks to Cardoza, and few people cared about Dante's chemistry knowledge.

And psychology, while fascinating in and of itself, was not his first love. Growing up, he'd found his escape in chemistry when no family seemed to want him long-term, not even his own. Formulas made sense, were the same today as they were tomorrow, and base elements always reacted precisely as he intended when the right catalyst was introduced.

Being in the lab again… only sharpened that ache to return to real science. Before lunch, he'd have said that was the highlight of the day. But as this was shaping up to be a stellar evening, he'd reserve judgment on his favorite part until tomorrow.

"Stop it. You're still you." She smiled at him with a touch of fondness that splashed through his chest, mixing with the physical reactions he could never quite keep under control around her.

The blend felt nice.

"I had fun today," he told her. "It was a nice reminder of why we're still friends all these years later."

Her eyes fairly glowed as she put her fork down. "I was thinking the same thing. Except I realized something. Maybe our relationship has evolved and I've been trying too hard to stick to the past. Maybe a little experimentation isn't a bad thing. How else are we going to figure out what's happening if we don't embrace the changes?"

His heart froze, jamming up all the blood in his veins. Because… holy hell.

"What are you saying?" he asked cautiously, in case her point wasn't anything resembling what he hoped it was.

She shrugged, but her gaze never wavered from his, bless her. *That* was the fearless, no-holds-barred woman he knew and loved.

"We've been friends a long time. Because we have a lot in common, and we prioritize our relationship. We care about each other. I've been scared I would lose that. But in the last few days, I haven't seen any evidence of that changing just because your mouth feels like pure electricity against my skin."

The atmosphere heated instantly as she dragged her tongue across her bottom lip, and he couldn't help but follow the trail. Because that electricity wasn't only on her side. "That's what I've been saying all along."

The conversation caught in his throat and it tasted a lot like victory. Harper was finally coming around. Why hadn't he started out with the science museum?

He started to speak but she held up a finger. "You just have to promise me that things won't be weird. Nothing is going to change. Right?"

"Not one thing." What would he change? Everything was perfect between them. Or at least it would be very soon.

"There's just one problem," she said casually and his pulse fell off a cliff.

"What? No. No problems," he countered in a rush.

They had enough problems that he'd spent an inordinate amount of time untangling. His body had already latched onto the original premise: Evolution. Experimentation. Mouths. Electricity. He wanted all that. Now.

"I'm being serious. I'm used to having at least a working theory before I start an experiment and with all of this—" she waved to encompass the condo at large but she really meant the chemistry that burned up all the oxygen between them any time they were in the same room "—I'm not the expert. You are."

"Seems like I've mentioned that a time or two," he murmured, mystified about where she was going with all of this.

"Yeah, but you're insisting that I go at my own pace. I have no idea what my pace is. What to do, how to do it, where to start. Show me."

That beautiful phrase made a perfect little bow of her mouth and Dante officially lost interest in dinner, the dining room table and anything that resembled respect for his hostess's effort toward feeding him.

He hoped she'd forgive him.

If that speech wasn't a green light, Dante needed to work on his ability to read a woman.

Pushing back from the table, he wordlessly held out his hand to Harper and waited for her to grasp it, then drew her to her feet so he could lead her outside onto the balcony that overlooked Victory Park. Downtown Dallas twinkled in the dusk to the left of Harper's condo and in the distance, the Mid-Cities sprang up out of the Texas prairie, marching toward Ft. Worth.

But he focused all his attention on Harper, who needed something from him. Instruction, guidance, reassurance. All of the above.

And he was going to give it to her.

The balcony was Harper's favorite spot in the whole house. Normally. The view always got to her—but she scarcely noticed the twilight-tinged skyline. Her heart climbed into her throat as she stared at Dante, nervous as hell about what she'd gotten herself into by laying it all on the line.

Were they about to put on a show for the entire I-35 corridor?

Or had he just taken mercy on her, realizing that she wanted something, but lacked the skills to properly articulate exactly what it was she wanted?

That had been the crux of Trinity's advice. *Tell Dante to take the lead.* As that fit with her inexperience, she'd approved that plan. Heartily.

"So here's how this is going to go," Dante began, but

before Harper could get her brain started again, he pulled her into his arms and stroked a lock of hair behind her ear. “You’re going to remember that part you said about how we care about each other. And then you’re going to stand here with me until I say you can move.”

His arms encircled her like they had at the museum and she greedily leaned into him. His heart thumped against her chest in a thrilling experience of connection that she wouldn’t have guessed would feel so intimate. “And then what?”

“I’ll let you know,” he murmured. “The point of this part of the experiment is to feel. That’s it. What happens next is up to you. But don’t worry, I’m going to give you choices.”

“Oh, really? Like a test?”

Despite her nerves, her inexperience and the swirl of uncertainty, she laughed. If nothing else, she appreciated the validation that admitting she wanted to explore the spark between them hadn’t ruined everything. They still could have fun together. Because Dante was still Dante, no matter what else happened.

This was going to work. And everything inside went taut with anticipation.

He nodded. “But the best kind of test because there are no wrong answers. And it’s multiple choice, with an all-of-the-above option you may invoke at any time.”

“I like the sound of that. What’s the first question?” Her voice had dropped a couple of notes and it darkened his eyes. Deliciously. Why did it make her so shivery to have that melty gaze on her?

“Do you want me to keep holding you like this?”

Easy. “Yes.”

“See, you’re a pro,” he said and dipped his mouth closer to her ear, like he had at the museum, and his breath stirred along her skin, sensitizing it. "Next, I'd like to touch you. Name a spot."

"You're already touching me," she pointed out breathlessly and gave herself a mental kick. He meant somewhere else on her body. And was asking permission because she had a habit of freaking out.

God, did his patience ever end? It was a little dizzying to know he could so carefully devise a way to assuage her fears. And not for the first time. This was, like, the fourth tactic he'd effortlessly switched to, all in the name of progressing their relationship.

All at once, she wanted to reward him. Boldness stole over her, encouraging her to take charge of this one small aspect of the long evening she hoped was in store.

"I like your hands on my back," she whispered. "I think I might like you to touch me other places. But I have some questions of my own. Like where you want me to touch you."

He sucked in a breath, heat simmering in his expression, and against her skin where they connected. "That might be a little too difficult a test at this moment."

Because she affected him when she touched him. Affected him by simply *talking* about touching him. That was thrilling. "What if I said that was what I needed? Show me what to do."

A groan rippled through his chest. "Fine. Put your palms on my chest. Explore to your heart's content. But then I get to do the same to you."

A wicked thrill shot through her at the thought of Dante stroking her in all the achy places under her filmy dress. "Okay. But—"

"No buts. Shhh." Dante put his palms over hers, and dragged them down his chest in a slow, careful sweep. "Touch me like this. There's not a wrong way to do it."

She took that at face value and let her fingers do some exploring. Amazing. There wasn't a part of him that wasn't hard and she reveled in the unadulterated lust that accompanied her perusal. Little firecrackers turned into bigger ones as he leaned into her palms, seeking deeper contact, which she would gladly comply with. Except there was too much fabric between her and the man.

No time like the present to jump in with both feet.

"Can I unbutton your shirt?" she asked, a little shocked that she'd actually gotten that whole sentence out. But holy hell did she want to see that dragon again, touch it, lick it maybe. If he would let her.

"No," he ground out hoarsely as his eyelids shuttered in response. "That's why we're outside, so nothing goes too far."

Her heart swelled a little. Even in this he was thinking of her. "Why do we need to worry about things going too far? Am I not being clear enough that I'm ready?"

"Ready?" The back of his hand came up, knuckles grazing her jaw as the crackle in the air grew to a fever pitch. "In the course of a few hours? Based on past experience, I'd rather make really sure. Like extra, extra sure because I do not have the strength to let you go again."

That set her back. She had been overly wishy-washy, hadn't she? The frustration in his voice wasn't directed at her, just at the situation, and that squished at her heart just as much as the realization that he'd been carefully leading her through her reservations. Which wasn't supposed to be happening. Had she forgotten all of Trinity's warnings about allowing emotions into the middle of this?

But how could Harper push away the fact that he'd had a place in her heart for ten years? Dante was only demonstrating how much he cared about her. That's what friends did, and she'd expect no less. Wasn't it possible that being together like this might actually make their friendship stronger?

"Then don't let go," she murmured. "I heard a rumor that sex is better when you're pregnant, so you don't even have to be very good—"

Dante cut her off with a growl, swinging her up into his arms, caveman-style, and she couldn't even squeak because holy crap, where had that come from?

He carried her into the house through the double French doors, taking care not to bump her, and set her down in the living room, forcing her to slide down the length of his body until she was locked against him.

That's when he kissed her, taking her mouth in his with almost savage possession and she could only cling to him as his tongue licked through the opening she'd given him. Her skin ignited under his hands as they raced across her back, nothing slow about it this time, caressing every millimeter he could reach.

At which point he started a trail of sensation down her bottom, to her thighs, gripping one in his strong fingers to draw it upward. Snugging their bodies closer together.

He lifted his lips long enough to mutter, "Now you can unbutton my shirt," but then he didn't give her a chance to say her fingers had gone numb. His own fingers tangled around the collar of his button-down and he ripped it sideways, pulling the fabric from between them. Half the buttons bounced to the floor, yanked unceremoniously from their moorings, and then the shirt drifted away, baring the sun-bronzed, dragon-enhanced, gorgeous torso that she'd seen in her need-soaked dreams.

Lightning forked through her core as she greedily drank him in and then she couldn't stop herself from tentatively reaching out, running her nails over the green tail where the dragon wound around his bicep. His hot-eyed gaze followed the movement, his muscle flexing along the trail she painted.

"Would it—" She cleared her throat, shocked at her broken speech, but she recognized it as the product of desire. Not fear. "Could I…taste you?"

In response, he groaned. "If you hurry."

That didn't sound very fun to her, so she took her sweet time, laying her lips on the dragon and then dragging her tongue up the scales of his back to where he spread across Dante's shoulder. His flavor exploded in her mouth, part excitement, part salt and all man. She had to stand on her tiptoes to keep going around the back. He accommodated her by dipping down, but she wasn't so involved in her perusal that she didn't notice his legs were shaking.

From her mouth on his flesh? That was so exciting she could hardly stand it.

Emboldened, she licked into the hollow of his collarbone, kissing him with little nibbles because he was delicious and she liked the way it made her feel, until he growled her name.

Before she could blink, he'd spun to capture her in his arms again, nuzzling against her ear in the way she'd come to truly enjoy.

"That was enough. More later."

"How can I go at my own pace if you won't let me experiment?" Seemed like there were a few more buzzwords he'd tossed around in his quest to get them to this point. Oh yeah, how could she forget? "I believe I was promised the opportunity to be in *control*."

Stressing the word did not have the desired effect of letting her continue her exploration. Instead, he backed her up to the couch, sat her down and knelt between her legs, his hands stroking up her thighs suggestively as he parted her knees.

"That was before," he informed her. "When I wanted to be sure you were on board. I've devised another method to figure that out, so we're just going to do that."

The wicked gleam darkening his brown eyes almost made her afraid to ask. But even in this, she preferred to get the data. "Which is?"

"I'm going to show you. As the lady demanded."

Without further ado, he hooked the hem of her dress with both thumbs, then gathered the fabric as he slid upward, baring her legs to his predatory scrutiny. That thrilled through her, sensitizing her core as he traveled oh, so leisurely up her calves, brushing her skin with the pads of his thumbs. His gaze roved over the flesh he'd uncovered as if he couldn't look his fill.

Except he'd seen her legs before. Lots of times. But never with this kind of appreciation. It puckered her skin with prickly goose bumps, but whether from the sudden chill of being bared, from his touch or simply having his full, undivided attention, she couldn't say.

Maybe it was all three. And it was strange, wonderful, nerve-racking. Slow. Way too slow and her nerves stretched taut the higher he went. Over her knees. To her thighs. Which quivered as he thumbed them and all at once, he stopped. Because he'd noticed that she was quivering.

He glanced up at her over the tops of his glasses, evaluating, and the sight of him at her feet, checking in with her when he so clearly wanted to keep going filled her with a different kind of warmth.

"It's okay," she whispered, and meant it. "That's my excited shake."

He flashed a smile that deepened his dimple and then

smoothed his palms over her thighs, leaving her dress bunched at the juncture of her legs. But instead of stopping, like she'd half expected, he bent and placed his lips on the inside of her knee in a long kiss that he didn't seem to be in any hurry to end.

Heat gathered under his lips and he spread the wealth as he mouthed her inner thigh, working slowly toward the bunched fabric covering her panties. His faint five o'clock shadow scraped her, and shot sparks up her leg.

She gasped, nearly twisting off the couch, but Dante apparently had anticipated that as his hands gripped her waist, smoothing downward to hold her hips steady as he added his tongue to the action along her thighs in a long slow lick. Dampness soaked her panties as she watched his tongue move closer and closer to her secrets.

He would stop before he got there. Wouldn't he? It would be weird if he—

Her lungs hitched as he gathered her dress in one hand, twisting the fabric high on her stomach, revealing her low-slung pink panties.

Dante licked at the hem in the crease of her thigh and flicked his gaze sideways to catch her watching him. "I like pink."

Hands fisted against the couch, she dragged air into her body, torso heaving as she processed that. "You're not going to…you know. Are you?"

Those gorgeous lips pursed and he nearly kissed the dampest part of her underwear. That didn't help the breathing situation. Because she ached for his lips to connect, for his magic mouth to relieve the restless achiness all of this was invoking. And she had a pretty good idea that he could accomplish that.

But to touch her *there*…with his tongue? She'd never get that image out of her head. Ever.

"Depends," he murmured and his breath brushed across her sensitive thighs, sending a spiral of white hot heat through her. But with his free hand, he gripped her hip in anticipation, keeping her in place on the couch. "What's *you know*?"

"Don't tease me," she shot back. "I'm not well-versed in all the lingo and it doesn't sound very sexy to use the clinical term."

"Not teasing you. Not yet," he clarified with a wicked smile. "I'm just gathering enough data to answer the question. Because there are several things I can do to you here. For example, I can touch you."

To demonstrate, he lifted one index finger and ran it down the flat of her stomach until he hit the dead center of her damp panties. Her thighs quivered again and clamped together involuntarily, but he just pushed them back apart easily with one firm hand to her knee. Opening her up, and it was decadent. Wicked. Unbelievably affecting.

"Or I can lick you."

Before she could move, he followed the line his finger had traced with his tongue, licking at her panties with little tugs that enflamed her and her hips rolled toward his mouth automatically. Her chest heaved as she blindly sought more.

"And I can do both at the same time."

His thumb eased under the hem of her panties, shoving aside the fabric. Cool air burned against her heated, exposed core as Dante's mouth covered her sex. She forgot to be embarrassed as his lips claimed the hard nub, teasing it as he nibbled and one finger toyed with her folds, finally plunging in.

*Oh, my.*

Her body bowed as he pushed her higher and higher,

sending her soaring on a flight to ecstasy until she saw pinpricks of light exploding across her vision. The reaction built on itself, her hips circling involuntarily, accepting his fingers deeper until the pressure pushed her over the threshold and the greatest sense of relief and release burst across her center as her muscles clenched and rippled.

Her first orgasm. She cried out with it, might have mumbled his name, might have been talking nonsense. And then she went limp, utterly spent and unable to get her brain to form thoughts. Words. Anything.

Dante covered her with her nearly ruined panties and kissed her thighs, once on each side of her still throbbing core.

"I guess that's a *yes*," he murmured. "I *am* going to."

"Was that one of those 'all of the above' deals?" she choked out, breathless, awed, a million things at once. "Because my answer is that. From now on."

# Eight

Dante had never seen a more gorgeous sight than Harper post-orgasm. And she was still fully clothed. His body throbbed with the promise of diving in. But he couldn't stop looking at her

Cheeks flushed, hands limp at her side, eyelids at half-mast. *Yes.* Exactly as he'd envisioned her a million times or more. He couldn't lie—being the man she'd let between her legs, the one who'd tongued her to that amazing finish, the only one ever to do so—it was a hell of a rush.

Best of all, he had a whole night of firsts ahead of him. He nearly felt like a virgin himself, with a raw sense of anticipation that he didn't recall from any of his sexual encounters.

With the honeyed taste of her still fresh on his tongue, he stood and held out a hand to her. He'd lost count of the number of times he'd done so, issuing invitation after invitation for her to follow him to a new place. Every time, she reached back and it thrilled him.

This time was no different. So trusting, she laid her hand in his and allowed him to pull her from the couch, then lead her to the bedroom. The master suite had a million-dollar view of downtown Dallas, lit for the night by this point, so he left the room's lights off, allowing the full wall of glass to provide the illumination he needed to get this woman naked as soon as humanly possible.

"Harper," he murmured, drawing her knuckles to his lips, and she looked at him, her eyes still warm and sated.

His breath tangled in his throat, freezing everything in his chest until he thought all his organs would burst from the pain of how simply stunning she was.

"Dante." Her throaty response thrummed through his erection. "Is it later? Because I'm ready for more."

Seems like he'd said something along those lines out on the balcony. She was asking for a turn to explore him in kind, but that was before she'd nearly taken him apart with her cries and sweet taste. "No. Definitely not. I'm not done with you."

She shuddered and he used that as an excuse to kiss her again, because clearly she needed his warmth. Her mouth opened under his, eagerly, her tongue already meeting his halfway because his darling did not hesitate when she forgot to be self-conscious. That was unbelievably hot and his groin let him know exactly how much by straining against his pants. He'd hesitated to strip off any more clothes than just his shirt—she'd already seen him without one—but since he'd touched her as intimately as possible and she hadn't fled…maybe it was time to take it up a notch.

"I'm going to take off your dress," he told her. "I want to see you."

She nodded and held still, allowing him to kneel at her feet to gather up that hem again, but unlike the last time, he didn't have the patience for a slow reveal. Drawing it upward, he kept going past the creamy expanse of her thighs, which nearly drove him insane a second time, past the pink panties that had frankly been as hot a shock as how quickly she'd come.

Watching her body in the throes, feeling her close around his fingers…highlight of the night, thus far. But he was keeping an open mind in case something else edged out her sharp responses to his tongue for the number one spot.

Finally, he got the fabric free of her body and let the dress float to the floor. Harper stood naked before him save the panties, and every drop of blood rushed from his head as he took in the perfection of her breasts. Tight, hard nipples stood at full attention begging for his mouth, but he couldn't, not yet. Not when she dropped her arms to her sides, letting him look his fill without flinching, and it practically choked him up.

How had he gotten so lucky as to gain this opportunity with such an amazing woman? Yeah, he'd been campaigning for it on and off for years, and in earnest over the last week. But still. Now that it was happening, he didn't actually believe he'd done one blessed thing that had turned the tide. This was one-hundred percent her choice and it humbled him.

"I need to touch you," he whispered and his voice ground out across vocal chords that had forgotten how to operate.

No problem. Everything else still seemed in working order. His erection pulsed with the promise of finally being free of its confines. Quickly, he pulled the condoms from his pocket, because there was no point in pretending that he hadn't hoped to need them, and threw them on the bed. Her eyes flicked toward the packages, questioning.

"Safety equipment is the first rule of any experiment, right?" he told her. It was also the first rule of anyone who had a major aversion to accidental pregnancies.

"But I'm already pregnant," she reminded him with a smile.

As this was not a good point to start discussing reasons why people should use a condom every time they had sex no matter what, he dropped it. All the reasons were on his side anyway, and he'd already forgotten every woman on the planet besides this one.

New subject. His pants hit the floor and she wasted no time checking out his briefs, which frankly weren't big enough to fully contain him, especially not when she reached out to trace the waistband. He sucked in a breath as she grazed the tip of his flesh and his hips jerked backward involuntarily.

"Maybe we'll save that," he ground out through clenched teeth.

"Why? You keep saying that, but this is my first time." Her lashes swept downward as her gaze lit on his crotch. "I want to do all the things."

"Because all the things will be over if you keep that up," he advised her, not even a little ashamed how desperate he sounded. "I'm skating on thin ice here and doing what I can to hold it all back."

"You didn't let me hold back. Why do you get to?"

Always the scientist. He couldn't help but laugh. Even in this, she had to question everything, seeking to understand. He didn't mind. Her curiosity was what had gotten her here. Finally.

"Fair enough." And he didn't even strangle over his surrender.

Eagerly, she let her fingers rest on his pecs before sliding the tips downward, her nails scraping across his skin with fire that threatened to undo. He groaned as she fingered the waistband of his underwear, dipping inside, then shifting around to the back.

And then without warning, she pulled them down, letting them drop to his ankles. Baring him to her hot gaze and his pulse bobbled as she looked at his erection with a sense of wonder, awe and pure fascination.

That was nearly the brink. His sanity was holding on by a thin thread and if he didn't slow things down, her first time would be disappointing indeed.

Before she could make good on the intent in her posture, which he was pretty sure meant her mouth was headed in the direction of his groin, he swept her up in his arms to deposit her on the bed, whether she liked it or not.

*He* liked it, especially as she rolled to her back and one knee fell to the side, opening her thighs. But not open enough. That pink underwear needed to go. So he stripped it off and took his time settling next to her on the bed, gathering her up in his arms.

"I know it's your first time. Trust me," he murmured, nuzzling the sweet flesh of her ear with his nose because that was where it smelled the most like peaches. "Let me make it good for you and then you can do whatever you want to me. All night. I will willingly submit to your every fantasy. But not right this minute."

She nodded against his neck, her lips grazing his skin. "I trust you."

And then she tipped her head up to take his lips in

a kiss so sweet and unassuming that he fell into it. Fell into her.

Rolling her onto her back, he went with the motion, snugging their bodies tight, and then he let go of his rein on his desire. For so long he'd been forced to temper it, but not now. There was no pretending he wasn't aching for her, no ignoring his need. This woman was his.

He kissed her with every ounce of his pent-up longing, which had been building for a decade. Her firm body under his vibrated with excitement and he groaned as her hands ran down his back, across his bare butt, down his thighs as if she couldn't get enough under her fingertips.

He chunked his glasses onto the bedside table, blessing his nearsightedness. Meant he could see Harper in all her glory just fine but the rest of the room was a blur. Perfect. He had exactly what he wanted to see in his field of vision.

Blindly, he fumbled for the condoms, managed to pull away from her for an eternity while he rolled one on and then he was back against her, tongues clashing in a battle of heat and raging desire. His body screamed to slide into her tight channel, which had never held another man before, and he could not hold back another second. She'd been so wet and swollen for him earlier; he had no idea how he'd stopped himself from taking her right there on the couch. Only a strong determination to give her a memorable end to her virginity kept him from it.

But he wasn't leaving that to chance now.

Ripping away from her lips, he trailed open-mouthed kisses down her throat in a straight line to her nipple, then sucked one between his teeth, rolling it gently as he tongued it and, yes, it did taste like heaven.

Harper's hips bucked against the mattress as he switched to the other nipple and she moaned with the sweetest little sound. Too bad he couldn't hang around doing *that* for another couple of hours. He was about to lose his mind as it was and those moans were sexier than all get-out. He kissed down her stomach until he hit the nirvana between her legs, spreading them wide to give him the full access he hadn't been granted earlier.

Dante groaned as he swiped his tongue across her nub, then dipped into her nectar. She was as hot and wet as she'd been earlier. Amazingly so, and as much as he wanted to bring her to another shattering climax this way, he wanted to be inside her with every fiber of his body so much more.

Shaking with need, he crawled back up her length, gathered Harper in his arms and gave himself the longest-denied pleasure of his life. Slowly, he notched his length at her entrance and caught her gaze in his so he could watch her expression as he pushed into her.

The ecstasy of it swamped his senses. She was tight, but so slick with her desire for him that he slid all the way in before he'd realized the resistance he'd felt was her maidenhood. She froze. Cursing, he fought his instinct to possess her, instead giving her a minute to acclimate.

"Okay?" he whispered.

Harper exhaled and her body relaxed under his. And then she nodded, allowing his heart to start beating again.

He meant to let his body go, let this fire between them rage to its natural conclusion. But all he could do was brush a thumb across her temple tenderly as they stared at each other, locked intimately in a timeless, hazy moment that forever imprinted on his memory as he made love to Harper for the first time.

But definitely not the last. Oh, no. He'd vastly underestimated how many times they'd have to repeat this experiment before they could even think about calling the spark extinguished.

The clear, bottomless depths of her gaze wrapped around him, holding him captive as surely as her body did.

"Dante," she breathed and the whisper floated over his skin, where he absorbed it like water on parched earth. "I'm sorry I held out for so long. I…needed this. So much. Needed you."

That made two of them. He nodded, too overcome to put the overwhelming emotions pounding through his blood into words. So he showed her instead.

Slowly, he withdrew and eased back in, watching her carefully, gauging even the slightest nuance of her expression so he could adjust the pace. He'd never done this with a pregnant woman, had no idea if he should change anything. He had to be careful.

She sucked in a breath and her eyelids drifted closed, her mouth partially open as he repeated the rhythm that felt so good, so right, that it nearly brought tears to his eyes.

Her hips rolled, meeting him on the next thrust, driving him deeper and pulling a gasp from her throat. Oh, she liked that, yes she did, and he was happy to give her more where that came from. Faster now, they came together, and he couldn't help but go a little further each time, pushing her limits with each stroke. And still she met him, fingernails biting into his back in a sweet burn that spurred him on.

He sought her center with his thumb, wedging his hands between their undulating bodies, and fingered her until her eyes went glassy. She bucked her hips faster, finally clenching around him in a tight glove, and he lost his fragile grip on the release he'd been fighting for an eternity.

In tandem, they climaxed, and he pried his lids open to watch her face as she came with him deep inside her, emptying himself as she cradled him. It was so beautiful that it bordered on spiritual.

Enlivened, he stroked her flushed face, drawing a smile from her that speared him right through the gut.

"I can unequivocally say that I now know what all the fuss is about," she said with a contented sigh.

He laughed and his heart wrenched as he lay there still half inside her, still wrapped in her arms. Still wrapped in the utter perfection of the emotional high being with her had created.

That was really, really...*not good.*

He shut his eyes but the feeling didn't go away.

As experiments went, he'd call that one an utter failure. Because nothing he'd hypothesized about the experience of being with Harper Livingston had been true. It wasn't a onetime thing, it definitely hadn't been "just sex," and they weren't going to wake up tomorrow and be friends again like nothing had happened.

None of this had been about one-upping Cardoza, or Dante beating his chest with territorial pride. He'd wanted more from her, more from their relationship, and used any means at his disposal to get it.

Because Dante was hopelessly and utterly in love with Harper.

When he'd taken her virginity, she'd taken something just as precious and unrecoverable—his heart. He needed her like he needed oxygen. She wasn't the closest thing to love he'd ever felt; she was it.

He loved Harper. Of course he did, and had for a decade. But he hadn't realized he was *in love* with her until this moment. Hadn't even realized it was something he was capable of or that it existed in such a pure form.

The sheer disaster of it swept over him, souring the gorgeous moment of clarity.

For the first time in his life, he had a woman in his arms that he could envision a future with, a relationship of equals. Maybe even put a ring on that third finger one day—like tomorrow. Why wait? They'd been moving toward this for a long time.

Except there was no happily-ever-after on the horizon here.

Instead of making their relationship better, he'd ruined it. But how could he have known the complications would arise after it was too late to start scouting for the rip cord?

His newly lost heart squeezed as her hand drifted across his face in a caress, and she shifted against him, stretching her back with a sexy lift of her breasts. He should be thinking about sinking into her again, letting her have her turn. Living in the moment of pleasure because that was all he could possibly hope to get out of this relationship with Harper.

When morning came, she'd still be pregnant with a baby Dante didn't want, who'd been fathered by a man he hated. And Harper didn't believe in love. What had she called it? *A nebulous emotion warped by greeting card companies.*

Before tonight, he'd totally agreed. Now he completely understood how faulty that logic was.

Somehow, he was supposed to pretend none of this had happened and find a way to get back to being friends. He'd promised. Multiple times. And after being let down by people time and time again as a foster kid, keeping his word meant something to him. His friendship meant something to Harper.

How had the simple decision to kiss Harper at the airport turned into his worst nightmare?

Harper took Dante's advice and hightailed it to the bath to soak her sore body in hot water. She'd half hoped he'd join her but he'd just smiled and said they had plenty of time for that later.

Always later. Dante had teased, licked, and rubbed not one, but two orgasms out of her, and it had been glorious. Really, the experiment had been a huge success and now that she had some data, she wanted a hell of a lot more.

Because while she had very little experience, she wasn't completely ignorant. There were a lot of things they hadn't done yet, all of which she wanted to do. The floodgates had been opened.

As she lay in her marble bathtub, the hot water soothed her raw places. Tipping her head back, she closed her eyes and let the images and memories assault her. And it was an assault in every sense of the word because…*wow.*

Hard and fast, all the incredible sensations Dante had elicited buzzed through her mind, and it was fascinating how even imagining him kneeling between her legs, his tongue hot on her sex, induced a similar physical reaction. A powerful lick of heat rippled through her core and she arched with it.

God, he wasn't even in the room and he could still affect her.

But the beauty of it was that she wasn't scared of those feelings anymore. He'd smashed all her barriers with his sweet patience and then taken her to places she'd never dreamed existed. The expert indeed.

And she couldn't wait for her turn to explore his beautiful, mostly unknown body. Find ways to pleasure him as he'd done her. Oh, yes, there was so much more he could teach her and she was a willing student.

When the water grew too cold, Harper climbed from the tub and pulled on a robe. She thought about getting dressed again but why be shy? Dante had seen everything she had to show. And besides, it was kind of wicked to be wandering around her condo naked except for a sheer robe as she searched for the man she hoped to spend a very long night with.

Dante was in the kitchen. Both of their forgotten dinner plates sat on the counter.

He flashed her a smile, but left off the dimple and she missed it all at once.

"Hungry?" he asked. "We never finished dinner. I was going to heat it."

"Sure. Gotta keep up our strength." She winked but he'd already turned around to stick one of the plates in the microwave.

No finer sight than that of Dr. Gates' extremely tight butt. He made khaki pants a work of art. And his shoulders… That dragon lay in exactly the spot she'd discovered tasted the best on his body. Emboldened by the activities of the evening, she put both hands on his back and slid her palms upward, exploring. Because she could. Because she wanted to understand his body better, wanted to please him. And he was hard, delicious and so masculine under her fingers.

Didn't matter if he was clothed. At some point, they'd pick up where they left off. No reason they couldn't indulge in a precursor while dinner heated.

Except he stiffened under her hands. Somehow, she'd envisioned touching him would be pleasurable for him.

That he might melt under her palms and make little noises of appreciation that would tell her she was doing it right.

"Dante?" He didn't answer or turn around. "Is everything okay? Am I not allowed to touch you like this in the kitchen? If there are rules, you better tell me now because I do not want to make a faux pas like stripping off this robe to show you that I'm n—"

"It's fine." His chuckle sounded forced and she wished he'd turn around so she could see his face. "You're allowed to do whatever you want. Your house, your rules."

She blinked and let her hands drop from his shoulders. "Well, in that case, there are no rules. If you want to walk around naked, I'm heavily in favor of it."

"Noted."

The microwave beeped and he made a huge show of removing the first plate and replacing it with the second. As soon as he pressed the start button, she waited for him to make a joke about her walking around naked in kind. When he didn't, a funny tickle started up in her throat.

She was making huge concessions here. Did he not realize that? At one point, she'd have been mortified by the idea of anyone walking around naked. This was all new to her, but she was willing to learn, to try new things, and he'd offered to be her guide. She needed that.

"I was thinking that it might be nice to go to the Kimball this weekend," she offered. Maybe a subject change would dispel the odd tension in the room that she'd somehow caused by touching him. "There's an ancient Egypt exhibit there for a limited time and I hear the mummies are cool. Of course, it's technically your turn to pick the date."

"That sounds great."

And then they stood in awkward silence and the

longer it stretched, the pricklier the back of her throat got. Was this some kind of post-coitus thing men went through? Like a withdrawal that was biologically necessary to replenish their strength?

But his reticence, especially in the face of the monumental experience they'd just shared, struck her oddly.

She opted to let it go. For now. What was she supposed to do instead? Besides, the scent of hot food was making her mouth water and that physiology was easy to interpret. She hadn't eaten dinner and Dante had stirred up all her juices.

Dante took both plates of warmed pad thai to the dining room table and settled in without another word to eat his own dinner. She shoveled noodles and chicken into her mouth as fast as she could, and let the silence stretch until she couldn't stand it any longer.

"This is the best date I've ever been on."

He glanced at her, and his eyes softened behind his glasses, turning that melty chocolate. "I'm glad."

"You didn't ask. But it was amazing."

His eyelids flew shut and he swallowed, clearly struggling, which was a little alarming. But then he looked at her dead-on for the first time since they'd untangled their bodies from each other. "I'm sorry. I should have checked in with you. It *was* amazing, more so than I was expecting. Much more. And my expectations were pretty high."

That put a warm glow in her chest. And other places. Which she liked, maybe a little too much. The glow spreading in her core was about to get out of hand very quickly now that she knew it was just the tip of the iceberg. "I didn't have any. So you definitely exceeded mine."

The smile he flashed her wasn't the wicked one he'd

adopted recently. The one she'd always reacted to and pretended she hadn't. And the tension hadn't fled one iota despite the break in the silence.

Her heart thumped in her chest and not in a good way.

"I am the expert," he intoned and she had the impression it was supposed to be a joke. She didn't feel like laughing all at once. This strange mood was starting to scare her.

"Dante?" She put her fork down and folded her hands. The appetite she'd developed had completely fled in the face of this whatever-it-was that laced the atmosphere. "Remember when we were on the balcony? I asked you to promise that things would not be weird between us if we slept together. I may not have a lot of know-how in the bedroom, but I do know you. And you're making it weird."

At least she thought it was him. A sense of foreboding prickled her spine. Or was this totally on her? Had she messed up by giving in to the lure he'd dangled in front of her?

All her misgivings, the hesitation—she should have listened to her brain, not her body.

Oh, God. He'd *promised.* She couldn't lose him, not now. Not after everything, with his incredible help with the samples, his support for her pregnancy despite not totally being on board.

Not after the cataclysmic lovemaking they'd shared.

Instantly, his face blanked. "I'm not trying to."

The panic sped up, zooming through her veins. "Well, you're not trying *not* to either. I was looking forward to having my turn. You promised me that, too."

He shoved his chair back and stood, gathering both of their plates. "Yeah, I guess I did."

Was that it then? The naked part of their relationship

was over? If so, it didn't bode well for their friendship because it sure seemed like that wasn't going so well, either, if he couldn't talk to her, couldn't even look at her.

All this time she'd thought she would be the one who wouldn't be able to look him in the eye after doing things to each other that she'd only had a vague awareness of after years of watching movies. And that education had been poor indeed compared to reality.

The prickling at her spine flared into full-on temper as she followed him to the kitchen. How dare he make things weird between them? How dare he call an end to the benefits side of their friendship before she was ready?

She needed him to help her understand all the strange, wonderful sensations, the rush of tenderness she'd felt when he touched her. She needed *him*.

"What if I want my turn right now?" She dogged his steps as he headed to the sink, temper rising the more agitated she got. "Right here in the kitchen. What if I wanted to untie this robe and rub myself all over your body?"

The plates clacked into the sink with a little more force than necessary. Dante spread his arms wide, gripping the counter as if holding himself up. His knuckles turned white as he stared at the mess in the sink. "How can that possibly be considered part of your turn?"

Exasperating, frustrating, stubborn, stupid *male*. "Because, Dante! I want to experiment. To see what makes you hot, to see if I can make you feel good like you did for me. How do I know what turns you on unless I try it? I want you to tell me, to teach me."

"The thing is—" He cursed, but kept his back to her. "That was a onetime deal, so we could burn off the spark, remember? We did and we're done."

Her brows came together. What the hell was he talking about? If he thought for one second the spark had been snuffed, there was something sorely lacking in her education on the matter. And the only person who could help her understand was turning her down. A chill crept through her blood.

"Turn around and say that to my face."

"What?" he growled. "Why?"

*Because I need you.*

She'd always needed him for emotional support, intellectual challenge, even just to make her laugh, and then he'd gone and added a brand-new, complex layer that was one hundred percent physical need—which might be the strongest need of all. For the first time in her memory, she didn't feel like she could express her consternation out loud and that scared her most of all.

So she went with logic. "My house, my rules."

Slowly, he turned, resting his butt against the countertop, arms crossed as he met her gaze. Instead of being blank as she'd fully expected, a thousand things darted through his expression—and all of them labeled him a liar.

They were not done. The spark was not snuffed. And in that moment, she learned he could still convey an enormous amount of affection for her through his melty chocolate eyes when he wanted to.

Her breath caught. "Dante."

He struggled to swallow and suddenly, she didn't care what the rules were. Her heart ached in a way her body never had or could and she wanted all of the weirdness gone. So she stepped into the space between his legs and wrapped herself around him despite his crossed arms because that wasn't anywhere close to enough of a barrier to keep her out.

Immediately, he dropped his defensive posture and

crushed her to his chest, holding her so tight she could hardly breathe, but she didn't mind. Emboldened, she snugged her face into the hollow of his shoulder, the spot she'd discovered earlier where it smelled most like him.

"I'm sorry," he said simply. "No more weird."

Her world tilted back into place as he rested his cheek against her head. Relief rushed into the cold, jagged holes inside, invigorating her, draining all her temper. All her fear. *Everything was okay.*

God, she needed this, needed his strength and his wit and his unique take on life in general. He felt good in her arms, divine under her palms. She spread her fingers to get more of his back muscles against her flesh.

His lips grazed the hair near her temple, his breath stirring against her scalp and it put a tinge of awareness into the embrace that snagged her body's attention.

She turned her head into his mouth, seeking a stronger connection. And was rewarded to feel a very prominent bulge in his pants. Languorously, she tilted her hips against it and his heart rate increased instantly, thumping against her cheek.

Well, that was just lovely.

Nuzzling his neck, she let the moment build, until the anticipation grew so heavy on her shoulders that she could hardly breathe. She wanted him to kiss her, to take her back to bed and light her up again. But there was so much more to explore.

So she did. Her tongue fit nicely in the dip where his throat met his torso and she traced the line of his collarbone. Dante groaned and it rumbled against her breasts, teasing them. She could get used to that. Nibbling her way upward, she concentrated on his earlobe and judging from his sharp exhale, she'd hit a good spot.

"Is this okay?" she asked softly in case he'd really

meant it about being done. He deserved the opportunity to say no.

"More than."

His hands spread across the small of her back, holding her in place and it was delicious, especially given his strange mood earlier. That had completely fled and she reveled in the rush of sensation, of feeling secure in their relationship again. In knowing that they could navigate bumps in their friendship.

"What can I do to pleasure you?" she whispered in his ear and he turned into her mouth, sliding their cheeks together.

"Everything," he murmured, his voice broken and raw against her skin. "Everything is pleasurable when you're in my arms."

And then their mouths connected and he kissed her, but it was so much more than just a kiss. She accepted it, desperate to fall into the connection they'd shared once already this evening.

Hustling her backward, he kissed her and guided her at the same time until she felt the hardwood floor of her bedroom under her feet. Perfect. She pulled away from his mouth—somehow—and backed toward the bed with a smile, shedding her robe as she went until she finally stood naked. Waiting.

He didn't make her wait long. Depositing his glasses on the bedside table, he then shed his own clothes and snugged her into his body as he rolled her onto the bed. She stared up into his beautiful eyes and experienced an odd moment of intimacy as she touched his bare face. Dante without his glasses was almost more intimate than when they were joined, as if she'd gotten a glimpse of him the rest of the world never saw.

And then he proceeded to shatter her a third and

fourth time, carefully avoiding her sorest spots like a master, as if he knew her body better than she did. Her soul sang with the pleasure. But afterward, the weirdness in the kitchen haunted her and despite the major exhaustion of her body, and the gorgeous man holding her, sleep never came.

# Nine

Dante woke in the morning still tangled with Harper and it was the most bittersweet experience imaginable. He'd like nothing more than to gather her close and whisper all the things in his heart. It sure as hell wasn't what he'd envisioned he'd want if he got past the threshold of her bedroom door.

And he doubted that she'd like to hear it anyway, especially since half of what was going on inside him was consternation over the permanent roadblocks between him and what he wished could be the next steps. But there were no more steps. No more stages of seduction. This could *not* go on. That was part of what he wanted to tell her, too.

As he blinked the sleep from his eyes, he stared at the ceiling, contemplating the spattered texture, looking for order in the chaos in hopes it would settle his racing mind.

Didn't work. And then Harper stretched against him,

clearly awake and looking to get a little closer. That second time last night had been the worst sort of concession, one he'd schooled himself against and then had been too weak to resist. He'd have to do better today because he truly did not think he could take the barb through the chest again.

"We should get going," he muttered and kissed Harper's temple in apology, though it was a distant second to what he'd rather be doing. "The strides we made yesterday on the formula were great, but we still have a lot of work to do."

"That's a switch. That's usually my line." She rolled to face him, her hair spilling into her face, and he couldn't stop himself from fingering the strands.

She was just so beautiful and perfect and responsive. His body had absolutely no problem adding additional complexity to Dante's anguish, springing fully alert as she slid a leg against his, snugging a thigh tight against his erection.

Oh, who was he kidding? When it came to Harper, he had zero will, and there was no way he could get out of this bed without a wholly conflicted heart anyway, so why not indulge in her sweet, tight body as long as he could?

Rolling her to her back, he dove into an open-mouthed kiss that she instantly responded to and within minutes, she'd moaned her way through a gorgeous climax that nearly pushed him off the edge.

He should leave it at that and get out of Dodge. Nothing wrong with going into the lab still sporting wood. Hell, lately, it had been his constant state, so he certainly had plenty of practice hiding it.

But she arched against him, her fingers questing until they hit his groin, then closed around him. A curse tangled in his throat as she eagerly explored his shaft, lithe fingers stroking the flames higher and higher until he couldn't stand being apart from her a second longer.

Sheathing himself, he slid into the heat at her core, nearly coming instantly, but he battled it back because this was the sweet part. The intimacy of being inside Harper surrounded him and he let his heart fly, unabashed, since this was the only time when he could.

She wrapped her legs around his waist, drawing him deeper, her eyes shiny as she watched him. And his pulse stumbled. There was no way he could give this up. Not anytime soon.

A powerful wave of emotion swamped him as he considered what compromises he could make to keep Harper in his arms. Maybe they could make a deal to be lovers until she had the baby. That gave him time. Eventually he might sate himself enough to go back to a platonic relationship. It could happen.

With that, his body shuddered and he came in a rush, closing his eyes as he let the emotional and physical reaction combine in a swirl of Harper that he couldn't have stopped at gunpoint.

Finally, they rolled from bed and got dressed for work, then drove to Fyra to spend several hours doing his second favorite thing—chemistry. Just after lunch, Harper popped over to his lab table and slid onto the next stool, her expression cluing him in that she was hoping for his undivided attention.

"I have a huge favor to ask," she began and then hesitated.

Which was silly. After the scene in the kitchen last night, he'd obviously lost the ability to deny her—or himself—anything. "Whatever it is, I'm pretty sure the answer is going to be yes."

"Will you go to the obstetrician with me?"

The bottom dropped out of Dante's stomach. He should have waited to hear the favor, obviously. "That's not something you'd rather do with Cass? You guys can compare notes."

There was literally nothing he'd enjoy less than sitting through a doctor's appointment where the major point of discussion would be the largest obstacle between him and bliss.

Harper shook her head. "She's in Austin for the rest of the week. It's Robbie's birthday."

Cass's husband and son lived in Austin and he knew she split her time between cities. Unfortunate timing. And Alex lived in Washington. "Trinity?"

The derision in Harper's snort came through loud and clear. "I'd have a better shot asking Trinity to come with me to get matching root canals. Please, Dante. I know it's not a guy thing, but when I came to LA, this is precisely what I meant when I said I needed you. I don't want to go by myself."

Holy God, if only his objection had anything remotely to do with whether he'd feel masculine enough while sitting in a roomful of pregnant women. "Plenty of guys go with their wives to the doctor's when they're having a baby. We're not married and I'm not that guy."

"Is this because we're…sleeping together?" Her voice dropped to whisper the words, her eyes darting to the two lab techs working on the other side of the room.

Which was frankly ridiculous when he was pretty sure everyone at Fyra knew what had happened between Dante and Harper last night. And again this morning. Trinity had even high-fived him in the breakroom earlier and offered a hearty, *Congrats. Took you long enough.*

"Of course not."

It had everything to do with that, along with the fact that Trinity's comment still stuck in his craw. If only he'd made a move sooner, he could have kept Harper happy enough to forget all about the idea of having a baby.

"It's okay. I'll drive myself." She shrugged, her mouth turning down. "You know, I drove Alex to the doctor and she can't even return the favor because of her own difficult pregnancy. Figures. I got pregnant at the worst possible time, I guess."

Her unhappy tone lanced through him and he groaned. Yeah, he should have just said yes from the beginning and shut up. There was no point pretending she didn't have him wrapped around her finger. "Forget I said anything. I'll take you."

She lit up, which hit him right in the solar plexus. "Thanks, I owe you."

And the gleam in her eye gave him a pretty good idea what she intended to use as currency. Which made the ride to the doctor's office uncomfortable for reasons beyond his emotional turmoil.

There were more than a few fans of Dr. Sexy in the waiting room, judging by the whispers and furtive looks, followed by mad texting. No one approached him for pictures or autographs, a rarity that Dante appreciated given the sensitive nature of their location. Though he wouldn't be surprised to get a couple of calls from his manager and publicist asking if there was something he'd like to tell them about his new girlfriend's condition.

The truth was so much less interesting than speculation, as he well knew. But Harper didn't, and he made a mental note to make sure she understood the downside of celebrity and how being in his orbit would undoubtedly lead to unwelcome exposure.

For now, he held her hand as she nervously beat out

the can-can against his chair leg with her sandaled foot. He distracted her with some funny stories about his TV crew, which only worked about half as well as he'd have liked, and somewhere in the middle of it, his manager called. That was fast. And an easy message to ignore.

Finally, a nurse called Harper's name and he followed her through the warren of hallways to an exam room.

The stark decor reminded him why he'd gone with chemistry instead of biology. He didn't like the idea of poking around in humans and he liked the idea of strangers doing the same to Harper even less. His protective instinct reared its ugly head and suddenly, he was glad she'd asked him to be here.

Especially when the nurse told the mother-to-be to put on a gown, then left the room so Dante could watch Harper strip. That was an unexpected bonus he wouldn't have been granted if they hadn't begun the "experimentation" phase of their relationship.

The doctor bustled into the room, introduced herself and asked after Cass. Huh. Harper hadn't mentioned she'd be seeing Cass's obstetrician, but of course the ladies would share recommendations.

"I'm Dr. Dean. And you must be the…?" The doctor stuck her hand out, eyebrows raised expectantly as she waited for him to fill in the blank to explain his role here.

Wasn't that the million-dollar question? "I'm the uncomfortable one who knows far less about this than he would like. But you can call me Dante. Or Dr. Gates if you like to stand on protocol."

The doctor smiled. "I thought I recognized you. As I'm sure we'll be seeing a lot of each other in the next seven and a half months, I'll stick with Dante. Welcome to fatherhood."

Dante didn't correct her, because all at once, it became an uncomfortable and unwavering fact of his current circumstances that he might very well be the closest thing to a father the baby would have.

God, what was he doing here in this sterile room? A picture of a woman's reproductive organs stared him in the face from the poster on the wall.

Things got even worse when the doctor announced that she'd like to do an ultrasound to determine Harper's due date. Pretty sure he was going to need brain bleach before the appointment was through, Dante gritted his teeth as the tech rolled the equipment from the corner and then gooped up Harper's stomach.

The technician rolled the wand over Harper's abdomen and a strong, strange sound emanated from the machine. *Wha-wha-wha.*

"That's the baby's heartbeat," she said with a smile and pointed at the blotchy screen. "And there's your little jellybean."

Transfixed, Dante gripped Harper's hand and stared at the black-and-white monitor. Would you look at that? It was really in there. The fetus did resemble a bean, or more precisely an ameoba, especially as the tech rolled the wand around to capture measurements, causing elongation of the image.

Out of the corner of his eye, he noticed Harper's flinch. He glanced at her. Tears streamed down her face in silent, powerful emotion and his heart twisted to the point of pain.

Wordlessly, he wiped the tears away and kissed her temple. But she didn't take her eyes off the screen.

"Look," she whispered. "It's my baby."

The rawness in her voice scraped at his soul. "I know, sweetheart. I see it."

And in a snap, it was real. Harper was going to have

a baby. She'd need someone to take care of her as she rounded with it, someone to help make decisions about things, to hold her hand when she went into labor. And then she'd have a baby, one who would also need a lot of care for a very long time.

God, when had he developed such an overwhelming urge to raise his hand and volunteer?

What a disaster that would be. He couldn't be anyone's father. His own crappy childhood had branded him, rendering him incapable of parenting. And even if he had the slightest inclination to figure out a way to get over that handicap—because Harper was totally worth it—what if he somehow transferred his hatred of Cardoza to the baby?

It was too big of a risk.

Harper deserved so much better. She needed someone for the long-term and Dante would only be in the way of that. Wow, if that wasn't a stick through the gullet, he didn't know what was. But it didn't change facts. He would have to encourage Harper to find someone else to be the baby's male influence because he wasn't the right man for the job.

They would have to go back to being friends with no benefits much more quickly than he anticipated and that was so physically painful that he feared his chest might explode from it.

But he had to fight through it. He had to be here for Harper because she'd asked him to come to this doctor's appointment and he was not going to fail her.

Harper let Dante run with the rest of the sample creation. They were almost done, which meant she could focus on the original tainted samples. Or try to focus.

The ultrasound still had her shaken up, even though it had been several days ago.

Pregnancy had merely been a state of being thus far, but she'd somehow divorced it in her mind from the actual, physical baby. Seeing it in 3-D had been one of the single most defining moments in her life, the others being when she'd received her doctorate, the day she, Cass and Alex opened the doors of Fyra, and the night she'd lost her virginity to her best friend.

All of those events shared a common element—they represented the start of something wonderful. And like all of the others, seeing the baby had given her the deepest sense of joy.

She'd made the right decision. The timing was perfect, especially with Dante by her side. All her doubt had instantly fled in that moment.

She hadn't expected the ultrasound to be administered at that initial appointment. Dr. Dean hadn't given Alex an ultrasound that early in her pregnancy, but as the doctor had explained, the fact that Alex had been carrying twins had caused her to change her policy.

Harper was glad. It had spurred her to start thinking about the future a great deal sooner than she'd intended to. Which meant she was trying desperately to figure out what she was going to do when Dante went back to LA in just a few days. Of course they'd see each other. They always had. But everything was different now that they were sleeping together—in every sense of the word.

She went to bed with him at night and woke up to his melty chocolate eyes every morning, something she'd never have dreamed she'd want or grow to crave. Unfortunately, it had an expiration date because of course he had to get back to his home in California.

It was going to suck.

The weeks and weeks ahead loomed long and cold as she'd most certainly be navigating the rest of the pregnancy alone. Ironic that one of the reasons she'd originally decided to have a baby right now was to have something in common with her friends, and they were so busy with their own lives that the only female friend who had time for her lately was the non-pregnant one.

The whole thing depressed her so much that she had to stop thinking about it. Her distraction of choice: throwing herself into the project of deconstructing the original lab samples. If the samples had been altered or substituted, she could prove it by pulling apart the molecular structure and analyzing it against what her formulary said was supposed to be in them. The work was tedious and difficult.

But she couldn't trust this to anyone else.

She'd already done some of the initial analysis back when the FDA first announced suspension of the request for approval. That was when she'd developed the theory that the samples were not the ones she'd submitted—because they weren't. There was no way. Her formula was sound. And she'd prove it.

Hours later, she had her answer. Dumbstruck to have the black-and-white evidence of sabotage, she stared at the data on her computer monitor, her stomach twisting with nausea.

Dante, bless him, must have sensed her distress because he glanced over at her from his lab table and immediately dropped whatever he was doing to cross the room. The warmth of his hand on her shoulder bled through her and she absorbed his presence as he came up behind her.

"What did you find out?" he asked quietly.

The answer was so huge and so overwhelming the

only thing she could do was swivel on her stool and bury her face in his chest. His arms encircled her, holding her close. She'd lost count of the number of times he'd done that over the years and the familiarity of it was the only thing that held her together.

"The samples are different," she said into his shirt and wasn't at all surprised when tears pricked at her eyelids. "Sabotage, for sure. This is *my lab*. My entire career. And someone undermined two years of my life with this stunt."

"I'm sorry, sweetheart."

He stroked her hair and let her cry on him because that was what he did. He was her rock, her go-to guy for everything. Miraculously, their relationship had gotten better and deeper with the addition of sex. Because she knew him so much more intimately now, and the depths blended with their history in a way that was great. Unexpectedly so.

Thank God he was here to soothe the jagged places inside.

She took a deep, shuddery breath. "I have to clean house. I can't trust anyone right now."

That was the worst part of this. She had twelve employees, all highly qualified technicians and scientists whom she'd handpicked way back when they'd started this company from nothing. All of them had been with her since the beginning, and one of them had *betrayed* her. Betrayed the entire company, including the women who were Harper's friends and business partners. It was unforgivable.

"Let's go home," Dante advised, drawing back a touch, and the concern and tenderness in his gaze nearly pulled apart her seams. "You can't do anything more today. You need to get out of here and take some downtime to process. Let me draw you a bath and then I'll take care of dinner."

Her eyelids slammed shut as gratitude washed through her. *Yes*. That sounded like exactly what she needed. Dante was her rock because he paid attention to her. Understood her. Knew what she needed often before she did. He'd always been like that but she'd never fully appreciated it. Until now. Why had it taken her this long to realize how much it meant to her?

She nodded. "That would be perfect. Except I have to tell the others. They need to know."

It was professional courtesy, of course, to inform the members of Fyra's C-suite what she'd discovered. But it was also personal. She'd brought this on Fyra and it was her responsibility to fix it.

Harper asked Melinda, the receptionist, to call an emergency meeting. Trinity, wonder of wonders, breezed through the door first, a neon-pink stripe decorating a lock of hair closest to her face.

"Hey, honey." Trinity slid into a chair and laced her fingers. "I'm guessing by the look on your face that this is not the meeting where you're going to announce that you and Dante are getting married."

Harper's pulse froze as the notion pinged around inside her. "Married? Why in the world would you say something so ridiculous?"

Marriage had never been on Harper's agenda, and she'd never heard Dante so much as breathe the word.

Trinity's expression grew crafty as Cass strode in and set up the TV to call Alex in DC. She fiddled with the controls until Alex's face popped up.

"Cass," Trinity called in a singsong voice. "Why in the world would I expect Dante and Harper to get married someday?"

Cass glanced at Harper with a smirk. "Because they've been in love with each other for like a million years."

Alex clapped. "Oh, did Harper finally figure that out? Is this an announcement?"

Her friends had all gone insane, obviously. "I'd ask if pregnancy hormones have melted all of your brains, but Trinity doesn't have that excuse. So instead, I'll say shut up. I am not in love with Dan—"

But suddenly, she couldn't say it as her throat closed. Romantic love was a chemical reaction gone really wrong at best. It was the psyche's way of putting a framework to sexual response. She'd swear it under oath.

But glancing at Cass and Alex, who were both happily married to amazing men who clearly would move heaven and earth for them…maybe things weren't as cut and dried as Harper had always made them out to be. Still…

"It's okay, honey. Give it a minute," Trinity said soothingly.

What was going on with this conversation? After all, Trinity had been the one to convince Harper that emotion-free was the only way to fly. "You said emotions have no place in sex. I heard you!"

She shrugged. "I told you what you needed to hear. You were letting your feelings for Dante get you all messed up."

"There's nothing like that between us!" Harper cried. "I do love Dante, but not like you're all talking about. Besides, if you really thought that was true, why hasn't anyone said anything before now?"

If they had, she'd have shot it down. The whole concept was ludicrous. Especially when you threw in the part about Dante being in love with her in return. The man had girlfriends coming out of his ears. Hot supermodels who probably knew way more than Harper did about how to please a man, in bed and out, one of whom he'd probably marry at some point if he was going to marry anyone.

Out of nowhere, her eyes started stinging as she imagined him twined with another woman.

Hormones. They were going to kill her.

Alex rolled her eyes. "This is one of those ruby slipper type deals. If we'd told you, you wouldn't have believed us. You have to learn it for yourself."

Sinking down in her seat, Harper thought about banging her head against the table. "Dante is not the reason I called this meeting. Can we please get back on track?"

Voice shaking, Harper told her friends what she'd found in the lab, and spent the next hour talking through the next steps. Grim-faced, they agreed to submit to the FDA the new samples that Harper had been keeping under lock and key. Then they'd do a careful analysis of the staff. Cass wasn't totally on board with a total sweep of the department due to concerns over severance costs and such, but she made a note to talk to Mike, their lawyer, as soon as possible.

Finally, Harper escaped the conference room and hustled Dante out of the lab to take her home, as his plan to put her in a bath and handle dinner was the only sane thing she'd heard in the last ninety minutes.

The bath went a long way toward making her feel human again, as did the back rub and medium-well steak Dante had delivered from Perry's. But of course the highlight of the day came when Dante took her by the hand and led her into the bedroom, then proceeded to undress her. When he kissed her with exquisite thoroughness and care, she nearly wept.

Off came his glasses, and her body flooded with so many feelings at once she could hardly stand under the storm. Which worked out well because Dante swept her up in his arms and rolled with her onto the bed, tangling their bodies so tightly together, it was hard to tell where one started and the other ended.

His gorgeous body…she couldn't get enough of it under her fingers, touching, marveling, letting the heat of his skin heighten her raging need. Then came her favorite part, when he finally entered her, sliding home as if he'd always been there. Her body accepted him easily as he filled her all the way to the brim. As he built the pressure and heat to the boiling point, she caught his gaze and stared into the depths of his gaze while he made love to her. The vastness of what he made her feel overwhelmed her and all at once, the conversation from earlier couldn't be ignored.

If every other female in her life saw something more here than friendship, why didn't she? Or was all of this huge and wonderful depth *exactly* what they were talking about?

Dante kissed her again as he touched her intimately in that way that never failed to make her body erupt with a thousand ripples, but this time, the contractions traveled all the way to her heart, squeezing it so tightly, she feared it might burst. He followed with his own climax—which was an amazing thing to witness, to know she'd had a part in bringing that exquisite expression to his face as he came.

Maybe she should start calling her heart arrhythmia by its proper name and stop pretending she didn't know why the thought of him leaving made her want to cry. She'd chalked it all up to hormones but maybe there was more here she'd been too afraid to examine.

She loved Dante. Always had, without reservation, without fear. He made sense in her life in his role as her friend. Until it made far more sense to be with him like this, and the transition had exceeded her expectations. But the one thing she'd never done was examine whether the emotion she'd always explained away as love for a male friend might be the same as the romantic kind she'd categorically denied existed.

She'd gotten pregnant solely because she'd thought a baby would fill a void in her life that no man could fill, when in reality, no other man could ever hope to compete with the one who already had a piece of her heart.

For someone so smart, she felt really stupid.

The whole concept made her want to curl up in a ball. Figure out unquantifiable emotions, especially after she'd *already* assigned them an ordered place in her mind? She could no sooner do that than she could turn invisible.

# Ten

Dante's manager finally got his attention the next afternoon with a pointed text message that someone claiming to be his birth father had been contacting him via his social media accounts. Dante never looked at those things. That's what his publicist was for.

A quick text message back took care of that problem: I don't have a birth father.

Likely it was yet another ploy to get sticky fingers on Dante's money. That had begun happening with alarming frequency once he'd hit the big time and it was one of the many aspects of being a celebrity that he did not enjoy. People had gall, that was for sure. As if he owed anyone money because of some sob story—and yet the sob story weighed on him. Because what if it was true? It haunted him to think he had so much and others had so little.

So he gave money to charities and went on. The benefits of having success, even in the field of psychology, offset the negatives. For now.

At loose ends, Dante prowled around Harper's condo, alone and not happy about it.

They'd finished the samples yesterday and Harper had flown to Washington, DC, to personally hand them over to Alex. Then Alex's husband would present them to the FDA approval board and that would be that. Filming started up on *The Science of Seduction* in three days, and his role in Harper's life would return to what it had been. Friends with fifteen hundred miles between them and a date for lunch in a couple weeks when he connected through the DFW airport on the way to God knew where...*if* their schedules coincided.

He wasn't ready for what had happened in Dallas to be over.

The thought of giving up the lab again was bad enough. But having to leave Harper behind, pregnant and probably scared, definitely gorgeous and funny and so amazingly sexy all the time...that was killing him.

Nor was he ready to talk about the reasons why he had to get on a plane to LA. It was critical that Dante separate himself from Harper and the baby before bad things happened.

Because he couldn't help himself, he pulled out his wallet and fingered open the folded ultrasound picture he'd charmed the technician out of when Harper was talking to Dr. Dean. The little blob had no features whatsoever. It was nothing but cells and a heartbeat. But half the DNA of that blob came from a man who had essentially destroyed Dante's long-term affair with chemistry.

It would be easy to envision a scenario where Harper eventually gave birth and the baby came out with dark hair and Spanish features. Because Cardoza came from strong bloodlines; otherwise Harper wouldn't have chosen him.

A little whisper that had started up at the doctor's office plagued Dante: *if only Harper had asked Dante to be her donor.*

Madness. Why hadn't she asked him? If she had—and he'd said yes—he wouldn't at this very moment feel like his soul was being torn in two.

Also madness. If she'd asked him, he'd have said no. Not just no, but hell no. For exactly the reasons he'd told her that he didn't appreciate being forced into the "male influence" role she'd delegated to him without his consent.

Babies were leagues away from his area of expertise. He had no business being a father. People who jumped into having kids could never be fully certain they'd continue to want kids, and by the time they figured it out, it was too late. The kid already existed and it was far too easy to dump one into the system. The pain of that experience would never leave him, even if he wanted to find a way to be there for Harper and her baby. He saw that now.

Cardoza was no longer the biggest reason Dante couldn't do this. Maybe that had never been the reason and Dante had used his old rival as an excuse to ignore the real issue—he couldn't get past his childhood.

He had nothing to offer Harper or her baby—no parenting skills, no role model to glean advice from. What if he tried and messed up? He'd ruin a kid's whole life.

The longer Dante stared at this picture, the worse the wash of emotions became. The catch-22 was brutal. He couldn't stay, but he didn't want to go back to Hollywood.

Maybe he could find a third option. What good was it to have a healthy bank account if he couldn't buy whatever he wanted? Once upon a time, he'd have given his right arm to have a benefactor fall in his lap who could fund his lab, and he wouldn't have minded one bit if that benefactor popped in occasionally to play around in the nitty-gritty details.

Before he could change his mind, he sat down with his laptop and spent two hours querying everyone he knew in hopes of getting a lead on projects outside the university system in need of quick cash. Grant proposals had too many strings and oversight. Private was the way to go.

Within thirty minutes, four different responses appeared in his inbox. Dante got on the phone and talked to some great people he hadn't touched base with in years. It was cathartic to learn that the scientific community as a whole hadn't shunned him and there were still labs out there hoping to change the world with a big breakthrough. All they lacked was funding.

On his third call, he connected with Val Gochnauer, a guy he'd worked with during his dissertation. Val had landed at a think tank in his native Switzerland and needed an infusion of cash desperately, or the doors would close within thirty days.

Harper's key rattled in the lock and she breezed through the door just as Dante was wrapping up with Val. He cut it shorter than he would have liked because he had a gut feeling Val's setup was exactly what Dante had been looking for. Of course, he'd have to fly to Switzerland to find out. Today. He was due back on the set Monday, so the timing was perfect.

Except for the part where he had to tell Harper he was leaving. His chest hurt already. How was he going to get through a whole conversation?

But as she set down her suitcases and flew into Dante's embrace, the scent of peaches nearly put him on his knees. Instead of pushing her away, like he should, he gathered her close and breathed her in for what was probably the last time.

If he funded Val's lab, he'd probably end up spending all his free time in Switzerland. The situation was tailor-made. If Dante was on another continent, he couldn't tempt himself with a quick side trip to Dallas to spend the weekend in Harper's bed.

"I wasn't expecting you back so soon, or I would have picked you up," he said gruffly into her hair. "I thought your return flight wasn't until tonight. Weren't you going to having dinner with Alex and her husband?"

Nodding, Harper pulled back just enough so he could see her face. "I was supposed to but Phillip had an unexpected thing come up. The busy life of a senator. I don't know how Alex does it."

Good. And not good. It would have been easier if he could have left before she got back. But that kind of cowardice didn't sit well anyway. Now he had a chance to come clean, especially about the part where he was going to opt out of being here during the pregnancy and birth. "I'm glad. I missed you."

That was so not what he'd meant to say.

"I missed you, too." She smiled and it ripped through him with jagged teeth.

Now came the hard part.

God, he did not want to disappoint her. But what was he supposed to do? Hilarious how she'd fought so hard against his seduction campaign because she didn't want to lose their friendship, and he'd been the one to convince her that would never happen because of how important she was to him.

Someone with as many advanced degrees as Dante sure as hell should have predicted the outcome of that a little better. But how could he have seen that he'd end up deciding to remove himself from her life *because* of how much he cared about her? The last thing he wanted was to negatively affect their relationship because of unalterable circumstances surrounding her child. It was much better to drift away, lose contact eventually like so many friends did.

"I have something to tell you," he muttered and dropped his arms far too quickly.

"Funny," she commented brightly. "I have something to tell you, too. I may have slightly misrepresented the thing Phillip had. They actually invited me to come with them but I wanted to come home. I had a lot of time to think about us on the flight and—"

"Us? Is there an us?"

Hope filtered through his heart greedily, and in two seconds, his mind whirled through a series of compromises that sounded incredibly selfish the longer he contemplated them.

Her expression froze and took his pulse along for the ride as she carefully picked her way to the long sofa overlooking the patio, where he'd given himself the first taste of her. She sank down on the cushions. "Well, of course there's an us. We're friends, silly."

She hadn't meant it the way he'd taken it. Harper wasn't looking for anything from him other than friendship. "Yes, always. And because of that, it's important that I tell you mine first. I'm...leaving."

Her brow wrinkled. "I know. On Sunday. That's what I wanted to talk about actually, because I have another doctor's appointment in two weeks and I'm kind of hoping you might be able to get away—"

"Today. In a few hours." He shut his eyes as the reality of it swept over him. She'd been about to ask him to be her official doctor's appointment hand-holder, probably for the remainder of her pregnancy. And he had to say no. "I'm going to Switzerland. There's an amazing opportunity there for me to get back into the lab. So I'll be splitting my time between LA and Zurich for a while. I don't think I'll be able to make it back to Dallas for your appointment."

The first bit of unease moved through Harper's gaze. "What are you talking about? I didn't know you were looking for a lab. What about your TV show?"

"I can do both." He shrugged. "There's a regular direct flight between LAX and Zurich, so it's pretty convenient. I just won't have time to come back here very often. I'm sorry."

She scowled. "Dante, what is going on with you? You promised to be here for me during this pregnancy. Couldn't you have just said no to the Switzerland deal?"

And here came the part where he had to twist the knife because she clearly wasn't getting the full, brutal point of the situation. "I've wanted to get back into the lab for a long time and working with your samples only solidified that. I can't say no because it's my deal. I put it together."

All the blood drained from Harper's face. "You did this on purpose? Help me understand. I want to be supportive of your career, but…this is coming from out of nowhere. What about us?"

"There is no us, Harper, that's the whole point," he said and yeah, it had come out a little more harshly than he'd intended. "I know you were expecting me to be involved in your pregnancy and with the baby, but it's… not going to work out."

She flinched as if he'd smacked her in the face. "You

don't even plan to be around later? After the baby is born? Switzerland is, like, a long-term thing?"

"Afraid so." He crossed his own arms in hopes that it might seal up his insides before they spilled out all over her pristine beige carpet.

"What if…things between us were different?" she whispered, as she stared at a spot on her skirt. "What if we were a couple?"

A couple of what? Idiots who thought that sex wouldn't complicate everything to the point of ruin? "But we're not. That's not even something you want. Right?"

Stupid, stupid, stupid. Why tack that question onto the end, as if the answer would make a difference?

But then she glanced up, tears gathering in her eyes, and said, "I think I'm in love with you."

*Oh, my God.* His insides fell out anyway, leaving a huge, dark hole where his vital organs should be as his soul processed the words he'd never have imagined falling from her lips. Words that could have made everything better—*should* have made everything better—but didn't. It was so much worse. Now he had to break both of their hearts. Push her away, hurt her, and do it well enough that there was no chance she'd hang onto the hope that her confession changed anything.

The irony. Harper had finally come around to what he'd known for a long time—they were perfect for each other.

Except for the part where they couldn't be together.

That was it—as open and as honest as Harper could be with another human being and all Dante had done with her declaration of love was sit down heavily on the floor, his head cradled in his hands.

"Did you hear what I said?" she repeated softly.

Admitting she was in love with Dante was a huge concession. One she hadn't made lightly and then only because her entire world was sliding away and she'd grabbed on with both hands, clawing back the destruction in the only way she knew how.

"I heard," he muttered. "Maybe *you* didn't hear what you said. You think you're in love? You *think*? I'm supposed to hang my life on the hope that you'll eventually be at least, what, seventy-five percent sure? Can I cross my fingers for ninety?"

"I don't know." Mute, she stared at him. He was angry. At her. For daring to say something so bold and huge as *I love you.* "I'm trying to—"

"You can stop trying. It doesn't matter because I don't believe you anyway."

"You don't—" She faltered. Had Dante just thrown her shaky admission back in her face and called her a liar at the same time? "You think I just randomly go around saying things like that? How dare you."

Dante rose up on his feet then, his expression black. Fierce. "Harper, you don't want to push me right now."

"I don't want to push *you*?" The Irish in her blood stirred and she leaped to her feet in kind, skin pricking with anger she'd never have guessed Dante could provoke. "I just flew three hours home from Washington after being on the ground a total of ninety minutes. Because I wanted to see you. To talk to you about how great things are between us. How becoming lovers is the best thing that ever happened to me. And you're *mad* about it. Please tell me how I'm pushing you."

All at once, he deflated, growing visibly weary as he slipped off his glasses, rubbing the bridge of his nose. "I'm not mad. I'm… I don't know what I am."

The sight of his bare face nearly undid her and she

wrapped her arms around her stomach, hoping to stem the wave of nausea that had risen up almost instantly as she realized she might never see him that intimately again. "You're my friend. Always. Me being in love with you doesn't change that. Isn't that what we've said all along? Becoming more only enhanced what we already had. I don't understand how everything just fell apart in the space of one afternoon."

Bleakly, he shook his head. "It didn't. It's been falling apart since you told me you were pregnant. Back in LA. I tried, Harper. But I can't be your baby's male influence."

The starkness in his expression sliced through her. Since LA. Since she'd flown to *Los Angeles*? That was a gut shot she'd never recover from. He'd not only rejected her love, he wasn't on board with her pregnancy. And hadn't been from the beginning. So what was all this? Simply a way to get her into bed? No. She could never believe something so monstrous.

"What are you saying? That you've been pretending all this time?"

"Yeah. Pretending there was a way this was all going to work out, when in reality, I'm the worst possible person for you to depend on."

"*That's* the lie, Dante," she whispered. "You've always been there for me. There's no one else in my life that I depend on more than you."

"In this, you can't. Not with a baby on the way. For a lot of reasons. But mostly because of who the father is."

His eyes burned like dark coals, unrecognizable. Unyielding. Because she'd asked Tomas to donate sperm.

And that's when her temper snapped. This boiled down to professional rivalry, nothing more. And *oh, my God.* Really? "That's a low blow, Dante. Never mind the loss of what I thought we were headed toward as we took our relationship to the next level. So we can't even be friends anymore? Because you can't get over the fact that a million years ago some guy beat you out for a prize?"

Wrong thing to say. Too harsh. Too much truth.

But her whole body ached with grief and disappointment and a dozen other things that she couldn't voice. She'd never done anything like this before, had no idea how to deal with the blackness swirling through her chest. Dante was her rock. He was supposed to make everything better, bearable. Not tear her apart with nothing more than a few words.

Dante's hands clenched and unclenched. He stretched his fingers out, examining them as he tried to find a measure of calm. But he just stood there and when he exhaled, his angry vibe hadn't diminished at all.

The look in his eyes scared her. She'd stepped way over the line.

"I can't," he finally ground out through clenched teeth. "The thing is, I tried. Don't you see how hard I tried? I don't tell you this because it makes me happy. It's killing me. I would have kept on trying but..."

His voice broke and took her heart with it. She ached to cross the small expanse of carpet because no matter what, he was still Dante, precious and special, and he'd always comforted her. But she didn't think he'd accept the same from her.

"But *what*?" she murmured. "Tomas? That's really so much of a deal breaker?"

If only... But filling in that blank was the path to madness. There was no *if only* in this scenario. She'd made an adult decision to have a baby and now she had to be an adult about the consequences of that decision.

Dante's nod was so imperceptible that it was hard to

fathom how that one small jerk of his head could bring her entire world crashing down.

Dazed, she fell back onto the couch. "So that's it then. You're done here. With me, our intimate relationship. With our friendship as a whole, I guess."

"Not because I want to be," he croaked. "Because that's the only way. I chose Switzerland on purpose, so there was no confusion."

The unfairness of it…the sheer injustice nearly overwhelmed her. "I didn't know I was going to fall in love with you when I asked another man to father my baby. Doesn't that count for anything?"

His brown eyes blinked shut for a moment and it was like all the light in the room vanished. When his lids opened, she knew the answer before he said it. "Sometimes we have to lie in the bed we made, no matter how lonely and cold it is."

And then Dante walked out of her condo, the place where he'd opened her world, introduced her to her first experience with physical pleasures, which in turn had become that much greater because her feelings for him had grown as a result. Only to ultimately give her the first taste of a broken heart.

# Eleven

Switzerland had been everything Dante had hoped for. Lab—check. Thousands of miles away from Harper and her baby—check. A large, multi-year project in the works that would definitely be a distraction from the morass of emotion weighing down his entire body—check.

Val was a great guy who deserved the funding Dante would provide. The whole team had welcomed him with open arms—no mystery when you packed your checkbook—but the marked lack of fans sold the deal. No one had even looked at him twice as he walked the halls of the think tank's building in an industrial section north of Zurich. The summer weather was similar to LA, so that even worked. He'd worry about the snow when it became a factor.

Best of all, *The Science of Seduction*'s producers had loved Dante's proposal to film a series in Europe that focused on new strategies he'd developed on the plane.

Nothing said romance like the quaint villages and breathtaking mountains of Switzerland.

Too bad Dante's enthusiasm was entirely faked. Looked like he'd learned to be a fairly decent actor while spending the better part of three years in front of the camera. No one had guessed that he'd left a large chunk of his heart behind in Harper's condo as he'd turned his back on the tears streaming down her face, a necessity because he couldn't be the man she needed. Couldn't be the father figure her baby needed. No matter how much he might want to.

Leaving had been, hands down, the most difficult thing he'd ever done. Even two weeks later, it still haunted him nightly. In the shower. At random moments when he should have been paying attention to a thousand other things. Because as she'd so eloquently pointed out, falling in love hadn't changed the fact that she was still his best friend. He'd lost far more than merely the woman he was sleeping with.

Ten times a day, he reached for his phone to text Harper a funny joke Val had told him, or lament the boredom he faced so frequently on the set as he waited for a costume change or makeup. But ultimately, he always put the phone back in his pocket.

He didn't know how to do life without Harper.

After two weeks back in LA to finish filming the current spate of episodes, Dante had the weekend off to pack and give Mrs. Ortiz some final instructions. Production was moving to a space the studio had found near the think tank and by this time Monday morning, Dante would be living in Zurich. For the next six months and more if he could swing it.

Harper would be late in her last trimester of pregnancy by then, and he did not have any intention of being near the States for the whole of it. Because he very much feared he'd run back to Dallas, desperate to see Harper again, to touch her, see her belly grow as the baby gained features, fingers, toes—things he'd never dreamed he'd want to witness until he'd already given up his right to do so.

But how could he be so selfish as to insinuate himself into Harper's life, and ultimately her child's, when he had no clue how bad of a father he'd be until it was too late? The risks were still too high. Nothing had changed just because he was miserable.

Dante's phone buzzed as he and Mrs. Ortiz wrapped up discussion on the relatively short list of things he'd given her to handle while he was gone. Funny how he lived in this house day in and day out but it didn't seem like much would change with him gone.

It was Howie, Dante's manager. Again. He'd been pestering Dante for a solid week about contacting the man claiming to be Dante's birth father. "What now?"

"It's about this guy, Edgar Gates," Howie said. "He traveled to LA to see you. I know you don't want to hear it, but before you leave for Switzerland, I really think you should talk to him."

Dante's lip curled. After the third round of unsolicited contact, he'd asked his lawyer to discretely check into the story and there was every possibility that Edgar Gates was indeed Dante's birth father. But why the man thought Dante would give him the time of day was the real mystery.

Obviously this problem wasn't going away anytime soon, and it wasn't fair to his team to continually subject them to this nuisance. A restraining order sounded like the most expedient solution. But suddenly, Dante had an inexplicable urge to face down the man who was the reason he'd had a miserable childhood.

"I'll talk to him. Tell him to meet me at Tango's on Santa Monica."

Dante ended the call. That was stupid. Why pick such a public place in the heart of LA to meet his supposed father? There'd be pictures galore plastered across the tabloids in no time flat. Too late now. And it was probably for the better. Odds were good Dante would think twice about making a scene.

This was the part where he'd normally call Harper. She'd tell him everything he needed to hear, that it didn't matter what this man said, Dante was still amazing and she was in his corner.

But he'd given up her friendship. For her own good. For her baby's good.

Dante arrived ten minutes early because he believed in being prepared. Still, his pulse jackhammered in his temples with no relief in sight, especially as a dark-haired man with a weathered face shuffled in the door. Dante recognized him instantly. Not because he'd met him before. But there was a certain familiar element to the man's features. His carriage. The way his gaze roamed over the crowd and then connected with Dante's—it jolted him into a near cardiac arrest.

Edgar Gates. No question about the man's claim. Dante didn't need a DNA test to know he and this man shared blood. But he didn't stand as his father loomed over the table, didn't offer to shake hands.

"Thanks for coming," Dante said politely because he had manners that he'd taught himself.

"You look just like you do on the TV." Edgar Gates stared at him as if he'd seen a ghost. "I watch you all the time. I thought I was imagining how much you look like your mother."

The man's voice coated Dante's stomach with thick nausea. He shook his head and bit back the years of anger, hatred and disappointment that had surged to the surface hearing this horrible human being speak of things he had no right to talk about. But really, what had Dante expected the outcome of this meeting to be?

He'd prepared himself for the possibility that it was a hoax. An extortion scheme. He had *mistakenly* thought he'd also prepared himself for the alternative, but that was far from true.

Swallowing the bile that had accompanied the surge of emotion, Dante waved at the opposing seat. "Please, don't hover. The time to be a helicopter parent has long passed."

"You're very successful." As he fell heavily into the chair, Edgar Gates's gaze roamed over Dante's face, taking it in but what he was looking for, who could say? "I would like to be proud of that."

"But you can't be," Dante broke in. "Because you had nothing to do with it. What do you want? You have five minutes to lay it out and then I'm leaving."

*Success.* What was the measure of that in Edgar Gates's world? Money? Fame? A Nobel Prize? Loving a woman until death do you part and raising a family with her because that's what people with honor, character and respect did?

Edgar nodded, wringing his hands. "I've got some medical problems—"

"And you want money." Dante nodded grimly. "How much? I'll write you a check and then you forget my name."

That was the easy part. His "father" would probably

do that the moment he walked out the door. It was Dante who would lay awake at night, wondering why he'd been unworthy of that simple family where he could thrive. Be loved.

"No." Edgar's lips trembled and his face turned ashen. "I wish it was that simple. You have to understand I'm here because I'm desperate. I got no right to be here, to ask anything of you."

"Agreed. So why are you here?" God, his arms wouldn't stop shaking. He crossed them and stuck his hands under his biceps, squeezing until he got the trembling mostly under control.

"I need a kidney. Or I'll die. Soon."

"That's almost too poetic for words. You're here because you suddenly remembered you have a potential match running around loose in the world. What's a dying man to do but look up the son he treated like garbage? It's been thirty years. What's a trip through the foster system between blood relatives, huh?"

Edgar didn't blink, accepting every harsh word as his due, which didn't earn him an iota of Dante's respect. "Is that what happened? Your mother put you in the system?"

"You don't know?" Disbelief squeezed what little civility remained in Dante's chest. "I was told by my caseworker that you left and she couldn't handle being a single mom. So yeah. Into the system. Until I was eighteen."

Why was he rehashing this? There was no changing it, no absolution. No reason to still be sitting here. Dante stood and Edgar followed him with his gaze, holding up a hand to stop him from storming out. It shouldn't have worked. But Dante froze in his tracks anyway.

"That's true." Misery pulled at Edgar's expression,

which was no less than he deserved. "I didn't do right by you or your mother. I took off. Had no interest in being your dad, but that had nothing to do with you. It was all on me. And I've paid for that, over and over."

"Oh, really. Your idea of absolving that debt and mine differ by leagues." His temper spiked, which was the only reason he was able to get the rest out over the knot of emotion in his chest. "No interest in being a dad, hmm? Guess what? It doesn't work that way. You don't get to decide whether you want to be a parent when the kid already exists. You man up and figure it out."

That was the rub. The thing he'd nursed in his gut for ages. And now he'd finally said it to the man who'd needed to hear it, which had been cathartic in a way he'd never expected.

A sense of calm came over him then, allowing him to sit back down so he could settle this once and for all. "Here's the thing. I'm pretty attached to my kidneys and I don't have a spare available for the man who was one half of the reason I never had a home."

Even now he didn't have one. The Spanish hacienda in the Hills had been so easy to walk away from because it wasn't his home.

Harper had been so hard to walk away from because she was.

Dante's temples throbbed as he stared at the man who had given him life but had nothing to do with who Dante had become. His success was all on him. Dante had made difficult choices, risen to impossible challenges, to create his own version of success. He'd studied enough psychology to know you didn't get pottery worth a crap if you didn't put it through the fire, and he could be man enough to accept that his childhood circumstances had driven him to succeed. Perhaps had even been the sole reason.

But he wasn't sure if he was man enough to admit he'd walked away from the only home he'd ever known because he didn't know how to succeed at loving Harper and being a real father to her child. Not because of Cardoza—that was a concern he'd almost gotten over. But because he had little faith in his ability to be a good parent because of how he'd been raised.

He'd chosen to let his pride and a fear of the unknown trump everything instead of letting the past go. That was on him, too.

Edgar nodded bleakly and stood. "I had to try. I appreciate your time. I won't bother you again."

"That's it? You came all this way, I say no, and now you're leaving? No, 'let's have a drink for old times' or 'maybe you could spare me a twenty to tide me over?'"

"I don't expect anything from you. I don't deserve anything. But I'm scared enough of dying that it was worth a shot."

This man was a coward. Through and through. The revelation thumped Dante between the eyes. It was the one thing they had in common—and Dante did not like thinking of himself that way.

But what else could he call a man who walked away from a pregnant woman, forcing her to be a single mom? The differences between Edgar's situation and Dante's weren't as vast as he would have said five minutes ago, and what Dante had done might actually be worse…because he'd done it to his best friend. A woman he loved more than anyone on earth. A woman who didn't have anyone else to lean on as she raised her baby.

Was he really going to choose fear over happiness?

Perhaps he might take his own advice and man up.

No, her baby wasn't biologically his. But if he made the choice to be a father, that would make all the difference. Who cared if the baby had Cardoza's DNA? Evidence that DNA didn't make the man lived inside Dante's own body and he would remember that he and Edgar had *nothing* in common every time he looked in the mirror.

Because Dr. Dante Gates, PhD, was not a coward.

In one of life's great ironies, Dr. Harper Livingston could not go into the lab at Fyra, the place she'd built from scratch, also known as her refuge. She could not walk through the door.

Too many memories. Too much association.

Chemistry and Dante had intertwined to the point where she couldn't separate one from the other, no matter its form. Her body cried for his touch as much as her soul missed his voice. They'd never gone more than a couple of days between phone calls.

She missed him keenly, in a way she never had before.

Morning sickness had walloped her the day after Dante left. Or as she liked to call it, *mourning sickness.* Because every fiber of her body felt black and sticky with grief. Why not throw an upset stomach on top, like the misery cherry on a desolation sundae?

The crackers and ginger ale Alex had recommended sat untouched on her desk. When Alex had gone through the horrific rounds of morning sickness, Harper had been the one to go to 7-Eleven to fetch whatever her friend had asked for. But Alex was on bed rest, and she'd already set the expectation that she'd take a six-month maternity leave. She wouldn't be around to fetch crackers for Harper. In fact, she wouldn't be around, period.

It wasn't that Harper needed someone at her beck and call—she'd been taking care of herself for a long time. It was the emotional support she'd hoped for. Long lunches where she shopped for baby clothes with her friends. Baby showers. Inclusion in the inner circle of motherhood.

Except Cass was spending more and more time in Austin and had started talking to a real estate agent about buildings near Round Rock. Of course the four founding members of Fyra would make the decision together, but everyone knew Cass hoped to move Fyra's headquarters to Austin before her and Gage's baby was born. Harper didn't have any particular ties to Dallas, and Austin was closer to her parents, not that it mattered. They'd never been an overly tight family.

Normally when she got in a mood like this, she'd call Dante and spill her heart about how lonely she was. He'd tell her a joke and say she would always have him to lean on. That small bit of encouragement would make her smile without fail.

Despondent and utterly helpless to change her attitude, Harper sat in her office and clicked through a few emails with zero enthusiasm. They hadn't heard back from the FDA committee about her new samples and the lure of creating something new in the lab had completely vanished.

She had enough new creation going on in her womb, thank you very much.

That thought cheered her slightly. It didn't matter if her friends weren't around. This baby would be her family. Always. The baby would be solely hers and wouldn't drift off to other relationships, other jobs, other cities.

Cue the waterworks. Pregnancy had thoroughly wrecked her. Or maybe it only magnified the reality of losing her best friend over the baby she'd conceived with the best of intentions. A woman with an analytical mind and zero ability to understand her own emotions had to create her own bonds in this world.

Harper sniffled into a tissue and when she looked up, the one man she'd never expected to see again filled her doorway.

"Dante."

Even saying his name hurt, rasping across vocal chords raw from morning sickness and crying jags that lasted until 3:00 a.m. She blinked but he was still standing there, watching her from behind his glasses, his eyes soft and tender. Completely unlike the last time she'd seen him.

"Can I come in?" he asked and when she nodded, he entered and shut the door behind him, leaning against it.

Hungrily, she took in the small details. New lines around his mouth and eyes that begged the question—jet lag? Or was he miserable, too, unable to sleep, unable to function without an anchor in his life?

"Of all the cities you could be in, this isn't the one I was expecting," she said and it almost didn't sound bitter.

He nodded, his spiky brown hair sweeping with the gesture because he needed a haircut but was probably too busy running around the globe to take the time. "I sold my house in LA."

That bobbled her pulse. "What? Why? Did you stop doing the show?"

"No. We're filming in Zurich now." He crossed his arms, his own gaze roaming over her in kind. "How are you? How is the baby?"

The laugh she managed wasn't the slightest bit amused. "Still in there. Still not fathered by someone acceptable."

"What if he or she could be?" he asked. "What if I said I wanted to be its father?"

The words hung in the air, laden with a promise that felt just out of reach.

"What are you talking about? You're an amazing scientist but gene replacement therapy is experimental, and even then only for the treatment of disease. You can't remove the Tomas Cardoza from my baby."

Nor would she if it was possible. She loved the baby the way it was already. No, this was a decision she'd made that Dante could not accept and everyone had to live with it. No matter how hard it was to see him again, to have him in her office, within touching distance.

He shook his head. "That's so far from what I'm saying. I don't want to fix anything about this situation. I want to embrace it."

Startled, she met his gaze and it burned through her with so much implication she couldn't interpret, but her breath caught because something had shifted. What, she couldn't tell, but the room no longer felt like Dante had sucked up all the oxygen when he'd breezed into her office.

"Embrace it?" That sounded an awful lot like he was saying he'd reevaluated...and had come back to tell her he'd changed his mind about them. But to what end—like he wanted to be friends again? Lovers until he jetted off to Switzerland? "How?"

He crossed the room in a flash, rounding her desk and then stopping short, as if not sure she would welcome his touch. In fact, she burned for him to take her into his arms and melt away all the dark, sticky places inside that he'd left behind.

"One hundred percent," he said huskily and leaned back on the desk as if he planned to stay awhile. "You. The baby. Us. Love. This is one of those all-of-the-above deals, in case I'm not being clear."

Something bright flared to life in her chest, nearly overshadowing everything else. But not quite. Because things were never that easy, not when it came to the unquantifiable. She had too much caution ingrained in her now. "You left, Dante. I told you I loved you and you threw it back in my face. You have no idea how hard it was for me to say that when I barely understand it myself."

Dante took that in stride without flinching and somehow, that broke the barrier. He reached out and slid his fingers into hers, then pulled her hand into the hollow of his thigh, trapping her palm against his heat, and holy hell did her Dante-starved body like that.

"I thought I was doing the right thing. For both of us. I tried to make it about Cardoza, but this was about my failings, my insecurities. My past. The problem is that I don't understand love, either. Obviously." His gaze caught hers, holding, evaluating. "Will you let me explain?"

She nodded and he told her the story of his birth father contacting him and how meeting him had surfaced so much anger about Dante's childhood. Some of which she knew about, of course, but she'd never realized how being in the foster system had poisoned him. His reaction when she'd told him she was pregnant made a whole lot more sense in that context. And her heart ached for the little boy who'd never been loved.

Which only made her love the man he'd become twice as much.

Dante concluded his confessional. "I should have stuck around and insisted we figure out how to interpret our emotions together. Instead, I left you. Alone. Because I was so scared of messing up fatherhood for your baby. That was a cowardly move and I'm sorry. So sorry," he murmured and lifted her hand to his cheek, kissing her palm so tenderly that tears sprang to her eyes.

"I forgive you." That hadn't been in question. She could never hold a grudge in any way, shape or form. "But I still don't understand. Why did you come back? If it was so easy to embrace all of this, why did you leave in the first place?"

His short laugh was anything but amused. "None of this is easy. The only thing that changed is that I figured out that you're worth the effort of leaving my past in the past, where it belongs. Being a father scares me. But being without you is worse. I tried that. It didn't work."

And that did it. The tears spilled over, falling down her cheeks as he smiled gently, wiping at her face with his thumb. Totally ineffectual when her hormones were driving the bus. Besides, they were happy tears. "It didn't work for me, either. Turns out I'm not a fan of sleeping alone. Who knew? That's what happens when you experiment. Sometimes you get results you didn't expect."

With a growl, he pulled on her hand until she came out of her swivel chair and fell into his arms. "I wasn't kidding about embracing this. I plan to spend a good chunk of the next six months in bed with you. Once the baby is here, we won't have much time to ourselves."

"I like the sound of that," she said, her voice muffled against his shoulder as she snuggled into his body.

"Which part?" he murmured in her ear.

"All of the above." And then she turned her head, just a little, until she got her nose right in the hollow of his throat, where it most smelled like him. Her insides quivered with unfulfilled need, but there was—apparently—plenty of time for that later.

"Harper?" Dante waited until she pulled back, brows raised, before continuing. His melty chocolate eyes speared her to the core as he looked at her and said, "I love you. Feels like I always have. And I know I always will."

Her heart filled so fast she almost couldn't stand under the force of it. But Dante had her tight in his strong arms, and he didn't let go. "The only question I have now is whether you're in the market for a permanent lab partner. Because I am."

"Depends," she said with a mischievous smile. "Do I have to wash all the beakers?"

He laughed, flashing his dimple. "I would be happy to hire as many beaker washers as the lady of the manor desires. I just want to be with you. For the rest of our lives. I want to wake up next to you and call you Mrs. Gates and put my name on our baby's birth certificate so he knows he's loved from the moment he's born."

Oh, God. That was the most romantic thing he'd ever said to her. She didn't even mind the tears so much anymore, which was a good thing since they didn't seem to have an end in sight. "In that case, yes."

"One additional small thing. Minuscule, really." He hefted her deeper in his arms, smoothing a hand over her back, and she felt it clear to her toes. "How do you feel about Swiss prenatal care? I hear they have one of the highest rated medical systems in the world."

Her eyebrows shot up. "Are you asking me to move to Switzerland with you?"

"I kind of already moved there. Before I knew I was going to ask you to marry me." He eyed her. "See, there's a think tank and I fully funded it for the next six months and our research is going so well, that I—"

"Yes." If Alex could live in Washington, Harper could live in Zurich. And if not, then when Cass moved the company to Austin, she'd sell her share in Fyra to the other three girls.

Nothing was more important to her than Dante and the baby they were going to have together. *Together.* It was nearly miraculous, nearly impossible to grasp how much she'd wanted that and had been afraid to hope.

"Yes? Just like that?" Dumbfounded, Dante gaped at her and she giggled at his fish mouth.

"I love you. I always have. You're everything to me, my whole world. No matter where you are, that's where I want to be, too. So you're stuck with me." The crackle in the air sent a shiver down her spine as he devoured her with his gaze alone. "Keep looking at me like that, Dr. Sexy, and you might find yourself naked in about four seconds."

"Oh, yeah?" he growled and, instantly, buttons started flying as he tore out of his shirt. "I like a woman who knows what she wants."

As they came together in a firestorm of passion that she'd never imagined would be so tender and meaningful, she murmured in his ear, "I forgot to mention that pregnancy does something wicked to me. I can't get enough of you."

"So," he mouthed against her throat as they slid together perfectly. "We're talking ten, maybe twelve, kids then?"

"Keep talking. I like what I'm hearing." And what she was feeling. *Loved.*

What an amazing series of chemical reactions, all of which had come together to make her a part of something—a family.

# Epilogue

When Harper got the text message from Cass, she almost ignored it. After all, it might be 3:00 p.m. in Dallas, but it was ten o'clock Central European Time and she had a hot date with her husband. Who walked in the door from the lab at that precise moment, draining her mind of everything but him.

"You work too much," she scolded with a smile, only for Dante to sweep her into his arms with a growl. "Careful. The doctor said you can resume normal activity next week. Not a moment before."

"If I'd known donating a kidney would limit how much sex I can have with my new wife, I'd have waited," Dante said with a mock frown.

"No, you wouldn't have. Your father was in bad shape and your heart is too big to have ignored his need." That was her favorite part of Dante's decision to become the father of her baby. He'd proven he had truly put his past behind him by offering something precious to a man he should hate for a lot of really good reasons. But the fact that he'd so generously given Edgar Gates the chance at life…it tugged at her heart. Dante was going to be a great father in spite of his lack of a good example.

Her phone beeped again and then again. She started to turn it off but then caught sight of the message. "Oh! Cass is calling a meeting. The FDA approved the samples."

So many emotions rushed into her chest as Dante whooped, hauling her close for a tight embrace. Tears of relief and happiness welled up at the corners of her eyes. And here she'd thought marrying her best friend in a small ceremony the week before had been the pinnacle of bliss.

Harper settled into her desk chair, and flipped on the computer to pull up the online meeting software, and the conference room at Fyra blinked into focus. Trinity was the lone C-suite member at the conference room table, but she owned it with a saucy toss of her head.

Cass popped up in a separate video window, her husband, Gage, also in the picture most likely because they were at home together. Then Alex's window appeared and of course Phillip had elected to attend as well since he'd been navigating the FDA meetings on Fyra's behalf.

"It's done," Phillip said without preamble. "The FDA approval is official. Full steam ahead."

Everyone clapped and Dante kissed Harper on the temple with a murmured, "Well done, sweetheart."

Trinity nodded. "Formula-47 never would have happened without you, Harper. You rocked this. Now let's tell the world about our product and watch all our hard work pay off."

"Yes," Cass agreed enthusiastically. "This is the best part, where everything comes together. The marketing campaign we've been working on can finally come to fruition. About that..."

She hesitated and Trinity's eyes narrowed, apparently honing in on that small blip in Cass's normally polished delivery. "What about that, Cass? This is my thing. I've got it."

"Well, the negative publicity over the tainted samples is a problem. Like we've discussed." Cass glanced at Gage, who put his arm around his wife in a sweet gesture that made Harper's heart happy. "I found a publicity consultant that I think we should speak to. Just to get some additional thoughts on how to mitigate the bad press."

Steam shot out of Trinity's ears and she nearly came out of her chair. "A consultant? I'm the CMO, hon. You can consult with me all day long."

"Trin, let the woman talk," Alex cut in mildly. "She's not saying you're not in charge. She's saying we need some damage control and why not outsource that while you focus on the campaign for the formula. That's all."

Cass chuckled. "No need. That's exactly what I was going to say."

Arms crossed, Trinity fumed a bit more and then said, "I'll listen to what the consultant says. But I get final say on everything suggested. Period."

"Cass?" Harper hated to bring it up, but it needed to be said. "We still don't know who was responsible for all of this. I think it's safe to say it's a lab employee and I'm too close to it to be objective. Thoughts?"

Whoever it was had a personal agenda, and they'd hurt all of these people in earshot. One way or another someone needed to pay for that.

Everyone grew quiet and finally Cass sighed. "That's on me. I need to close that down once and for all. Give me a day to come up with a plan of attack."

They talked for a few more minutes and then signed off in deference to Harper's pointed comments about the time difference.

And then she let her gorgeous husband take her to bed where he kissed her belly and murmured to their baby while she stroked his hair. The chemistry between them did indeed come with a hell of kick—in the heart.

* * * * *

# THE BEST MAN'S BABY

KAREN BOOTH

For Bryony Evens, my sweet and lovely friend.
May the handsome guy in the flower
shop always flirt with you.

# One

Julia Keys ducked out of the cab in front of her childhood home amid a hailstorm of camera flashes and shouts from reporters.

*Where's Derek, Julia? Is he flying in from LA for your sister's wedding?*

*Is it true you and Derek are shopping for a house together?*

*Any chance you and Derek will tie the knot?*

Ludicrous questions, and yet they kept coming. She wouldn't date Derek, her current costar, if her life depended on it. The idea made her queasier than her first trimester morning sickness, and that was saying a lot.

Dodging reporters and lugging a week's worth of designer clothes in a roller bag, she marched up the walk, past the rhododendron that had been in full bloom at the beginning of summer, the last time she'd been back in Wilmington. That was also the last time Logan Brandt had stomped on her heart. The very last time. Or at least that was the plan.

Her father raced down the stairs of the wraparound porch and folded her into his arms. "Y'all need to learn some manners," he yelled to the media militia assembled at the curb.

At least the local press had enough respect to stay off private property. The same could not be said for the paparazzi in a big city like New York or Los Angeles. A film career spanning nearly a decade had left Julia a reluctant pro. Judging by the frantic phone call from her publicist that morning, when the story of her nonexistent romance first broke, the press would be arriving in waves over the next several hours.

"Sorry about that, Daddy. Don't talk to them. They'll go away if we don't say anything." She pressed a kiss to her father's clean-shaven face. It was framed by thick, chocolate-brown hair—the same color as Julia's, except his had gone salt-and-pepper at the temples. The few wrinkles he had showed deep concern. Of course he was worried—one daughter was getting married, and the other, according to the strangers still yammering at them, had questionable taste in men. When her real predicament—the one that would make her father a granddad—finally came to light, she could only hope he'd stay as relatively calm as he was now.

Her father ushered her inside, which was only about ten degrees cooler than the eighty-degree day. She knew better than to ask her dad to adjust the thermostat. As far as he was concerned, it was September, and therefore autumn, which meant air-conditioning was no longer needed. Never mind that summer in coastal North Carolina could stretch on until Halloween.

Her mother strolled into the living room wearing a pink

sleeveless blouse and white capri pants, auburn hair back in a ponytail, pearls completing the look, as always. She wiped her hands with a checkered kitchen towel. Julia's younger sister, Tracy, brought up the rear. Spitting image of their mother and the bride-to-be, Tracy was a fresh-faced vision in a turquoise sundress, staring down Julia as if she were evil incarnate. Julia was now liking her chances with the school of piranha masquerading as the media outside.

Mom offered a hug and a kiss. "It's good to see you, hon. I feel so spoiled having you home for the second time in three months."

*Three months. Just enough time to get pregnant.* "The high school reunion was one thing. It's not every day my baby sister gets married." Julia went in for a hug from her sister.

Tracy was having none of that, planting her hands on her hips. "How long are we going to pretend that Jules isn't ruining my wedding? If y'all are going to stand around and chitchat like nothing is wrong, I'm asking Carter to fix me a stiff drink."

It physically hurt to know that her arrival didn't warrant a hug, but Julia couldn't blame her sister. If the roles had been reversed, she'd be mad as a hornet about the frenzy in the front yard. "I'm sorry about the mess outside, but it's all a stupid lie. The press has been hinting at something between Derek and me since before we even started filming. Trust me, I'm not involved with him."

"I saw the photos. You're practically kissing him." Her mother's sweet drawl teetered on *practically*. "Are you denying it because you're not proud of the way he's behaved? They said he's been arrested for public intoxication seven times. Why would you want to be with a man like that?"

Julia shook her head, sweat already beading up on her skin. If the press could sell this contrivance of a story to her own mother, they could convince anyone. "Mom. Listen to me." She grasped her shoulders. "I swear there's nothing going on with Derek. Yes, it looks like a kiss. We were rehearsing a scene. I have zero interest in him. And he has no interest in me." *And he has the world's worst breath.*

"Then go outside and tell those buzzards precisely that." Julia's father teased back the drapes, peering outside. "We spent an awful lot of money on this wedding. I'm not about to see it ruined."

If only her father knew the lengths to which Julia was already going to *not* ruin her sister's wedding—namely keeping a pregnancy under her hat, which was absolutely killing her. Why couldn't things be normal? Just once? If her life were normal, she'd walk into this room and tell her parents she was pregnant. Her mother would probably burst with excitement, then sport the start of a nine-month-long smile and ask a million questions. Her father would sidle up to Julia's loving, handsome husband and congratulate him with a firm handshake and a clap on the back. But of course, things couldn't be normal. No husband had materialized in Julia's twenty-nine years on earth, and that was of little consequence compared to not knowing whether her ex or Logan Brandt was the baby's father. Oops.

"You have to trust me," Julia said. "If we say anything, they'll just ask more questions. We should ignore them and focus on Tracy." *Please. Anything so I can stop fixating on wanting to blurt out that I have a tiny top-secret bundle of joy in my belly.*

Tracy snorted and shook her head. "Focus on me." Plopping down on the end of the couch, she broadcast her anger by aggressively flipping through a bridal magazine. "That's rich coming from you right now." Tracy had never been much for mincing words. Why start now?

Their father sat in his wingback chair. "Jules, I know you think you know what you're doing, but I've had my own experience with the media." Julia's father had been a state senator for two decades. Twenty-one squeaky-clean, scandal-free years. "If they've fabricated this much, they'll speculate until the cows come home. Who knows what they'll come up with next."

A heavy sigh came from her mother. "I can't even think about this anymore. I need to keep myself busy in the kitchen. Maybe open a bottle of chardonnay."

"See? Now your mother is upset. I didn't pay all this money for a scandal and an unhappy wife."

"Is that all you care about?" Tracy blurted. "The money? What people will say?"

"I have a reelection campaign to run next year. My family should be an asset, not a political liability."

Tracy tossed the magazine aside. "I swear to God, it's like I'm not even getting married. Julia and money and Dad's job are obviously far more important."

"We've never had a family scandal before, Trace. I intend to keep it that way."

*Family scandal.* If only they knew. Julia took a deep breath, but it made her head swim. A smooth start to Tracy's wedding was out the window, and it was all her fault. The guilt of that alone was overwhelming. Tracy had played second fiddle in the Keys family for the last decade, simply because of Julia's success. People were always making a fuss, as much as Julia tried to deflect. It was time for her sister to have center stage. Then Julia could avoid the family microscope and find the perfect time to break the baby news, only after the wedding was over and the happy couple was on a cruise ship to the Bahamas.

Tracy's fiancé, Carter, came downstairs. "Logan just pulled up."

*Logan.* There was that to deal with as well. Her stomach sank, adding an entirely new and unpleasant aspect to pregnancy queasiness. His hundred-watt smile painfully flashed in her memory. Then came the visions from their last time together. They'd spent nearly the entire weekend in bed. His bare chest, naked shoulders…and other glorious stretches of his tawny brown skin were all that wanted to cycle through her mind. *Damn pregnancy hormones.* Her pulse raced, stirring emotion—anger over the way Logan had ended things after the reunion, frustration over once again being the girl who never managed to do anything the right way. In between all of that was a churning sea of uncertainty. And some churning of her stomach as well. She was going to be a mom. And Logan might be the father. Or he might not. Either way, she had no choice other than to tell him, deal with his reaction and move on. There was nothing more than moving on between them, and that was to be done as two separate parties. Logan had seen to that.

But first she had to find the right time to tell him. Maybe she'd take the approach her mother did when she had potentially upsetting news to break to her father—she'd tell him while he was driving. A man could only freak out so much with two hands on the wheel.

Parked on the narrow tree-lined street, several houses down from the grand Victorian the Keys family had lived in since he could remember, Logan Brandt bided his time in his rental car. Sunglasses on, flipping the keys on his finger, he studied the reporters milling about, consulting their phones. Waiting.

"What a mess," he mumbled. The buzz of activity was normal when it came to Julia. Even if she'd never become a box office hit or had her stunning face land on the cover of countless magazines, drama still would've found her. As to the cause, Logan was so tired of this scenario he could hardly see straight. Julia was once again romantically entangled with a disastrous guy. One of her projects, no doubt, as he referred to them.

His phone rang. Carter, the groom-to-be, his best friend from high school. "Hey," Logan answered. "I'm just now getting to the house."

"Liar. You're sitting in your rental car because you don't want to deal with Hurricane Julia."

"How'd you know it was me?"

"Nobody in Wilmington drives a car that expensive. Well, nobody but you."

Logan snickered. He did have an appetite for nice cars, especially if they were fast, and if anyone knew him well, it was Carter. He and Logan had met freshman year of high school at baseball tryouts. Logan landed a spot on varsity, a harbinger of things to come—full scholarship to UCLA, eight years as a major league pitcher. Record-breaking seasons. Record-breaking salaries. Then a World Series, a loss, and a career-ending injury. His trajectory had never suggested it'd all be over by the time he was thirty.

Julia was a loss of another kind, although it dogged him in much the same way. His high school sweetheart, the woman who understood him better than most, and yet she'd hurt and disappointed him countless times. He must be a glutton for punishment, because he was still wrestling with his need for Julia.

"You have to come inside and talk to Julia about getting rid of the press. Tracy is freaking out," Carter pleaded.

"I doubt she's going to listen to a thing I say after what happened after the reunion."

Julia and Logan saw each other every year at their high school reunion. The meeting had several time-honored traditions that only they were a part of. First came the downing of a cocktail, followed by merciless flirting—laughing, innocent touches, pointed glances, the flipping of hair from Julia. After the second drink came a spirited round of one-upmanship, including desperate attempts to convince the other how "happy" they were. Once full tipsiness was achieved, the painful stroll down memory lane could commence, usually ending with a heated make-out session. In those instances, one of them was to cut it short before things went too far. It was customary for the other person to stomp on the brakes the following year.

The last reunion had veered off course. They'd both walked in wounded—Logan hated his new career as a network commentator covering the sport he missed terribly, while Julia had just been offered a role playing a much older woman. She'd also made mention of having been dumped by another boyfriend, but Logan had tried to ignore that part. They'd needed each other that balmy June night, and that translated into two unforgettable days in bed, making love, laughing and talking for hours.

Unfortunately, Logan had been shaken back to reality when he got to the airport at the end of their weekend and saw a tabloid story saying there was romance brewing with her next costar—the hapless movie star named Derek. True or not, it was too powerful a reminder that Julia wasn't capable of settling down. She was too busy trying to save the world, too drawn to an endless string of loser guys. Logan refused to be one of her losers. He'd had no choice but to end things before she hurt him again.

"Sorry you had to find out about her new boyfriend like this," Carter said. "It's gotta be tough."

"I'm fine. I'd already seen the papers. I knew all about it." *Just like last time. And every other time.*

"Will you please get in here so I can offer you a beer

and not feel guilty about having one myself at four in the afternoon?"

"I'll be right there."

Logan did his duty as Carter's best man, strolling down the aged sidewalk to the Keyses' house. The reporters yelled after him—mostly requests to get Julia to come outside, although there was one question about life as an athlete-turned-sports commentator. Logan didn't reply; he just waved. He wasn't about to chime in if they asked about Julia and her new boyfriend.

Mrs. Keys opened the door, welcoming him with a smile and a hug. "Logan Brandt. If my eyes don't deceive me. I hope you and Julia can play nicely today. We have enough drama for a lifetime."

Logan nodded, stepping inside and keeping an eye peeled for Julia. "Don't you worry about us." *I'll do it for you.*

Carter waved on his way into the kitchen. "Two beers, coming up."

Tracy rose from the couch, but grabbed Logan's arms rather than taking the hug he offered. Her eyes were ringed in pink. "Will you talk to her? You might be the only person she'll listen to about getting the press to go away."

"I don't know that I have any sway with..." Her name was poised on his lips when Julia waltzed in from the kitchen. Midstride, she froze. He couldn't move, either. Their eyes locked, and he felt as though he was up to his knees in a concrete block of memories, the most recent ones the strongest—watching her sleep in the early morning as his hand followed the contour of her lower back and a smile broke across her face. When Julia was happy, the world was a beautiful place, and she gave in to it, heart and soul.

For an incoherent instant, he wished he could take back

the message he'd left for her. The one that ended everything. Her pull on him registered square in the center of his chest—a tightening that said two opposing things: he couldn't live without her, but he had to stick to his guns or he'd end up romantic roadkill. "Jules."

"Logan." Julia didn't come closer, which was a good thing, albeit disappointing. She crossed her arms, building a fortress around herself. Still, her vanilla scent found his nose and warmed him from head to toe.

"How are you?" he asked. If ever there was a loaded question, that was it. Stress radiated off her, but she was as stunning as ever. Her silky chestnut hair fell about her face in waves, effortlessly sexy. His hands twitched with the memory of what it was like to have his fingers buried in it. Her peachy skin had a summer glow he couldn't place—she usually avoided the sun. It suited her. Perfectly.

"I'm fine. I'm ready to start talking about the wedding and stop talking about me," she said.

*I bet.*

"That's a wonderful idea," Mrs. Keys said. "I have a special treat for Carter in the kitchen, and then we'll get started. Trace, why don't we go over the schedule and you can fill us all in on the jobs we need to do."

Tracy pulled out a binder and perched on the middle cushion of the couch. Carter handed Logan a bottle of pale ale and took a seat next to his bride-to-be, putting his arm around her and kissing her temple. Logan had given Carter plenty to envy over the years, but when it came to this, Carter had him beat. Aside from a temporary breakup, Carter and Tracy's love story was uncomplicated and sweet. Logan would've done anything to have that.

Mrs. Keys triumphantly presented a platter of her world-famous deviled eggs to her future son-in-law.

Carter lunged for one the instant they were on the coffee table. "Oh, man. Thank you. I love these things." He popped it into his mouth and moaned in ecstasy.

Julia made a wretched sound and pursed her lips, turning away.

"You okay?" Logan asked as Mrs. Keys took the remaining spot on the couch, next to Tracy.

Julia clamped her eyes shut and nodded. "Bad experience with deviled eggs on set a few weeks ago. I'm fine."

"Oh, honey. I didn't know," Mrs. Keys said, as her husband grabbed several of the offending eggs. "I can put them away if you like."

Julia shook her head. "Don't worry about me. I know how much everyone loves them."

Mr. Keys sat in his chair, leaving the love seat for Julia and Logan. Once again, their gazes connected, and he had to fight to make sense of what his body was saying to him. The problem was, whenever she was in a foul mood, he had a deep longing to kiss her out of it. He was practically wired to do it.

Logan offered her a seat. "Please. Ladies first."

Julia rolled her eyes. "Such a gentleman."

"I'm just being polite."

"It's a little late for polite."

"No fighting," Tracy barked. "Julia, I swear to God, you're going to kill me. I need the maid of honor and best man to get along. The reporters are bad enough. Not that you don't have the ability to make them go away."

Julia sat, snugging herself up against the arm of the love seat, preemptively distancing herself from him. "I can only say it so many times. The story is fake. I know you all think I have the world's worst taste in men, but don't worry. I did manage to avoid this one. And if we just ignore the press, they'll leave."

Relief washed over him, followed by surprise. No romance with Derek? Really? "Julia's probably right. They'll get bored if you don't talk to them." Feeling considerably more at ease, Logan joined Julia on the love seat. "We're getting along just fine. No fighting."

Tracy's eyes darted back and forth between them. She seemed unconvinced, but returned her focus to her binder. "Give me a minute to figure out what I want everyone to do. Mom, can you look at this?"

Mrs. Keys slid closer to her daughter and the two became immersed in conversation. That left Carter and Mr. Keys to feast on deviled eggs.

Logan was still computing the revelation about Julia's costar. If the story was fake, had it always been? "So, no love connection with Derek, huh?" he asked under his breath.

"No."

"Never?"

"No, Logan. Not ever," she snipped. "After that lovely message you left for me, I'm surprised you care."

*Ouch.* "I never want to see you with the wrong guy, Jules."

"Okay, everybody. Listen up." Tracy straightened in her seat and started rattling off orders about the florist and picking up wedding bands, the baker and final dress fittings, like a four-star general about to lead them into battle. That left no time for Logan to continue his conversation with Julia, although he wanted to. At least to smooth things over.

Julia was scribbling notes as fast as Tracy could talk. "Got it. I'm on florist and cake duty. Don't worry. I'll take care of it. The only hitch is that I didn't rent a car." She cleared her throat. "Logan, maybe you can drive me."

"You're at the same hotel. It only makes sense," Mrs. Keys chimed in.

True. It *did* make sense, but he couldn't escape the feeling that Julia had ulterior motives. Something in her voice told him that she did. Whatever her plan, hopefully it didn't include ripping his head off and sticking it on a stake in the front yard as payback for the post-reunion breakup. "Of course. Whatever Tracy and Carter need us to do to help make this the perfect wedding."

# Two

Julia was sure there was no sound more unhinging than that of reporters politely, but incessantly, rapping on the windows of Logan's rental car, raising their voices as he tried to pull away.

"These people are ridiculous. Somebody's going to get hurt." Logan inched the car out of his parking space. The second he had a clear path, he gunned it.

Julia jerked back in her seat. Her stomach lurched along with it. "Logan. Cool it." She whipped around to look behind them. The reporters were climbing into their cars. "They're following us. Of course."

Logan watched via the rearview window. "We have to get out of here. Now."

He took a sharp turn and ducked down a side street. He knew the shortcuts like the back of his hand. They both did. They'd both learned to drive on these streets. The house Logan grew up in was only seven or eight blocks away.

Logan was intensely focused, eyes darting between the mirror and the road. He ran his hand over his close-cut ebony hair. Being so near him, it was hard not to fixate on what his stubble felt like against her cheek when he kissed her. Or the way his warm and manly smell, citrusy and clean, begged her to curl up in his arms. Everything about being around him again made her chest ache. Things were so much simpler three months ago, for that brief forty-eight hours when she could kiss him and lose herself in him without reservation. Before he ended it forever.

His hands gripped the steering wheel. With the sleeves of his deep blue dress shirt rolled to his elbows, she couldn't have ignored the flex of his solid forearms if she'd wanted to. His arms could make her feel as if she were made of feathers—light as air. Ready to be taken anywhere he wished to have her.

Logan cut over again, navigating the city grid. All while inducing an acute case of nausea.

Julia crossed her arms at her waist. Maybe she'd be too busy barfing to worry about telling Logan about the baby. "Can you take it easy? I'm feeling carsick."

"First the deviled eggs, now this? You're the girl who wanted to eat corn dogs and go on every upside-down ride imaginable at the state fair. Twice."

Logan had thrown down the gauntlet, only he didn't know it. Logan was a smart guy. She could only keep her secret from him for so long. As soon as she turned down a cocktail this weekend, he'd know something was up. His eyes were trained on the road. Time to put her mother's theory to the test.

"I need to know if you can keep a secret." She rummaged through her purse. It was better if they were both busy doing something that precluded a lot of eye contact.

"About what?"

"I can't tell you or you'll know the secret."

He shook his head, taking a left onto the main road to the hotel. "Fine. As long as it doesn't involve a murder, I can keep a secret." He stopped at a yellow light. Normally, Logan would've gunned it through the intersection, but there was a police car parked at the corner.

Why had her mother never briefed her on the protocol for stoplights? This was *not* the way this was supposed to go. Her heart raced, but the secret was going to suffocate her if she didn't tell him. She had to tell him. At least the first part. Then she'd reevaluate. "I'm pregnant."

The light turned green, but he didn't go. "You're what?"

Julia pointed ahead. "It's green."

"Oh." Logan had them again under way. "You're pregnant?"

"I am." She choked back her breath, unable to come out with the part that came next. *And you might be the father.*

"I take it nobody knows? Your family didn't say a thing about it."

"Nobody knows. I've only known for about three weeks and I didn't want to overshadow Tracy."

"You have to tell your family, Jules. They won't be happy you kept this from them."

Julia swallowed hard. *And how does the maybe-father feel about me keeping the secret?* "You saw how Tracy is. She's a wreck already. It wouldn't be fair."

Julia caught sight of the hotel. They'd be there any minute. That was bringing up a whole new set of feelings. If only her mother hadn't turned her old bedroom into an office. If only there was another good hotel close to home. If only she and Logan hadn't slept together the last time she was here. Then she wouldn't be suffering from vivid flashes of hot, bittersweet memories—his welcoming pecan-brown eyes, smoldering, telling her every sexy thing he wanted to do to her, all without a single word leaving his tempting lips. He was a man of action in the bedroom, not big for talk, but when he did speak, it was usually a doozy. *You're so damn sexy, Jules. You make me want to lock the door and throw away the key.*

He'd done such a number on her. She'd been stupidly hopeful when she was last here, foolish enough to think that finally she and Logan had gotten their act straight. Then hours after they parted, he left his message. *We'll never work. Let's just admit it. Once and for all.*

And of course, if they hadn't slept together, there was a very good chance she wouldn't be in the business of keeping secrets at all. She cupped her belly with her hand. However difficult, she wanted this. She wouldn't regret her time with Logan, however painfully it had ended, if it had brought her this baby. Her baby wasn't the problem.

Logan turned into the hotel drive. "I don't know why I bothered to try to outrun anybody. The bastards are already here." He pointed to a handful of news vans in the parking lot out front.

"There are only so many hotels between here and Wrightsville Beach. It wasn't going to take them long to figure out where we were."

They pulled up to the valet stand, reporters waiting, but no attendant in sight. Logan grabbed her arm. "Hold on one second. Let me come around to your side of the car. I don't want you out there on your own. You know what these guys are like, and we're on public property now. It's not like it was at your parents' house."

"I can handle myself."

"Look, Jules. Just cut a guy some slack and let me have my macho moment, okay?"

She cracked a smile. At least chivalry wasn't dead.

"I owned up to it, didn't I?"

"Yes. You did." She folded her hands in her lap to wait.

Logan climbed out of the car. The reporters shouted his name, swarming him like bees. He was at her door in a flash. "Take two steps back, everybody, and let Ms. Keys out of the car."

She put on her sunglasses and opened her door. At this point, nearly a dozen people with cameras and microphones had them surrounded. She hated this more than pretty much anything.

*Julia, where's Derek?*

*Are you having an affair with Mr. Brandt?*

The valet pushed his way through the crowd. "Oh. Wow. Mr. Brandt. Ms. Keys. I'm so sorry I wasn't out here when you pulled up."

Logan surrendered his keys and a ten. "If you could have our bags brought in, that would be great."

"You got it, Mr. Brandt. I'm a huge fan. A huge fan."

Logan smiled wide. He was always gracious with his fans. "I'll be sure to sign something for you before I check out." He held back the press with one arm while he put the other around Julia.

This probably wasn't the right message to send, not with the reporters here, but she liked feeling protected by Logan.

"Are you two a couple?" someone asked. If only they knew the extent to which they were *not* a couple, even if he could be the father of her unborn child.

Logan picked up their pace as they neared the door. Still, the throng crushed in on them. "Everybody, back off." His voice boomed above the incessant chatter. He swiped off his sunglasses and straightened, employing all six feet and several more inches of him as intimidation. His audience actually shut up for a moment. Hard to believe. "One step inside and I won't bother with hotel management. I'll call the police. Leave her alone and find some other story to chase." He took her hand, and they escaped through the revolving doors.

"Are you okay?" Logan asked, not letting go of her as they made their way through the lobby.

His touch sent tingles throughout her entire body—unrequited, one-way tingles that served no purpose other than to frustrate her. "Yes. I'm fine." She stepped up to the front desk. "Checking in. The reservation is under Brady."

"Marcia?" Logan chuckled.

"Jan Brady. I'm no Marcia," she mumbled under her breath.

The front desk clerk, who looked familiar, smiled and winked, seeming to enjoy the idea of being in on the joke of a celebrity using a false name. "But, Mr. Brandt. I see you have a reservation with us as well." Confusion washed over his face as he glanced back and forth between them.

It was then that Julia recognized the man—he'd been working the front desk when she and Logan had had their tryst. They'd ended up staying in Logan's room that time. Julia hadn't bothered to check in before the reunion, and by the time they'd arrived at the hotel, they were about to tear off each other's clothes in the lobby. Two rooms had seemed laughable.

But not anymore.

Room keys in hand, Logan and Julia filed into the elevator. An elderly couple had joined them. No one said a thing, and the quiet gave Logan's mind plenty of space to roam. Too much space. *She's pregnant? And it's a secret? Who in the hell is the dad?* He glanced over at her. *No baby bump yet. She's known for a few weeks. She can't be very far along. Wait a minute...* How far along was she? Could he? No. Not that. But wait. Could he be? The dad?

The elevator came to a stop. Logan held the door to afford the other passengers some time. He caught the uncertainty in Julia's eyes. There was more weighing on her. He could see it, and he had to know it all, even if it might hurt. They made it to the top floor—as Logan remembered it, the only floor with suites. Judging by their room numbers, they'd be across the hall from each other.

"We should talk some more," Julia said when they'd arrived at their doors. Her voice was ragged at the edges, an apt reflection of her nerves. Considering the pressure from the reporters, her family and having to keep her secret, she had to be exhausted.

"Yes. We should. I want to hear more about your, um, situation." He felt idiotic the minute he'd worded it that way, but at least he'd kept his promise to not say anything.

"I need food, too. I'm really hungry."

"Even after being carsick?"

"Yes. It's one of the weird things about...it. I feel queasy, but I'd give my right arm for fried chicken and a peach pie. The whole pie."

He was still getting used to the idea of Julia being pregnant. Talking about it wasn't helping. It was only making it more bizarre. "With the vultures outside, we probably shouldn't leave the hotel until we need to."

"Can we order room service and talk after I have a chance to change?"

The bellman came strolling down the hall with their two roller bags.

"Looks like your change of clothes is right on time. My room? A half hour?"

"Perfect."

Logan brought his suitcase inside and ordered food—grilled pork for himself, and with no fried chicken on the menu, he chose a steak for Julia, medium rare. Just the way she liked it, and she never turned down a steak. He then unpacked his suit for the rehearsal dinner Friday night, as well as the rest of his clothes, and changed into jeans and a T-shirt. He might as well get comfortable for whatever it was that Julia was going to spring on him tonight. One thing was for sure. She had a talent for catching him off guard.

Room service was wheeling in the cart when Julia came out of her room. "Sorry I'm a little late. I nodded off for a few minutes."

She *was* tired—enough to nod off. That was so unlike Julia, he could hardly wrap his brain around it. She never slowed down. There was always something brewing, always something to do, someone new to meet, some new adventure on which to embark. So this was her new adventure. A baby.

A sweet smile that was tinged with melancholy crossed her face as she stepped inside. It struck him as she padded past, leaving her soft and sensuous smell in her wake—she seemed smaller. Was it because she was as out on a limb as a person could be, all while trying to hide? Although she rarely allowed herself to be vulnerable, Julia was a very open person. Keeping this secret from her family must've been one of the most difficult things she'd ever decided she had to do.

She'd changed into a loose-fitting pink top and a pair of black yoga pants. Julia could work a fancy designer dress like nobody's business, but he really preferred her like this—relaxed. And he had to admire the rear view as he trailed behind her. "We can sit on the sofa and eat."

They started in on dinner, Julia confirming her claim that she was starving. She'd always been an enthusiastic eater, even when she was skinny as a rail in high school, but this was an impressive showing. "I've been craving red meat, too. So thank you. This is perfect."

He smiled and nodded, not really tasting his meal, still getting accustomed to the notion of the pregnancy. He'd already psyched himself up for her to tell him who the dad was, although he dreaded the answer—some hotshot CEO, a power-hungry producer or one of her toothy costars. And then there was the voice in his head asking if he might be part of the equation.

The moment was still fresh in his mind—back in his room after the reunion, peeling away her dress, drinking in the vision of her curves, it all hitting him in an avalanche—he'd waited for a very long time to be with her again. The way she moved told him that she was far more comfortable with her body than she'd ever been in high school. As she unbuckled his belt and kissed him softly, she'd said they wouldn't need a condom. She was on the pill. She'd also quipped, "When I remember to take it." Then his pants had slumped to the floor and further clarification of birth control was the last thing on his mind. That night alone they could have conceived a baby many times over, and it had been only the start of their weekend together.

"So. Pregnant. That's big. Really big." Why he suddenly had so little vocabulary was beyond him. He only knew that his palms were starting to get clammy.

"I know. It is." She gathered her napkin and placed it on the table. "I was surprised, to say the least."

"So this wasn't planned."

"No. It wasn't."

"How far along are you?"

"Three months."

*Just say it.* "And how is the dad feeling about all of this?"

She twisted her lips and turned to look at him with her

wide brown eyes. He'd never seen them so unsure. "I don't know, exactly. The truth is that I'm not completely certain who the father is."

His heart was thundering in his chest. He knew she had men falling at her feet, but was it really this extreme? "Oh."

"It's either my ex, the guy who dumped me right before the reunion, or…it's you."

His heart came to a complete stop. In fact, the only thing that gave him any indication the earth was still spinning was the bat of Julia's dark lashes. He sat forward and rested his elbows on his knees, nodding. Thinking. Processing. Once again, she'd surprised the hell out of him. He'd prepared for either answer. Not *both. I might be the dad? Or I might not?* He couldn't live long without knowing for sure. He sat back up. "We have to have a paternity test. Right away."

"I knew you were going to say that, but I don't really see the point. It's not going to change anything."

"It'll change a lot for me." His brain hurt from the suggestion that they not find out who the father was..

"It doesn't matter. Either way, I'm pregnant by a man who chooses not to be with me. Do you have any idea how terrible that feels? I need to focus on the good, for my own sake. I'm choosing to focus on the baby."

Logan still couldn't believe what she was saying. "I'm going to go insane sitting around for the next six months wondering whether or not I'm about to be a dad."

"I'm sorry, but that's just too bad. It's not going to change the fact that we aren't together. We'll have to wait until the baby arrives and then we'll know. It should be fairly obvious once the baby is born. I doubt we'll need a paternity test."

*Ah. I see.* "So the other guy isn't black?"

"He isn't."

Well, that certainly made that aspect of things convenient. But still the logistics made no sense. Was he supposed to sit in a waiting room with her ex and hope like hell that the baby came out with a skin tone closest to his own?

"I've thought about it, and the most sensible thing is to wait until then and you can decide how involved you want to be. We'll have to negotiate all of that. I'm hoping I can count on you to be sensible and flexible. I don't want to bring in lawyers," Julia said.

His head pounded. She was discussing this as if they were two multinational corporations preparing to merge. "What did the other guy have to say about all of this?" He winced at the thought of her having this conversation with any other man, even when he had no claim on her.

"He's out. Like all the way out. He wants nothing to do with me. He was pretty sure I made up the baby so I could get him back."

A low grumble left Logan's throat. What kind of scum would think a woman like Julia would make up a baby to get him back? And how did she end up with a guy like that? "He's out? What does that even mean? You get a woman pregnant, you accept responsibility. That's the first chapter of the book called *How to Be a Real Man*."

A tear rolled down her cheek. She wrapped her arms around herself and settled back against the couch. "Apparently he doesn't agree."

Logan had to fight back his rage. He sucked in a deep breath. If the baby was his, he'd take responsibility. "If it's mine, we have to get married."

A dismissive puff of air left her lips. "This is not the time for jokes."

"It's no joke. We're getting married if the baby is mine. You grew up with both parents. I..." His voice cracked, thinking about his father. "I grew up with both parents until we lost my dad. A kid needs both parents. I won't be able to live with it any other way."

"I'm not getting married to you. That's not happening."

"Yes. You are. Unlike this other guy you were with, I'm a man and I accept my responsibilities. We have to get married if the baby is mine." He wasn't even sure what was coming out of his mouth anymore. It seemed perfectly sensible in his head a few seconds earlier.

"And none of that matters, Logan. You don't love me. You want nothing to do with me romantically. Remember? You were very clear with your message after the reunion. Painfully clear. I can recite it if you want. It wasn't hard to commit it to memory."

He'd ended it definitively, there was no question about that. Clarity had been for the sake of them both. Of course, he'd never imagined she'd memorize his message. Had he been too cold? "What was I supposed to do? I get to the airport and you're on the cover of a magazine that says sparks were flying when you were auditioning with Derek. That was a week before the reunion and you'd just come off a breakup. That told me everything I needed to know about any future between us."

"There were no sparks with Derek. Why doesn't anyone believe me?"

"There's always some other guy around the corner, isn't there? Some mess of a guy who you can try to fix."

She shot him a final look of disgust before she bolted from the couch and stalked to the front door. "You can be such a jerk. Really. You have an uncanny ability to say the most hurtful things."

He rushed to follow her. "Wait a minute. We're still talking."

She squared her body to his and poked the center of his chest, hard, even though he had a good fifty pounds on her. Maybe more. "If you think the next six months are going to be difficult for you, how do you think the pregnant woman feels? How about the woman who got dumped by both of the men who might've knocked her up? Did you even take two seconds to think about that?"

"I asked you to marry me. I'm willing to play my part."

"You did not ask me to marry you. You were issuing a mandate. And that's not happening, anyway. I'm not marrying someone out of obligation, and certainly not a man who broke up with me. I'm done making mistakes when it comes to you." She opened the door and stormed out. It closed with a *thud* behind her.

Logan turned, his eyes wide open. No way he was getting any sleep tonight. Julia had given him more than enough to chew on.

His phone beeped with a text. *What now?* He wandered across the room and picked it up from the coffee table. It was from Julia.

We have to leave for the florist by ten.

*Great.* A whole day of wedding errands with the pregnant woman who drove him crazy, refused to marry him and might be carrying his baby.

# Three

Logan had been a royal jerk last night—selfishly worrying how he'd survive the next six months of uncertainty, informing Julia that he expected her to marry him. That was *not* happening. She could do this all on her own. She didn't need help from Logan.

Although she didn't mind the view.

"Oh. Hey. Good morning." He flashed a sheepish smile, standing in the doorway of his room, nothing more than a towel wrapped around his waist, beads of water dotting his shoulder. "I was just getting the paper." Bending over to pick it up, he showed off his perfectly defined back.

Julia stood stuck. His velvety voice delivered a too-sexy memory of their last morning in this hotel—Logan's long, warm naked body pressed against her back in the wee hours, his giving lips on her neck as he slid his hand between her knees, lifted her leg and rocked her world with the most memorable wake-up call, well, ever.

"Jules? You okay?"

"Morning," she sputtered, pushing a room service cart out of her room and into the hall. "I ordered bacon with breakfast, but the smell was making me queasy. If you want the leftovers." *Sexy, Jules. Real sexy.*

He looked both ways, flipped the latch on his door and crossed the hall. He raised the stainless cloche from the plate, grabbing some bacon. "Just two. The camera adds ten pounds."

"You're fine." She stole a glimpse of his stomach, just as hard and muscled as ever. He might not be paid to be an elite athlete anymore, but he maintained his body like one. And to think she'd reaped the benefits—those strapping arms wrapped around her, keeping her close, making her feel for two whole days that she belonged nowhere else. The price of admission had been far more than she'd been willing to pay—every shred of her heart. A big chunk of her pride, too.

"Ready in fifteen?" She braced herself against her door. Being around nearly-naked Logan was making it impossible to stand up straight.

"Definitely. I called down to the valet. We can go out the side entrance. They'll have the car waiting for us."

"You don't think the press will be tipped off by the eighty-thousand-dollar gleaming black sports car you just had to rent?"

He shrugged. "I'm not about to drive anything less. You'll have to suffer through it, babe."

*Babe. As if.*

Julia retreated to her room and tried not to obsess over her makeup or hair, but it was hard not to, knowing she'd be spending her day with Logan. He deserved to be tortured by what he'd so solidly rejected. It would likely be her only measure of revenge. She dressed in a swishy navy blue skirt that showed off her legs, black ballet flats and a white sleeveless top with a cut that left her expanding bustline on full display. Boobs. At least she was getting *something* out of this whole single-and-pregnant thing, other than a baby, of course.

She met Logan in the hall, and he just *had* to be stunning. So effortlessly hot in jeans and a white button-down, sleeves rolled up just far enough to again mesmerize her with his inexplicably alluring forearms. He led her out through the side exit and to his rental car. His plan to remain incognito was working perfectly until he peeled out of the parking lot.

"Why did you do that?" Her vision darted back to the hotel entrance. Sure enough, reporters were racing to their cars. "They're following us now." She shook her head. He always had to have his manly moment.

"Don't worry. I'll lose them."

He tried to shake the media as he had the day before, but they got stuck at a red light and he was left to lead a dysfunctional caravan to the florist, with his fancy car front and center. They found their destination a few minutes later, and Julia dashed for the door while Logan took his chance to reprimand the reporters yet again and tell them to stay outside.

Julia swept her hair from her face as a red-haired woman came out of the back with an enormous bucket of flowers blocking her view. "Can I help you?" she asked in a lovely singsong British accent. She plopped her armful onto the checkout counter. "Blimey. You're…her."

*Her. Yep.* Julia smiled warmly. It was the only way to put people at ease and get them off the subject of who she was. "Hi. You're doing the flowers for my sister Tracy's wedding on Saturday. She asked me to come by and look over everything. She's more than a little picky and I want everything to be perfect for her."

The woman nodded. "Yes. I'm Bryony. And I remember your sister. Very well. Come with me."

The bell on the door jingled as Logan walked inside. With a nod, Julia motioned for him to follow her, and he trailed behind her into a back room. While Bryony pulled buckets of blooms from a cooler, Logan assumed what Julia called his jock-in-command stance—feet nearly shoulder-width apart, hands clasped behind his back, shoulders straight, chest out proud. This was his way of taking in the world. She'd first noticed him doing it their junior year of high school, eyeing him when they played softball in gym class. What a joke that had been—like sending in an Olympic broad jumper to play hopscotch. No one had ever beaned a softball as hard as Logan.

He'd been so far out of her league in school that it took her nearly a year to get up the guts to talk to him, and only after he accidentally showed up at a party at her parents' beach house. Imagine the horror when it dawned on her during that first conversation, as she drank in the mesmerizing beauty of his eyes up close, that he didn't actually know her name. She must have done something right, though…he was her boyfriend a week later.

And when it came to part a year after that, as they both went off to college at far-flung schools, she'd taken the initiative and broken up with him. It had been a bit of a preemptive strike and her attempt to be mature about something. She was terrified to leave home, but she was even more scared of how badly it would hurt when Logan called her from UCLA and said he'd met another girl. Or more likely, another fifty girls. It wouldn't have taken long. In the end, Logan became the guy in her past she couldn't have. That was all there was to it. Circumstances, fate or other women—there was always something standing between them.

Logan waited dutifully next to her while Julia checked the array of flowers set aside for her sister. Her mother's penchant for gardening had left Julia more knowledgeable than the average person. She checked each selection off the list her sister had given her. Hydrangea, snapdragons and roses in white. Pink was for tulips, more roses and… *Oh no.*

"These aren't peonies," Julia said.

"Our supplier was out," Bryony answered. "We had to substitute ranunculus."

Julia shook her head. "No. No. No. Peonies are Tracy's favorite flower. She'll pitch a royal fit if she doesn't have them."

Bryony shrugged. "I'm sorry. That's the best we could do. They aren't that dissimilar."

"Logan, don't you think Tracy's going to be mad about ranunculus?" Julia asked.

"I wouldn't know a ranunculus if it walked up to me and introduced itself." He flashed a wide and clever smile.

The florist tittered like a schoolgirl at Logan's comment. "I'm sorry, but I can't make pink peonies magically appear this time of year. I told your sister there might be a problem getting them."

"I have to fix this." Filled with dread, Julia pulled her phone out of her purse and dialed her assistant, Liz. If Tracy didn't have the right flowers, not only would she freak out, by the transitive property of sisterly blame, it'd be Julia's fault.

"Julia. Is everything okay?" Liz answered.

"Hey. I need you to do something for me. Can you call your flower guy and have four dozen stems of pale pink peonies overnighted to the florist in Wilmington?

We need a very pale pink. Not rosy. Not vibrant. Does that make sense?"

"Yes. Of course. I'm on it."

"I'll text you the address. And make sure he knows it's for my sister. I need this to go off without a hitch."

"Got it. Anything else?"

Julia felt as if it was now okay to exhale. "That's it for now."

"Is everything else going okay? The press is really hammering you on this Derek thing, aren't they? And I saw you're hanging out with Logan. How's that going?"

Liz had worked for Julia for years. She might've heard her complain and wax poetic about Logan a few dozen times. Or a few hundred. "Oh, um, it's been fine." She couldn't say more, not with Logan in such close proximity.

"You know, if you wanted the press to go away, you could tell them that you're with Logan," Liz said. "They'll run off and speculate about it for at least a day or two. Or they'll turn it into more of a spectacle. Hard to know, but my gut is they'll take pictures, write their stories and hound Derek with questions about being heartbroken."

Julia watched Logan as he chatted up Bryony, who was blushing like crazy. If any man knew how to make a woman feel good about herself, it was Logan. His presence alone—just breathing the same air he did—made a girl feel special. Precisely why it hurt so much when he took it away. "Well, that's one idea. I'll think about it. Thanks. You're the best."

Julia hung up and took the florist's business card, texting the address to Liz. "The peonies will be here tomorrow morning. Everything else looks great. Thanks for your help."

She turned to Logan. He had the funniest look on his face—both bewildered and amused. She loved that expression, although if she were honest, she loved everything about his face—full lips shaping his effortless smile, square chin with a tiny scar obscured by scruff, and eyes so warm and sincere it was hard to imagine him ever doing something hurtful.

"Your sister is really lucky she didn't put me in charge of this," he said. "I mean really lucky. Imagine how horrified she'd be if she ended up with ranun…you know. Those flowers."

Julia granted him a quiet laugh. "Ranunculus. And you know how much I love my sister. I'm just trying to make the mess I made a little better. Now let's go deal with the cake."

The throng of reporters outside had grown. Either Julia was losing her patience or they were getting pushier. Logan made sure she got into the car safely, making her truly thankful to have him there. On the way to the bakery, she stole a glimpse of his handsome profile, allowing herself to think about what would've happened last night if he'd proposed for real, because he loved her. If he'd never called it off. If the baby was his. They could hold hands, they could stay up late talking for hours, they could make *plans*. Perhaps that was why she was so dead-set on making everything perfect for her sister. If she couldn't have the fairy tale, at least her sister could.

Fifteen minutes later, they arrived at the bakery and again had to sprint for the door as reporters shouted at them. They seemed to be at the end of their rope. There was much speculation about the reasons why Julia was running around town with Logan Brandt and not Derek. Not good.

Inside, one of the bakers led them to the work space where all three cakes were being decorated—one for the rehearsal dinner, the groom's cake and of course, the grand, three-tiered wedding cake. Julia took pictures with her phone and sent them to her sister. She got a quick response that, to Julia's great relief, everything except one of the shades of pink frosting passed muster. After straightening that out, and double-checking the delivery times and addresses, she crossed the bakery visit off the list.

She and Logan stood at the bakery window. The reporters were waiting, clogging the sidewalk out front. Logan was finishing a cookie he'd talked out of the girl working behind the counter.

"What happened to 'the camera adds ten pounds'?" Julia asked as he wiped crumbs from the corner of his mouth.

"I will always relax the rules for a chocolate chip cookie. It's my one weakness." He cleared his throat. "Well, that, and my desire to pop one of these reporters in the mouth."

"I don't even want to go out there." Julia hitched her purse up onto her shoulder.

He rolled his neck to the side as if working out a kink. "I don't know if I can take an entire weekend of this. I'm tempted to just tell them I'm your boyfriend to get them to go away."

*Exactly what Liz suggested.* "It might work," Julia muttered. Of course then she'd have to live with the story. And the myriad ways in which her sister would pitch a conniption. "I'd say we could go out through the alley, but we're still going to have to walk right past them to get to the car."

He took her hand. "It'll be okay. I won't let anything bad happen." He opened the door and out they went, back into the belly of the beast.

They narrowly escaped the reporters outside the bakery unscathed. One of them, a brutish man with a camera lens so long that Logan wondered whether he was compensating for some shortcoming, had become particularly curt with his questions. It was clear he just wanted an answer. And Logan was inclined to agree, only because he himself had reached the boiling point.

Now they were being followed in the car again. "Maybe it's better if you just say something, Jules. The only thing you seem to be accomplishing is frustrating them."

"I wouldn't even know how to say it. You know me. Give me a script and I can deal with it. In front of cameras, with unfriendly faces barking at me, I get panicky. The next thing you know I'm tripping over my words and accidentally telling the press I'm pregnant. And I'll have to spill the beans then. I'm a terrible liar."

"That's probably an argument for just telling your parents about the baby before you mess up and the secret comes out."

"No way. As long as you keep your end of the bargain and keep your mouth shut, it'll be fine."

"Personally, I don't think it's a risk worth taking. Just tell them. Then you can relax and enjoy the wedding."

Julia directed a piercing glare at him. "That's the most harebrained thing you've ever said. My plan is not only the best plan, it's the only plan. My baby. My plan."

Her plan. Jules was doing what she always did—putting her head down, forging ahead and ignoring what everyone else said. Like a beautiful steamroller. She was far better at handing out advice than taking it, which would make it impossible to change her mind. "And what exactly is the rest of your plan? What are you going to say to your parents about the baby's father?"

"I'm going to have to tell them the truth. You might be the dad. And you might not."

Hearing her say that didn't sting any less today than it had last night. "Have you taken the time to think about how they're going to react? Because there could be a lot of fall-out, and I'm sorry, but most of that is going to fall on me."

"You have to make everything about you, don't you?"

"No. I don't. I'm just thinking this through to its logical conclusion. Do you remember what your dad asked me the night I took you to senior prom?"

Her eyes narrowed. "What does that have to do with anything?"

"Just answer the question. Do you remember what he said?"

She reached into her bag, pulled out a lip balm and rolled it across her lips. Logan was thankful he was driving and only caught a glimpse of what she was doing. He had a soft spot for her mouth, especially for the things it could do to him.

"My dad asked you what your intentions were with his daughter. Doesn't every dad ask that?"

"Maybe in old movies, they do. My point is that your dad is an old-fashioned guy. And that's part of what I love about him. He's going to want to know if I'm accepting my responsibility. And I told you I'm willing to do that."

"Logan. You dumped me three months ago." She turned sideways in her seat and confronted him. "*Dumped* me."

He didn't want to feel remorseful about ending things with Julia, but he was starting to. Even though he was also certain that they wouldn't have made it through the summer. Julia would've gotten flighty. She would've started doing the things that made him question whether she wanted to be with him, and he never handled that well. "But that was before the baby."

"Precisely the reason this won't work. A baby is not a reason to be together. And I'm not going to be with some man who didn't want me three months ago, just because he's worried about what my dad might think."

"A child deserves two parents." It bothered him to hear his voice crack like that. A few words and the pain of losing his dad returned to the center of his chest, just as it had the night before. After all these years, it hadn't gotten easier; there were merely longer stretches of time when he could focus on other things. It was hard enough to think about how difficult it'd been on his mom to shoulder the responsibility of three boys, a mortgage and law school. It was even more difficult to recall the promise he'd made at the age of twelve, to his father, his hero, as he slipped away. *Don't worry. I'll be the man of the house. I'll take care of Mom and my brothers.* "I have to accept my responsibility. I owe you that much, and I won't allow your dad to think anything less."

Logan pulled up to the curb out in front of the Keyses' house. The reporters were parking their vans and cars. They'd be descending on them in no time. "We have to make a run for it, Jules. Now."

She gathered her things. Logan hopped out of the car and hurried around to Julia's side. They squeezed past the reporters, walking upstream against a rush of people coming at them. The obnoxious man with the big camera elbowed his way next to Julia, butting into her with his shoulder. The woman behind him pushed ahead. Too many people. On a narrow sidewalk flanked by parked cars and azalea bushes.

Julia stumbled. Her fingers splayed to brace her fall. Her purse flew out of her hand. Muscle memory took over. Logan lunged like an outfielder going for the ball. He curled his arm around Julia, pulling her into him. Everyone came to an abrupt stop.

"Are you okay?" he gasped. Adrenaline surged through his veins. That was too close. She could've been hurt. The baby could've been hurt.

She shook like a leaf, telling him exactly how rattled she was. "I'm okay."

"Don't move." He plucked her purse from the sidewalk and handed it to her. Turning back, he positioned himself directly between Julia and the reporters. He spread his arms wide. If they were going to come another step closer to her, they'd have to go through him. He set his sights on the reckless cameraman. "If you come within fifty feet of her again, you're going to be a very unhappy guy." *More like you're going to be in traction.*

The man puffed out his chest. "Are you threatening me? The sidewalk is a public right-of-way. We have the right to ask questions."

If only there weren't so many cameras trained on him. Two minutes and this guy would know not to get in Julia's face again. Reluctantly, Logan lowered his arms. He hated to do it, but he had to back down or this would escalate. He couldn't manage to unclench his balled fists, though. "Why don't you show some decorum? We're here for a wedding."

"Yesterday she was linked with one of the biggest stars in Hollywood, and now she's at her sister's wedding with her old boyfriend, one of the most successful athletes of the last decade. You can't blame us for wanting to know what's going on."

"Julia, just tell us if you dumped Derek for Logan and we'll leave you alone," one reporter shouted.

"Yeah. Just tell us," another voice chimed in. "Are you cheating on Derek? Is that why he's not with you for your sister's wedding?"

*Oh hell no. Cheating? With him?* Steam was about to pour out of Logan's ears. He turned back to Julia. The color had been sapped from her face. She looked so defenseless, not at all the self-assured woman he knew. All he could think about was the other helpless person in the middle of this—the baby. God, he'd been an ass last night. Julia was stuck at the center of two crises—Derek and the pregnancy—and he'd let his ego get in the way. The question of paternity was painful for him, but she had to live with much more. He did an abrupt about-face. "Julia and I are together. We're a couple. There's nothing with Derek."

For a second, everyone shut up. Then came a single question. "Is it serious?"

He had to act. And he had to say yes. What kind of man says he isn't serious about the woman he got pregnant? Once the baby news got out, that would be the media's logical assumption. "Yes. It's serious. Now leave us alone, please. Her sister is getting married and the family would like some peace."

"Give us a kiss for the cameras first," one of the reporters said. "So we know it's real."

"Don't push it," left Logan's lips before he realized what he was saying. He couldn't help it. Telling the press no was his gut instinct. And a kiss? As if his feelings weren't confused enough. Not that he didn't want to kiss her. He'd spent a good deal of time in her parents' living room yesterday wishing he could do exactly that. Before things got complicated. Again.

The reporters complained and grumbled. *Just a kiss and we're out of here.*

He was about to tell them to forget it when delicate fingers slipped into his hand. *Julia.* He turned. A sweet smile crossed her face. The color had returned to her cheeks. Although by the way she was now gripping his hand, he was fairly certain the flush was anger, not acquiescence.

"If you guys promise to let my sister get married in peace, you can have your kiss. But you have to promise." The words were for the reporters, but she directed them at

Logan. Her lips—the lips he'd fixated on so many times, were waiting right there for him. Pouty and plump.

*We promise.*

He didn't risk waiting another second, threading his arm around her waist. He witnessed the graceful closing of her eyes and took that as his cue to do the same, to shut out the press and tune out everything around them. When it was Julia and him, all alone, things could be right. It was the rest of the world that made things complicated. Her lips sweetly brushed his—a hint of warmth and sugar, enough to make the edges of his resolve melt and trickle away.

Pressing against her, he felt the newness between them. There was no visible baby bump yet, but there was undoubtedly something new there—a slight, firm protrusion of her belly. That hadn't been there at the beginning of the summer. New life. Was the baby his? Could it bring Julia back to him? Could it bring him back to Julia? Could he really get past that feeling that things would never be right between them?

Just like that, Julia ended the kiss and stepped away, turning toward the house. There was no sentiment, no moment of recognition for what had happened between them.

Logan cleared his throat, trying to conceal how disoriented he was. He was as thrown for a loop by her choice of tactics with the media as he was by his own. Julia, and that kiss, had turned his thinking upside down. "There you go, guys. I expect you to hold up your end of the deal." He turned to Julia and grasped her elbow to usher her ahead, but she stood frozen on the sidewalk. He caught the surprise on her face as she stared ahead at her parents' front porch. He followed her line of sight. The whole family was standing there—Mr. and Mrs. Keys, Tracy and Carter. Judging by their expressions, they'd heard—and seen—it all.

There were car doors closing and engines starting behind him. Probably the vultures on their way to the closest Wi-Fi hotspot to break the news. Or in reality, his little white lie.

"Tell me you didn't just start what I think you did," Julia muttered under her breath, smiling and waving at her parents.

Logan adopted the same phony grin and began walking up the sidewalk, squeezing Julia's hand.

"Tell me you didn't just do what I think *you* did. A kiss?"

"What about you? It's serious?"

His pulse was thumping, but he was sure he'd done the right thing. Mostly sure, at least. "I didn't have a choice," he mumbled. "Somebody was going to get hurt. You were going to get hurt. I had to make them go away. And you're worried about ruining your sister's wedding. That was going to ruin your sister's wedding."

# Four

Tracy wasted no time letting her opinion be known. "Nice job making my big weekend all about you." She whipped around and stormed into the house.

Logan grimaced and shrugged, apparently at a loss for words. Julia wasn't doing much better. She was too busy trying to get her bearings after the kiss.

*We're together?*

This was a bad idea.

Fake romance or real, there would be no opening of those old wounds.

And yet here she was, holding Logan's hand, scaling the stairs to the wraparound porch and filing inside her parents' house. Logan closed the door after her, while her father clapped him on the shoulder.

The grin on her dad's face was as wide as the beach at low tide. "Sounds like I'll be marrying off a second daughter soon. Julia's mother and I had always hoped this day would come."

*Married?* Good God, what was it with the men in Julia's life assuming marriage was the next logical step? "Dad, isn't that a little presumptuous?"

"The man said serious. What else am I to presume?"

"We're so happy, Jules. We've always thought Logan was the only one for you." Her mother's ability to radiate warmth and happiness made everything worse. How would her parents feel when she told them her secret on Sunday? Would they only be happy for her if Logan was indeed the dad? Precisely the reason she didn't want a paternity test. She didn't want her baby to be judged because of who his or her father might be. It was such an old-fashioned fixation, anyway. She could be a mom on her own, with no need for a man. The baby was Julia's, and that was all anyone needed to know.

Julia sucked in a deep breath, not knowing what to say. Logan had put them in a horrible position. And admittedly, Julia had probably made it worse with the kiss, but the press had said they'd go away. She wanted that insurance. Still, playing fast and loose with the truth… Julia might be an actress, but she sucked at lying. "Logan and I aren't together. He just said that to make the press go away."

"I knew it!" Tracy exclaimed, breaking her momentary silence. "At least Logan cared enough about me to do something about the problem." She shot Julia a pointed stare. "Unlike my sister."

"What about the kiss? That's what really made them go away."

Logan nodded in agreement. "True. The kiss was definitely Julia's idea."

*Don't remind me.*

"The kiss was fake?" Her mother's voice was rife with distress, just as it had been the day before when this all started. "No. It couldn't have been. It was so sweet. It looked real."

*I bet.* Julia still felt that kiss all over every inch of her body. Damn Logan and his resolve-destroying lips. "It was just what they asked for. A kiss for the cameras. Nothing else. I am a halfway decent actress, you know."

Julia had thought she'd have to fake her way through it, that she was still too mad at Logan for the way he'd treated her. That wasn't the way it had gone at all. The second his lips fell on hers, her body cast aside any hurt feelings and went for it. Her traitorous mouth knew exactly what to do, and sought his warmth and touch, his impossibly tender kiss. Her body knew how perfectly they fit together, physically at least, and was all too eager to find a way for them to squeeze three months of lost time into a few short heartbeats.

Logan stepped forward. "Actually, it's not entirely true that Julia and I aren't together."

If Julia could've clamped her hand over Logan's mouth and make it look like an accident, she would have. Tracy threw up her hands, stomped once on the hardwood floor with her jeweled beachcomber sandal and began pacing the room. "Which is it? Will you two get your act together so we can go back to enjoying my wedding week?"

And to think that earlier today, Julia's big concern had been shades of pink frosting. Now she was far more worried about shades of red. Namely the various hues of crimson coloring her sister's face. Volcano Tracy was about to blow.

"I spent the last six months worrying about everything that could go wrong," Tracy continued, circling the room. "Would the church put us down for the wrong date? Would I find the perfect dress? Would the caterer serve fish instead of chicken? I never imagined that the person who would ruin it would be my own sister. You just can't let me have the spotlight. You *have* to create all of this drama. You can't live without it, can you?"

Julia's father stuffed his hands into the pockets of his flat-front khakis. "Now wait a minute, Trace. We're just having a conversation. Your mother and I would like to know what exactly is going on with Logan and Julia."

*Yeah, Dad. Get in line.*

"Julia and I had a long talk last night about..." Logan started, looking over to Julia as if he was waiting for her to say that now was a good time to come out with the baby news, which it absolutely was not.

Julia felt as though she was going to be sick. She tried to send him direct messages with her eyes. *One word and I'll never speak to you again.*

"Julia and I had a long talk about things," Logan finished, scratching his head. "No one should put the idea of Julia and me, together, out of the realm of possibility."

Julia would've let out a massive sigh of relief about the baby secret still being under wraps if she weren't so annoyed. The two of them together was out of all realms. She'd wasted enough of her life on men who didn't love her.

The smirk on Tracy's face showed zero amusement. She wagged her finger in the air. "Oh no. I'm calling BS on this. Jules, you told me you two were done. And with good reason, remember? I didn't spend all those hours on the phone listening to you cry for nothing."

Tracy had indeed clocked a lot of time listening to her sob into the phone. She knew Julia and Logan's long history, the one that had taken its first horrible turn when Julia broke up with Logan before they both went off to college. Tracy had listened to Julia complain year after year about the women Logan was linked to in the tabloids—always models, always stunning and perfect, one of them even becoming his fiancée for a short time. Even though his engagement hadn't lasted, it ate at Julia like crazy, and Tracy had to suffer right along with her sister. Tracy knew exactly how dysfunctional they were together.

"Tracy Jean. I don't know why you'd be so rude to your sister," their mother said.

"Come on, hon." Carter walked up behind Tracy and set his hands on her shoulders. "Why don't you and I go in the kitchen and get a nice, cold drink?"

Tracy shrugged her way out of Carter's grip. "Oh, please. I love you, but you don't see what's going on, and you're yet another person who thinks Logan can do no wrong. And Mom, don't even start with rude. All I'm saying is that Julia and Logan have zero business being together. That ship has sailed. I mean, seriously, Jules? After what happened after the reunion?"

*Well, then.* Was Tracy about to air Julia's dirty laundry in front of their parents? Julia's mind raced for diversion tactics. If only an earthquake could hit the coast of North Carolina right now. Or a hurricane, at least.

"Did I miss something?" Julia's father asked.

Logan cleared his throat and bugged his eyes at Julia. As if that was going to help her figure a way out of this mess. Or keep Tracy's mouth from running. Sweat dripped down Julia's back, part nervousness, part the iron fist her dad used to rule the thermostat. "Dad, can we please turn on the air-conditioning?"

"Julia and Logan slept together," Tracy blurted, not giving her dad a chance to answer. "And then he dumped her."

Julia braced for a gasp of disgrace from her mother or a disapproving grunt from her father.

"I'm sorry to hear that," Julia's mother said. "But couples have rough patches. You and Carter should know that better than anyone. You two broke up for an entire year before you got back together and got engaged."

"You're both smart. I'm sure you'll work everything out," their father said, easing into his wingback chair as casually as if they'd all been discussing where to go to dinner.

*I'll be damned.* That in itself was pure evidence of how much her parents adored Logan. Talk of premarital sex—words spoken out loud, in the living room of the scandal-free state senator from New Hanover County and his wife no less, and not a judgmental peep came from either of them.

"This really doesn't seem like a topic for polite conversation," Julia said. *Or even impolite conversation.* "Let's get back to focusing on the wedding. Logan got the press to go away. Let's be thankful for that."

Tracy arched her eyebrows and cracked a fake smile. "The only way it stays that way is if you two put on a convincing show. For everyone. The wedding guests, the people at your hotel. All of our friends and family. They can't all be in on your little lie, or it'll just get out and that will bring back the press with a vengeance."

*Oh no.* Julia's stomach sank. Tracy was right. They couldn't trust anyone beyond these four walls with the truth. Julia didn't even want to think about the return of those awful reporters, especially the guy with the big lens. They were going to have to put on a show. A convincing show of love and affection and romance. Great. Julia sighed. If that was what it would take, then fine. For now, she only wanted peace and calm. And somewhere to sit. And maybe a cheeseburger.

Her grandmother's antique cuckoo clock in the foyer chimed three o'clock, which really meant it was two thirty. The thing had never worked right. "The afternoon is wasting away. Trace, don't you and I have a date to decorate the beach house for the rehearsal dinner? It's our only real chance for sisterly bonding this weekend." *And I can unruffle a million feathers.*

"Honestly, Jules, you ruined it. I need a nap so I can calm down. I'm worried I might strangle you if we spend any time alone."

Julia swallowed, hard. That certainly clarified things. "Okay. I understand."

"Tell you what," Logan interjected. "Jules and I will take care of the decorating."

*There he goes.* Logan Brandt to the rescue.

"That would be wonderful," her mother said. "Plus, it sounds like it'll be good for you two to have some alone time."

*Alone time. Good Lord.*

"Happy to do it," Logan said.

"Yep." Julia nodded. Speaking as little as possible seemed like the only way to make a graceful exit from this house. Her entrance had been anything but.

After a quick trip to the bathroom, Julia joined Logan in the car, and they were on their way to perform their new wedding duties.

"I'm starving." Julia tore open the wrapper on a protein bar she'd stuck in her purse. Her stomach rumbled, but gladly accepted the sustenance. "And this isn't going to be enough. I need real food."

Logan nodded, surveying the road ahead, a wide stretch of shopping plazas, gas stations and eateries. "Unless you want to find a sit-down restaurant, your options are chain fast food or biscuits."

*Ooh.* The dilapidated sign for Sunset Biscuit Kitchen was straight ahead. It'd been years since she'd eaten there. It wasn't exactly camera-friendly cuisine, but her pregnant appetite had her salivating at the thought of their fluffy, buttery pieces of heaven. "Biscuits."

"I was hoping you'd say that." Logan pulled into the parking lot of the restaurant, which was really more like a shack, with a battleship-gray exterior and a faded red roof. There was no drive-through or dining room—just a walk-up window and if memory served, lightning-fast service. "The usual? Fried chicken biscuit and a hash brown?"

"How do you remember this stuff?"

"I remember everything."

That was indeed her standard, very unhealthy order. But she wanted more than that. "Can you also get me a sausage and egg biscuit? And an extra biscuit with honey? You know. Just in case."

Logan nodded and smiled. "I like this whole pregnant and hungry thing. It's adorable."

"Adorable?"

"It's a nice change of pace. I spend entirely too much time with women who order side salads and nothing else."

As if Julia wanted or needed the vision of Logan's penchant for supermodels planted in her head. "Yeah, well, I'm going to have to spend every waking minute in the gym after this baby is born. But for now, I want to eat everything."

"I'm on it. One order of everything, coming up."

Logan hopped out of the car and strolled up to the ordering window. Maybe it was the aftershocks of the kiss, but she had to admire him as he walked away. How could she not? From a purely objective standpoint, one having nothing to do with hurt feelings or history, he was a spectacular specimen.

Luckily, the line wasn't long in the middle of the afternoon. Julia didn't think she could endure much of a wait. Logan was back in a few short minutes, white parchment bag, two bottles of water and a fat stack of paper napkins in hand.

He opted to drive and eat, and they went for an entire fifteen minutes without argument or conflict, Julia's stress level dropping with each artery-clogging but oh-so-delicious bite—crispy buttermilk fried chicken tucked inside a light-as-air biscuit. But then Logan finished his sandwich.

"I can't believe you couldn't keep our secret until we had a chance to talk about it. I had it all worked out and you ruined it."

"Our secret? Oh, no. That was your secret, not mine. You need to have your head examined. You made everything fifty times more complicated."

"I made the press go away, didn't I?"

"Yes. And apparently my parents would like to present you with a key to the city for doing so. In the meantime, they're going to be that much more confused on Sunday when I tell them about the baby. They're going to be asking themselves what exactly did all of that mean. Especially when you had to tell them that we talked about us last night."

"It doesn't have to be confusing, Jules. If you'd think about reality for a minute and realize that I'm your best shot at giving the baby a real father."

She knew for a fact he wasn't thinking straight. He was letting his macho brain run the show, and that never went well. He was relishing the idea of being her knight in shining armor, and although she appreciated the gesture, she knew how empty a promise it was. As soon as he realized the reality of what he was saying, of what he was getting into, he'd take it back. And then where would she be? Right where she was the last time he rejected her.

Plus, she knew Logan. He hated every guy who had

come along after him. Every last one. There was no way he would want to play Dad if it turned out that her ex was the father. She always stopped herself before she got much further in her thinking, wondering what that moment would be like. It was better for her to think of the baby only as hers—50 percent of her DNA, 100 percent of her heart. Julia wouldn't allow paternity to cloud her feelings for her child. Her future was the baby, making it work, finding happiness in what would become the new normal. Mother and child. Everyone else could worry about themselves.

"Right now, I'm focused on the only thing I can control, which is being a good mother. I can't afford to depend on anyone else, especially not a man."

"It's not a sign of weakness to count on someone."

"I'm not worried about how it might look if I agree with you. I'm worried about how bad it would feel if and when you changed your mind. Plus, let's not forget the most damning detail."

He stopped at the stoplight that T-boned into Lumina Avenue signaling for the left turn. It was as if they'd turned back the clock thirteen years and he remembered exactly where they were going. "Well? I'm waiting for the most damning detail."

Julia sighed quietly and looked out the car window, admiring the gorgeous shades of pink and purple that colored the edges of the darkening late-afternoon sky. So beautiful. So romantic. "We aren't in love, Logan."

*Well, one of us isn't.* The realization had been there in her head from the moment she saw him yesterday. Everything she'd convinced herself of over the summer was wrong. She wasn't over him at all. She was just going to have to try harder. It was a matter of survival. Of course, that wasn't going to be easy when they were keeping up their charade for the public and the array of guests at the wedding. She could see it now. Holding hands. Pet names. Kissing. Good God, kissing. How was she supposed to try harder to fall out of love with him at the same time they were expected to kiss? This would require her greatest acting skills. No doubt about that.

"Maybe we just need to figure out a way to fall back in love," he said, as if the statement was of little consequence.

The mere fact that he suggested they figure it out proved that he didn't love her. No one who was in love found it necessary to figure it out. "You can't force it. Either it's there or it isn't." Talk about a damning detail. If ever there was one, that was it.

Logan slowed down the car and pointed up ahead. "That's it, right?"

"Yep."

"I'm so used to finding it in the dark. I was worried I might not recognize it."

"Well, it just got a new paint job. My parents did some sprucing up for the wedding. I can't wait to see inside. This will be my first time."

Logan turned into the driveway of her parents' beach getaway, the one that had once belonged to her grandparents on her mom's side. The parking area was tucked underneath, the house up on stilts for the times when mid-Atlantic hurricanes lapped an extra twenty feet of water up over the dunes. She opened her car door and a waft of briny ocean, carried on a sticky breeze, hit her nose. It brought with it a wealth of memories, many starring Logan. He pulled plastic bins of party decorations from the trunk, and Julia led the way to the wood stairs up to the front door. Even with a fresh coat of butter yellow on the shaker siding of the house, every sensory cue shuffled images through her mind, like flipping through the pages of an old photo album. With the roar of the waves, the wind catching her hair and having him so near, distant moments felt like yesterday, the most palpable of which were the times when Logan had been her everything. And she had been his.

"You okay, Jules? Carsick again?" Logan was at her side as she paused at the front door with the key in the lock. His hand went to her lower back, true concern in his warm and gentle eyes.

*It isn't even funny how not okay I am.* She nodded. "Yeah. I'm good. We should probably go inside and get started, huh?"

"No time like the present."

Yes, it was now time to start, right where it all began.

# Five

Logan followed Julia into the beach house, hardly believing his own eyes. Was this really the same place? Once dark, cramped quarters, the kitchen seemed nearly twice its original size. It was completely open to the living room thanks to the obliteration of an entire wall, the space crowned with high-beamed whitewashed ceilings. Where there had once been dark cabinets, wood paneling and avocado-green appliances sat their modern-day counterparts in white and stainless steel. "Your parents practically gutted the place. It looks incredible."

Julia nodded, appearing pleased as she admired the room. She ran her hand along the edge of the gleaming marble countertop on the center island, another new addition. "It does look great, doesn't it? I really hope Tracy's happy with it."

In Logan's estimation, Tracy was a complete brat if this didn't show her just how hard her family was trying to make her wedding as perfect as could be. "She'd better be happy. She'd better be thanking your parents for days."

Julia wandered into the living room, past a sprawling white sectional couch. Judging by the immaculate upholstery, it was brand-new. The old brick fireplace had undergone a makeover of stacked stone, topped with a distressed wood mantel hosting an array of framed family photos. He was oddly thankful for the considerable house renovation. It took an edge off the memories. It was difficult enough to be here with her, trying hard to keep from kicking up the dust of old memories, all while dealing with the issues of the present.

"How'd your parents afford to do this? There's no way a state senator makes a big salary, and your mom's a teacher." Logan joined her at the expanse of glass doors at the far side of the room that led to the sprawling deck. White rocking chairs pitched forward and back in the wind.

"They didn't afford it. When Tracy told me she wanted to get married here and that Mom and Dad were going to take out a second mortgage to spruce it up, I just sent a check. It seemed silly for them to be spending money on this."

"Wait a minute. I thought they were just doing the rehearsal dinner here. The ceremony's in town at the church down the street from the River Room, isn't it?"

"Yes. As soon as Tracy realized how hard it'd be to wear heels in the sand, she changed her mind about getting married on the beach."

"You spent tens of thousands of dollars so your sister could have a nice place for a rehearsal dinner and not have to worry about her shoes?"

"You haven't seen the shoes. They're really cute." She grinned and shrugged it off. "This is as much for my parents as anything. They're so close to retirement. I wanted to do something nice for them."

Julia wasn't one of the most generous people Logan had ever met, she was *the* most generous. Logan had been on the receiving end of her generosity many times, especially when it came to advice and support. If you called Julia in the middle of the night, she'd answer. And she'd listen, no matter how long it might take to unravel a problem. It was a wonderful quality, but it also meant people took advantage of her. Especially men.

Had Logan taken advantage in June? That night when she was a damning mix of long legs and a laugh that was like truth serum? That night when she was all open ears and sympathy? That night when her touch electrified him and reminded him that busted baseball career or not, he was still alive? "That was awfully nice of you. You'd think Tracy would lay off the extra-demanding routine considering all of that."

"It's her big day. I get it. It doesn't matter what I did last week or last month to help out. Right now is what matters, and she wants it to be perfect."

Julia stared off at the surf as if she were hypnotized. Daylight was fading, coloring the sky with a swirl of pink and orange that only made her more radiant. It wouldn't be long until the moon would be making its appearance on the horizon; night would be falling. They'd be all alone in this beautiful house, no one expecting them anywhere, all while his body persisted in sending potent reminders of the kiss they'd shared mere hours ago.

He cleared his throat. If he thought for too long about her lips on his, he might do something stupid—namely acting like they could kiss without hurting each other. "And you want to give that to her."

"My sister and I fight, but we love each other a lot. We still talk almost every day."

Precisely the reason why Tracy knew what had happened at the reunion. "So I gathered by her reaction to the idea of you and me together."

She shook her head, seemingly bringing herself back to reality. Without so much as looking at him, she headed back to the kitchen island and began pulling party supplies out of the bins. "I had to tell somebody. I was pretty wrecked by the whole thing."

He'd been so certain at the time that it was the right call. Now, alone with her, part of him wanted somebody to smack him upside the head. Regardless of right or wrong, no matter if it had been smart to want to save himself, he'd messed up. "I'm sorry, Jules. Really, I am. It was never my intention to hurt you."

She shot him a look of pure skepticism, then unloaded strands of Christmas lights. "You knew it was going to hurt. I don't buy it for a minute that you didn't know that."

He *had* known that, but in the heat of the moment, angry that their frustrating past was repeating itself again, he hadn't worried about it much. "I figured you'd get over it pretty quickly. It's not like you don't have a million guys falling at your feet."

She chuckled, but it wasn't in fun. "Oh, please. Remind me to call you the next time I'm sitting around at home with absolutely zero guys at my feet. It happens all the time."

He had to stop himself from unleashing his own laugh. She was deluded about what she could have if she'd just settle on one person. "That's a choice you make and you know it. As soon as you finally decide you want to be with one person, you'll have no problem."

The look of hurt that crossed her face made him wish

he could take back his words, even though they had been the reality, and something she needed to hear. "That's hilarious coming from you. And I haven't decided anything. The men in my life have a real talent for making those decisions before I have a clue what's going on."

"Probably because they're the wrong men."

"Probably." She crossed her arms, pressing her lips together tightly, telling him without words that she considered him a member of the group of men labeled "wrong."

"Oh, come on. I'm not like those guys. It's not the same thing at all. What you and I had was different."

"Is it really that different? You think it's some special snowflake? Because the end result is the same. I'm on my own. Except this time I have a baby to worry about."

"You're just being stubborn about that. I told you I'd accept my responsibility."

Her jaw immediately tensed. Normally that might make him worry that he'd angered her, but the truth was it made her lower lip jut out in a very sexy way. So he'd take it. Her eyes blazed and she balled up her hands. That wasn't quite as sexy. She grabbed a roll of streamers and nailed a sofa cushion with it.

"Nice throw."

"I was imagining the couch was your face."

"Oh." He kneaded his forehead. He no longer had to wonder how mad he was making her.

She closed her eyes and took a breath so deep her shoulders rose to her ears. "Can we please talk about something else? After everything else today, I really don't want to get into this right now."

Logan stuffed his hands into his pants pockets, fighting his own brand of frustration. The circles he and Jules could talk in had worn a hole in his psyche. He didn't have the mettle to push her more tonight if it would only lead to an argument. "Fine."

"Let's focus on the wedding." She returned to rummaging through the box. "Make yourself useful and get the stepladder. I think it's in the laundry room."

"I'll be right back."

He wound his way down the hall past the bedrooms to the laundry room in the back corner of the house. This space hadn't seen much of a makeover aside from a fresh coat of white paint and what appeared to be a new washer and dryer.

Feeling nostalgic about a laundry room was odd for sure, but he and Jules had once had a pretty epic, albeit brief, make-out session in this exact place. He'd been invited over for a family cookout and bonfire a few weekends after they became boyfriend and girlfriend. Julia had spilled mustard on her top and was headed inside to change and treat the stain. After an exchange of pointed glances, Logan had gone with her, saying he needed to use the bathroom. With her parents watching their every move, they'd both known it was likely the only time alone they would get. She'd practically slammed the door shut once they were inside the laundry room. *I need to take my shirt off or this stain will never come out.* Logan had never before been thankful for an accidental condiment spill.

His hand had been up her shirt before then, but that moment had been different. He could finally see her—every beautiful vulnerability. They'd known they only had about five minutes before Julia's very observant father came looking for her. They'd made the most of it—frantic kisses against the door, tongues winding, hands everywhere. It took Logan hours to cool off that night, and he couldn't help but lie in bed when he got home and think about Julia and how perfect she was and how lucky he was that she was his girlfriend.

A few days later they had sex for the first time. Julia had been a virgin, making him that much more nervous. He hadn't been particularly experienced, either. After that, their young love had grown so fast it was as if it had been rushing to fill the corners of the universe. Every day was magical, even when they fought, which was often. Even so, they'd been incapable of getting enough of each other. Never enough.

Just thinking about how all-consuming it had once been was a little overwhelming, since it eventually led to unhappy memories. It had been such a shock to the system when Julia ended it. The girl who had lifted him out of the fog of losing his dad had removed herself from his life. Of course he'd kept a stiff upper lip that day, playing it off, agreeing that it was for the best. What else could he have done? They were both going off to college. And everyone had preached to them for months that high school sweethearts never made it long-distance.

He took a deep breath, stopping himself from exploring this train of thought. The past was only clouding up the here and now, and he only had a few days to convince her they needed a solid plan. If the baby was his, he was not about to be the guy negotiating weekends and joint custody.

He found the stepladder in the corner storage closet and brought it out to Julia. "You put on some music," he noted.

"You and I could use the distraction." Julia fanned a piece of paper in the air. "Tracy drew up a schematic of how she wants the room decorated."

"Wow." Logan studied the drawing, which had all the specifics about where streamers and strands of lights were to go. He hadn't seen such attention to detail since the team manager laid out the team strategy for game seven of the World Series. "Seems like we could've paid someone to do all of this."

"This was supposed to be my quality time with my sister. And honestly, she's way too much of a control freak."

*Runs in the family.* "It's a lot of work for a cookout for the wedding party and family."

"Doesn't matter. As big sister and maid of honor, I'm obliged to carry out her wishes." Julia handed Logan the trail end of a string of lights. "As best man, you are similarly obliged. So let's get to work."

Logan followed orders, scooting the ladder all over the room, moving furniture when needed, and looping lights and streamers as instructed.

"How's the new job going?" Julia asked, carefully looking over his work. "I have to say the wardrobe department puts you in some pretty interesting ties."

He wasn't sure how he felt about the fact that all she'd noticed was what he was wearing. At least she'd tuned in. "Do you watch often?"

"Every now and then. If I'm flipping through the channels."

"So I'm not a destination so much as something you pass by." The irony of that statement wasn't lost on him.

"What about you? How many of my movies have you seen in recent history?"

Logan didn't watch Julia's movies. The reigning queen of romantic comedies, she almost always had at least one on-screen kiss and sometimes even a bedroom scene. He couldn't handle that. Pretend or not, even when she wasn't his, the idea of her with another man made him crazy. "You know me. I don't get to the movies."

"That's such a lousy excuse. They're all on TV. *Losing Mr. Wonderful* is practically on a continual cable loop."

She shook her head in dismay. "And you're just avoiding my question. Do you like your new job?"

Yes, Logan had deflected on this subject. It wasn't that he hated his job so much as it wasn't the same. It wasn't taking the field and playing. "I like it. It's a challenge. But I'm getting used to it."

Julia handed him another string of lights. "You don't have to try to convince me. I know you better than anyone."

He sucked in a deep breath and climbed a rung higher on the ladder. He didn't want to tell her the truth. It led to a place where she pitied him, and he hated that more than anything. "I don't want to talk about it."

"Logan, just tell me. You know I'm a good listener."

"I know you are. I don't need the advice right now. I'm fine." He glanced down to see a doubtful smirk cross her face.

"If you don't like your job, you should just quit. Go do something else."

Why had he even bothered to deflect? She wasn't about to let it go. "It's not that. It's that nothing is going to replace baseball. I can't do what I really want to do, and you already know that."

"You know what you should do? You should write a memoir. You've led this amazing life, and you've always been an excellent writer. I'm sure it would be a bestseller." She waltzed off to one of the bins and fished out more bundles of lights.

"See? You're trying to fix my problems. Maybe I don't need you to fix me. Maybe I'm just fine the way I am."

"Why is it so hard for you to accept a little encouragement from me? It's okay to stop being the big, strong man for a few minutes, you know."

"I could ask you the same thing. Why is it so hard for you to accept my help?"

"If you're referring to your offer to marry me, we should agree that it's best if we're just friends."

*Friends. Yes.* Could they ever get beyond that? Three months ago, his decision had been absolutely not. But that was before the baby. That was before she needed him. Finally, for once, she needed him. "Maybe we could make another try at more than friends." This was a different and softer approach than the one he'd taken last night, one that might actually work if she'd listen.

"Ummm. No." Julia crossed her arms over her chest, then gazed up at the ceiling, scrutinizing his work. "And no to that, too." She pointed at the spot where he'd just hung lights. "Redo that."

"What's wrong with it?"

"They're not looped at the same height as the other ones. It doesn't match."

Logan grumbled and hopped off the ladder to grab a drink of water, partly annoyed by being bossed around by his high school sweetheart about holiday lights. The other part of him bristled over her quick dismissal of the notion of being more than friends. "A few cocktails tomorrow night and no one's going to notice, you know."

"Well, I don't get to drink, so I'll notice." She stepped onto the ladder, grabbing the top rung and making it clear she was on her way up. "I'll do it."

He rushed over to her, not thinking, just reacting. One hand landed on the ladder, the other on her hip. "No, you don't. You are not climbing up there."

She turned in his arms, gorgeous locks of hair cascading around her face. "Oh, please. I'm fine."

He should've stepped back, let her get down from the single step she'd taken, but he didn't want to. His body wanted this. And this was the one part of their chemistry that Julia had a hard time resisting. So let her resist. Let her tell him that she didn't want to at least explore things when he had his arms around her. "You and the baby are not getting hurt. Not on my watch."

"Please promise me you won't accidentally say something like that out loud in front of my family."

"I'm serious, Jules. I'm not kidding around. You and the baby. It's a game changer for us. You can't deny that." He gripped her waist and carefully lifted her, lowering her to the safety of the floor. He didn't let go. The notion of game changers had him wondering how he could ever do the same to her mind. As if fate was trying to give them both a nudge, a song came over the radio that had powerful memories for them both.

Recognition crossed Julia's face and she smiled, pressing her hand to her chest. "This song. Oh my God. I love this song."

The arrival of this song was about as ill-timed as could be. It had been Logan and Julia's make-out song when they were in school. Only a few notes in and Julia was already melting, probably not a good idea considering whose arms she was in. And yet she wasn't really sure she cared that this was a bad idea. After twenty-four hours of painful truths and uncomfortable secrets, it was too easy to give in to the one thing that felt good—Logan's hand at her waist, carefully sliding to her back, as if he was hoping to do it undetected. This was comfortable. Familiar. And she wanted that now more than anything.

He took her hand and began swaying them both back and forth.

"Typically, a guy asks a girl to dance. He doesn't just

launch into it without an invitation." She felt the need to at least feign a protest.

He smiled, sending a trickle of electricity down her spine. "I'm not big on asking. And you'll just say no."

Forget the song—she had little defense for Logan when he was acting like this. Romantic. Slightly bossy. Sexy as all get-out. This was precisely the version of Logan she couldn't resist at the beginning of the summer. This was the Logan who could leave her undone with a single glance. Dancing was the least of her worries—all he had to do was look at her in the right way and she'd be clay in his very capable hands.

"I'm worried about what might happen if there's too much touching."

"It's just a dance. We're taking the room for a spin. Seems like part of our due diligence as best man and maid of honor. We wouldn't want Tracy to tell us tomorrow that something's wrong with the way the lights are strung."

"You're just saying that because I'm trying so hard to keep her happy."

"Okay, then. How about this? You and I have to convince a whole lot of people that we're a couple. Consider it practice."

She couldn't argue with him on that. And at least she felt like she had someone on her side, stuck in her proverbial boat. Where would she be right now if she didn't have Logan? Feeling even more alone than she already did. At least someone knew her secret. And someone understood how she felt about making her sister happy. It was merely an unfortunate coincidence that her ally in secret-keeping and wedding planning also happened to be the man who broke her heart.

Logan continued with the dance, committing to it with a more deliberate sway. He squeezed her hand and pressed into her back with his other hand. Julia admired the handsome and cocky grin on his face as each musical note pulled her further under his spell. It was like his lips were sending her secret messages. *Just another kiss, Jules. You know you loved the one from earlier today.*

His eyes drifted lower, and she couldn't help but be amused by the way he unsubtly ogled her cleavage.

"My eyes are up here, mister."

A guilty smile crossed his lips. "What? It's impossible not to look. I mean, they're right there."

"They've always been right there."

He cocked an eyebrow. "Not like this, they haven't." He shook his head. "Never mind. Forget I said anything."

"No. What were you going to say?"

He pulled her closer, pressing their chests together, his mouth drifting to her ear. "I'm not saying another thing on the subject. I'll just get into trouble." The heat of his breath grazed her neck, sending a rush of warmth through her.

"Fine. Then dance with me." She gave in to the moment, settling her head against Logan's shoulder. He pulled her even closer and held her tight. Side to side, slow and steady, feet moving only slightly, their dance continued into a different song—less meaningful in terms of their shared history, but still laid-back and sexy. His warmth poured into her, wrapping her up in contentment.

"I was thinking about the parties you and Tracy used to have here. The ones your parents didn't know about," Logan said.

"They were fun, weren't they?" So many of her memories of this house were tied to those parties. After Julia had gotten her driver's license, she and Tracy used to sneak the keys to the beach house and invite friends over. Neither girl had been particularly wild, and Julia always insisted the guest list be small and they leave the house immaculate, but they certainly did things they shouldn't have been doing—drinking beer and kissing boys, mostly, although Tracy had far more luck in that department than Julia. That was until the night Logan showed up.

"Of course, I think the first one I came to was the most fun."

She had to smile. "It might have been the best night ever." It had been the best—a huge turning point for her. Emboldened by half a can of light beer, Julia finally had the guts to talk to Logan. She'd been pining for him for more than a year before that. "We talked forever that night."

"A lifetime."

Indeed, they'd had an hours-long conversation out on the dunes, Julia with her knees pulled up to her chin and Logan stretching his legs and digging his feet into the sand. She'd never listened to anyone so eagerly, hanging on every word as Logan told her about losing his dad, about trying to be the man of the family, about baseball. Summer wind swirled, whipping at the beach grass as the roar of the ocean swelled and receded over and over again. It was literally a dream come true… Logan Brandt, the most perfect guy she'd ever laid eyes on, had not only noticed her, he'd talked to her. He'd held her hand. And then, beneath that impossibly beautiful midnight-blue sky, he'd done the thing she'd worried no boy as amazing as Logan would ever want to do. He'd kissed her.

Logan cleared his throat and began trailing his fingers along her spine. It felt so good. Too good. "I know I rambled on and on that night. I was nervous about kissing you."

"I don't believe that for a second. You were so smooth. You've always been the smooth guy."

"Something about you made me question my kissing ability."

She laughed quietly. "You were perfect. Absolutely perfect." Julia could've sworn she floated on air for two days after that first kiss. Even if nothing else had ever happened between them, she could have lived off the memory for a lifetime. When he'd asked her a week later to be his girlfriend? She was so gone, up to her neck in her first love, the then-shy Julia didn't even bother with an answer. She'd thrown her arms around his neck and kissed him like her life depended on it. Was there any better feeling than that? Julia didn't think so, even now. That love had transformed her. It had made her believe that she was lovable. She'd never really been sure of it before that.

"I'm not sure I buy it when you say you felt nothing from our kiss in front of the cameras." Logan's voice was low, resonating throughout her body. It wasn't just the kiss that made her feel something. Everything about him made her feel, and that was a terrifying feeling. Leaving herself open to him eventually led to hurt. Always.

A heavy sigh escaped her lungs. "It was a kiss. It didn't change my world," she lied.

Logan reared back his head and brought their dance to a stop. "I don't believe you."

"They're my feelings. I think I know what I did and did not feel." She tried to avoid his gaze, but he followed her with his, as if he was pleading for a retraction. "Fine. It was a nice kiss. You've always been a good kisser. Is that what you want to hear?"

"I'm not fishing for compliments. I felt something, and I think you did, too. I think you're trying to convince yourself of something that isn't the way it actually happened."

She shrugged, but she didn't like dismissing it. The temptation to give in and tell him how much she'd loved it was too great. He was wearing down her resolve, and she had to put a stop to it. "It was hours ago. I hardly even remember it."

"Then let me refresh your memory."

He clutched her neck and lowered his lips to hers. His mouth was warm and soft. Giving. Like Logan had an unlimited supply of affection and he was going to hand it out like candy. He dictated the pace—languid and dizzying, suggesting they deserved to take their time, and for the moment, she believed they did. Here they were, all alone, in this big empty house, all the time in the world. His mouth drifted to her cheek, his stubble scratching her nose, then he traveled to her jaw and kissed her neck. She kept her eyes closed, luxuriating in every heavenly press of his lips to hers, not wanting it to end.

"Tell me you don't feel anything," he whispered into her ear.

"I don't feel anything." She reasoned that she was merely following orders, but she'd actually become a fountain of fibs. She was surprised her nose wasn't growing. The truth was that she was feeling everything right now. Her entire body was so alert she could probably stay awake for the next twenty-four hours.

"You said it yourself earlier today. You're a terrible liar."

*And you're a ridiculously good kisser.* "I know what I said. You don't have to remind me."

# Six

The ride back to the hotel was long. And quiet. Part of Julia was glad she'd had the sense to lie to him and pull them back from the precipice before bodies slipped out of clothes. And her sense slipped out of her brain. The other part of her, the hormonal part, was downright annoyed. She'd been in the arms of an eager Logan and she'd said she felt nothing. She'd lied and denied herself sex, all in the same breath. They could've christened the brand-new sofa. Regret was starting to needle her.

*Focus on the baby.* That was her key to keeping Logan where he belonged—in the strangest friend zone she could imagine. She had to keep her life in order for the sake of the baby. A child needed stability and normalcy. Allowing herself to be tangled up with yet another man who didn't love her was a recipe for anything but what she wanted to give her baby.

Logan pulled up in front of the hotel, and thankfully

the press had kept their promise. They'd stayed away. Finally, Tracy could be happy.

"Oh my God," Julia blurted. "Tracy."

"What now?" Logan asked, turning off the ignition.

"We can't stay in different rooms. Everyone thinks we're a couple. You saw the way that guy at the front desk looked at us when we checked in. He thought it was weird, and it was, because we stayed in the same room last time. If anyone is likely to tip off the press about something out of the ordinary, it's the guy working the front desk."

The valet approached. They were about to lose what bit of privacy they had. Julia's mind was whirring. She'd been psyching herself up for holding hands at the wedding reception and ignoring her feelings while doing it, not preparing for a roommate.

"Pardon me if I find this weird coming from the person who just told me she didn't feel anything when she kissed me."

"And I'm also the person worried about her sister's wedding. The press comes back and I'm sunk. But I have no clue how we're supposed to explain this to the people at the front desk."

He rubbed the side of his face as if he couldn't possibly stand another minute of thinking about this. "Don't worry about it. I'll come up with something."

Easy enough for Logan to say. Right now, Julia was worried about everything, especially the realization that she and Logan were about to share a room.

Logan turned the keys over to the valet and they went inside. The man with the familiar face was again manning the front desk.

"Yes. Hi," Logan started, clearly stalling. So much for coming up with something. "I need to check out of my room. I had a cold when we arrived, and I didn't want Ms. Keys to get sick when she's…"

Julia kicked Logan's foot. "He didn't want me to get sick right before my sister's wedding. It would be a disaster."

The desk clerk hesitated, looking back and forth between them, the moments ticking by at half speed. "Of course, Mr. Brandt. I'll send a bellman up to your room to move your belongings for you." He tapped away at his keyboard while Julia silently let out a sigh of relief.

"No need for that. I'll manage fine on my own."

"Let me know if you change your mind." The clerk swiped a room card. "And here's your extra key." The look he gave them said that he was in no way fooled, but Julia figured this guy had probably seen it all at this point.

They proceeded to the elevator. Today's second kiss seemed even more ill-advised now that she and Logan would be staying in the same room. Why did everything with Logan have to exist on such a slippery slope? She'd dipped her toes into those warm, inviting waters, and now it felt like she was up to her waist in trouble.

Logan went to collect his things while Julia quickly changed into pajama pants and a tank top. Apparently he was a light packer—he was opening her door minutes later, just as she was downing the second of the chocolates the maid had left on the pillows. She put her hands behind her back and crumpled the wrapper. Logan didn't need to know she wasn't just eating for two, she was eating chocolate for two.

"Hey, roomie," he quipped, flashing that beguiling smile of his and breezing into the room.

"Roomie is right. Platonic roommates. I don't want you getting any ideas." She discreetly dropped the evidence of her clandestine candy-eating into the trash.

"Getting ideas. You make me sound like a horny teenager. Don't worry about me. You made it pretty clear where you stand when you told me you didn't feel anything after our kiss." He wheeled his roller bag next to the bureau. "Which was a little odd considering how much you were actually participating in it."

"I plead hormonal insanity."

He toted his garment bag to the closet. "Where exactly do you expect me to hang my suit? You have enough clothes in here for a week."

"Oh, please. You're exaggerating." She walked over and began sliding hangers across the rod, cramming her clothes together. She took his suit from him and squeezed it in at the end.

"If it gets wrinkled, you're ironing it."

"Whatever it takes to appease you, Mr. Brandt." She turned and he was right there, peering down at her breasts. "You have got to stop staring at my chest."

"I'm sorry, but when it's just the two of us, it's really hard not to look." A sly grin crossed his face, and he looped his finger in the direction of her chest. "They're spectacular. And it's hard not to think about the reason why they look like that. It's surprisingly sexy."

Julia's head was swimming. She hadn't been prepared for that. Did he really feel that way? Pregnancy had made her feel anything but sexy—tired and starving most of the time, although she had to admit that being around Logan had a way of helping her find her more alluring side. "Thank you. I just wish they didn't hurt so much."

"Hurt?" Logan traipsed across to the other side of his room and kicked off his shoes.

"Yes. They're sore. You blow more air into a balloon, it stretches. Same principle."

"You paint a lovely picture." He turned and began unbuttoning his pants. "You're totally taking the fun out of the idea of you with larger breasts, though."

Before she knew what was happening, he'd shucked his jeans and was folding them neatly. In black boxer briefs that showed off his long, lean legs, he was doing far too efficient a job of helping her feel sexy. Probably because she couldn't have him. He was forbidden fruit, the shiny apple she wasn't allowed to take a bite out of, no matter how tempting he was, all because she'd promised herself she wouldn't. And now Mr. Temptation was unbuttoning his shirt.

"Will you please go change in the bathroom?" she sputtered, clamping her eyes shut out of self-preservation.

"You can't be serious. I'm getting ready for bed. It's late and I'm wiped out. Drama makes me tired."

"So put on your pajamas already."

"These are my pajamas."

"You can't just sleep in your boxers. You have to put on something else." Every breath out of her was coming way too fast. Her heart was hammering.

"I didn't pack anything else. And it's not like you haven't seen me in way less than this."

*Holy crap.* His voice was so close. Much closer than it had been a moment ago. She sensed him moving closer. She could feel the warmth radiating from his body. She was too scared to open her eyes. She already knew how amazing he looked half-naked.

"If you aren't nice, I'll just sleep in the nude."

She wrestled with the threat—be mean and have him take his clothes off. Dangerous, but not the worst deal in the world. "Fine. I'll be nice."

"Then open your eyes. I promise you'll live through it."

*Yeah, right.* She opened her eyes all right, but just as quickly whipped around to avoid the sight of him. That meant she was now confronted with the image of a king-size expanse of luxury linens atop what she already knew was a very comfortable mattress.

Guilt ate at her, about a lot of things—bogarting the chocolate, not telling him the truth about the kiss and knowing she'd be in the bed while Logan was stuck on the couch. "I got the extra blanket out of the closet for you. You can take one of my pillows."

"What are you talking about? There are plenty of blankets." Logan pulled back the duvet, slipping under the covers. Well, his legs were blanketed. His stomach and chest weren't. No, those parts of him were too busy building their torment in her body. Judging by the way her body temperature was spiking, they'd built an entire torment city. He patted her side of the bed. "Doesn't the mom-to-be need to get some rest?"

"Oh, no. You're sleeping on the couch."

"No way. Have you seen how short that thing is? It wouldn't fit a guy who's six feet tall, and we both know I'm a lot taller than that."

This was not happening. She could see it now—in bed with Logan, fast asleep, somebody's hand wanders, somebody starts spooning, one body part finds another body part and the next thing they know, the baby-making parade is under way again. "Fine. Then I'll sleep on it."

He bolted upright in bed. "I'm not letting a pregnant woman sleep on that couch. Stop being ridiculous. We're capable of staying in the same bed and things not turning to…you know. Sex."

"Why would you think that? We've never slept in the same bed without it turning to sex. Ever."

"That can't be right."

She nodded and dared to step closer to the bed, even though she was being dogged by memories of the last time they were sharing a room in this hotel. Everything she saw—the bedside tables, the lamps and of course half-naked Logan—brought her back to that magical weekend. "Think about it. Never. Ever."

He reclined against the pillows, placing his hands behind his head. Good God, now it was like he was posing for the cover of a men's fitness magazine. And she had to act as if she wasn't fazed, even when her eyes were drawn to his well-defined chest, his abs, that narrow trail of dark hair beneath his belly button. Deep down, she was anything but ambivalent—she wanted to read every square inch of his body like she was studying braille. *Deep breaths. Enjoy the view. You're fine.*

Stupid straight and narrow. Of course she wasn't fine.

He pursed his lips and nodded slowly. "Huh. Maybe you're right. Well, first time for everything, right? Unless you'd rather fully immerse yourself in the role of my fake, serious girlfriend and seduce me." He rolled to his side and propped up his head with his hand.

"I have plenty of roles to play right now, thank you. Let's just get some sleep, okay? We have a long day ahead of us and I'm exhausted." She gingerly climbed beneath the covers. That one movement caused goose bumps to pepper her arms. Why her body had this unrelenting reaction to Logan was a mystery. She only knew it was a constant, and even after all the years of ups and downs, showed no sign of abating.

She flipped off the lamp, plunging them into darkness and quiet. She rolled to her side, away from him. He shifted in the bed, but he did what he always did, which was more of a flop than a gentle roll. She tried to ignore it. Tried to pay no attention to what her body was telling her, to snug herself up to him, let him envelop her in those arms, keep her warm, make her feel safe.

He shifted in the bed again, except this time she heard his slow and measured breaths. He'd dozed off already. He'd always been like that. His body seemed to have little trouble finding sleep.

She turned to her other side, which was far more comfortable. That put her close enough to touch him, to feel his soft breath against her face. It was hard not to continue to cling to an alternate version of what had happened after the reunion. Thoughts of what this moment might be like if things had been different, if he hadn't called things off. If they'd kept it together all summer. If he'd just believed that they belonged together. The same way she did, however much it pained her to acknowledge it.

Reaching over, she pulled the covers up over his arm. She'd always care for him. That wasn't going anywhere. She knew that much. And he might be the father of her child. That wasn't going anywhere, either. Her mind leaped ahead to the end of the weekend, to that moment when she would tell her parents. Maybe she should've had the DNA test. But then again, if she had, and the baby wasn't his, Logan would remove himself from her life forever.

She placed her hand on her lower belly. If she was being completely honest with herself, there were far too many moments when she really wished that Logan was the dad. She wouldn't treat the baby any differently if he wasn't the father, but her heart really wanted it to be Logan. At least there had been love between them at some point. And despite their problems, they were friends. If there was a problem, she'd be able to call him, and she knew with certainty that he would help her. He would play the role of dad beautifully if that was what he became. As to the question of the role of husband and whether that day would come with her, the answer was no. She was too certain that friendship and attraction were not enough to sustain them. She needed him to love her.

# Seven

"Ow! Ow!"

Logan opened one eye to darkness.

"Ow!" Jules yelped again. The bed shook.

He flipped on the lamp, wincing at the light, but alert. He hadn't really been asleep. Just dozing and replaying the kiss, along with her insistence that she'd felt nothing. "Are you okay? What's wrong?"

"Sorry. It's my leg. A cramp." She tossed back the covers and practically folded herself in half.

Scrambling out from under the comforter, he raced around to the other side of the bed. "Give me your leg." He grabbed her ankle, using both hands to flex her foot.

"Ow!" She reached for him, her face scrunched up in agony.

"Just lie back and try to relax." He gently raised her foot and planted it against his chest, massaging the calf muscle to unwind it from its painful contraction.

Julia knocked her head back on the bed and rocked it back and forth, a smile breaking across her face. "Oh, thank God. It's going away."

Logan pressed on her foot a little harder with his shoulder to get the full stretch while caressing her leg. Her skin was impossibly soft, conjuring so many pleasurable memories, accompanied right now by enticing visuals. Her pajama leg had slipped down to the middle of her thigh, revealing the part of her that he most loved wrapped around him. His hand spanned the back of her leg, rubbing from ankle to knee, up and down, the feel of her velvety skin slowly driving him mad, and yet there was no way he was about to let go. "Better?"

"Much. I keep getting charley horses in my sleep. It's a pregnancy thing. I'm sorry I woke you up."

"You didn't really. I was basically awake."

"I hope I wasn't snoring."

He laughed quietly. "You weren't. I was thinking about last night."

Several heartbeats of silence played out. "Last night?"

"The kiss. I don't want to give you a hard time about it, but am I crazy? Was there really nothing there?"

She chewed on her lower lip. Something of substance was running around in that beautiful head of hers, and he really hoped it wasn't the endless loop of denial. She sighed and looked him in the eye. "There was something there. There's always something there. Can't we leave it at that?"

Back and forth, he continued rubbing her leg. She was perfectly fine now. Her cramp was gone. He could walk away. Except that he couldn't, especially not after she'd finally told the truth. There in the soft, early-morning light, he couldn't get past how gorgeous she was. Rich brown hair splayed out against the white of the sheets, pleased grin on her face as she gave in to his touch, and then there were the sounds coming from her mouth. He kneaded her leg a little deeper with his fingers.

"That feels so good." Her voice was a sweet purr, uttering words he'd heard her say many times over their reunion weekend. She arched her back, then settled into the bed. Through the thin fabric of her tank top, he couldn't help but notice that her nipples had responded in a positive way. It took everything not to reach out and touch them. Not to lower himself to the bed and slip those skinny straps from her shoulders, cup her voluptuous breasts in his hands. Kiss her. Make her admit again that she felt something.

"Good. I'm glad. I like making you feel good." He couldn't have cared less that his words dripped with innuendo. All of the troubles and rough spots between them seemed so inconsequential right now. With the morning hours stretching out before them, all he wanted was to make love to her. He'd not only satisfy the thirst for her that never went away, he was certain that he'd know how she felt. He was tired of trying to interpret everything she said and did. The two rarely matched up.

With each pass of his hands, he made his journey a bit longer. He reached her slender ankle at the top of the pass, and now he was venturing beyond the back of her knee, lower and lower on her thigh.

"I could just stay like this all day." She put her hands behind her head and smiled. "My legs were killing me after all of that running around and standing all day yesterday."

"We don't need to be anywhere until your dress fitting, right?" That was at noon. He glanced at the clock, rubbing her leg, never losing contact. It was only a few minutes past seven. They had time. Oh boy did they have time. Everything in his body tensed at the idea, blood now fiercely coursing through him. Breathing became tougher, nearly forced. Thinking wasn't much easier. Would his way back in really be this simple?

"Yes. But don't talk about the wedding. It'll ruin the mood." She closed her eyes, her full mouth relaxed, a look of near-bliss on her face.

*The mood.* There was no mistaking that phrasing. He slowed the pace of his hand, dipping below her knee, inching lower along her thigh. All he could hear was his own heartbeat thumping in his ears and a breathy hum from Julia. He knew that hum, and it meant only one thing. His hand kept going, inches beyond previous passes. She didn't flinch. Her eyes remained closed. His body reacted with an abrupt stiffening in his chest, warmth creeping down his torso and below his waist, the most primal of responses to the beautiful creature in his clutches. Was this going to happen? Or was he still asleep, and stuck in a dream?

Whatever Julia could say about Logan and the ways in which he made her mad or hurt her, the man had amazing hands—one might go so far as to say he was gifted. And then there was his incredibly firm chest. With her foot planted against the muscular plane, she appreciated how solid it was.

His hands might have started as givers of therapeutic massage, but there was no mistaking their new role as tools of seduction. She had zero inclination to fight it. She didn't care to think about it. It was too good to be bad. Maybe this was what they needed to figure things out—work out their problems in bed.

He dipped his hand lower, his grip on the back of her leg just strong enough to tell her his intentions. Or at least what she surmised as his intentions. She begged the universe—please don't let this be another time when she'd managed to read him wrong. Her body was becoming far too accustomed to the idea of what could be coming next—Logan's sleeping attire on the floor, followed quickly by her own.

His thumb rode along the inside of her thigh, his other fingers clamped around the outside of her leg, his palm creating heat and friction. Slow and rhythmic, his movements brought about a trancelike state, one in which she didn't care about repercussions or what might happen to her stupid heart if she let Logan back in. She only knew that she wanted him in. Inside. Her.

She opened her eyes, one at a time, nervous she'd built this all in her head, and all she'd see was a disinterested Logan. Her truth-seeking brought a rich reward—his eyelids heavy with desire. How she loved seeing that expression on his face. It was the sexiest thing she could imagine. So sexy that she was sure there was no luckier woman anywhere on the planet right now. They were all alone. The door was locked. Clothes coming off and kissing and touching and lovemaking…they all felt possible now. She squirmed against the bed, goose bumps popping up along the surface of her skin. Her face flushed with dry heat, as if she were basking in the sun. Every inch of her wanted him.

"Have I mentioned how good that feels?" she asked, pleased with how genuinely seductive her voice was.

"It feels good to me, too." His gaze was so intent, eyes dark and focused on her, as if he had nothing on his mind but consuming her.

But he wasn't making a move, and now her brain was searching for the next thing to say. He hadn't left her with an opening. He hadn't led her to the next step. Perhaps he was waiting for her to take charge. Not surprising considering the way things had gone since Wednesday afternoon. She'd put him in his place more than once.

She wiggled her toes, then dug them into the skin of his chest. His hand was on one of the heavenly downward passes. He was mere inches from her center now. Her pajama pants were as bunched up around her upper thigh as they could be. If he wanted to go any farther, he'd have to slip his hand beneath the fabric.

"My pajamas are in the way." She held her breath, waiting for his response.

"I noticed. What do you want to do about that?"

The low rumble in his voice made her back arch again. He wanted her to say it. If she was going to repay the pleasure of the last few minutes, he deserved as much. "I want you to take them off."

His eyebrows bounced, conveying a cockiness he'd earned. "I'm a big fan of that answer." He gently lowered her leg until it was hanging off the edge of the bed like her other.

He towered over her as her vision drifted across his strong shoulders, down his muscled chest and defined stomach. Her eyes dipped lower, and she relished the thought of what would soon be hers, as there was no hiding his current enthusiasm—and readiness—for sex. His warm fingers curled under the waistband of her pajama pants, sending a shiver down her spine as he shimmied the fabric down her legs. She never wore panties under her pj's; it always felt like an unnecessary extra layer of clothes. Aside from her tank top, she was as bare to him as she could possibly be.

They hadn't marked this first moment of vulnerability when they first made love after the reunion. They were both too eager, all action, stopping for few words. At least the first time. There was a stillness to this moment, an anticipation that left her breathless. Perhaps it was because this time they'd arrived by chance, the two of them falling together, as was their natural inclination.

He stepped out of his boxers and she had to shift up

onto her elbows to admire him, all chiseled physique and masculinity. A sly smile crossed his heavenly lips as he stretched out on the bed next to her. He cupped her face and kissed her softly, gently. He took his time. She loved that about sex with Logan. He rarely rushed, and she was always the priority, even when they were both feeling frantic. His tongue wound in languid circles with hers, enough to make her feel dizzy. Their two kisses yesterday had taken hours to shake off. She'd be lucky if she could stand up straight anytime soon after this one.

He flattened his hand against her belly and slipped it underneath her top. She sat up for a second and removed it, then settled next to him again. His hand slowly crept to the flat plane in the center of her chest, fingers smoothing up over the top of one breast; blood rushed to flood her skin, tightening her nipple.

"I don't want to hurt you. You'll have to tell me what's too much." He gently circled the hardened peak with the tip of his finger, teasing and making her crazy in the process.

"It all feels good right now. All of it." She watched as he lowered his head and gave her nipple a soft lick, swirling his tongue around it before drawing it into his mouth. She closed her eyes and reached down between them, wrapping her fingers around his steely length and stroking.

A low groan left his throat and his mouth returned to hers, kissing her with greater vigor than before. He rolled to his back and pulled her with him, inviting her to press her full body weight into his. They fell into a kiss both soft and intense, different from the other kisses this weekend. There was a freeness that hadn't been there before—probably the feeling of setting aside her reservations. She rocked her body against his, craving deeper contact, everything between her legs hungry for him.

Luckily, no birth control was necessary. She straddled

his hips, not giving up on their mind-blowing kiss, their tongues winding in circles as the scruff on his face faintly scratched at her cheeks and chin. He had the most amazing smell in the morning—the faintest traces of woodsy cologne, blended with sleep. It was intoxicating and all his own. She raised her bottom and took his erection in hand, guiding him inside her. Her eyes drifted closed as he filled her perfectly, inch by inch. The sense that she'd reached the promised land was immense, probably because she remembered exactly how good this would be, but it was an odd sensation—her body immersed in quiet jubilation and eager anticipation at the same time.

He took her breasts into his hands, squeezing, then raising his head and sucking on each nipple. The tension inside her had been quickly building already, but that sent her racing for her peak. She kissed him again, wanting to languish in this beautiful moment, knowing that whatever happened this weekend, she would at least have another beautiful memory to stow away in her head. He slipped his hand between their bodies, his thumb finding her apex. He wound it in tiny circles, knowing exactly how to play this, and she luckily could dictate the pressure with her body weight. Still, it was as if he'd been born with the instruction manual for her body inside his head, and he pursued a tempo that perfectly matched the rhythm of his thrusts.

His breaths came shorter now, much like hers, and the muscles of his torso and hips began to coil tighter beneath her. The peak was upon her, her breath hitching in her chest, and everything around her was falling away… everything except Logan. The waves kept coming, and then he cried out with a forceful thrust, his arms reining her in tightly. She collapsed against him as contentment enveloped her. She was exactly where she'd wanted to be from the moment she first saw him two days ago—safe in his embrace.

Logan didn't hesitate to pull her back into their kiss, the motions of his lips helping her savor this blissful moment.

Then Logan's cell phone rang.

It registered as a minor annoyance with Julia, but he ended the kiss, rolling away from her. "No no no," he groaned.

She smiled and smoothed her hand over his stomach. She wasn't about to let technology cut this short. "Let it go to voice mail. We have all morning." She drew a lazy circle in the center of his chest with her finger. "Now where were we?"

He closed his eyes and moved her hand. "I hate to say this, but we're done for the morning." The phone continued its interruption. "That ringtone is literally the only sound that can ruin the mood." He rolled away again and strode across the room.

"Just ignore it. Come back." She patted the mattress, wishing she could transport him back to where he'd just been.

"It's my mom. I have to answer it. She'll just keep calling if I don't. Plus, the mere thought of my mom makes a repeat performance impossible."

Julia sighed and scooted back on the bed, resting her head on the pillow. She pulled the sheet up to her chin. The moment was indeed over.

"Mom, hey. I'm sorry I haven't called. Things have been crazy busy since I got here." He cradled the phone between his ear and shoulder, pulling a pair of basketball shorts out of his suitcase and tugging them on.

*And there went my view.*

"Oh. Yeah. Right. Jules and me. We should probably talk about that." He shook his head and looked down at the floor. "I know. You're right. I'm sorry you had to find out from the news."

*Oh crap.* Right there was proof that Logan had put little thought into his plan. Of course his mom would find out about it. She not only lived in town, she was as connected as could be—lifelong resident and a district court judge. The rumor mill had probably started churning the instant Logan told his tale to the reporters. It was a miracle she hadn't called him last night.

"I know. I know." He nodded eagerly. "Hey, Mom, let me put you on speaker for a second." He pressed a button on his phone and placed it on the bureau, then threw a T-shirt over his head and threaded his arms into it.

Logan's mother's voice rang out over the speaker. "I know you're busy with the wedding, but I'd like to see the two of you together before tomorrow. Otherwise I might not get any time alone with you at all."

He closed his eyes, kneading his forehead, clearly wrestling with the conversation. Difficult to explain or not, they were going to have to come clean with his mom as well. "Don't you need to be in court today?"

"As luck would have it, there's a gas leak at the courthouse. I swear it's something new every day. They really need to put some money into that building. Normally I'd complain, but if it means I get to see my handsome son and the girlfriend I'd always hoped he'd find a way to be with, I'm happy. So, no, court is not in session today."

# Eight

The press had stayed away. Logan was able to retrieve the car from the valet like a civilized person—no more sneaking around. Whatever his fabrication had done to annoy Julia or infuriate Tracy, it had been worth it. Now he just had to find out how much it would irritate his mother when she, too, learned it was a lie. *Great.*

Only after what had transpired with Julia that morning, he wasn't entirely sure it was a lie. They hadn't had a conversation about it. During his time on the phone with his mom, Julia had received a call from Tracy. He'd hopped in the shower while she talked about lunch plans with her sister, then it had been Julia's turn to commandeer the bathroom. Room service arrived with breakfast; he got a few texts from Carter about the two of them picking up the rings. Julia bustled around the hotel room, Logan did much of the same, and it all just went back to the way it had been twenty-four hours ago. Except now there was sex with Julia fresh in his mind, and he couldn't stop thinking about the surreality of that moment when it was clear she wanted him.

Was Julia experimenting? Was she trying to sound him out? Was she finally coming around to his way of thinking? That they should figure out a way to forgive each other and move forward? He wasn't about to see his child go without a father, no matter how much he worried that Julia might not be capable of loving him, at least not forever.

Unfortunately, Julia was on the phone with her Aunt Judy for the duration of the drive to Logan's mom's. Meaning, yet again, no conversation or clarification. The wedding had taken center stage. And there wasn't a damn thing Logan could do about it.

When they arrived at the house, Logan took Julia in through the side door that led to the kitchen. The room never changed—simple white tile countertops, checkerboard dish towel draped over the oven handle, a ceramic cookie jar shaped like a cupcake, and the picture window above the sink, overlooking the backyard. Coffee was on, also no surprise. His mom was an all-day-long coffee drinker, just as his dad had been. He couldn't imagine his childhood home without it. And that one particular aroma brought back more than memories, good and bad; it transported him to a time when he was a different person, a kid trying to figure out how to be a man.

As much as he loved this house, he never stayed here when he came back into town. Sleeping in his old bed would've invited too much introspection, along with a sore back. Luckily, his mom had converted his room into a sewing and craft space, and the one his brothers had shared still housed their old bunk beds. His mom didn't seem eager to nudge time ahead, and he'd be the last person to push.

His mother waltzed into the kitchen, her chin-length curly dark hair tied back with a colorful scarf. Even with a day off from work, she was the epitome of put-together. Jewelry. Makeup. "I should've known you'd come in through the side door." She beamed as they beelined for each other, arms wide open.

"It just feels weird to go to the front. The mailman and strangers go to the front door." They embraced, both holding on tight. Hugs from his mom always lasted a heartbeat longer than most, a powerful reminder of how much they'd needed each other after his father's death. She'd lost her best friend and husband of fifteen years. Logan and his brothers had lost their hero, mentor and coach. If any family had ever held each other up, they had.

"And here's the lovely Julia." His mother hadn't let go of his shoulders, but she was now looking back and forth between them, a prideful smile on her face. "I always wondered if you two would find a way."

Logan's stomach wobbled at the tone in his mother's voice. It was different from Julia's parents. They were always full of sunny optimism. His mom was an upbeat person, but she also had an unflinching critical eye. She could pick apart any charade. Could she see what was lying beneath the surface between them? That they were drawn to each other, however messed up things happened to get? Or was his mom hinting that she knew what was going on and was simply waiting for him to come out with it?

"Mrs. B. You look amazing. As always." Julia stepped closer, and that was enough to coax his mother from his arms.

"Coming from one of the most beautiful women in the world, I'll take that compliment any day."

He stood back and admired the two of them. Even his mom and Julia looked right together.

"It's all smoke and mirrors, you know," Julia said. "They put me in so much makeup for my movies and photo shoots, it's ridiculous. You have me beat with those high cheekbones."

"Well, thank you. Flattery will get you everywhere." Logan's mom draped her arm across Julia's shoulders. "Can I get you two some coffee? Followed by an explanation of what in the world is going on that I find out from the newspaper that you're a couple after all this time?"

There was his cue to come out with it. "Mom, I had to say that to get the press to go away. To make them stop asking Julia about her costar."

She nodded as if the news was no surprise. "I see. Well, that's a disappointment, but I thought it seemed a little out of the blue." She directed her gaze at Julia. "Coffee?"

His mom pulled two mugs from the cabinet, but Julia had cut way back on coffee because of the pregnancy.

"Oh, no, Mrs. B. I'm good. I had plenty at the hotel. In fact, may I use your powder room?"

"Of course. You know where it is." Logan's mom filled a fresh cup for Logan and topped off her own mug as Julia left to go to the bathroom.

"So?" his mom asked, leaning back against the counter and arching her eyebrows at him. "Anything else you want to share with me?"

There it was—the only invitation she'd extend for him to apologize. "I'm sorry you had to hear the story from the news. It's just complicated. Like most things with Jules."

His mother shook her head. "That's not what I was asking. How far along is she?"

Logan nearly choked on his coffee. "What?"

"One of the most successful actresses in Hollywood is

getting a little thick in the middle? I don't think so. And she's glowing. Good God, if ever a woman glowed, it's her." She sipped from her mug. "Declining the coffee was the final clue. Julia has never turned down a cup of my coffee. Ever. I spent an awful lot of years as a prosecutor. I'm good at figuring things out."

*I'll be damned.* Logan leaned back and peered through the doorway into the hall. "She's three months along. But it's a secret. Nobody knows." The rest was sitting on his lips. He wasn't keen on saying any of it, but his mother was likely one or two pointed questions away from figuring everything out. He cleared his throat, then came clean—the reunion, the phone call. And the worst of it—her ex.

His mother took another sip of coffee. "So you're telling me there's a chance I'm about to become a grandmother, but you aren't together. Do you love her?"

Just then, Julia ducked into the room. "I didn't want y'all to think I got lost. My sister called and I need to call her back. I'll just be in the living room if that's okay."

"Of course. Feel free to use my office if you need it," his mother replied.

Julia retreated to the other room. Logan was still mulling over his mother's question.

"Well? Do you?" she asked.

He knew the answer, but he wished he didn't have to qualify it. "I do, on some level, but it's not as simple as that. If the baby is mine, we have to get married. I don't see any other way it's going to work. I have to accept my responsibility."

"Of course you do. You've always stepped in and done what was right. You did that when your father passed."

"See? Exactly. Similar situation, but Julia doesn't agree. There comes a time when things happen and you just have to man up and do your job. But she doesn't see my point.

If she'd listen to me and get a paternity test, it would make this much more clear-cut."

His mother shook her head in slow motion, as if she wanted him to feel every bit of condemnation that was coming from her expression. "Please tell me you haven't actually said that to her."

"It's a legitimate request. Any man in the world would ask the question."

"Of course they would, but that doesn't mean I don't expect my son to see the problem. A paternity test does nothing more than give you a free pass to walk away if the answer is that you're not the father, and makes you beholden to her if you are."

"I'm not looking for a free pass. That's not what this is about. But I don't know how I'm supposed to make a decision without that information."

His mother cocked both eyebrows, her lips pursed. She clunked her coffee cup in the porcelain sink. "Logan Brandt, I thought I raised you better than that. How do you think Julia feels?" She then proceeded to say virtually everything Julia had said to him about living with complete uncertainty, all on her own. "Not only that, but her career is on the line here. She's going to have to take time off from films, quite possibly raise a child on her own. It's not easy, Logan. I'm speaking from experience. I had to be a single mom after your dad passed away. Trying to work my way through the prosecutor's office and raise three boys? It was hard."

"I know, Mom. I do. I was there for the whole thing, remember? I did my best to step up to the plate then, too. I'm not going to walk away from her if the baby is mine."

"And I'm telling you right now that if I was Julia, that would not be my misgiving. I'd be far more worried about what you'll do if the baby isn't yours. It would be difficult for any man to step into that role with another man's child. But take your history with her and it's got to be twice as hard. She has prepared herself for you to walk away. Again. That's why she was not particularly enamored of your line about accepting responsibility."

He stared down at the kitchen floor, realizing how much Julia had let her guard down that morning when they'd made love. How would he and Julia ever get past this? It was a catch-22 unlike any he'd ever experienced. "I just don't know what to do anymore. I only want to do what's right, but I feel like I'm damned if I do and damned if I don't."

"It's not just up to you. You both have to arrive at the same decision. That's the only way you both end up happy."

"That's the exact thing we're horrible at."

"What did your daddy always say when he was helping you with your pitching? He told you that practice makes perfect. You have to keep trying."

He kneaded his forehead. Everything going through his mind was starting to give him a headache. "Honestly, I'm not even sure what to try with Julia anymore."

"Something tells me you'll figure it out." She reached out and clasped her hand over his. "Hold on one minute. I want to run upstairs and get you something."

Logan poured out the last of his coffee and rinsed the sink. His mother always kept a spotless kitchen. He stood and looked out at the backyard, exactly the spot where his father had played catcher while Logan perfected his pitch. The mound they'd built with load after load of dirt from the back of the lot was barely visible now, covered in grass and mostly sunken in with the rest of the lawn. Still, the traces remained. Just as the traces of his father remained in his head—James Brandt's proud stance, kind ways and deep voice, which became rough and grumbly as the cancer slowly took him away. Logan could still hear his dad's words—not his final utterance to his son, but the one that made the deepest impression, echoing for years, never shared with anyone until Julia. *You have to be the man of the house now, son. Take care of your mom and your brothers. I can't be here to do it.*

Talk about life's patterns repeating—he had to take care of Julia and the baby. Something deep inside him told him it was the only way. But would Julia let him? And would she want him to stay?

Logan jumped when his mom pressed her hand to his back.

"Logan, hon. You okay?"

He nodded and turned, choking back those memories of his dad. "Yeah. Of course."

She held out a small gray felt drawstring pouch. "This is what I went to get."

Logan was in shock. The last thing he'd expected her to give him today was his grandmother's ring. He'd been told from a young age that he would get it whenever it came time to propose to a woman. He hadn't even asked for the ring with his previous engagement, the one eventually broken, to a woman he'd never bothered to bring home. He'd made every excuse in the book, but the truth was that he'd known his mother would see right through the facade. What he'd had with his former fiancée wasn't real. "Mom. Really?"

She nodded and opened the pouch, revealing the large pale pink diamond in the center, surrounded by white diamonds, all set in platinum. "Yes, really. I have a feeling you're going to need this in the coming days or weeks, or maybe hours. Hard to tell with you two. I don't want you to be unprepared. She'll take you more seriously with a ring." She pulled it from its resting place, turning it in her fingers. "I always forget how beautiful it is. It will look perfect on her hand."

Julia's voice filtered in from the hall. "Okay, Trace. I'll see you in thirty at the boutique."

Logan's mom dropped the ring back into the tiny bag, yanked the drawstring and folded it into his hand. He shoved it into his pocket, still disbelieving that his mother had given it to him, all while wrestling with what would have to happen for Julia to accept it from him.

Julia wandered into the kitchen and tucked her phone into her purse. "It's a modern miracle. My sister doesn't hate me today. Or at least not as much as yesterday."

Logan's mom nodded and stepped closer to Julia, eyeing her belly. He watched in horror as the look on her face changed, as if she was turning into a grandmother before his eyes. "Don't worry, hon. She won't hate you at all once she finds out your little secret."

Julia smiled politely and waved at Logan's mom as they said their goodbyes, but she could only sustain her pleasantness until the side door was closed and Mrs. Brandt was out of earshot. "I can't believe you told her." She should have waited until Sunday to tell Logan. She never should've given in to that little voice inside that said he deserved to know as soon as she'd had her first chance.

"I didn't have to tell her. She guessed."

"What?" Julia stopped at the bottom of the driveway. "How could she guess that I'm pregnant?"

Logan grabbed her hand and pulled her toward the car. "Come on. Let's not have this discussion in the middle of the street. You're worried about keeping your secret, all we need is for some hapless dog walker to wander by and overhear you."

"Okay. Fine," Julia grumbled and got into the car. "I don't understand how she possibly could've guessed."

Logan wasted little time driving away from the curb.

"I'm telling you right now, there's no way you make it through this wedding without everyone figuring it out. The clues are there. Your chest is bigger. You pass up coffee. You're glowing."

"Glowing is such baloney." Julia dismissed the comment with a flip of her hand.

"What? You *are* glowing. I probably could've figured out what was going on if I hadn't been so busy thinking about how hot you look right now."

Heat rushed to her cheeks. Logan and his compliments—so disarming in an argument. "That's not fair. You're flirting so I won't give you a hard time."

"Nope. Just being honest. The only way I can get to you is with total honesty."

She sat back in her seat and wrapped her arms around her waist. Her plan was starting to feel more and more stupid, only it was too late to veer off course. "Thank you. That was nice of you to say."

"If we're being honest, I want to know what happened this morning."

She nearly laughed. "You know what happened. You were there. And I'm pretty sure you enjoyed it."

"That's not what I mean." He quickly cut onto a side street. He put the gearshift into Park beneath the shade of a looming oak tree. "I need to know what's going on. What you're thinking. Last night you insisted you felt nothing when I kissed you and then this morning you change your story. I need to know what you're thinking."

If Logan wanted the truth about her feelings, it would take several hours to unravel it. They were messy. And complicated. And ever-changing. She glanced at the digital clock on the dash. "I'm thinking that if you don't get me to my dress fitting in the next fifteen minutes, my sister is going to blow a gasket."

"I really don't care. I'll deal with your sister if I have to, and I'm tired of the wedding putting everything else on hold. Not talking about this isn't going to help us navigate the maze ahead of us."

She sucked in a deep breath. Dealing with the wedding was a pain, but at least it had afforded her a few moments where she could stop worrying about what the future held. Her mind drifted to those heavenly moments just a few hours ago, when nothing else mattered but the two of them, perfectly in sync. "I wanted you this morning. You touch me and all I want is to give in. And it was wonderful. But that just makes everything more depressing."

Logan blinked in disbelief. "I'm not sure what about that was depressing."

The frustration was building inside her again. "I hate that we can only get our act together in bed. That doesn't feel great."

He sighed, tugging the keys out of the ignition and tossing them down into the cup holder. Apparently they were going to be there for a while. "We do have that problem, don't we?"

She'd been bracing for an argument from him. Instead, he agreed, which felt far worse. "So I don't know where we are, other than at an impasse."

"An impasse with benefits. That's a new one."

"Very funny. You know, even if I forgive you for dumping me after the reunion, that doesn't change the fact that you did it. That's the thing I can't get past right now."

"I said I was sorry. You're the one who doesn't want to accept my apology."

"It's not about that. It's not about saying that you're sorry." *It's that you don't love me. And I can't make you do it.* She blew out a breath, and the quiet felt like it might suffocate her. There were no words she could say aloud to erase the empty feeling he'd left her with the day he took his love—or at least the promise of his love—away.

"Then what is it about?" He turned and reached for her hand, enveloping it in his. "Talk to me. Tell me whatever it is you need to say so we can get past this."

How did she even put this into words? She looked up at him, fighting tears. It felt as though she was about to scratch open her own wounds. "You have to understand, I was so happy when I flew home to California that day after the reunion. I was so thankful that the planets had finally aligned and we were on the same page."

He nodded. "I know. I felt that way, too."

"And then you called and left me a message." She shook her head and closed her eyes, praying for strength. "I remember it so clearly, too. I'd gone outside to get the mail and my phone was inside on the coffee table. You have no idea how my heart leaped when I came inside and saw that you'd called." Just telling the story was making her heart feel impossibly heavy, as if it might fold in on itself from the weight of the past. "And then you told me that I was wrong. That we wouldn't work. That our weekend had been fun, but we had to admit it was over. It felt worse than having the rug pulled out from under me. It felt like the earth had disappeared. One minute I saw a future for us and the next minute it went away. Poof. Disappeared."

"I'm sorry I hurt you. I don't know what else to say. I can't undo what I did."

"And then we talk in your hotel room the other night and you tell me that this all started because of the Derek thing. It's so stupid."

Logan sucked in a deep breath. "It's not just that."

She waited for him to say something else, but he didn't. "Then what?"

"I was a mess walking into that reunion. Feeling sorry

for myself, depressed about my job. And that's the one time, out of all of the reunions that we've seen each other at, that you decide you want to be with me? You didn't want me. You just wanted another project."

She narrowed her stare at him. "I don't even know what that means."

"You're always trying to fix guys. They always have some tragic fault that you seem to think you can fix. And it usually just bites you in the butt at the end. Either that or you actually accomplish what you set out to do and then you're looking for the next person to save. And frankly, I don't care to belong in either of those camps."

"That's so untrue." She crossed her arms and stared out the windshield. Or was that true? Was that really her pattern?

"Just think about it, Jules. When we first started going out, I was a project, wasn't I?"

"That's not the reason I liked you. That's not the reason I wanted to go out with you. I thought you were cute and I couldn't believe that you would even pay attention to me, let alone like me."

"But once you got to know me, you realized just how lost I was. I needed your help. And you did help me. I will always be grateful for that. But once you were sure I'd be fine on my own, you dumped me. I wasn't about to go through that with you again."

*Oh. That.* All these years later and they'd never, ever, talked about their first breakup. Never.

"I don't want to dredge up the past," he continued. "But it hurt a lot."

"We were kids. Did it really mean that much to you?"

Disbelief and disappointment crossed his face. Julia wasn't sure which one hurt more. "I don't know, Jules. We were in love, weren't we? Did we mean that much to you?"

She nearly choked on the answer. "Of course we meant that much. Of course we did." She stared down at her hands in her lap. "But I thought it was inevitable. You were going off to UCLA, destined to be the famous baseball player. You were going to have every girl in the world you ever wanted. I couldn't compete with that."

He shrugged. "Fair enough. I get that. Maybe we wouldn't have been able to make it work. Very few people do. But it doesn't change the fact that everything bad between us started right then."

They were both quiet, Julia trying to absorb just how badly she'd hurt him. Did it all even out? Was that the way love was supposed to work? "Just so you know, you were not a project. I've never, ever thought of you that way. Not when we were seventeen and not three months ago. You have to believe me when I say that. I just wanted to help you." *Because I love you.* The words were right there, but she couldn't say them. They would go unreturned, and nothing would be more painful than that.

He nodded, but didn't seem entirely convinced. "Okay. That's good to know."

"You know, you said that there was no telling how things would've played out the first time, but can you really say that about this summer, too? What if we'd done well? What if we'd worked it all out? What then? Just think of how different this weekend could be. We wouldn't have to be sitting here wondering what the future held."

Except that the question of paternity would still be hanging over their heads. They might be together, they might even still be in love, but if she'd had the test and taken away the uncertainty, there was a chance that in itself would've been the end.

"Look, I'm sorry if I misread the situation," he said. "I'm sorry that I hurt your feelings. But you have to understand that I did what felt right at the time. It wasn't pleasant for me, either. The summer was hard. I missed you a lot."

"You did?" She looked up at him. Funny how that one tiny admission softened her heart. "Why didn't you call me? I would've talked to you."

"I could ask you the same thing, since you found out you were pregnant with what might be my child."

Well then. The phone *did* work both ways. "Yeah. I see your point."

"So now what?"

Facing him, she scanned his handsome features, wondering if he felt better about any of this. She was still processing. "I don't know. I don't know what to think anymore."

"Okay. Well, let me ask you this. What do you want from me? Let's not even put the question of the baby in the mix. As a man, what do you want from me?"

Talk about a loaded question. It was hard to separate the baby from the equation, but he'd asked her to. That meant she could only go to one place for the answer—the way she'd felt after he'd broken up with her, before she'd found out she was pregnant. "I want you to love me." It was as much a plea to the universe as it was a request of Logan.

"I'll always love you, Jules. There will always be love between us. And you know, I could ask the same of you. I would love it if you could find a way to love me. For real. For the long haul. I realize you were hurt, but you didn't call me when you found out you were pregnant. That doesn't really feel like love."

She felt as if the air had been squeezed out of her. She'd spent an entire summer cursing Logan's existence and a month wishing she didn't have to tell him about the pregnancy. Then she'd spent the last two days thinking he was being nothing but a selfish jerk about the baby. Now who'd been the selfish jerk? She was pretty sure it was her. "You're right and I'm so sorry. That was wrong." *Really, really wrong.* "So now what?"

"Kiss and make up?"

"Yeah, I guess it's time for us to forgive each other. It's not like we don't have other problems to deal with."

"Okay. I forgive you. But they don't just call it kiss and make up. We make up, we kiss."

She dropped her head and hoped to convey admonishment with a single look.

"Think of it as a fact-finding mission. We're both trying to figure out how we feel right now, and we both admit this is the part we always get right. And honestly, I feel like I break through some of your stubbornness every time I kiss you."

"I'm not that stubborn."

"Now you're being stubborn about being stubborn."

Before she could say another word, he clasped the back of her neck and pulled her mouth to his. She insisted on a few seconds of hesitation, but gave in to it quickly, tilting her head as he opened his lips and sent that familiar tingle right through her. She pressed into him. He pushed right back. *Hello, slippery slope.*

She pulled back, her mind buzzing, but he held her head close, their foreheads pressed together, noses touching, both of them breathing heavily. "Logan, we can't. You're going to get me all riled up again. And I'm going to be late."

He blew out an exasperated breath. "Yes. Of course. God forbid we disappoint the bride."

# Nine

Julia opened the door for Belle's Bridal Boutique to one of the most unfunny pieces of music she could imagine right now. Electronic chimes played "Here Comes the Bride," announcing her arrival. *Ding ding ding-ding. Here comes the bride. Ha ha ha.*

The woman working behind a tall counter near the entrance looked up and gasped. "Your sister said you would be coming." She hurried out from behind her post and thrust out her hand. "I'm Tiffany. I'm the manager. I told myself I wouldn't get too excited, but I can't believe you're in our little shop."

Julia smiled and nodded. "Well, your little shop is just darling." Her eyes glazed over at the racks of white dresses surrounding them. It was hard to imagine she would ever find herself in this situation of her own accord—picking out a wedding gown. That would mean she'd not only managed to find the right guy, she'd managed to hold on to him, and the entire world knew she was incapable of that.

Her father, sitting in the center of the showroom in a fussy white upholstered armchair, waved her over. He'd been stationed in an area with a carpeted pedestal and three-way mirror. "Hey, Junebug. Where's Mr. Baseball?"

"He went with Carter to pick up the wedding bands. He'll be back in about a half hour." Julia plopped herself down on a love seat, thoughts of her talk with Logan still tumbling around in her head. He'd asked how she felt, but he hadn't offered his own take on much of anything beyond their painful past. She wasn't ready to slap a label on anything, but that kiss had sure given her something to chew on.

"Your mother is in the back with Tracy and the tailor. They should be out any minute."

"Can I get you something to drink?" Tiffany asked. "Your mother and sister are enjoying a glass of champagne."

*Not for me.* "Water would be wonderful."

"I'll be right back. Surely you remember Ms. Sully from your first fitting." Tiffany's drawl was so thick that the seamstress's name came out as one word—*Mssully.* "She'll bring out your dress as soon as she finishes up with your sister."

Right on cue, a billowing white skirt peeked out from behind the expanse of mirrors. Tracy floated into view. Julia didn't even have a second to process the vision before the tears started. She loved her sister to the very depths of her heart, even when Tracy was being a pain in her backside. Seeing her in a stunning off-the-shoulder gown that would've made Cinderella jealous enough to spit, all she could do was cry. Her mother wasn't doing much better, hand held to her mouth, shaking her head, a blubbering mess.

Julia rose from her seat and went to Tracy as she stepped up onto the platform. "You are the most gorgeous bride I have seen in my entire life."

Tracy gleamed into the mirror, turning side to side and smoothing the dress. She looked down at Julia with pure elation on her face. "Thank you so much. I can't believe this is finally happening." This was what Julia had hoped for this weekend—her sister, blissful and basking in the glory of being the bride. "And honestly, I can't believe that something is actually going right for once. As soon as you got here the other day, I was sure this wedding was going to be a disaster."

And just like that, Julia was thunked back down to earth.

"I really don't think the dress needs any more alterations, Trace," their mother said. "It's perfect. Absolutely perfect."

"I agree." Ms. Sully added as she filed out from behind the mirror with a pincushion on her wrist and a pink measuring tape around her neck. "Now let's get your sister into her dress. This should be quick. It was close to perfect for the first fitting, but I do want to check the length."

Tiffany sidled out from the back room and handed Julia a bottle of water.

"No champagne, Jules?" Tracy asked. "We're celebrating."

She'd worried about this, especially after Logan had made the comment about the secret being impossible to keep. Julia rarely passed up a glass of bubbly, especially not celebratory. "I have a bit of a headache." Not entirely a lie. The summit with Logan in the car had given her more than her head could handle.

"Maybe it'll loosen you up," Tracy countered.

"I'm good." Julia hoped like heck her sister would just drop it.

"Your fitting room is right over here," Tiffany said, thankfully taking the focus off what Julia was and was not willing to drink.

Ms. Sully followed as Tiffany directed Julia to a small room with an upholstered bench. Next to a standing mirror hung Julia's dress, the one she'd tried on the last time she'd been in town. It was pretty, albeit maybe not what Julia would've picked out—pale pink organza with a strapless bodice and puffy skirt—so fluffy that Julia had commented that if the dress were yellow, she'd look like a lemon meringue pie. Tracy had not found that funny.

Julia's mother joined them, closing the door behind her. "The bridesmaids' dresses are so lovely."

"Everyone else had their final fittings weeks ago," Ms. Sully said, unzipping the dress, taking it from its hanger and handing it to Julia. "I would've preferred to have done the same for you."

Julia slipped out of her sundress and into the gown. "I'm sorry. My schedule has been crazy." Stepping in front of the mirror, she tugged up the dress to her armpits, holding it to her chest.

Ms. Sully took the zipper in hand, but judging by the sound of it, and the way the dress had not snugged up around Julia, she didn't get more than a few inches. "It's too small in the bust."

Julia's mother tittered. "That can't be right. The Keys women are blessed with childbearing hips and that's about it. We did not get much in the boob department."

"Look for yourself." Ms. Sully struggled to pull the back of the dress closed, cutting off Julia's oxygen supply in the process.

Julia felt the blood drain from her face. *Oh no no no no no.* She hadn't accounted for this. She'd tried the dress on with a padded bra the first time—a very padded bra. The one she was wearing right now had only a thin lining. She'd been sure that would be enough difference to accommodate her expanded endowments. Apparently not.

Julia's mom let out a snort of frustration. "This doesn't make any sense. I was here when you tried it on the first time. Are you sure this is the same dress? Did you grab one of the other bridesmaids' dresses?"

"The other girls have all taken their dresses home. This is the last one."

A knock came at the door and Tracy walked in, back in her preppy fuchsia-and-lime-green sheath dress, bottle of champagne and three glasses in hand. "I brought the party and I'm not taking a no from Jules this time." The smile on her face didn't last long when she saw the back of Julia's dress.

"Oh no, Jules. What did you do?"

"Me? Why do you immediately blame me?"

Tracy set the bottle down on a small table and hurried over, elbowing Ms. Sully out of the way and yanking on the back of the dress. "Suck it in. Come on." She grunted and tugged, but it wouldn't budge. "What on earth have you been eating?"

"It's not her waist, although that's definitely tighter, too. It's her bust. Her chest is too large for the dress." Ms. Sully pulled the tape measure from around her neck.

Tracy rounded out from behind Julia, confronting her head-on and staring at her bust. "You got a boob job and didn't tell me?" She poked her right in the chest.

"Ow." Julia winced.

Tracy's eyes grew wide. "Oh my God. You *did* get a

boob job. Before my wedding? Now you're trying to steal my thunder by having bigger boobs?"

"I did not get a boob job." Julia wished she would've thought about that answer for even two seconds. That would've given her an out. But it would've been a lie, one that would eventually come to light.

"The only other thing that could make this dramatic a difference is pregnancy," Ms. Sully said nonchalantly, as if she were telling everyone that it might rain next week.

Tracy's eyes practically popped out of her head. "No."

"Pregnant?" Their mother let out a whimper. Julia wasn't sure she'd ever heard a sadder sound.

"Oh. My. God." Tracy's face turned that shade of red again. This was getting to be far too common a sight. "That's why you won't drink any champagne. I *knew* something was up."

Julia's heart was about to pound its way out of her chest, but she wasn't going to deny something she'd have to come clean about in two days. Plus, she was tired. Flat-out exhausted. "Yes, I'm pregnant. I didn't want anyone to know until after the wedding was over. The spotlight is supposed to be Tracy's right now."

Tracy shook her head, practically boring a hole through Julia with her piercing eyes. Her jaw was so tight, it was making the veins in her neck stick out. "You really are trying to ruin my wedding. You knew this was going to happen. You knew your dress wouldn't fit." She turned, poured herself a glass of champagne, and downed it.

"I had no idea it wouldn't fit. I didn't think it was going to be that big of a difference."

"And you just had to orchestrate this to suck the air out of my happiness, didn't you? Right after I'd tried on my dress and we'd all cried together and had such a beautiful moment. The big famous actress had to go for maximum drama." Her voice was ice cold.

Their mother was apparently still catching up. "A baby? I'm going to be a grandmother? Who's the father? Please don't tell me it's that terrible Derek."

"Mom. It's not Derek." At least she had one answer she could give without hesitation.

Ms. Sully leaned over Julia's shoulder. "I've got the measurements I need. I'll do my best to let it out before tomorrow, but no promises. Bring me the dress when you've changed your clothes. I need to get right to work."

Julia grasped the woman's arm. "I'm begging you. Please don't say anything to anyone about this."

"Of course, dear. You can count on my discretion."

"I'm out of here. I can't deal with this." But Tracy wasn't *really* out of there, because she got back in Julia's face. "You make me wish I hadn't made you my maid of honor. I just want you to think about that." A single tear rolled down her cheek, which felt like a knife in Julia's heart.

"Tracy, please don't say things like that. I understand it's a shock. But maybe Julia had a good reason for hiding this from us," their mother said.

"But that's the thing. She wasn't hiding it, really. She was just waiting for the worst possible time to tell us. I'm tired of her grandstanding. Every five minutes there's another fire to put out and it's all her doing."

Julia couldn't have moved if she'd wanted to. Her sister's words were consuming her whole, eating at her from the inside out. Her shoulders drooped; she closed her eyes, part of her wishing she could just psychically beam herself back to her New York apartment or to her house on the beach in Malibu. Anywhere else but here, where everyone was mad at her and her sister despised her very existence. She dared to open her eyes. Staring down, she was mocked by the field of billowy pink. *I'm here.*

Another knock came at the dressing room door. "Is everything okay in there?" Julia's father asked. "There's an awful lot of yelling. And did somebody say something about a baby?"

"I'll be right out, darling," Julia's mother answered, collecting her handbag. "I don't even know what to say," she said to Julia, her voice unsettled. "You know I don't like it when Tracy flies off the handle like this, but she's not wrong this time. You've created so much upheaval since your arrival."

Julia cast her eyes at her mother. The look on her face was difficult to pin a word to, but both *sad* and *disappointed* came to mind.

"I don't know what's going on with you, but I think you'd better get your act together, at least until this weekend is over. Otherwise, it's only going to get worse for all of us."

A puff of air left Julia's lips as she clutched that stupid bridesmaid's dress to her chest. She'd just told her mom that she was going to have a baby. It was a moment she'd thought about many times—one that was meant to be joyous and cheerful. Instead, she was standing in a fitting room, and it had come and gone in as unhappy a fashion as Julia could've imagined. It many ways, it mirrored her future…and her past, for that matter—the ways in which she couldn't stop messing up. "Aren't you going to say anything about the baby?"

Her mother's eyes were watery. "I'm excited for you sweetheart, really I am, but I'm in shock. And this really isn't a good time. I hope that we can talk about it later this weekend. After the wedding is over."

"Exactly why I wanted to keep the secret in the first place."

"How long have you known?"

"Three weeks. Or so."

"Three whole weeks? Oh, Jules. Three weeks?" She shook her head. "And you didn't tell me? Your sister would've been annoyed, but she would've been over it well before her wedding day arrived."

Julia sat down on the bench and buried her head in her hands. Her stomach burned as she realized that her mistake was much worse than she'd thought. "I'm so sorry. Really. I am. I didn't want it to be like this."

"I believe you. I do. Now we just need to wait for your sister to cool down. Speaking of which, let me see if I can find her and talk to her. And somebody's got to get your father up to speed."

"I'm coming with you." She had to fix this. She had to explain.

"It's probably best if you give your sister some space. I'm guessing you're the last person she wants to talk to."

Right now it felt as if there was an insurmountable divide between her Tracy. There was no telling how long it would take for her sister to calm down. When was the next ice age expected? That might be enough time.

"Let me talk to Daddy, then."

Her mother reached for the door. "I'll talk to him. He thinks you can do no wrong. He doesn't want to believe you might ever be untruthful with us. He'll probably be even more disappointed than I am that you kept this from us."

*Disappointed.* If ever there was a dagger to the heart of a child, that was it. She sat back and knocked her head against the wall as her mother closed the door. If she thought she'd felt alone in all of this when she arrived, she felt that tenfold now. She wrapped her arms around her waist, and the dress gaped in the back. All she wanted was someone on her side. All she wanted was someone who believed she'd had the best of intentions. All she wanted was someone who knew she was trying her best.

All she wanted was Logan.

# Ten

After their trip to pick up the wedding bands, Logan and Carter pulled into the parking lot at the bridal boutique. Logan turned off the car and opened his door. Carter, however, seemed content to stay put.

"Everything okay?" Logan asked. "You've been quiet since we left the jeweler."

Carter nodded. "I'm good. Just thinking about everything. To be honest, I keep waiting for the other shoe to drop. When is my luck going to run out?"

Logan closed his door and turned the ignition on in order to roll down the windows. They might be there for a while. "I'm not sure I understand what you're saying. Are you getting cold feet? Because that's perfectly normal." *Hell, I'm the king of cold feet.*

Carter stared straight ahead as if he were pondering the very meaning of life. "When I'm with Tracy, I feel so lucky, especially thinking about the fact that we'd broken up for a whole year. What if she hadn't gotten a flat tire?

What if I hadn't driven by her that day? We might never have gotten back together. My whole life turned around because of dumb luck."

"It's fate. Nothing dumb about it."

"I just think about what I would be doing right now if things hadn't turned out the way they did. I'd be living in my crappy condo, dragging myself to work every day, nothing to look forward to. I look at what that was like and I can't believe I lived through a single day of the year we were apart. It was pathetic."

*Wow.* Did that sound familiar—that was Logan's life. Sure, swap out the crappy condo for a sprawling home on a wooded lot in Connecticut with a pool and manicured grounds. And yes, he had an array of cars to choose from whenever it was time to head up to the network offices for a production meeting or to the airport to travel to a game, but his life was only a more glamorous version of bachelorhood than Carter's. At its essence, at its core, it was the same. And there was zero indication it was going to get any better. He dated some wonderful women, a pleasure to spend time with, but he never found himself wondering what was next, or even worrying whether they wanted to stick around. Whenever it came to a conclusion, it was almost always the same goodbye. *That was fun. Good luck. I hope you find the right woman someday.*

Logan reached over and grabbed Carter's shoulder. "You know, most guys don't appreciate what they have. Or they don't until it's too late. I'm glad you aren't one of those guys."

"So what about you? What about the stuff you were saying yesterday about not counting out the idea of you and Julia getting back together?"

Now it was Logan's turn to stare anywhere but at his best friend, choosing to fix his eyes on his own hands as he picked at his thumbnail. "I want us to try, but there are a lot of moving parts. I'm not sure it can happen until we resolve one or two things."

"No. Dude. Let me stop you right there. There is no resolving a few things. There are always going to be problems."

"Some problems are bigger than others." *Like having a thing for a woman who might be carrying another man's baby.*

"Listen to me. That day when Tracy got the flat tire? Do you think I was standing on the side of the road thinking about how much we used to fight? Or that she gets up at five and I can't sleep before midnight? Because I wasn't. All I was thinking about was how much I wanted to kiss her. All I was thinking about was how being with her felt right." Carter was clearly worked up about this—his cheeks were flushed and his blue eyes blazed.

"I see your point. You've given me a lot to think about."

"Look. You are my best friend in the whole world. You're the brother I never had. I want you to be happy. And you might have a lot of what most men want, but you don't have it all. I want that for you. If you love her, you have to lock things down with Jules. Otherwise, she gets on a plane on Monday morning and you two just go back to whatever in the heck you've been doing for the last dozen years. Tracy and I call it Olympic flirting. It makes the rest of us crazy to watch you two *not* figure it out."

*Olympic flirting.* He and Julia *were* really good at that.

Just then, Tracy burst out of the door to the boutique. The instant she saw Logan and Carter, she beelined for them, but she didn't go to her husband-to-be's side of the car. She went straight for Logan. "You. I don't know what your problem is, but I'm tired of this. First you dump her and then you get her pregnant?"

"Well, to be fair, it happened the other way around." Logan swallowed hard. What in the hell happened in the last forty-five minutes? And how bad was it going to be when he walked in there?

"Don't joke around about this. I'm in no mood. I'm telling you right now that you need to straighten things out with Julia." She leaned down and looked into the car at Carter. "Carter, honey. Please get me out of here. I just want to turn off my phone and eat ice cream and hang out with you. Everyone else is insane."

Carter practically leaped out of the car, rushing to Tracy's side, wrapping her up in his arms and kissing the top of her head. "Everything's going to be fine," he muttered to her. He then shot Logan the look he'd gotten far too many times since he'd arrived in North Carolina. "Pregnant? And you're sitting in the car wondering what you should do?"

Logan was about to explain, or at least retort that it wasn't as simple as that, but he and Carter had already had that conversation. Enough talking in circles. "You two go. I'll tend to Julia." Logan climbed out of his car as Tracy and Carter got into hers.

He strode into the boutique. He had to shake his head when the door chime played "Here Comes the Bride." Mrs. Keys was standing at a counter, rummaging through her purse, while Mr. Keys looked on. Neither of them were pleased. In fact, Logan had never seen either of them look so unhappy. "Everything okay?" he asked, bracing for the answer.

"Sounds to me like you and Julia are the ones to answer that question." Mr. Keys's voice was stern and cold, a complete one-eighty from the way he'd greeted Logan on Wednesday.

"Logan? Is that you?" Julia stuck her head out from behind a door. She'd been crying. "Come here. We need to talk."

He looked at Julia's parents, desperate to explain. "Can we talk about this in one minute? Jules needs me right now."

"I'd say she needs you now more than anything. And we're on our way out." Mr. Keys ushered his wife out of the shop. She wouldn't even look at Logan.

He headed right over, stepping inside the dressing room. "What happened?"

She blew out an exasperated breath as she latched the door. "My dress didn't fit and now everybody knows. Tracy is furious with me."

"Uh, yeah. I ran into her in the parking lot. I already got on the wrong end of your sister's fury."

"I didn't even have time to explain that I don't know for certain that you're the dad," she whispered. "Plus, I knew it was just going to make it worse. Tracy said the most awful things to me. She said she wished she hadn't asked me to be her maid of honor."

It felt as if ice ran through his veins. That was the worst possible thing Tracy could have said. "What do you want to do? Tell everybody the truth?"

"Surely it's occurred to you how messy the truth is."

"I've been thinking about little else since I first saw you on Wednesday." *And especially in the last ten minutes.*

Tears streamed down her face. "Do you want to know why I didn't do the paternity test? Because I knew that the minute I did, if you weren't the dad, you would never ever want anything to do with me again."

He pulled her into a hug, wishing he could squeeze the sadness out of her. "I would never feel that way." His mother had been absolutely right. This was the real thing holding Julia back. The breakup was one thing, but this was quite another. "We just have to get through the wedding. Tell me what you want to do and I'm on board with whatever it is. Okay?"

"Anything?"

"Anything."

She sucked in a breath and plopped down onto a bench, her dress poofing up around her. She looked as defeated as a person could be. It was no surprise. Her sister, the wedding, her parents…everyone and everything putting pressure on her in their own way. Never mind her worries about the baby. Logan had to give her whatever she wanted right now. It was only fair. He crouched down next to her, pushing aside the mounds of puffy pink dress. She sat straighter and peered into his eyes. Hers were so warm and inviting, sweet and vulnerable. They were like home.

"I just want everything to be okay. I want to feel safe. I want to feel normal. And happy," she said.

Logan reached out and wiped the tears away from her cheek. They were welling in his eyes, too. "I hate seeing you cry, Jules. It kills me."

"I'm sorry."

"I don't want you to be sorry. Please. Stop being sorry."

Again, she sought his eyes. In some ways it felt as if they were having a conversation that was separate from the one that came from their lips. Every part of him wanted to wrap his arms around her and take her away. He took her hand, grasping her delicate fingers. The irony that they were in a bridal boutique while he had his grandmother's ring in his pocket was not lost on him. He would've popped it out and brought her to tears for an entirely different reason if he didn't know that it would take baby steps with Julia. He had to open his heart to her. If he was having a hard time trusting her, she felt the same way.

"Let me keep you safe," he said. "Let me make things

normal. We'll get through the wedding, and then we'll talk about everything when the pressure is off. I think we need to take some of the drama out of your life."

"It's not polite to have the bride kidnapped." A slight smile crossed her face. She pulled up the neckline of her dress, trying to hitch it up. "So you're going to have to tell me what you mean."

"Everyone already thinks we're together. And now your parents and Tracy know about the baby. And between the hotel room this morning and everything that happened in the car this afternoon, you and I both know that staying away from each other never works. Neither one of us is very good at it."

"Yeah. I noticed."

"So let's just try to be together. For two days. Let's be Julia and Logan. Together. A couple. No putting on a show."

"What will we do if people ask us about it? Because you know they're going to. They're going to ask about the baby and whether we're getting married. And I don't think I can pretend about that. I need it to be real."

"We'll just say that we're together and we're focused on Tracy and Carter right now. That's the truth, and if that's not good enough for them, then too bad. We'll just have to walk away or get really good at changing the subject."

"What do we tell everyone later? After the wedding?"

He took her other hand and gripped them together tightly. They were both putting a lot on the line here, willingly creating a tangle that could become an unholy mess to clean up. It didn't matter. Their past was littered with mistakes that couldn't be undone and their future was uncertain at best, but it was theirs. And it was up to the two of them to figure it out. "All we can do is our best right now. If anyone wants to fault us for that after the fact, then that's their problem. And if someone needs to take the heat, I will."

"You don't have to do that. I can take it. I'm used to it."

"You know what? I don't want you to be used to it. Let me shield you from this."

Julia swallowed. "Do you have any idea how many times I've had a guy say he'd stick up for me like that?"

He shrugged. "No idea. You know it's not my favorite subject."

"Zero. Zero times. You're the only one."

"Really?"

"Really. Believe me, I wouldn't lie about that." She stood and hiked up her dress again. "Okay. Let me get out of this silly get-up so we can get it to the seamstress and she can hopefully finish the alterations before tomorrow. I need to get out of this place."

He straightened, now keenly aware of the privacy they had, in a way that hadn't made an impression before. He really wanted to kiss her again. "I don't get to stay?"

She shook her head. "We're in a bridal boutique in the South. Let's not invite more scandal into our lives by being the unmarried pregnant couple making out in the fitting room."

His hand nearly twitched. The ring in his pocket might help to shut everyone up. But he couldn't go there until he knew for certain that she would say yes, and that they were ready. They needed their trial period. They needed to lean on each other again. "Okay, then. Out I go."

Logan quietly exited the dressing room and closed the door behind him. A few steps into the main room of the boutique and the eyes of the women working at the shop were all on him. He was used to women staring at him every now and then, but this was different. There was a whole lot of judgment being aimed at him right now and he didn't like it one bit. Julia thankfully emerged from behind the white door, the pink dress in her hands. One of the women working in the shop rushed over to take it from her.

A fraction of a smile crossed Julia's face as she walked up to him. Relief settled in. As much as she needed reassurance that everything would be okay, he needed it, too. He wasn't going to ask for it, but hopefully that grin from her meant that he could start trusting his instincts again. It was time.

"So? What should we do?" he asked. "We have hours until we need to be at the rehearsal."

"You know what would be awesome?"

Logan hoped she would suggest they go back to the hotel and have sex all afternoon.

"Let's go to the beach."

# Eleven

Julia rolled down the car window and leaned against the door frame, letting the wind sweep her hair from her face and the sun warm her skin. Closing her eyes, she breathed in the familiar salty breeze.

"Any particular place you want to stop?" Logan asked.

"Anywhere quiet. I do not want to see people. And if you see a single member of my family, turn around and go in the opposite direction. I don't care how fast you drive."

He laughed, further improving her mood. If ever there was a sound worth listening to, it was Logan's laugh—not as deep as his speaking voice, but close, and it was always unguarded. "If we want privacy, then I think we both know where we need to go."

Privacy. "Yes. Go there."

A short fifteen minutes later, Logan pulled the car over to the side of the road in the perfect spot, right where a long string of rental houses stood between two of the bigger beach hotels. The undertow was particularly strong in this stretch and the sand extra pebbly, making it far less popular with swimmers. With school back in session, it wouldn't be too busy.

Julia kicked off her flats and collected them in her hands while Logan sat on the edge of the public access walkway, taking off his black leather shoes and removing his socks. He rolled up the legs of his jeans. Julia just watched, admiring him. A stunning ocean vista might have been waiting on the other side of the dunes, but the line of Logan's athletic shoulders as he hunched over was more enticing. He stood and gathered his things in one hand, while doing something that she had once taken for granted. He reached for her. Surely he'd done it thousands of times over the years, but it nearly knocked the breath out of her now. So much was expressed in that single gesture—everything she'd wished for, the thing that had left an unimaginable void when it was taken away. She'd felt heartbroken every time she and Logan had ever parted, even when she'd done the walking away.

"Hey, Logan," she said as they advanced over rickety gray wooden slats glazed with sand. Tall beach grass rustled and whipped at their legs. "Can we make a deal?"

"Tentatively, yes."

She stepped ahead of him and came to a stop, taking his other hand and peering up at him. His aviator sunglasses glinted as a curious smile spread slowly across his lips. Between the glare and his grin, it was a wonder she wasn't blind. "No more questions today, okay? Even when it's just the two of us. Let's practice being happy. I think I've forgotten how to do that."

He wrapped an arm around her shoulders, pulling her close and pressing a kiss to the top of her head. At moments like this, his tenderness was unmatched, a gift. "I think we both could use the practice."

Julia sighed, her legs feeling a bit like they were made of rubber. Being in his arms gave her exactly what she'd been craving—a refuge. "Good."

A few dozen steps and they crested the dunes and descended the stairs to the beach. Aside from an older couple sleeping on lounge chairs beneath an umbrella and a man casting a line into the water, the shore was nearly deserted, stretching north for what looked like a mile without another person. Julia let Logan lead the way down to the water. Midafternoon, the tide was low, revealing millions of tiny shells and scattered strands of seaweed.

Julia ventured in to her ankles, but Logan went midcalf, tugging on her hand. "Come on," he insisted. "It's so warm today."

"I don't want to get my dress wet."

He shook his head. "Don't be lame. Just come here."

There was something so sexy about being beckoned by Logan, somewhere between the tempting trouble of a dare and the thrill of an irresistible man wanting you close. She waded deeper. She had to. There was no denying Logan. Not when he was like this. She stood right next to him, the waves indeed threatening to soak the hem of her dress. They both looked off at the horizon, holding hands, leaning into each other as the Atlantic lapped at their legs. His thumb rubbed the back of her hand in a steady rhythm. The sun warmed her shoulders. Between Logan and the rock of the tide, the stress and worry were slipping away.

"Are you ready to give your toast tomorrow?" she asked.

"Yep. I have it all typed on my phone and everything."

"How very efficient of you."

"The best man should be prepared."

"I, of course, went old school and wrote mine on paper.

I'm a little worried it's corny, though. Either that or I'm thinking too hard about it."

"Do you have it with you?" He tugged on her hand.

"I do. It's in my purse. Want to trade?"

"We should probably at least practice."

"On dry land?"

"Yes."

They took their time, Julia kicking at the water as they made their way back up onto shore. They found a dry patch of sand and sat. The wind blew Julia's hair in a million directions as she dug around in her purse for the paper. Amid lip balm, gum and a pack of tissues, she finally found the carefully folded sheet torn from a legal pad. She handed it to Logan as he surrendered his phone to her.

It came as no surprise that Logan's was pure poetry from the first word, but the real curiosity was his subject matter. A few sentences in, she had to say something. "Logan. This is practically the same thing I wrote. Well, I mean, yours is written far better than mine, but that's no shock. You know, you really should write a memoir. I wasn't trying to fix your problems when I suggested it."

"I wouldn't know where to start with that, and I'm not sure anyone would want to read it in the first place."

"But you're an amazing writer. You'd figure it out. I know you'd do a fantastic job."

He returned his sights to the page, which ruffled in the breeze. Forearms resting on his knees, he shook his head and smiled. "Shhh. I'm reading."

Like she was supposed to do the same when he was being so adorable. Still, she returned to what he'd written, just to hear his voice in her head. It only took a few more lines before goose bumps were racing up her bare arms, even in the glow of the fading sun. "Fate returning two souls to each other? Isn't that the exact same thing I said?"

"You said fate *bringing* two souls together."

"Of course. I don't have your flair, Mr. Memoir-Writer. I'm calling you that from now on, just so you know." She went on reading, soon stumbling over another parallel. "We both told the same story, about that night at the beach house when Tracy cut her foot on that rusty old can in the sand. About Carter carrying her inside and how sweet they were to each other."

"Is it really that surprising? It's a great story."

She shrugged. "It is a great story, but it also happened an eon ago. It's still a weird coincidence."

"When you and I are on the same page, we're really on the same page."

Julia's skin tingled with recognition. "It's true. There's not much stopping us when we're in sync." She handed him his phone and tucked her speech back into her purse. "Yours is so good. It's almost too good. I feel like I should change mine. Otherwise people are just going to get bored or say that we copied each other."

"Yours is perfect. Keep it just the way it is. I'll tweak mine. I'm sure I can come up with something else to say."

"See? You can't *not* write." Julia leaned back on her hands, digging her toes into the sand. "You know, I think about that night with Tracy and Carter and I'm still sort of in awe of it. It's still so vivid. It was like watching a movie. We saw them fall in love with each other. It was so romantic."

He reached back for her hand. "Maybe we're watching the same thing."

Warmth rushed to her cheeks. "It's not the same. We're participating. And we're a lot older now. We already fell in love for the first time."

"First off, I think it's better that we're older. It means more. And people can fall in love more than once. My grandmother used to say that the secret to a long marriage was falling in love over and over again. She'd been married to my grandfather for sixty-seven years when he passed away."

Leave it to Logan to break out an especially poignant story, made even better with his impossibly romantic turn of phrase. As competitive as they could be with each other, she'd gladly be outmatched by him when it came to romance. "Yeah? What makes you think things will suddenly work now that it's all so much more complicated?"

He shook his head and raised a finger to her lips. "We aren't asking questions today. No worrying about tomorrow. We only do what makes us happy. We do what feels right." He moved his hand to the side of her face and raked his fingers through her hair. "Like this."

Her heart wouldn't stop fluttering at the anticipation as he rubbed her jaw with his thumb and caressed her neck with his fingers. When his lips finally met hers, the kiss was soft and tender, but passionate. Focused. She sensed a different sweet sentiment with every move of his mouth, which still amazed her, even after all this time. She arched her back, craned her neck, desperate to keep doing the one thing that they knew they couldn't get wrong, no matter how hard they tried. His lips became more insistent, the heat building, his tongue gentle but unsubtle in where this was going. He wasn't kidding about doing what felt right—this was every kind of correct she could imagine. She shut out the bad thoughts that wanted to creep in and went with the moment. Old wounds would take a long time to heal. She couldn't expect it to happen overnight. And the kiss was definitely helping.

Logan really wished they had a blanket, so they could lie back on the sand, roll around a little. But they didn't, which meant he could take this kiss only so far. Not to mention that they were in public, however quiet the beach was that afternoon.

Julia's lips were as sweet now as they'd been every other time he'd kissed her over the last few days, but there was something else behind the kiss now…a promise that they were going to try to find a way. If Julia would just give a little bit, try to understand his hesitation and at least acknowledge that it was okay for him to feel the way he did, he could do the same. Give an inch here, an inch there, until finally they could meet in the middle.

Her hand clutched his biceps, her hair whipped at his face, as they both became more emphatic with the kiss. It was as if they were in their own little world and they were doing nothing but one-upping each other, a familiar part of their dynamic. *I want you. I want you more. I want you the most.* Logan's brain wouldn't stop thinking about what might lie ahead…a continuation of the heavenly fun they'd had that morning. They did, after all, have a hotel room to return to. They did, after all, have several hours until the rehearsal.

Julia's phone started beeping in her purse. She wrenched herself from the kiss and turned away from him, grabbing at her bag and digging in it.

"No, Jules. Let it go." *This is too good.* His eyes were half-open, his breathing labored. Every part of him was poised and ready to have her, make love to her.

"It's not a call. It's the alarm on my phone. We should head back to the hotel to get ready for the rehearsal."

The hotel. Bed. Privacy. "Yes. We should go." Logan grabbed his shoes and stood up, even when it was difficult to fully straighten. Everything below his waist was ready to have her, and it felt as if the blood had left his limbs. Julia scampered up the dunes to the stairs and Logan had no choice but to follow, every step painful, especially as he watched the sway of her hips in that summery dress and the way the wind carried it up to the middle of her thighs.

Logan grabbed a pair of flip-flops he'd left in the back seat and put them on, wanting to hurry as much as Julia did. He started the car and cranked the air-conditioning, needing to cool off. Julia had him way too warmed up. That morning had been wonderful, but it wasn't nearly enough, and everything had been a mystery then. There was far less gray area between them now.

They arrived at the hotel in record time, but Julia didn't seem to notice the liberties he'd taken with the speed limit. She was preoccupied with texting and checking things on her phone. The guy at the valet stand greeted them and took care of the car quickly, and they lucked out when they didn't have to wait for the elevator inside. Down the hall to their room, each step only made Logan's pulse race faster. He would have her. Right now.

He took her into his arms the instant they were inside their room, his hand quickly finding the zipper on the back of her dress and drawing it down. She kissed him back, moaning softly. He loved the sound, until he realized it was a complaint.

"Everything okay?"

"Why did you have to kiss me at the beach that way?" Her gorgeous chest was heaving.

"We were going with it, remember? And being around you is making me crazy, Jules. I want you. Now."

"I know. I want you, too." She kissed him, her tongue winding with his. "But we can't. There's no time. If we're late for the rehearsal, Tracy will literally kill me."

Julia's moans might have conveyed annoyance, but he was about to register a grievance of his own. "Just a quickie. Or a shower. We'll call it multitasking."

She shook her head and kissed his cheek. "You're cute,

but I have to do my hair and makeup from scratch and I haven't shaved my legs."

"See? I'll help."

"Do you really want to rush through this? If we're going to make love do you really want to hurry it? After the day we've had and everything we said to each other?" She pressed her hand flat against his chest. "I want us to be able to take our time with each other." She bit on her lower lip. "I want to be able to be thorough. If you know what I mean."

A low rumble came from the center of his chest. Oh, he knew exactly what she meant. And thinking about it all night was going to make him insane. Still, she was probably right. If they were going to get back to where they used to be, it needed to be more than a quickie. They needed hours to reconnect on every level. "Okay. You shower first. Just be sure to use all of the hot water. Every drop. I want mine ice cold."

"I'm sorry. Really. I am." She popped up onto her tiptoes and kissed his cheek. She flashed a smile and hurried off to the bathroom, shutting the door behind her.

Logan flopped down on the bed, frustration about to eat him alive. *This is going to be a really, really long night.*

# Twelve

Logan now knew what it was like to be on the outs with the Keys family. And he didn't like it one bit.

"I have to talk to your dad," he mumbled into Julia's ear as they both stood in the church, waiting for the rehearsal to start.

"Not now," she whispered.

"At dinner."

She shot him a look. "Can we talk about this later?"

He was about to retort that they'd agreed there would be no questions, but the minister had begun delivering orders. Stand here. Stand there. Walk like this. Wait for this. Get out the rings. Wait again. This was going to take forever. All while enduring the cold shoulder from Julia's parents.

Carter and Tracy were wound as tight as he'd seen either of them, but it was seeing Mr. and Mrs. Keys like this that really ate at him. If he and Julia were going to find a future, he couldn't be at odds with them. Surprisingly, the person who seemed somewhat relaxed, or at least comparatively so, was Julia. Whether she'd wanted to admit it or not, keeping the secret of the baby had been a big burden to bear.

By far, the high spot of the rehearsal was standing at the altar with the other groomsmen, watching Julia walk up the aisle. Step by measured step, she was both graceful and statuesque, wearing a gauzy navy blue dress that fluttered at her feet and showed off her gorgeous shoulders. Their gazes connected, and he couldn't have contained his grin if he'd wanted to. Similarly, a smile broke across her face; petal pink washed over her cheeks. She shied away, casting her sights to the red carpet runner. His mind raced with excuses they could use to skip the rehearsal dinner—a horrible headache, a painful splinter. The truth was that he and Julia had shared a roller coaster of a day—from the high points of making love and spending time on the beach, to the low of that moment in the fitting room. They were finally back on track. She knew how he felt about the things that had bothered him for years, and he had begun the process of accepting that he might not be the baby's father. He'd been working hard to see past that possibility. And because of the things they'd patched up today, he craved more togetherness. He longed for them to be alone.

Once the ceremony run-through was done, and the bride and groom had shared their practice kiss, it was time for Logan and Julia to walk down the aisle arm in arm.

"You are so beautiful in that dress," he muttered out of the side of his mouth, pulling her close. "I know I told you at the hotel, but really. It's mind-boggling."

"You told me in the car, too. And don't act like I can even come close to matching the way you look in that suit." She glanced up at him, putting every nerve ending in his body on high alert. "The tie really brings out your eyes. Much better than the ones they put you in on TV."

Damn, it felt good to be admired by her. It was intoxicating enough to be in her presence, but when she was solely focused on him? Forget it. The rest of the world hardly existed. Step by step down that aisle, all eyes on them, he couldn't help but wonder what it would be like to go through this ritual with her. He had some fences to mend with the Keyses, but that would pass. With the ring in his pocket, he was still waiting to find the right moment to ask, the perfect point in time. There'd been twelve years of build-up to a proper proposal. It had to be right, and it had to be romantic.

Would Julia be as much of a wreck for her own wedding as she was for her sister's? He could just see it now—guest list a mile long, a wedding planner buzzing about and bossing everyone around, a big fancy church and an even fancier reception. Between her Hollywood friends and his legion of former teammates, it did seem to call for a grand affair. One rule would have to be strictly adhered to, by both of them—no exes. No exceptions.

Tracy insisted Julia ride with her out to the beach house for dinner, which left Carter and Logan some guy time in Logan's car.

"I can't believe you didn't tell me about the baby," Carter said. "That's huge."

He and Julia didn't enjoy the business of keeping secrets, but they had agreed to keep the question of paternity under wraps for now. They had enough obstacles to overcome, and they didn't need the world weighing in on their future. "I know. I'm sorry. I promised her I wouldn't say anything and I had to keep my word."

"Are you nervous? First-time dad and you have to figure out a way to make things work with the one woman who makes you crazy? That's a big challenge."

Logan felt the corners of his mouth turn down. It was so much more than that, and Carter had no idea. "When you put it like that, yes. I'm nervous."

"I didn't mean to sound all gloom-and-doom. I'm just in awe of you for trying. I think it's awesome. You're going to make an amazing dad."

Logan took the left onto Lumina Avenue toward the Keyses' beach house. Carter's words were still ringing in his ears. Was he really going to make a good dad? He wanted to think so. He wanted to believe he was up to the challenge, even if it meant raising a child who wasn't biologically his. "If I can be half as good of a dad as my father was, I'll be doing pretty well."

"I'm bummed I never had a chance to meet your dad. He sounds like he was such an incredible man."

"He was. I never would've gotten as far in baseball as I did without the things he did for me. I just wish I could've done it all. I still feel like I let him down. Or at least his memory." Logan always missed his dad, but it was especially palpable today. The conversation he'd had with his mom that morning would've been different with his father. Backward or macho or whatever anyone wanted to call it, his dad would've understood Logan's perspective fully. He wanted the baby to be his.

"I don't see any way your dad would've been anything less than totally proud of you."

"I guess. But if we'd won the World Series, I wouldn't have any doubts."

Logan slowed down as they approached the Keyses' beach house, which was all lit up, glowing against the darkening night sky. The parking area under the house was full, so Logan took a spot on the road. He turned off the ignition. "Ready?"

"I want to say one more thing. I know it's only been a year, but you need to find a way to let this go. Stop being so hard on yourself."

It wasn't that Logan needed the affirmation, but he'd take it. "Do I need to start paying you by the hour? Or are you hoping for a future in career counseling for athletes?"

Carter laughed. "I get that you're competitive and that you want it all. But not every ballplayer wins a World Series. Not every dad has a chance to see his child fulfill their dreams. It's sad, but it's life."

*I know. Do I ever know.*

Tracy pulled up behind them. Logan and Carter quickly hopped outside. Carter walked double-time to Tracy's side of the car, opening her door for her. By the time Logan got to Julia, he was too late to do the same, but he was at least able to close it for her. Tracy and Carter made their way to the house; Logan and Julia lagged behind.

"When do we get to get out of here?" he muttered.

"We haven't even eaten yet. My sister will freak out if we leave early."

"I know, but all I want is to be alone with you."

She stopped just shy of the door. A sly smile crossed her lips. "You're cute when you're desperate for sex."

"I'm not desperate. Just ready." It was about more than the physical urge, though. He needed that connection with her, especially after everything today.

He wrapped his arm around her waist and pulled her forward. Julia kissed him this time and it was so natural, as if they were falling together in perfect sync. It was as if he'd stepped into a dream. She pressed into him, arching her back, hinting at everything he wanted with a welcome side of enthusiasm.

They went inside where everyone was gathering for dinner—aunts, uncles and distant cousins had arrived at the house during the rehearsal, with their Aunt Judy, who lived up the coast in Elizabeth City, in charge. Lined up neatly on the kitchen island were chafing dishes of North Carolina chopped pork barbecue, coleslaw, hush puppies, collard greens and baked beans. Logan's stomach growled, but something else inside him begged for attention as he again exchanged looks with Julia's dad. He had to speak to him.

After dinner and many long toasts, Logan saw Julia's dad step outside onto the deck. Julia was immersed in conversation with her aunt, so he took his chance. He didn't want an argument. He wanted to fix this.

"Mr. Keys," Logan said, closing the sliding glass door behind him. The night air was humid and blustery. "Do you have a minute?"

Mr. Keys was standing at the railing, looking out at the surf. "Always. I always have a minute for you."

Logan finally felt as though he could breathe. "About today. I know this all came as a shock, but I don't want everyone to be too hard on Julia. She really was doing what she felt was right. You know her. She's always worried far more about everyone else than she is about herself."

Mr. Keys let out a quiet laugh. "I do know that about my daughter. That's for sure. She's been like that since she was little. The number of stray animals she brought home over the years would make your head spin. And don't even get me started on the charity lemonade stands."

Now it was Logan's turn to laugh. He loved the image of a young Julia, out there, trying to save the world one project at a time.

"So is this what you were hinting at yesterday?" Mr. Keys asked. "That business of not counting you two out?"

Logan nodded. "You could say that. I know this is unconventional, but things with Julia and I have been rocky over the years. We're doing our best to put it together."

"Unconventional? I'd call it putting the cart before the horse." Mr. Keys's words nearly made Logan's heart seize up. He turned, leaning back against the railing and folding his arms across his chest. He nodded in the direction of the party inside. Julia and Tracy were talking, right on the other side of the sliding glass doors. "You'll understand it much better when you're a dad, but those two girls are my greatest gift. I would do anything to protect them. Keep them safe."

"I understand. I really do."

"But you know, what you and Julia do is none of my darn business. I just want my daughters to be happy." There was an unmistakable wobble to Mr. Keys's voice, underscoring the reasons he'd been testy with Logan.

"I admire you for doing anything to protect your girls."

"I have to admit, I'm more than a little excited by the prospect of being a grandfather." He elbowed Logan in the stomach. "And what if it's a boy? I could have a major leaguer for a grandson."

Logan caught the look in Mr. Keys's eye, a glint of pride. Something about that moment made the baby much more real, far less of an abstract. Would the baby be a boy? A girl? Regardless, he saw ten small fingers and ten small toes, chubby legs and cheeks, a sweet baby face. In his mind, his head, and his heart, the baby looked like both Julia and him. He couldn't see the baby any other way. It might not be the right vision to cling to, but it was an idea firmly planted, and he'd just have to deal with the reality when the time came.

"I want you to know that I won't let Julia down. And I won't shirk my responsibilities. You'll have to trust that we're doing our best to work things out." He watched Julia through the glass—the way she focused intently when someone spoke to her, the way she tossed her head back when she laughed, and the way her smile reflected the light inside her. She was so beautiful, inside and out. Mr. Keys had called her a gift. Logan understood now how true that was. *I love her.* He wasn't sure what he'd done to be lucky enough to have a second chance with her. Or in reality, more like his tenth chance. He only knew that he wouldn't let Julia wonder whether he was there for her. She said she needed to feel safe and like everything was okay. He could do that.

After two plates of food, three lemonades and countless uncomfortable questions about the future, Julia allowed herself to relish the part she'd played in making the rehearsal dinner a success. Tracy had completed the process of softening to her sister, although it had taken some intense conversation during the car ride to the beach, topped off with Tracy downing several glasses of wine. She actually seemed happy with the way things had gone. The food had been wonderful; the cake had arrived on time and exactly as Tracy had wanted it. Everyone raved about the house renovations. Tracy even remarked that the decorations were "perfect." Aside from an uncle from Indiana liberating himself from his pants before heading out for a late-night swim, the evening had been largely free of controversy. Now the final guests were filtering out of the beach house.

Julia was helping clean up the kitchen when Logan came up behind her, wrapping his arms around her waist and kissing her neck. "Mmm. You smell so good." His words and a single kiss sent electricity racing along her spine. And it felt so good to have his broad frame and warm body pressed against hers.

"Thank you. Shouldn't be too long and we can get out of here. Just a few more dishes."

"Can't someone else deal with this? You've worked your butt off today." With that, he gave her bottom a gentle squeeze. "Save some for me, please."

Julia turned around and playfully swatted him on his arm. "You're bad."

"I said please." His eyes scanned her face, amping up the anticipation. Sure, she and Logan had been to bed before. Just that morning, in fact. But not like this. Not when so much was on the line and she was so very well aware of how easily it could fall apart. She decided it was best to celebrate the fragile nature of what was between them. It was new life, just like the baby, and that was to be nurtured and cared for.

"Aunt Judy, do you mind finishing up?" Julia asked.

Her aunt looked up from the living room where she was fluffing couch cushions and picking up plastic cups. "Of course, darling. I'll take care of it. See you in the morning at the church."

"Have I told you how much I adore you, Aunt Judy?" Logan asked.

"You didn't need to. It's all over your face." She smiled wide. "Now shoo, you two."

Julia grabbed her purse and cardigan, took Logan's hand, and out they went into the night. The roar of the ocean was off in the distance, warm breeze sweeping against her skin as Logan took her hand and led her to the car. They climbed inside and Logan went for a kiss instead of turning the key in the ignition.

Julia reared back her head. "If we start here, we'll never be able to leave. And I really don't want Aunt Judy walking by while we're steaming up the windows."

"So true." Logan started the car, and after quickly looking both ways, made a U-turn in the middle of the street and raced off to the hotel. This late at night, they thankfully hit more than their fair share of green lights. Julia hoped it was symbolic of the future—no more stopping. Just moving forward.

By the time they turned the car over to the valet, speed-walked through the lobby, rode the elevator and raced down the hall to their room, they were both laughing. It was a fun and nervous laughter, filled with hope and happiness. Julia couldn't think of a time when things had felt more perfect.

"Before we go in, phones off," he said.

"Yes. You're so smart." She dug hers from her purse and shut the power off. "Good to go."

Logan opened the door and had his hands all over her the instant it closed behind them. "This dress has got to go."

"I thought you liked it."

"I do. I love it. I love it so much I want to see what it looks like on the floor. I think it will go with the carpet quite nicely."

"Just like your suit."

"I feel like we should hang up the suit."

"And not my dress? Talk about a double standard."

He wrapped his hand around her neck and rubbed her jaw with his thumb. "Kiss me and tell me we can worry about laundry later."

"Gladly," she purred, tugging on his necktie as his mouth crashed into hers. He smelled so good—the fragrance she could only describe as Logan, like a good glass of bourbon, warmed in the summer sun.

She took off his tie and he wrestled his way out of his jacket. Her fingers flew over the buttons of his shirt and as soon as that was gone, he turned her around, unzipping the back of her dress. He teased it from her shoulders, pushing it to the floor before pressing his body against hers. She felt the cool metal of his belt buckle in the curve of her back, and lower…a firm declaration of how turned on he was. He took her hair in his hands and swept it back from her neck, kissing her softly with a gentle brush of his tongue. She loved having him stand behind her. There was something so sexy about it, as if he expected no reciprocity, but of course she would be giving.

She reached back, finding his erection, which strained against the front of his pants. She pressed against it with her hand, eliciting a low groan from him. He backed up slightly and unhooked her strapless bra, a double dose of relief—the boning had been digging into her armpits for hours. She hummed with happiness over the reprieve from the torturous garment. Logan turned her in his arms, admiring her breasts with both hands, both eyes and a whole lot of commentary.

"I've always loved your breasts, but I just love how full they are right now."

Heat rushed to her cheeks. "Thanks."

"I meant it. They're stunning. Truly stunning."

"I'm glad you're enjoying them."

He cupped them with his palms, rubbed her nipples with his thumbs, drawing them into tight peaks. A week or so ago, that would've been torture, but the initial tenderness had subsided and between his touch and the pregnancy hormones, she was writhing with anticipation of more. As if he'd heard the wish she'd made in her head, he lowered his head and drew a nipple into his warm mouth, sucking softly and flicking at it with his tongue. She cradled his head in her hands, caressing his temples, leaning down to kiss the top of his head. He switched to the other breast and did the same, ramping up the intensity with licks and hot breath, causing her skin to bead so tightly she already felt as if she might unravel the instant he touched her most intimate parts.

He lowered himself to his knees, clutching her rib cage, then dragging his hands down her sides to her hips. He kissed her lower belly, gazing up at her. The only light in the room came from the nearly full moon, which was low in the sky tonight and cast soft beams through the window sheers. He was unbearably handsome in any light, but she couldn't have imagined him looking any more so than he did at that moment—his eyes and face full of adoration.

"I meant what I said earlier about your current state being a turn-on. Your body is so ripe right now. Every inch of you has a little more to squeeze and I love it. I absolutely love it." He grasped her hips, curving his fingers into the fleshy part of her buttocks, then tucked his fingers into the waist of her black satin panties and dragged them down to her ankles. She stepped out of them, reaching out to the arm of the chair behind her to steady herself. Logan seized the opportunity and backed her up a step, urging her to sit, but making it clear with his hands that he wanted her perched on the edge of the seat. Still on his knees, he coaxed one of her legs outward and hitched the other leg over his shoulder, opening her up to him. "Sit back for me," he said.

She watched his every move as his hand found her center and teased apart the folds. She gasped when he slipped two fingers inside her and rocked his thumb against her apex, slowly but deliberately. Her eyes opened and closed in an unpredictable pattern as her mind warred between wanting to luxuriate in the pleasure and wanting to watch what this incredible man was able to do to her. His fingers continued to glide inside her, and he curled them into the spot that made her arch her back and moan. Every inch of her marveled at how good it all felt, but there was a whole lot of anticipation of the main event going on in her head. "That feels so good," she muttered, feeling as if she might break at any moment. "But I want you inside me, Logan."

He kissed her lower belly. "I love hearing you say that. But we have all night, and I plan to enjoy every inch of you." He then moved his thumb aside from the tender bundle of nerves he'd been working and lowered his mouth to that spot, enveloping her with warmth as he wound his tongue in lazy circles.

Her thoughts were hazy, pleasure coiling tightly in her belly, and all she could do was unwind and let Logan have his way. Her breaths were ragged. Her chest heaved. Her body temperature was climbing steadily, warming her skin. With every pass of his tongue, the release crept closer, until finally she could take the pressure no longer and gave in to the orgasm. She called out his name and grasped his head, as every wave of joy and warmth unraveled her a little more. The minute she got her wits back, she sat up and brought Logan's face to hers, kissing him deeply as the remnants of the release still teased her body. In some ways, he hadn't satisfied her need for him so much as he'd heightened it.

He rose to his feet and stood before her, a tower of defined muscle. She tugged him closer and wrapped her hand around his steely length, rolling her thumb over the tip and watching his reaction. He closed his eyes and his head dropped back as her fingers rode up and down, gripping him until he became impossibly hard.

"Make love to me, Logan," she whispered.

He reached down and took her hand, bringing her to standing. They wrapped their arms around each other, kissing deeply, lips warm and wet. They turned in circles on their way to the bed, an incoherent couple's dance that eventually brought them to their landing spot. They collapsed on the bed in a heap and Logan rolled her to her back. He positioned himself between her legs and pushed himself up with one arm. Julia gasped when he finally came inside, at first only a little, before he flexed his torso and thrust with one strong and fluid movement.

He kissed her passionately, his tongue exploring her mouth and lips, as she wrapped her legs around him and they rocked in a rhythm that was all their own. Julia's mind became a swirl of serene thoughts. Many things in her world had felt wrong lately, but this undoubtedly felt right. It was the one conclusion she could make with zero deliberation. Logan rode in and out of her, lowering his head to her breast and flicking at her nipples with his tongue.

She was already poised for another release, but she focused on relaxing, even when her body was tensing in waves. His breaths were becoming short and labored, and she could tell from the tension in his back that he was close to his own climax. He kissed her again, this time with reckless urgency, his open mouth skating over hers, her cheeks and her neck. His thrusts came faster and more forceful until finally his body froze and a deep groan left his throat. He shuddered in her arms, and that was all it took for her to come undone once more, her body clutching his as he took a few final thrusts.

In utter exhaustion, he collapsed next to her on the bed, not hesitating to pull her against him and kiss her softly. "That was so incredible. Totally worth the wait."

She laughed quietly and shook her head, resting her head on his magnificent chest. "You mean the wait since this morning?"

"This morning was wonderful, don't get me wrong. But this had a lot of build-up. Makes it better." He raked his fingers through her hair. "I want you to know one thing,

Jules. I have always loved you. No matter what happens, I always will."

The confession took her by surprise, but not of a happy nature. It left her with that familiar sinking feeling, mostly because of what he hadn't said recently. Ever since they'd been doing well as a pair, he'd dropped all of his talk of marriage. What did that mean? Was he just trying to get through the weekend? He'd been so insistent about it before, bringing it up whenever he had the chance. Now the subject of marriage, and the future, and the baby were all absent. "You never stopped?"

Logan groaned. "Jules. No questions, remember?"

But she did have a question. More than one, actually. Starting with this—why did "I will always love you" have to sound so much like "goodbye"?

# Thirteen

Waking up next to Julia was more spectacular than Logan had remembered. Perhaps because it meant more now. They had managed to reclaim what they had three months ago, only this time he would not mess up.

She stirred in his arms and kissed his chest, bringing his entire body to life. “Good morning,” she murmured sweetly.

“It is a very good morning.” *Every morning will be good with you.*

“The big day is here.”

“It is.” The big day was indeed upon them, and not just for Tracy and Carter, although Julia had no idea. Logan had monumental plans for after the wedding—he was finally going to propose. He’d decided last night after Jules fell asleep, spending hours—literally—thinking out every scenario. The way he might feel if the baby wasn’t his. The way he would feel if the baby was. What it would feel like to build a family with Julia, the woman he’d never stop loving. He wouldn't take this lightly, as she'd suggested he might. He was ready. They were ready. He would convince her of it. And he was an idiot if he waited even another day. He wasn't about to risk something going wrong. He had to tie up these particular loose strings, ASAP.

"Yep. Won't be long now and it'll all be over. I'll be flying back to LA to finish the movie. You'll be flying home to Connecticut."

He could tease her about this later, right after he'd popped the question. "Back to reality."

She abruptly sat up in bed, turning her back to him. "Have you figured out what you're changing in your toast?"

"Not yet, but I will." With everything else going on, he hadn't had a spare second to think about it. Hopefully something would happen during the ceremony to spark an idea.

She grabbed his T-shirt from the floor and put it on, then made a beeline for the bathroom.

"You aren't leaving me, are you?"

"Gotta hop in the shower. It's my last chance to have an entire day where I don't make my sister mad. I don't want us to be late."

She closed the bathroom door and Logan got up, pulling on a pair of basketball shorts. He began to collect the belongings he would need for the day. He reached inside the pants pocket where the ring was safely tucked away, and gave it a squeeze for good luck. Wouldn't be long until it was on Julia's finger.

Julia had left a tote bag sitting on the floor, which had fallen over, causing several things to slip out, including a book about pregnancy. Curious, he flipped through the pages, quickly becoming immersed and sitting in the chair to read. There was so much to learn. Julia's body was going to do a lot of incredible things over the next six months. As would the baby. Apparently, she'd soon be able to feel the baby kick. *The baby.* It was still difficult to wrap his head around it, but it was getting a little easier with every passing minute, and a kick he could understand.

Julia seemed in a bit of a mood when she got out of the bathroom, but Logan knew the wedding weighed heavily on her mind, so he didn't bother saying anything, preferring instead to keep things light and upbeat. After he showered and dressed, they were off to the church by nine thirty. The ceremony was at eleven, to be followed by lunch and dancing until early evening, which suited Logan just fine. It meant more time for his night with Julia, the one where they finally set their future on the right path.

They ran into the woman from the bridal shop in the church parking lot.

"Everything go okay with the alterations?" Julia asked.

The woman nodded as she handed over a garment bag. "It did. There was enough fabric in the side seams to let it out. Good luck with the pregnancy."

Julia smiled, but Logan knew that particular grin, and it wasn't one she used when she was happy. It was for those moments when she had to fake it. "Uh-huh. Thank you."

The woman left while Logan and Julia walked inside.

"You okay?" he asked.

"Doesn't it seem weird that she mentioned the pregnancy out loud?"

Logan shrugged. "I guess. But isn't she the one who figured it out?"

Julia clutched the garment bag to her chest. "We asked the women in the shop not to say anything. Do you think somebody could've said something? I really don't want us to have to deal with the press again."

Logan hated seeing her so on edge, just as much as he

hated the idea of battling the media again. He gripped her elbow and kissed her temple. "Don't be paranoid. It'll be fine."

"Okay." She didn't seem at all convinced. "I have to go get dressed. Then I need to check on the flowers one last time."

"Sounds like a plan. I have to do a few things for Carter, but I'll meet you in the chapel if I can."

"Okay." Her tone was annoyed, but she was worried about the notion of the press returning. Precisely the reason to wait for peace and calm to pop the question.

They parted, Logan finding the room where the groomsmen were camped out. "How's Tracy's future husband?" Logan asked Carter, who was in his tux and pacing, about to wear a path in the carpet.

Carter tugged at the collar. "I already hate this thing. And I can't stop sweating."

Logan clapped him on the shoulder. "Just sit and relax. You're going to do great today. It'll all be fine. I promise." Logan had apparently been put in charge of keeping everyone calm, a job he readily accepted today. For once, he felt as though he could see ahead, to the future. He had a clear course to take. A purpose. "I need to get dressed."

Logan ducked into a small adjacent room to put on his tux. He was putting in his cufflinks when Carter poked his head in. "Julia's out in the hall. She says she needs to talk to you right away. I think she's panicking again."

*What now? Please don't let it be the press.* "Okay. I'll be right out." He slipped into his jacket and rushed out into the hall.

She knocked the breath right out of him when he saw her. Sure, he'd seen her in the dress at the bridal shop, but this was different and not just because it actually fit her now. Her hair was up in an elegant twist; the morning light from the arched windows that lined the hall cast her in a heavenly glow. She was so gorgeous—so perfect. And his. Now he understood what Carter had been saying about waiting for the other shoe to drop. Logan was damn lucky and he knew it.

"We have a problem," she blurted.

"Just one?" He stepped next to her, inhaling her sweet scent. "Then I'd say we're doing great. You look absolutely gorgeous, by the way."

"Don't be so dismissive."

"I could say the same thing about you. You didn't even acknowledge my compliment." He circled his arms around her waist, wanting her close.

She took a deep breath and forced a smile. "Thank you. Now come with me." She grasped his hand and marched them into the chapel. "Look. It's a complete disaster."

His eyes darted all over the room, searching for evidence of catastrophe. "What is?"

"The peonies. They aren't pale pink. They're pale purple. They're practically lavender." She forged ahead up the aisle, and Logan had to hustle to keep up. "See what I mean?" She pointed to an arrangement attached to the end of the pew as if it were the most repulsive thing she'd ever seen.

She wasn't wrong. They were clearly purple. And who really cared at this point? "Considering everything that has happened over the past few days, this is so unimportant. You did your best, and that's all anyone can ask. In the end, Tracy and Carter will be married, and that's what really matters."

"You don't think she'll freak out?"

"If she does, tell her to freak out at me. You've done so much to make her happy, and that includes keeping a secret that totally backfired on you."

"Please don't say I told you so."

"I won't. I think you know now that it was a bad idea to keep the pregnancy from your family."

She bowed her head. "I do. I messed up. I completely ruined that moment with my mom and there's no getting it back. I think that's my problem. I'm trying to keep any more moments from being ruined."

He put his arm around her and pulled her close. "It will all change when the baby arrives. Your mom will forget all of that. You'll have your moment with her then." All he could think about was the proposal later. He wanted that to be perfect, too. He understood exactly how she felt. "You know, I was reading your pregnancy book this morning while you were in the shower."

"You did?"

"I did. I read all about how big the baby is right now and about how big it's going to get. I read about when you'll be able to feel it kick. That's exciting stuff." *I hope I get to be there.* There was still part of him that knew Julia could panic. Or change her mind. Or say no. And her reaction to something as simple as the color of flowers wasn't doing much to assuage his worry.

She bit into her lower lip, her mouth quivering. "That's so sweet."

"Why are you crying?"

"Because I don't know what to think anymore, Logan, that's why. Two days ago you were all hot to get married and then the minute we start getting along, you drop it. All I can think is that you're just waiting and hoping..." A sob came out of her. "Hoping that the baby is yours."

He pulled her into a hug, holding her close, not wanting to ever go. "Of course I hope that the baby is mine. How could I not hope that?"

Julia's body tensed in such an immediate way that he knew he'd messed up.

He stood back, holding on to her shoulders. The sadness in her eyes had become more profound. "That's probably not the right way to put it. In fact, I know it's not the right way to put it." He couldn't explain himself further. It would ruin his plans for tonight. Guests would be walking into the church any minute now. There was no time.

"No. It's okay. I know what you mean. And you're just being honest."

He breathed a huge sigh of relief. "Exactly."

"You're just saying what's really in your heart. Which is that you only want to be with me if the baby is yours. You've convinced yourself that's the only way this works."

*No no no.* "That's not what I'm saying. I haven't convinced myself of anything. I love you, Jules, I told you that."

"You told me that you will always love me. It's not the same. And I need you to love the baby, completely. That's the only way this works. Unconditional love. No questions asked."

Visions of Julia's legion of scummy boyfriends shuffled through his mind, the guys who always treated her so badly. Was he strong enough to love a child who was a product of one of those pairings? The pairings that had ripped his heart out, and hers for that matter, over and over again? He wanted to be able to say that he would love the baby unconditionally from his or her very first breath, but the truth was that it might take some getting used to. Not much. But possibly a little. He would get there. He knew he would. But if he was being honest, there was a chance it would take time. "Am I not allowed to have a single doubt?" He took her hand and led her to the far side of the rectory as guests began to file in.

She crossed her arms, the hurt and betrayal radiating off of her. He wasn't doing any better. How had they ended up back at square one again? Neither of them truly trusting that the other would do what they said they were going to do? "No, Logan. You aren't. You aren't allowed to have a single doubt. I don't see any way that two people stay together for the long haul without setting aside every last doubt in their head."

A low grumble escaped Logan's throat. "Love isn't a destination. It takes work. A lot of work. And you're being so stubborn about this."

"I have no choice but to be exactly that, Logan. I can't let you break my heart again. It nearly killed me the first time."

*Nearly killed me.* "Then we work it out. Again." He couldn't hide his irritation with all of this.

She shook her head, tears welling at the corners of her eyes. "My original plan was the safest. You and I make great friends. We make great lovers. I think we'll make a good mom and dad, but I think those are separate things now. I don't know that we'll make a good husband and wife."

"What are you saying?"

She wrapped her arms around her waist, tears now rolling down her cheek.

"No. No. Jules, don't bail on me." It felt as if his stomach was diving for the floor. This was classic Julia—form an opinion and steamroller ahead, even when her take on things might not be based in reality.

"You know what, Logan? This is part of me correcting my past mistakes. You said you didn't want to be with me when I viewed you as a project. Well, this is me telling you that you're not a project. You don't want me to fix you, fine. I'm done fixing. You figure it out."

"Hoping that the baby will be mine isn't the most selfish thing in the world. It's human. I'm human."

She shook her head. "Do you have any idea how lonely I felt the day I found I was pregnant? That was supposed to be a purely happy day. But all I could do was wonder how I was going to make this work." Her hand went to her belly, cupping the tiny mound that was there. "This child needs love, Logan. Pure and simple. Doesn't matter what color his skin is or how tall she ends up being. In the end, this tiny human being growing inside me is going to need love. If I have to be the only person who gives it, I'll do that. Because I can't sit by and wonder if and when you're going to get with the program. I won't do it. It's one thing when it's my heart on the line, but I won't hurt this child."

"I'm not trying to hurt anyone. I'm just being honest."

Now the tears were really streaming down Julia's face, streaking her makeup and blanching her skin. "You questioned my stance on the paternity test, but this is the exact moment I feared. I knew that the minute I did and we got an answer you weren't going to like, that would be the end of Logan and Julia, forever. I wasn't ready to shut the door on us. But unfortunately, this just makes it feel like you do. I can't let you do it again, Logan. I have to be stronger than that."

"Jules. Come on. Let's just talk. I beg you."

"I can't stay. Not like this." With a swish of her dress, she was gone. Straight down the aisle and right out of his life.

*I should've known. I should've known it was too good to be true. Things aren't perfect for Logan and he has to take off. Just like last time.*

Julia raced down the hall to the room where her sister was getting ready. She stopped in the doorway, unable to step inside, although she wasn't sure why. Her mom was there, standing by Tracy's side.

"No tears." Tracy looked into the vanity mirror as she adjusted a clip in her hair. "There will be no tears on my wedding day."

"The mother of the bride is entitled to cry, honey. It's practically a tradition." Their mother pulled a tissue from her purse and blew her nose.

Julia stood frozen, sucking in deep breaths as inconspicuously as possible. And to think she'd been worried that flowers or cakes or of course, her pregnancy secret might ruin her sister's wedding. The reality was she was one unkind word away from collapsing into a pathetic pile of pink organza on the floor.

"Hey, Jules. I didn't see you there," Tracy said.

"Yep. Just got here." Julia's lip trembled, but she tried to ignore it.

"Everything good?" Tracy asked.

"Yes. Of course." Her sister would have her perfect day if it killed her. Which meant Julia had to keep her desire to blubber her eyes out to herself.

"Are you okay, darling? Your voice sounds funny. And why are you practically standing out in the hall? Come inside or Carter might try to sneak a peek at the bride."

Julia stepped into the room and closed the door behind her. "I'm fine. Just a little choked up, that's all. It's Tracy's big day and we've been waiting for it for so long. I'm so incredibly happy for her."

Tracy caught her sister's gaze in the reflection of the mirror. She jutted out her lower lip. "Now you're going to make me cry. That's the sweetest thing I think you've ever said to me. Come here." Tracy turned and reached for Julia and good God, Jules couldn't have kept it together if she'd been paid to do it. "I'm so sorry about my behavior over the last few days," Tracy said. "I know I've been hard on you and I'm sorry. Someday, you'll be in my place and you'll understand why I got so caught up in everything. I swear, it'll make you crazy."

*In my place.* Julia was convinced she would never, ever be in her sister's place. Ever. She wasn't capable of keeping a relationship together. Call it self-sabotage. Call it something else. She messed it up every time, and there was no sign of her changing this pattern any time soon. She and Logan had their breakthrough, the one they'd tried to reach for years. Then it all came tumbling down.

"I'm sorry I caused so many problems. It was never my intention," Julia said.

"I know you didn't do it on purpose. And you'll understand when you're a bride."

A single tear leaked from the corner of Julia's eye and she felt it about to happen—an avalanche of emotion was starting, trembling and quaking, threatening to crush her flimsy composure. "I'm not ever going to be a bride. I'm never going to get married. I'm going to die alone." The crying started. She'd cried more in the last month than she cared to admit. It wasn't a good thing to feel so on edge all the time.

"Don't say that."

"It's true. I get involved with the wrong guys over and over again. I can't help myself."

"Did something happen with Logan? I thought you two were working things out."

"We were, but then he had to go and say something that made me realize he doesn't really love me the way I need him to love me."

"What happened?"

Julia got very quiet, realizing there was a lot more to this explanation than simply recounting what happened.

"The thing is, about the baby, I'm not sure if it's his. It might be the boyfriend I had briefly before him."

"Oh no." Her mother closed her eyes and scratched her temple.

"Please don't freak out. I'm sorry I'm dumping all of this on you right now. We have to walk into that church in a few minutes and everything. I just… I thought he and I had worked it out and that he'd come to terms with the possibility that the baby isn't his, but he clearly still has doubts."

"Well, of course he has doubts. It's okay to have doubts," Tracy said, grabbing a nail file from the vanity and shaping one of her nails. "Carter had all kinds of doubts when we got back together. About whether or not it would work. He was gun-shy, to say the least. I was the one who'd broken up with him, and I think he was afraid I was going to break his heart again."

Many of Logan's words echoed in Julia's head…everything he'd said about the ways in which he'd been sure Julia would break his heart. "But you worked through all of it. You're getting married. Everything is perfect now."

"Everything is not perfect. We worked through enough to say that taking a chance on each other is a good idea. It doesn't mean we don't still have doubts. That's just part of being a couple. If you sit around waiting for the moment when everything is perfect, you're going to miss out on a lot."

Julia couldn't believe what was coming out of Tracy's mouth. "But Logan said that even though he loves me, he's still nervous about how he'll feel if the baby isn't his. And he was dead-set on getting married two days ago. Now that it's a little more real, he hasn't said a word about that. Doesn't that seem like an awfully damning detail?"

Their mother stepped forward and shook her head. "Jules, do you have any idea what you're asking of him?

It takes a big man to accept another man's responsibility, if that's the way this ends up. Of course he's going to have doubts. He's a first-time dad. Being a parent means you doubt everything and most of it comes down to worry that you won't measure up. Look at the relationship he had with his own dad. I'm sure he's worried about filling those shoes. It's not necessarily a reflection of you or the way he feels about you. Logan is a good man with a big heart, and he's wanted to be with you for more than twelve years. I think it's time you finally gave him the benefit of the doubt."

Julia's stomach sank. "So you're saying I messed up. Again."

"Yes. Yes, I am."

*Nothing like being real, Mom.*

"The good thing about mistakes is they can almost always be fixed."

A knock came at the door. "Five minutes until we're ready for the bride."

"Are you going to be okay, Jules?" Tracy asked.

*Once again, totally not okay.* Julia composed herself, glancing in the mirror and wiping away a smudge of mascara with her pinkie. "Yes. I'm great. My sister is getting married. That's all I really care about right now."

# Fourteen

The ceremony was torture. Standing up there, feet away from Logan, all while the room was filled with the heady scent of flowers and the knowledge that everyone in attendance was witnessing true love. Julia knew they were, and she was happy for her sister, but it only underscored one fact—this was one place she would never be.

When it came to the vows, Julia did everything she could to keep it together, but it was nearly impossible. The gasps and cries coming out of her mother in the front row weren't helping. Then there was Logan. She watched as he listened intently. The man had enough good looks for seven men, but that wasn't what she loved about him. She loved him for his persistence with her; she loved him for the ways he pushed for what he wanted. She loved him for his heart, which she knew from experience was the best place to ever be.

How could one person be everything she ever wanted

and still feel impossible to hold on to? Where was the fairness in that? Nowhere, that's where. But did it really matter? She might not have pushed him away the last time, but she'd pushed him away today, just as she'd pushed him away before. The pushing had to stop. The insecurities inside her, the ones that said she would never be good enough for him, were just going to have to learn to shut up. She had to make things right. She had to find a way to claim her one millionth chance to turn things around.

When it came time to walk down the aisle with him, she didn't waste a second. "We have to talk," she muttered out of the side of her mouth, with a big smile plastered to her face.

Logan smiled, too, but she knew it was for show, not his reaction to her. "Tell me about it."

They stood in the receiving line for a good half hour, shaking hands, kissing cheeks. Then it was time to go in to the reception. Every time Julia thought she'd catch a stray minute, someone would come up to her and start talking. Or they would drag Logan off to chat with someone else. It was a nightmare—no privacy, no alone time, no chance to just talk this out.

When it came time for toasts, she operated on autopilot. She read it exactly as she'd written it, not nearly as well as Logan, the man with the wonderful way with words. All she could think about was being on the beach a mere twenty-four hours ago, the world falling apart and coming together all at the same time. Her entire existence changed with Logan. It was different. It was better. And she was desperate to get back there. Again. Her mother and sister were right. It was horrible of her to hold Logan to such unrealistic standards.

"Let's all raise a glass to Tracy and Carter," she said, lifting her champagne glass, which was full of ginger ale.

The bubbles tickled her nose; tears tickled her eyes. The room was so full of love it nearly made her sick. Would Logan accept hers? What reason did he have aside from the baby? It would be easier on him if he just walked away. There was no doubt in her mind about that.

Logan clinked his fork against the side of his glass and stood. His focus was on Tracy and Carter, exactly as it should have been, but she longed for even a glance, a single flicker of his warm eyes. One look that would tell her that everything would be okay. That he would forgive her. "Just as Julia spoke of fate, I had originally planned to talk about the same thing today. And why wouldn't I? We all look at Tracy and Carter and know that they're meant to be together. It feels like fate that they found each other. Julia said exactly that." His normally strong voice wobbled, and he cleared his throat. "But what I want to talk about and toast to is perfection, or more specifically, the need to cast aside the notion of finding the perfect person. Because the truth is that Carter and Tracy aren't perfect. Neither one of them."

Carter shrugged and slugged back the last of the champagne in his glass, which brought a laugh from the guests and a welcome moment of levity.

"But together, as a couple, Carter and Tracy are perfect. They are there for each other. They don't let each other down. And when they do, they know how to say they're sorry."

Julia's breaths had grown so shallow she thought they might evaporate. Was this Logan's way of telling her that she'd done exactly that? She'd let him down. She would own up to it. She would say she was sorry. If he gave her the chance.

"They know how to forgive and ask for forgiveness,"

he continued. "They know to hold on to each other and not let go, because that is more important than anything."

With that, Logan looked at Julia intently, their gazes connecting, sending a steeplechase of goose bumps over her skin. His expression was difficult to read though and that filled her with familiar doubt. She wanted to think that she saw openness in his incredible eyes. She wanted to believe he would listen to her one more time, and that he wasn't instead holding her up as an example of the ways people don't manage to hold on to each other.

Logan turned his sights to the room of family and friends before them. "I'm not perfect," Logan continued. "I have made every mistake in the book. I have fallen short and I have failed. I've failed some of the most important people in my life. I'm not perfect. We're all imperfect." He glanced over at Julia again, this time looking much more deeply into her eyes. She was hanging on every word, still finding it nearly impossible to breathe. "But the beautiful thing about life is that if you find another person to love, your imperfections aren't important. Two imperfect people can make a perfect pair." He pressed his lips together and looked away. "With that, I want to wish Tracy and Carter a long and happy life together."

Logan sat down after his toast, hoping like hell that had done the trick. What else could he do? If Julia had decided that whatever he had to offer simply wasn't enough, there wasn't much to be done. How many times could he plead his case? It was nearly impossible to convince her of anything, but at least he could say that he'd made a strong argument.

The DJ made an announcement that it was time for Carter and Tracy's first dance. He watched as they made their way out to the dance floor, Tracy in her elegant white gown and Carter in his charcoal-gray tux. They seemed as happy as two people could be. *I want what they have.* His plan to get one step closer to his own wedding now seemed stupid. He should have given Julia the ring yesterday, when she was happy. He should have remembered just how tenuous things were between them and been more mindful of that.

Carter and Tracy started their dance, staring into each other's eyes, and gracefully swaying back and forth in each other's arms.

Julia, however, was playing musical chairs. She slid into the seat her sister had been occupying minutes ago, one seat closer to him. She patted the empty chair that had been Carter's. "Come here," she whispered.

He nearly asked if this was a trick, but he couldn't deny his natural inclination to want to be closer to her. He obliged. "Yes?"

"I wasn't kidding when I said that we need to talk."

"Okay. When?"

"Now?"

"The bride and groom are having their first dance. Don't you think we should stay to see that?"

She looked out at the dance floor and bobbed her head three times. "Okay. We saw it. Time to talk."

He laughed quietly. "For someone who was so concerned with making her sister happy, you don't seem to care much about it now."

She grasped his arm and squeezed, hard. "I'm more concerned with making us happy."

His breath caught in his throat. Maybe his speech really had worked. "Okay. Where?"

"Come with me." She took his hand and they made a careful and quiet exit, going out through the side of the reception hall, outside, and up a set of stairs to a wide stone balcony with a view of the Cape Fear River running alongside the downtown river walk.

When she stopped, she turned to him and took both hands, squinting into the sun. "I'm an idiot. I'm a total dummy and you're just going to have to find a way to forgive me. Let's get a paternity test right away. I'll do anything I can to have a shot at keeping you for real. We'll put all of it to rest and I'll have to trust that fate will keep us together somehow. We'll just do it. Rip it off like a Band-Aid."

If only she knew the thoughts that had run through his head during the ceremony, about the things he'd said. "We don't have to rely on fate, Jules. I don't want a paternity test. Frankly, you're as much of a test as I can handle."

She smiled softly. "Funny. I could say the same thing about you."

"Believe me, I know." He looked down at his feet, then out at the water, searching for the right words to say. Thoughts of Julia, of the baby, and of his dad had been cycling through his head all day. "I've spent an awful lot of my life hoping to live up to what my dad had wanted for me, the accolades and awards. Trying like hell to win a World Series. But after talking to your father last night, I really realized how much my dad loved his kids. He didn't catch a million pitches for me because he loved baseball. He did it because he loved me. This child deserves the same, and I know I'm capable of giving it. I'm not going to pass up the chance to do that. I don't need a test to prove to myself that I can."

"It's okay to have your reservations. I can live with them. I was being unreasonable and expecting you to conform to everything I wanted. I can trust that it will all work out." She smiled up at him, her face so eager and hopeful. "I can trust that we will work out."

"You don't have to worry about my reservations. There aren't any anymore. The last few hours, thinking about losing you again, all I could think was that I didn't doubt for a second that I wanted this. I wanted us, with the baby. The only hitch is that I need to know that you're on board. I need to know that you're in it for the long haul."

She blew out a breath and her eyes lit up, even out there in the bright sun. "I'm more than in it. I'm so sorry about this morning. I freaked out because it took me right back to that place where I was terrified of seeing you walk away."

He nodded, taking in every word, everything he'd wanted to hear from her. There was no way he was waiting another minute to start their future together. It had to start now. "Before I ask you what I need to ask you, I need to say one thing. No more talk of a paternity test. It's a dead issue."

"Okay…" A quizzical look crossed her face. "I know that's been difficult for you."

*Here goes nothing. And everything.* He dropped down to his knee, holding her hand.

Her other hand flew to her lips. "No."

"You're saying no already?"

Her head nearly rattled back and forth. "Not what I mean. I'm sorry. Go ahead."

He snickered. "Julia Keys, will you marry me? Will you be my wife? Will you parent with me and live happily ever after with me?"

She nodded, but a word didn't come out of her mouth.

"Marry me and have our baby. Nobody needs to think anything else. I don't care if the baby looks like me. Hell, if we're lucky, the baby will just look like you." He reached into his pocket for his grandmother's ring, something he'd thought about hundreds of times since his mother had given it to him. He slid it out of the pouch and held it up for her.

"Where did you get that?"

"It was my grandmother's. My dad's mom. My mother gave it to me the other day when we were over at the house."

"You've had it all this time?"

"You know, when you first told me that you were pregnant, and I insisted that we get married, that was my way of being a man and taking care of things. That was my way of trying to be a dad. And given that I was only a few minutes into it, I realize now that I wasn't doing that great of a job."

"What does that have to do with the ring?"

"I'm trying to say that I don't give this ring lightly. I've never even thought of putting it on another woman's finger. I think it's because I knew all along that I was waiting for you. I'm dying to put it on your finger. I'm dying to hear you say that you'll be my wife and we can have the happily-ever-after that we've spent more than a dozen years waiting on."

"I love you so much, Logan. Of course I'll marry you."

He stood and slipped the ring onto her finger. It didn't quite fit. "I'm sorry. It's a little tight."

"Bloating." She crammed the ring the rest of the way on to her hand. "Normal pregnancy stuff."

He leaned over and kissed her. "You make it sound so sexy."

She rested her forehead against his and they fell into a snug embrace. "I'm worried about one thing, though."

"No. No worrying. We're done worrying. I don't care if the forecast is for hail and the sky is going to fall. No more worrying."

She bugged her eyes at him. "I was just wondering

whether it's rude to get engaged at someone else's wedding."

"Considering all of the very rude things that have happened at our hand over the last few days, an engagement is the least of our worries. We'll just have to keep it our little secret."

"Oh, because we all know how good we are at doing that."

"This one is different. We're both fully invested in it."

"What about the actual wedding? We should probably talk about that at some point."

Good thing he'd thought about this yesterday during the rehearsal. "Yeah, about that. I guess we should do it here in town. For our parents?"

"Yes. Perfect. How about Monday morning?"

"Monday? But that's the day after tomorrow. There's no time to plan. We have to get the license and you'll have to find a dress. And then we'll have to find someone to officiate."

She shook her head and planted her hands on her hips. "If only we knew a judge..."

"My mom."

"Yes. I don't want to go through what Tracy just went through. I just want to get to the good part. Being with you."

He pulled her against him and gave her another kiss, soft and steamy. "You are so brilliant. I can't wait to get you back to the hotel."

She grabbed his wrist and consulted his watch. "Cake gets cut in fifteen minutes. Everyone should be hammered by a half hour after that. I say we make our escape then." Still holding his arm, she turned to head for the stairs, attempting to pull him along.

"Hey, Jules?" He tugged her back.

"Yes?"

"I think you were right. I should write a memoir."

She smiled the most beautiful smile he'd ever seen, which was saying a lot. "What changed your mind?"

"Now I know it's going to have a happy ending."

# Epilogue

Julia stopped in her tracks in the hall outside the master bedroom of Logan's Connecticut estate—*their* estate, now that they had been husband and wife for five and a half crazy, but ridiculously happy, months. She slapped her hands against the wall, pushing her hands into the plaster. The pain was unlike anything she'd experienced, a relentless tightening starting in her back and coiling around her midsection. It left her restless, with a desire to do conflicting things—sit and stand, move and freeze, stay silent and scream.

As she'd learned to do in childbirth class, she tried to visualize anything that felt good. Right now, mental images of their dreamy honeymoon in French Polynesia were the only thing getting her through the contractions. She and Logan had spent two weeks in a thatched-roof villa several hundred yards offshore, on stilts above the clear, emerald-green sea. Their days were filled with exquisite food, skinny-dips in their private pool, lovemaking and a nap every afternoon. At night after dinner, they climbed into the hammock and spent hours talking, snug in each other's arms, warmed by soft ocean breezes, body heat and the deep satisfaction that came with knowing they belonged together. They'd made it. And it was perfect.

"You've got this. A few more seconds." Logan continued to apply counterpressure on her lower back with his hand.

As if his words were magic, the tightening released her and she could move again. "Oh, thank God."

He consulted the stopwatch on his phone. "Still eight minutes apart. About forty-five seconds per contraction. Do you want me to call the hospital again? I feel like this isn't moving very quickly."

"They told us it can take a really long time the first time. I don't want to end up in a hospital bed for hours on end. I'd rather be here with you."

He sweetly brushed her hair away from her face. "I know, hon. I just want to make sure you and the baby are safe and healthy." Approaching from the side to avoid her impressive belly, he wrapped his arms around her shoulders and kissed her temple.

She smiled and took his hand. "And I love you for it. Let's just keep walking and we'll call after a few more contractions."

"Sounds like a deal. Which way are we headed?"

"Kitchen. I need food."

The trip downstairs was slow and deliberate, Logan's arm around her as she gripped the ornate wrought iron banister. She loved this house—it was grand, but homey, and they had all sorts of privacy. She loved being permanently on the same coast as her parents, Logan's mom, and Tracy and Carter. It would be a quick trip for the grandparents to fly up to dote on their grandchild. If Tracy and

Carter decided to have a baby, it would give them more chances to get the cousins together.

Julia toddled from the bottom of the stairs into the kitchen, her belly leading the way. "I just want something simple. Orange juice and an English muffin."

"Good, since that's the extent of my culinary skills." Logan went to work while Julia perched on the edge of a bar stool at the kitchen island, surveying the view through the stretch of multiple French doors overlooking the grounds behind the house. Early March and snow was still on the ground, something she was getting used to. She usually spent this time of year at her beach house in Malibu, just to stay away from the cold. "We need to call about having the pool fence put in as soon as the snow has melted. Otherwise, time will get away from us and the next thing we know, the baby will be walking and we'll both be worried sick about him or her getting outside and falling in."

"I already called this morning. After your first few contractions. I figure we'll have our hands full in the next few weeks. I didn't want to risk forgetting."

"Good thinking."

"That's why you love me." He handed her a glass of juice and smiled that electric Logan smile.

"That's part of it." She grinned back at him. There were days with Logan when she was tempted to wonder if this was all a dream. It was about far more than ending up with the charming, ridiculously handsome athlete. He was her best friend. They made each other whole. She'd spent a dozen years convinced they'd never get on the same page at the same time. But this certainly wasn't a dream—it was better. They hadn't been handed this on a silver platter. She and Logan had worked hard for their life together.

The toaster popped, and Logan buttered the English

muffin, bringing it to her on a small plate. Ravenous, Julia took a huge bite, but that was all she got before her body decided to take over. She leaned against the kitchen counter, bracing herself, dropping her head and breathing through the pain.

Logan was quickly at her side again. "Do you want me to rub your back?"

She shook her head vigorously, the pain nearly impossible to take. "Honestly? Don't. Touch. Me."

He took a step back as if she were a bomb about to go off. "Are they getting more intense?"

She couldn't speak. She nodded.

"I think we should go to the hospital."

Finally, her muscles began to uncoil. Her shoulders dropped in relief, and she caught her breath as warmth rippled down her upper thighs. She wondered for a moment if it was just being around Logan. He did have that effect on her, but as much as she loved him, she was feeling anything but romantic right now. The heat trailed down her leg. Liquid trickled onto the polished wood floor. She stared down as the pool of fluid grew. "Oh my God. My water broke."

"Your hospital bag is already in the car. I'll get your coat. And a towel."

*He's so calm and collected in a crisis.* "No coat. I'm a human furnace right now. And I'd get two towels if I were you."

"One minute."

He flew up the stairs and she soon heard the slamming of cabinet doors. He was back and ready to go before she could finish her English muffin. Frenetic energy radiated from him as he nervously nodded his head and helped her up from her seat. He was ready to go. He was ready for this to happen. She was ready, too. She was tired of feeling like a human beluga.

* * *

Rushing to the hospital ushered in a chaotic mix of excitement, anticipation and worry. Logan felt too much as if everything was happening *to* them and not because of them. They certainly had no control over the things Julia's body was doing, the immense pain she was having to endure. She suffered through the car ride, but remained quiet and focused. He admired her strength, but was not surprised by her determination to make it seem as if she had everything under control.

Now that he was putting their new minivan through its paces, navigating S-turns and tight corners, Logan was happy to learn just how well it handled. He'd never expected he'd own a car like this, nor did he expect that being behind the wheel of this car would make him feel more like a man than any of the expensive sports cars he owned. It made him feel like a dad.

He got them there in record time and zipped into a parking spot near the emergency entrance. An orderly dashed outside to help Julia into a wheelchair and get her inside. Logan juggled a clipboard a nurse had handed him, along with his phone and Julia's bag. He fielded questions about contractions and Julia's due date as she was wheeled into an exam room.

It didn't take hospital staff long to get her into a gown and up on the exam table. A doctor checked her, then rolled back on a stool and scribbled on Julia's chart. "She's nearly five centimeters. You're lucky you didn't stay at home much longer. You might've been having your baby in the car. Let's get you admitted and up into Labor and Delivery."

Julia's sweet eyes flashed up at Logan. They were filled with both optimism and fear. She seemed to be feeling much as he did—like they were riding a corkscrew roller coaster on Christmas morning.

He leaned down and kissed her forehead. "You're doing such a good job. I'm so proud of you."

"Thanks. I'm nervous."

*Yes, darling. Me, too.*

They were quickly registered and taken to a Labor and Delivery room. The nurses were a godsend—calm and capable through countless unfamiliar experiences: monitors that beeped, cords that lit up, and a constant parade of people in and out of the room. Julia got something to take the edge off the pain, but it was still very much there, and Logan would've done anything to take it all away from her.

She endured the contractions for hours. Logan did his part, talking her through it, reminding her to breathe, holding a cool washcloth to her forehead and giving her ice chips. Still, he felt so helpless that it had turned into a test of his mental endurance. How long can you watch the person you love most in the world suffer? He was desperate to make this easier for her and there was absolutely nothing he could do.

After nearly six hours, they were both exhausted, but Julia was showing the greatest effects of it. Her face was red and puffy, her eyes tired. They'd been left alone for at least the last forty-five minutes, and he was really starting to worry. Why wasn't anyone helping them? Why wasn't the baby here yet? He was just about to call someone when a nurse they hadn't yet met barged through the door.

"I think you're ready to push, Mom." The nurse bunched up the sleeves of the shirt she was wearing under scrubs and washed her hands. "Baby should be here very soon."

"Um, okay," Julia said, seeming as confused as Logan felt.

"I'm sorry. Who are you?" he asked.

"I'm Maria. I just came on shift about twenty minutes ago." She snapped on a pair of latex gloves. "I've been watching your contractions on the monitor. I think you're ready."

How someone could know it was time for the baby to arrive merely by looking on a television monitor was beyond Logan, but he was in no position to argue. "Okay. What can I do?"

"Help me get her feet in the stirrups."

Logan did as he was asked while Julia moaned with the pain of another contraction.

Maria did the quick examination. "Ten centimeters. Fully dilated. I can see the top of the baby's head, if you want to look, Dad."

Logan was struggling to keep up—holding Julia's hand, wanting to see the baby while also being scared to see the baby. The only logical question sprang from his lips. "The doctor?"

"Should be here any minute. But don't worry. I've caught lots of babies." She blew her curly black hair from her forehead and winked at Logan. "Another contraction, Mom?"

Julia nodded and scrunched up her face.

"Dad, help her sit up to push."

Logan took Julia's arm and again did as he was told.

"Bear down. Push as hard as you can. That's great. You can do it." Maria was a font of encouragement.

"Childbearing hips, my ass," Julia grunted, followed by a low and agonizing groan. When the final sound passed her lips, she collapsed back on the bed and turned to Logan. "Even though I love you, I hate you."

He smiled wide. "So nothing has changed."

"Very funny."

He leaned down and pressed a kiss to her forehead, which was damp with perspiration. "I love you more than you'll ever know."

"The baby is crowning. I think only one or two more

pushes like that last one. Looks like he or she has a pretty impressive head of dark hair.'"

"That's a good sign," Julia muttered.

Indeed, it was, although Logan would've taken a bald baby or a baby with clown hair at this point. He just wanted the little bugger to get here.

Julia pushed like a champ through two more contractions. "I don't want to stop. I can't not push."

"That's good. Just keep going. The baby is almost here," Maria said.

Logan didn't bother to bring up the fact that the doctor hadn't arrived. Maria had more than convinced him she knew what she was doing.

"Here comes the head. One more push and you're home free." Maria stood and kicked the stool out from under her.

Julia folded herself in half, her face turning nearly purple, not a sound coming from her. Instead, a squishing noise came from the end of the bed. Followed by a cry.

"It's a girl," Maria exclaimed, pure joy in her voice.

Another nurse walked in and saw what was happening. She rushed to help Maria clean up the baby and swaddle her.

Logan turned to Julia. Tears were running right down her face, but she was smiling ear to ear. He was in a similar state—consumed by happiness and relief. "A girl. It's a girl."

"I know. Oh my God. It's so amazing. I want to see her." Julia was still catching her breath.

"It'll be just a minute," Maria answered as the baby continued to cry. "Then we'll get her to you."

"You're going to be stuck in a house with two women," Julia said. "How's that going to work for the guy who grew up with only brothers?"

He leaned down and kissed her cheek at least a dozen times, wiping away her tears with his lips. "I think it sounds wonderful."

"Here's Baby Girl Brandt," Maria said, presenting Julia with a tiny bundle of baby tightly wrapped in a striped flannel blanket. "I'll leave you three some time to get acquainted. She's perfect. Congratulations."

Julia held the baby looking like she was born to do this. "Sophie?"

He nodded. "After my grandmother."

"The original owner of my ring."

He reached out and rubbed Sophie's cheek with the back of his hand. Her skin was a bit purple and splotchy, but tender and new. Her lips were sweet and pink and she had the most adorable tiny nose. She was incredibly quiet, eyes wide open and alert. "She's beautiful. Just like her mom." Logan couldn't even comprehend how lucky he was. It was unfathomable. He only knew that he was blessed.

Julia peeked under Sophie's hat. "Looks like some serious curly hair under there."

Logan leaned closer and looked. "So she does."

"A little bit like you had when you were younger."

Logan didn't need to weigh in on it. There was so much better left unsaid. They were a family. And a happy one at that.

* * * * *